Warriors of Blood and Dream

ooooo

* A night clerk at a 7-Eleven discovers that the path to enlightenment leads to a beer-guzzling, redneck *sensei* named Bubba.

* A human combatant enters the ring to face a fearsome Ektra shapeshifter before the home planet crowd in the 57,463rd Annual Games of the IntraGalactic Interworld Multicultural Amateur Wrestling League.

* A woman warrior crouches in the darkness, waiting to kill what she loves most.

* When martial arts and Virtual Reality meet, the result can be murder.

WARRIORS *of* BLOOD *and* DREAM

Edited By
ROGER ZELAZNY

AVON BOOKS • NEW YORK

To all of our teachers

AVON BOOKS
A division of
The Hearst Corporation
1350 Avenue of the Americas
New York, New York 10019

Cover art by Dorian Vallejo
Published by arrangement with the editor
Library of Congress Catalog Card Number: 94-96561
ISBN: 0-380-77422-4

First AvoNova Printing: June 1995

AVONOVA TRADEMARK REG. U.S. PAT. OFF. AND IN OTHER COUNTRIES, MARCA REGISTRADA, HECHO EN U.S.A.

Printed in the U.S.A.

RA 10 9 8 7 6 5 4 3 2 1

Contents

INTRODUCTION
Roger Zelazny

A teacher affects eternity;
he can never tell where his influence stops.
—Henry Adams

1

In the only photo I have of Phil Cleverley he is throwing me to the ground with an effortless aikido technique which perfectly controlled my attack. He is somewhere in his mid-thirties. His shoulder-length hair is unmussed, his *hakama* draped, almost artistically, over hip, thigh, leg. My feet are high in the air; his expression is emotionless above his neat beard. The photo was taken by a passing photographer for the *New Mexican*, out early on a Saturday morning looking for human interest material.

It was a balmy spring day, sunny, with a bit of birdsong and a small breeze about us, as I recall. There had been some rain the night before but the ground was not wet, only a little damp. There would be a few grass stains on the *gi*. Nothing that a little bleach wouldn't remedy. Nobody else had shown up for class that morning in the park, and I was getting a private lesson. I think I had my brown belt at the time.

Phil taught a very soft style of aikido; that is, there

were no jerks, wrenching movements, hard grabs—except from the person doing the attacking. There were times when I didn't even feel his touch, just felt myself suddenly off-balance, turning, falling. Not at all like the judo I had studied back in college. As effective, though.

I spent seven summers with Phil in that place, Patrick Smith Park, between Canyon Road and West Alameda, in Santa Fe, New Mexico. April through October, usually. Winters, Phil would rent space in a dojo, Kerry Li's or Cody Templeton's, where we would throw and be thrown on mats. He liked the grassy ground of the park best, however—often remarking that it was our real school—partly because one is seldom attacked for real when standing on a mat, partly because he was very fond of the outdoors. I never learned till the day of his funeral that he'd been an Eagle Scout as a kid.

Soft style. Hard style. . . . I remember Bill Gavel, a former Marine unarmed combat instructor, telling me in my earliest judo classes that when you are pulled you push, that when you are pushed you pull. He taught a lot of pure combat stuff, too, as opposed to the sport, things involving crushing larynxes, breaking necks and spines, and it all seemed good and useful, and the push-pull business really did work—after lots of practice. Later, Phil was to tell me that when you are pushed or pulled you turn. He was aware of the push-pull response as well, and when I questioned him upon the distinction he'd shrugged and said, "Not better. Not worse. Just different."

Phil had come to aikido with a background in Shotokan karate, kempo, and t'ai chi. One day when I was hunting for more distinctions he told me, "In karate when you block and counterpunch, you reject the attack, you reject the attacker. In aikido you embrace the attack, you embrace the attacker, and you turn."

"What's wrong with rejecting the attack and the attacker?" I'd asked.

He shook his head.

"Nothing," he said. "Neither way is right or wrong. They're just different approaches. Look at them as metaphors."

So, later, I did tae kwon do for six months, twice a week, on the side, to improve my attacks for aikido. It was not so much that I wanted the first, beginner's, belt in that art, but Phil's attacks—and those of the other people in the class who had done some form of karate—were so much cleaner than my own, that I felt a need to improve my attacking half of things. While it is true that aikido is mainly a defensive art, half of the time in class is spent being an attacker (*uke*), so as to give one's partner (*nage*) a chance to practice the defenses.

The concept of blocking and attacking was not totally unfamiliar to me. It had been there when I fenced for four years, as an undergraduate at Case Western Reserve (then just Western Reserve, as it didn't get together with Case till 1967), receiving varsity letters in the sport in my sophomore, junior, and senior years. I'd taken fencing in lieu of regular Phys Ed, as I couldn't stand team sports. Individual performance was something else, though. After the first year, the teacher had suggested I try out for the team, and I did. I wound up as captain of the épée squad in my final year, possibly by virtue of a certain double-jointedness which permitted my drawing my elbow back at an unnatural-seeming angle out of reach of riposte while going for a wrist touch. And parrying and attacking, beating a blade aside and attacking, is but an extended version of blocking and punching: Reject the attack, reject the attacker. Point!

Somewhere along the line, I learned the Japanese martial arts term for what I'd always sought in all affairs: *suki*. It means an opening. One can get all philosophical about yin and yang and mutual arisings, but basically it means that whatever you do you make yourself vulnerable somewhere. A skilled defensive player invites the attack and moves into the opening, the *suki*, which it creates. Even powerful, focused blows create their own *suki*, for strength is put forth in a wavelike pattern—exert, relax, exert, relax—and a soft-style martial artist will tell you that every moment of strength in the hard-style player's effort is followed by a moment of weakness. Avoid or parry the blow, and there is the *suki*. The soft stylist tries to avoid personal moments of strength and weakness himself by letting his strength flow at the same level at all times. No exertion, no lapse, enter the opening, embrace the attack, turn.

I am facing one of the pupils in the class I taught. I ask her for a munetski *punch to my midsection. Initially, I face her squarely. As the attack commences I am moving forward and turning. If the punch connects, it does not matter. It will roll off of me in the course of the rotation. I apply the technique. I reverse my turning. She is on the ground.*

Hard, soft, push-pull, reject-reject, circular-linear. None of this was unfamiliar, once I understood what the terms meant in practice. "The martial arts are a microcosm of the big world," Phil said. "It's all there."

"So what do you do if the person attacking you has studied silat or capoeira or some kung fu form you've never heard of?" I asked him.

"You can't learn them all," he told me. "I'll tell you one thing not to do, though: Never enter another man's universe, because in there he's God."

"What do you mean?"

"Don't try to play by his rules. He knows them better than you do. Try to make him enter your universe."

"How?"

"You might have to provoke his *ki*."

"What do you mean?"

He gave me the finger.

End of Zen parable.

2

Winter, in the late fifties: The skies were ashen and sober and there were small ridges of snow at the curbsides on East 185th Street. It was a Friday. My parents always did the week's shopping on Fridays, in the stores that lined that thoroughfare. While they were about it I browsed the Woolworth's and Neisner's five-and-dimes, the one bookstore, and the drugstores' magazine racks. At one point, I waited for a break in the traffic and then hurried to cross the street. Partway over I struck a patch of ice and felt my feet go out from under me. I was pleased that I did a breakfall without thinking. My right arm struck the pavement at a forty-five-degree angle out from my body simultaneous with my turning my hip and spreading the force of the impact along the outside of my right leg just as my left foot made contact with the street. It was a good breakfall, and I picked myself up, brushed myself off, and continued on to the store I was headed for. I recall thinking, "At least I've gotten this much out of judo." I'd been doing it for a year or so then.

A few years ago I was walking down my steep, blacktop driveway one winter day to pick up the morning papers when I struck a patch of ice. This time, as I felt myself slip forward I relaxed my upper body; it felt as if everything from my shoulders down to my waist instantly drained into my center. I sank into the slide and rode with it as if I were skiing. When I came to the edge of the ice I stepped off, straightened to my full height, and continued on down the hill. Later I tried it again intentionally, just for the hell of it, and I responded the same way each time. I embraced it and went with it. I had been doing aikido for three or four years at that point.

One does the same *ukemi* (breakfalls) in aikido as one does in judo or jujutsu; one also does a rolling version which brings one back to one's feet. The appropriate species of *ukemi* depends on the vector of the throw, and after a time one's body just knows which sort to employ, from somewhere down at the level of the spinal nerves. One learns to fall from one's center as well as to move from it in the vertical.

One member of my aikido class was Leroy Yerxa, Jr., son of the old Ziff-Davis science fiction writer of that name. Later, widowed, his mother had remarried—William Hamling, who soon had Leroy reading the slush pile of his magazine, *Imagination.* Leroy and I are the same age, and he was reading it in his teens at the same time I was writing and trying to sell. It is likely that he'd rejected some of my early stories, though I've never mentioned the possibility to him. I wonder, after all these years, whether he was the one who penned me the "Sorry, try again" on one of those early slips. One of life's odd turnings or returnings.

Behaviorism strikes me as an awfully cynical view of human nature: We run the maze because we're paid to, or because we fear the consequences if we don't. But, on the other hand, I've often wondered whether Freud himself believed, as so many of his followers seemed to, that every human action is the result of some hidden compulsion. I wondered whether some people might not simply choose values and conduct themselves in accordance with them. Or was that too naive? I remember my Political Science professor, Dr. Hotz, cautioning the class never to place too much trust in any system which relied heavily on the rationality of the human animal for its operation. He refused to guess as to the exact nature and extent of human irrationality. Just being aware of its existence is sufficient, he'd once told me. It was obviously there, though, I later came to realize, as humanity's collective *suki.*

* * *

I was impressed by Noel Perrin's book, *Giving Up the Gun* (''Japan's Reversion to the Sword, 1543–1879''), wherein he tells of firearms first being introduced into that country in 1543 and during the next thirty-some years pretty much replacing the sword save for a few diehard samurai. But this produced a reaction, when the warlords realized that they could spend years training great fighting men and then have them shot down by someone who'd learned only how to aim and fire, before the warriors could even close with them. So, the last engagement of the period in which firearms played a major role was the Shimabara Rebellion in 1637, wherein Christianity lost its last chance for success in that country. Afterward, the warlords licensed all of the gunmakers, regulated and purchased their total output, and locked the weapons up in warehouses; and the samurai went back to fencing, the monks to making arrows, the smiths to armoring. Firearms were then used only for hunting and display. It wasn't until the breaking of the samurai in the Satsuma Rebellion in the late 1870s that firearms came back—this time to stay—well over two centuries later. The author makes no overt comparisons concerning this and any voluntary abandonment of nuclear weapons; he simply describes what once happened, resulting in a culture's putting aside a form of military technology.

But, never place too much trust in any system which relies . . . I am reminded by memories of my Morgenthau-trained mentor. And there are plenty of holes to be found in attempted comparisons of one culture with another.

I do find stories like this fascinating, though, possibly only because I'm a technology junkie. The Greeks had an aeoliple, a rotating steam-powered novelty machine. With that technology, they could easily have learned to distill wine and make brandy, adding to the amenities (not to be confused with the Eumenides), but look how long the wait for spirits really was. The interaction of technology and society is one of the fascinations science fiction has always held for me. Even if there are no easy answers.

While doing push hands with a friend awhile back I gave a very liberal answer to a political question he'd asked me, and it made me think of something much more general.

People have told me that they can't tell my politics from my stories. The reason is something that probably smacks of perversity, save that I was the way that I am long before I'd thought it through: When the country's political climate is conservative I tend to grow liberal. When it swings the other way I find myself feeling more conservative. This goes back to a basic mistrust of extremes. I don't know whether, ultimately, this makes me radical or extremely conservative. More likely, it shows me as being basically mistrustful of both government and the temper of the times in general. I am aware of a somewhat paranoid element in my makeup when it comes to anyone or anything capable of exercising power over me. Whether this reaction is push-pull or turning, it is hard to say. Whether it is hard style or soft style depends upon how active, and in what ways, I choose to become on any matter. I mistrust principles, too, and tend to stick to values. That is as close as I can come to a principle.

"Aikido is purely defensive," Phil told me one day, as yellow and gold cottonwood leaves blew by us in the park, "teaching one to respond to aggression. But when does an attack really begin? When the other person takes a swing at you? Or when that person forms the intent to do so? Are there ways of detecting this intent before it becomes action?"

"If you've got an example, please give it to me," I said.

"I once worked in a hospital," he responded, "where a patient who seemed disturbed cursed me and began moving toward me while we were waiting for an elevator. That might be taken as an intent to attack."

"What did you do?" I asked.

"I raised my hands before me," he said, "and I smiled."

"And the man?"

"He changed his mind. Maybe it was the hands. Maybe it was the smile."

I read *A Brief History of Time*, by Stephen Hawking, a while back, because I feel obliged to read popular books in this area when written by anyone with such impressive credentials. While most of the book summarized general matters familiar to everyone who writes science fiction, the final chapters, which gave his cosmological thinking, were of interest. Even more interesting, however, was the man's triumph of sorts over that terrible wasting disease, amyotrophic lateral sclerosis (ALS)—Lou Gehrig's disease—which, while it racked his body, did not stop his mind in its turning through time, space, gravitation, from the quantum to the relativistic, in search of unities. In *Neuro* ("Life on the Frontlines of Brain Surgery and Neurological Medicine"), author David Noonan says:

> . . . [I]t is generally recognized that ALS has three different rates of progression: the typical rate, in which the patient survives two to three years; an accelerated rate, in which death occurs in a matter of months or even weeks; and a very slow rate, in which the patient survives for ten years, twenty years, or even longer.

One doesn't know whether to bless or curse in a case like Dr. Hawking's. One can but wonder at the warrior heart that continues to face the cosmos down that slow rate, working, working for maximum understanding, unable to push-pull or reject his own accelerated entropy, able only to turn, between riddles personal and universal.

* * *

"Once some guys attacked me on the street," Phil said one chilly evening after class as we pulled on street clothes and gathered our gear at the picnic table. "One of them threw a Coke bottle. I blocked automatically. The bottle shattered against my left forearm—still a few slivers in there—and the pieces flew off to the side. It was rather spectacular. I must have looked as if I knew what I was doing, because they backed off."

"Sounds like rejecting the attack rather than turning with it," I suggested.

"Yes, it was," he agreed. "Everything you know in the martial arts eventually flows together. What you're left with is your own style. You will do what is most appropriate."

Phil died on Monday, February 26, 1990, of amyotrophic lateral sclerosis, at the typical rate. It had eroded him for about two years. He turned with it, embracing the attacks and putting forth the best responses he could to each of its grapplings, with his own diminishing energies. He did block and punch, too; he did push and pull. But he had no choice but to enter its universe, to play by its rules. I taught his classes, under his guidance, during that time—and later by general consent of the class itself when he was no longer able to come in, periodically reporting back to him by telephone and seeking advice. I continued the teaching for several years after that, also.

He was buried in Santa Fe, New Mexico, on Thursday, March 1. He was survived by an amazing lady, Karen, a lovely daughter from a previous marriage, Carissa, and by all of those whom he had taught. Leroy Yerxa, Jr., Jamii Corley (herself an aikido, kenjutsu, and aikijutsu *sensei*), Claudia Hallowell, and I were at the service and the graveside with the family. Donna Lubell (a karate *sensei*) was there in spirit, as were some of the others I could not reach in time, or who could not travel the distance.

I wanted to open with a pair of tales representing the yang and the yin of martial arts—and they don't come much yanger than this one. Damn! this man's a vivid writer.

OOOOO

MASTER OF MISERY

Joe R. Lansdale

To the memory of my father, Bud Lansdale

Six o'clock in the morning, Richard was crossing by ferry from the Hotel on the Cay to Christiansted with a few other early-bird tourists, when he turned, looked toward shore, and saw a large ray leap from the water, its blue-gray hide glistening in the morning sunlight like gunmetal, its devil-tail flicking to one side as if to slash.

The ray floated there in defiance of gravity, hung in the sky between the boat and the shore, backgrounded by the storefronts and dock as if it were part of a painting, then splashed almost silently into the purple Caribbean, leaving in its wake a sun-kissed ripple.

Richard turned to see if the other passengers had noticed. He could tell from their faces they had not. The ray's leap had been a private showing, just for him, and he relished it. Later, he would think that perhaps it had been some kind of omen.

Ashore, he walked along the dock past the storefronts, and in front of the Anchorinn Restaurant, the charter fishing boat was waiting.

A man and a woman were on board already. The man was probably fifty, perhaps a little older, but certainly in good shape. He had an aura of invincibility about him, as if the normal laws of mortality and time did not apply to him.

He was about five-ten with broad shoulders, and, though he was a little thick in the middle, it was a hard thickness. It was evident, even beneath the black, loose, square-cut shirt he was wearing, he was a muscular man, perhaps first by birth, and second by exercise. His skin was as dark and leathery as an old bull's hide, his hair like frost on scorched grass. He was wearing khaki shorts and his dark legs were corded with muscle and his shins had a yellow shine to them that brought to mind weathered ivory.

He stood by the fighting chair bolted to the center of the deck, and looked at Richard standing on the dock with his little paper bag containing lunch and suntan lotion. The man's crow-colored eyes studied Richard as if he were a pile of dung that might contain some kernel of rare and undigested corn a crow might want.

The man's demeanor bothered Richard immediately. There was about him a cockiness. A way of looking at you and sizing you up and letting you know he wasn't seeing much.

The woman was quite another story. She was very much the bathing beauty type, aged beyond competition, but still beautiful, with a body by Nautilus. She was at least ten years younger than the man. She wore shoulder-length blond hair bleached by sun and chemicals. She had a heart-shaped face and a perfect nose and full lips. There was a slight cleft in her chin and her eyes were a faded blue. She was willowy and big breasted and wore a loose, white tee shirt over her black bathing suit, one of the kind you see women wear in movies, but not often on the beach. She had the body for it. A thong, or string, Richard thought the suits were called. Sort of thing where the strap in the back slid between the buttocks and covered them not at all. The top of the suit made a dark outline beneath her white tee shirt. She moved her body easily, as if she were accustomed to and not bothered by scrutiny, but there was something about her eyes that disturbed Richard.

Once, driving at night, a cat ran out in front of his car and he hit it, and when he stopped to see if there was hope, he found the cat mashed and dying, the eyes glowing hot and savage and terrified in the beam of his flashlight. The woman's eyes were like that.

She glanced at him quickly, then looked away. Richard climbed on board.

Richard extended his hand to the older man. The man smiled and took his hand and shook it. Richard cursed himself as the man squeezed hard. He should have expected that. "Hugo Peak," the older man said, then moved his head to indicate the woman behind him. "My wife, Margo."

Margo nodded at Richard and almost smiled. Richard was about to give his name, when the captain, Bill Jones, came out of the cabin grinning. He was a lean weathered fellow with a face that was all nose and eyes the color of watered meat gravy. He was carrying a couple cups of coffee. He gave one to Margo, the other to Hugo. He said, "Richard, how are you, my man?"

"Wishing I'd stayed in bed," Richard said. "I can't believe I let you talk me into this, Jones."

"Hey, fishing's not so bad," said the captain.

"Off the bank at home in Texas it might be all right. But all this water. I hate it."

This was true. Richard hated the water. He could

swim, had even earned lifeguard credentials as a Boy Scout, some twenty-five years ago, back when he was thirteen, but he had never learned to like the water. Especially deep water. The ocean.

He realized he had let Jones talk him into this simply because he wanted to convince himself he wasn't phobic. So, okay, he wasn't phobic, but he still didn't like the water. The thought of soon being surrounded by it, and it being deep, and above them there being nothing but hot blue sky, was not appealing.

"I'll get you some coffee and we'll shove off," Jones said.

"I thought it took five for a charter?" Richard said.

Jones looked faintly embarrassed. "Well, Mr. Peak paid the slack. He wanted to keep it down to three. More time in the chair that way, we hit something."

Richard turned to Peak. "I suppose I should split the difference with you."

"Not at all," Peak said. "It was my idea."

"That's kind of you, Hugo," Richard said.

"Not at all. And if it doesn't sound too presumptuous, I don't much prefer to be called by my first name, unless it's by my wife. If I'm not fucking the person, I want them to call me Mr. Peak. Or Peak. That all right with you?"

Richard saw Margo turn her face toward the sea, pretend to be watching the gulls in the distance. "Sure," Richard said.

"I'll get the coffee," Jones said, and disappeared into the cabin. Peak yelled after him. "Let's shove off."

The sea was calm until they reached the Atlantic. The water there was blue-green, and the rich purple color of the Caribbean stood in stark contrast against it, reaching out with long purple claws into the great ocean, as if it might tug the Atlantic to it. But the Atlantic was too mighty, and it would not come.

The little fishing boat chugged out of the Caribbean and onto the choppier waters of the Atlantic, on out and over the great depths, and above them the sky was blue, with clouds as white as the undergarments of the Sacred Virgin.

The boat rode up and the boat rode down, between wet valleys of ocean and up their sides and down again. The cool spray of the ocean splattered on the deck and the diesel engine chugged and blew its exhaust across it and onto Richard, where he sat on the supply box. The movement of the water and the stench of the diesel made him queasy.

After a couple of hours of pushing onward, Jones slowed the engine, and finally killed it. "You're up, Mr. Peak," Jones said coming down from his steering. He got a huge, metal ice chest out of the cabin and dragged it onto the deck and opened it. There were a number of small black fish inside, packed in ice. Sardines, maybe. Jones took one and cut it open, took loose one of the rods strapped to the side of the cabin, stuck the fish on the great hook. He gave the rod to Peak.

Peak took the rod and tossed the line expertly and it went way out. He sat down in the fighting chair and fastened the waist belt and shoulder straps and put the rod butt in the gimbal. He looked relaxed and professional. The boat bobbed beneath the hot sunlight and the minutes crawled by.

Margo removed her tee shirt and leaned against the side of the boat. The bathing suit top barely managed to cover her breasts. It was designed primarily to shield her nipples. The top and sides of her bathing suit bottom revealed escaped pubic hair, a darker blond than the hair on her head.

She got a tube of suntan lotion out of a little knit bag on the deck, pushed the lotion into her palm, and began to apply it, slowly and carefully from her ankles up. Richard tried not to watch her run her hand over her tanned legs and thighs, and finally over her belly and the tops of her breasts. He would look away, but always his eyes would come back.

He had not made love to a woman in a year, and for the first six months of the year had not wanted to. Now, looking at Margo Peak, it was all he could think about.

Richard glanced at Peak. He was studying the ocean. Jones was in the doorway of the cabin, trying not to be too obvious as he observed the woman. Richard could see that Jones's Adam's apple rode high in his throat. Margo seemed unaware or overly accustomed to the attention. She was primarily concerned with getting the suntan lotion even. Or so it seemed.

Then the line on the rod began to sing.

Richard looked toward the ocean and the line went straight and taut as the fish hit. The line sang louder as it jerked again and cut the air.

"I'm gonna hit him," Peak said. He tightened the drag, jerked back on the rod, and the rod bent slightly. "Now I've got him."

The fish cut to the right and the line moved with him, and Peak hit him again, said, "He's not too big. He's nothing."

Peak rapidly cranked the fish on deck. It was a barracuda. Jones took hold of a metal bar and whacked the flopping barracuda in the head. He got a pair of heavy shears off the deck and opened them and put them against the barracuda's head, and snapped down hard. The head came part of the way off. Jones popped the head again, and this time the head hung by a strand. He cut the head the rest of the way off, tossed it in the ocean, put the decapitated barracuda in the huge ice chest. "Some of the restaurants buy them," he said. "Probably sell them as tuna or something."

"Good catch," Richard said.

"A barracuda," Peak said. "That's no kinda fish. That's not worth a damn."

"Sometimes that's all you hit," Jones said. "Last party I took out, that was it. Three barracuda, back to back. You're next, Mrs. Peak."

Jones baited the hook and cast the line and Margo strapped herself into the fighting chair and slipped the rod into the gimbal. They drifted for an hour and finally Jones moved the boat, letting the line troll, but nothing hit right away. It was twenty minutes later and they were all having a beer, when suddenly the gimbal cranked forward and the line whizzed so fast and loud it sent goose bumps up Richard's back.

Margo dropped the beer and grabbed the rod. The beer foamed out of the can and ran over the deck, beneath Richard's tennis shoes. The line went way out. Jones cut the engine back plenty, and the line continued to sing and go far out into the water.

"Hit him, Margo," Peak said. "Hit him. He's not stuck, he's just got the bait and the line. You don't hit him, the sonofabitch is gone."

Margo tightened the drag, pushed her feet hard against the chair's footrests, and jerked back viciously on the line. The line went taut and the rod bent forward and Margo was yanked hard against the straps.

"Loosen the goddamn drag," Peak said, "or he'll snap it."

Margo loosened the drag. The line sang and the fish went wide to starboard. Jones leaped to the controls and reversed the boat and slowed the speed, gave the fish room to run. The line slacked and the pole began to straighten.

"Hit him again," Peak said, and Margo tried, but it was some job, and Richard could see that the fish was putting a tremendous strain on her. The sun had not so much as caused her tanned body to break a sweat, but the fish had given her sweat beads on her forehead and cheeks and under the nose. The muscles in her arms and legs coiled as if being braided. She pressed her feet hard against the footrests.

''It's too big for her,'' Richard said.

''Mind your own business, Mr. Young,'' Peak said.

Young? How had Peak known his last name? He was pondering that, and about to ask, when suddenly, the fish began to run. Peak yelled, ''Hit him, Margo, goddamn you! Hit him!''

Margo had been working the drag back and forth, and it was evident she had done this before, but the fish was too much for her, anyone could see that, and now she hit the big fish again, solid, and it leaped. It leaped high and pretty, full of color, fastened itself to the sky, then dived like an arrow into the water and out of sight. It was a great swordfish, and Richard thought: when we drag him onto the deck, immediately it will begin to lose its color and die. It will become nothing more than a dull gray dead fish to harden in some taxidermist's shop, later to be hung on a wall above a couch. It seemed a shame, and Richard suddenly felt shamed for coming out here, for wanting to fish at all. At home, on the banks, he caught a fish, it got eaten. Here, there was no point to the fishing but to garner a trophy.

''I want him, Margo,'' Peak said. ''You hear me, you don't lose this fish. I mean it, goddamn it.''

''I'm trying,'' Margo said. ''Really.''

''You know how it goes, you screw it up,'' Peak said. ''You know how it works.''

''Hugo . . . I can't hold him. I'm hurting.''

''You'll hold him, or wish you had,'' Peak said. ''You just think you're hurting.''

''Hey,'' Richard said, ''that's ridiculous. You want the goddamn fish, take over.''

Peak, who was standing on the other side of Margo, looked at Richard and smiled. ''She'll land it. It's her fish, and she'll land it.''

"It's ripping her apart," Richard said. "She's just not big enough."

"Please, Hugo," Margo said. "You can have it. It could have been me caught the barracuda."

"Look to the fish," Peak said.

Margo watched the water and her face went tight; she suddenly looked much older than she had looked. Peak reached out and laid a hand on Margo's breast and looked at Richard, said, "I say she does something, she does it. That's the way a wife does. Her husband says she does something, she does it."

Peak ran his hand over Margo's breast, nearly popping her top aside. Richard turned away from them and called up to Jones. "Cut this out. Let's go in."

Jones didn't answer.

"He does what I want," Peak said. "I pay him enough to do what I want."

The boat slowed almost to a stop, and the great fish began to sound. It went down and they waited. The rod was bent into a deep bow. Margo was beginning to shake. Her eyes looked as if they might roll up in her head. She was stretched forward in the straps so that her back was exposed to Richard, and he could see the cords of muscle there; they were as wadded and tight as the Gordian knot.

"She can't take much more of this," Richard said. "I'll take the fish, if you won't."

"You won't do a goddamn thing, Mr. Young. She can take it, and she will. She'll land it. She caught it, she'll bring it in."

"Hugo," Margo said, "I feel faint. Really."

Peak was still holding his beer, and he poured it over Margo's head. "That'll freshen you."

Margo shook beer from her hair. She began to cry silently. The rod began to bob up and down and the line on the reel was running out. The fish went down again.

Jones appeared from the upper deck. "I've killed the engine. The fish will sound and keep sounding."

"I know that," Peak said. "It'll sound until this bitch gives up, which she won't, or until she hauls it in, which she will."

Richard looked at Jones. The watered gravy eyes looked away. Richard realized now that not only was Jones a paid lackey, he had actually made sure he, Richard Young, was on this boat with Hugo Peak. He had known Jones a short time, since he'd been staying on St. Croix, and they had drunk a few together, and maybe he'd told Jones too much. Not that any of it mattered under normal circumstances, but now some things came clear, and Richard wished he had never known this Captain Jones.

Until now, he had considered Jones decent company. Had told him he was staying in the Caribbean for a few months to rest, really to get past some disappointments. And over one too many loaded fruit drinks, had told him more. For a brief time, two defenses, he had been the Heavyweight Kickboxing Champion of the World.

Trained in Kenpo and Tae Kwon Do, he had gone into kickboxing late, at thirty, and had worked his way up to the championship by age thirty-five, going at a slow rate due to lack of finances to chase all the tournaments. It wasn't like professional kickboxing paid all that much. But he had, by God, been the champion.

And on his second defense, against Manuel Martinez, it had gone wrong. Martinez was good. Real good. He gave Richard hell, and Richard lost sight of the rules in a pressed moment, snapped an elbow into the side of Martinez's temple. Martinez went down and never got up. The blow had been illegal and just right, and Martinez was dead and Richard was shamed and pained at what he had done.

He had the whole thing on videocassette. And at night, back home, when he was drunk or depressed, he sometimes got out the cassette and tormented himself with it. He had done what he had done on purpose, but he had never intended for it to kill. It was an instinctive action from years and years of self-defense training, especially Kenpo, which was fond of elbow strikes. He had lost his willpower and had killed.

He had told this to Jones, and obviously, Jones, most likely under the influence of drink, had told this to Peak, and Peak was the kind of man who would want to know a man who had killed someone. He would want to know someone like that to test himself against him. He would see killing a man in the ring as positive, a major macho achievement.

And those glowing yellow shins of Peak's. Callus. Thai boxers built their shins up to be impervious to pain. Used herbs on them to deaden feeling, so they could slam their legs against trees until they bled and scabbed and finally callused over. Peak wore those shins like a badge of honor.

Yeah, it was clear now. Peak had wanted to meet him and let it lead up to something. And Jones had made at least part of that dream possible. He had supplied Richard, lured him like an unsuspecting goat to the slaughter.

Richard began to feel sick. Not only from the tossing of the sea and the smell of the diesel, but from the fact that he had been handily betrayed, and that he had to see such a thing as a man abuse his wife over a fish, over the fact that Peak had caught a lowly barracuda, and his wife, through chance, had hooked a big one.

Richard moved to the side of the boat and threw up. He threw up hard and long. When he was finished, he turned and looked at Peak, who had slid his hand under Margo's top and was massaging her breast, his head close to her ear, whispering something. Margo no longer looked tan; she was pale and her mouth hung slack and tears ran down her face and dripped from her chin.

Richard turned back to look at the sea and saw a school of some kind of fish he couldn't identify, leaping out of the water and back in again. He looked at the deck and saw the bloodstained shears Jones had used on the barracuda. As he picked them up, and turned, the line on the rod went out fast again, finishing off the reel. Peak began to curse Margo and tell her what to do. Richard walked quickly over to the rod, reached up with the clippers, and snapped the line in two. The rod popped up, the line snapped away, drifted and looped, then it was jerked beneath the waves with the fish. Margo fell back in the chair and sighed, the harness creaking loosely against her.

Tossing the shears aside, Richard glared at Peak, who glared back. "To hell with you," Richard said.

Two days later Richard moved out of the Hotel on the Cay. Too expensive, and his savings were dwindling. He got a room over a fish market overlooking the dock and the waters of the Caribbean. He had planned to go home by now, back to Tyler, Texas, but somehow the thought of it made him sick.

Here, he seemed outside of the world he had known, and therefore, at least much of the time, outside of the event that had brought him here.

The first night in his little room, he lay fully dressed on the bed and smelled the fish smell that still lingered from the closed-up shop below. Above him, the ceiling fan beat at the hot air as if stirring chunky soup, and he watched the shadows the moonlight made off the blades of the fan, and the shadows whirled across him like some kind of alien, rotating spider.

After a time, he could lie there no more. He rose and began to move up and down the floor beside the bed, doing a Kenpo form, adjusting and varying it to suit the inconvenience of the room's size, the bed, and the furniture, which consisted of a table and two hardback chairs.

He snapped at the air with his fists and feet, and the fan moved, and the smell of the fish was strong, and through the open window came the noise of drunks along the dock.

His body became coated with sweat, and, pausing only long enough to remove his drenched shirt, he moved into new forms, and finally he lay down on the bed to try and sleep again, and he was almost there, when there was a knock on his door.

He went to the door, said through it: "Who is it?"

"Margo Peak."

Richard opened the door. She stood beneath the hall light, which was low down and close to her head. The bugs circling below the light were like a weird halo for her, a halo of little winged demons. She wore a short summer dress that showed her tan legs to advantage and revealed the tops of her breasts. Her face looked rough. Both eyes were blacked and there was a cut on her upper lip and her cheeks had bruises the color and size of ripe plums.

"May I come in?" she asked.

"Yes." He let her in and turned on the bare bulb that grew out of a tall floor lamp in the corner.

"Could we do without that?" she said. "I don't feel all that presentable."

"Peak?" he asked, turning off the light.

She sat on the edge of the bed, bounced it once, as if to test the springs. The moonlight came through the window and settled down on her like something heavy. "He hit me some."

Richard leaned against the wall. "Over the fish?"

"That. And you? You embarrassed him in front of me and Captain Jones by cutting the line on the fish. He felt belittled. For a moment he lost power over me. I might have been better off you'd stayed out of it and let me land the fish."

"Sorry. All things considered, you shouldn't be here. Why are you here?"

"You didn't work out like he wanted you to."

"I don't get it."

"He wants to fight you."

"Well, I got that much. I figured that's why Jones got me on the boat. Peak had plans for a match. He knows about me, I know that much. He knew my last name."

"He admires your skill. He has videos of your fights. It excites him you killed a man in the ring. He wants to fight a man who's killed a man. He thought he could antagonize you into something."

"A boat's no place to fight."

"He doesn't care where he fights. Actually, he wanted to get you mad enough to agree to come to his island. He has a little island not far out. Owns the whole thing."

"He thinks he can take me?"

"He wants to find out . . . Yes, he thinks he can."

"Tell him I think he can, too. I'll mail him one of my trophies when I get home."

"He wants it his way."

"He's out of luck."

"He sent me here. He wanted you to see what he'd done to me. He wanted me to tell you, if you don't come to the island, he'll do it again. He told me to tell you that he can be a master of misery. If not to you, then to me."

"That's your problem. Don't go back. You go back, you're a fool."

"He's got a lot of money."

"I'm not impressed with his money, or you. You're a fool, Margo."

"It's all I've got, Richard. He's not nearly as bad as my family was. He at least gives me money, attention. Being an attractive trophy is better than being your father's plaything, if you know what I mean. Hugo got me off drugs. I'm not turning tricks anymore. He did that."

"Just so he'd have a healthy punching bag. A good-looking trophy. Course, he's not treating you so good right now, is he? Listen, Margo, it's your life. Turn it around, you don't like it. Don't come to me like it's my fault you're getting your ass kicked."

"I could leave a man like Peak, I had another man to go to."

"You sound like you're shopping for cars. You see what kind of money I got. You'd leave Peak for this? You want a dump like this? A shared toilet?"

"You could do better. You've got the skill. The name. You've got the looks to get into movies. Martial arts guys can make lots of money. Look at Chuck Norris. Christ, you actually killed somebody. The media would eat that up. You're the real McCoy."

"You know, you and Peak deserve each other. Why don't you just paint bull's-eyes on yourself, give Peak spots to go for next time he gets pissed."

"He knows the spots already."

"Sorry, Margo, but good-bye."

He opened the door. Margo stood and studied him. She moved through the doorway and into the hall and turned to face him. Once again the bugs made a halo above her head. "He wants you to come out to his island. He'll have Captain Jones bring you. Jones is taking me back now, but he'll be back for you. It's a short trip where you need to go. Hugo told me to give you this."

She reached into a loose pocket on her dress and brought out a piece of folded paper, shoved it toward him. Richard took it but did not look at it. He said, "I'm not coming."

"You don't, he'll take it out on me. He'll treat me rough. You see my face. You should see my breasts. Between my legs. He did things there. He can do worse. He's done worse. What have you got to lose? You used to do it for a living. We could do all right together, you and me."

"We don't even know each other."

"We could fix that. We could start knowing one another now. We knew each other, you might not want to let me go."

She moved toward him and her arms went around his neck. He reached out and held her waist. She felt solid, small, and warm.

Richard said, "I've said it. I say it again. You can leave anytime you like."

"He'd have me followed to the ends of the earth."

"I'd rather run like a dog, than heel like one."

"You just don't know," she said, pushing away from him. "You don't know anything."

"I know you're still turning tricks, and Peak's a kind of pimp, and you're not even aware of it."

"You don't know a goddamn thing."

"All right. Good luck."

Margo didn't move. She held her place with the bugs swarming above her head. Richard stepped inside his room, and closed the door.

Richard lay on the bed with the note in his hand. He lay that way for a full fifteen minutes. Finally, he rolled on his side and unfolded the note and read it in the moonlight.

MR. YOUNG:

COME TO THE DOCK AND TAKE JONES' BOAT BY MIDNIGHT. HE'LL BRING YOU OUT TO MY ISLAND. WE'LL FIGHT. NO RULES. WE FIGHT, IT'S BEST FOR MARGO. YOU WIN, I'LL GIVE YOU TEN THOUSAND DOLLARS. I'LL GIVE YOU MARGO. I'LL GIVE YOU A RESTAURANT COUPON FOR FIVE DOLLARS OFF. YOU DON'T COME, MARGO WILL BE UNHAPPY. I'LL BE UNHAPPY AND THE COUPON WILL EXPIRE.

AND YOU'LL NEVER KNOW IF YOU COULD HAVE BEAT ME.

HUGO PEAK

Richard, dropped the note on the floor, rolled onto his back. *It's that simple for Peak,* Richard thought. *He says come, and he thinks I'll come. He's nuts. Margo's nuts. She thinks I owe her something and I don't even know her. I don't want to know her. She's a gold digger. It's not my problem she hasn't the strength to do what she should do. It's not my fault he'll kick her head in. She's a grown woman and she has to make her own decisions. I'm no hero. I'm not a knight on a white charger. I killed a man once by accident, by not staying with the rules, and I'll not fight another man without rules on purpose. The goddamn sonofabitch must think he's a James Bond villain. I won't have anything to do with him. I will never fight a man for sport again.*

Richard lay in the dark and watched the fan. The shadows the fan cast were growing thicker. Soon there would be no shadows at all, only darkness, because the moonlight was fading behind clouds. A cool, wet wind came through the open window. The smell of the fish market below was not as strong now because the smell of the sea and the damp earth had replaced it. Richard held his arm up so that he could see his watch. The luminous dial told him it was just before ten o'clock. He closed his eyes and slept.

When he awoke, rain was blowing in through the window and onto the bed. The rain felt good. He didn't get up to shut the window. He thought about Hugo Peak, waiting. He looked at his watch. It was 11:35.

Peak would be starting to warm up now. Anticipating. Actually thinking he might come. Peak would believe that because he would consider Richard weak. He would think he was weak in that he wanted to protect a woman who had no urge to protect herself. He would think Richard's snipping the fishing line was a sign of weakness. He wouldn't think Richard had done it to make things easier on Margo. He would think he did it as some sort of spiteful attack, and that Richard really wanted to fight him. That was what Peak would be thinking.

And Richard knew, deep down, Peak was not entirely wrong.

He thought: *If I were to go, I could make it to the boat in ten minutes. It's not that far. I could be there in ten minutes easy, I walked fast. But I'm not going, so it doesn't matter.*

He sat on the side of the bed and let the rain slice into him. He got up and went around the bed and opened the closet and got out his martial arts bag. He unzipped and opened it. The mouthpiece and safety gear were there. He zipped it back up. He put it in the closet and closed the door. He sat on the side of the bed. He picked the note up and read it again. He tore it into little pieces and dropped the pieces on the floor, frightening a roach. He tried not to think about anything, but he thought about Margo. The way her face had looked, what she said Peak had done to her breasts, between her legs. He remembered the eyes of that dying cat, and he remembered Margo's eyes. The same eyes, only she wasn't dying as fast. She was going slowly, piece by piece, committing suicide. He remembered the horror of killing the man in the ring, and he remembered, in some hidden, primitive compartment of himself, the pleasure. It was a scary thing inside of him; inside of humankind, especially mankind, this thing about killing. This need. This desire. Maybe, he got home, he'd go deer hunting this year. He hadn't been in over ten years, but he might go now. He might ought to go.

Richard got up and took off his clothes and rubbed his body down with ICY-HOT and took six aspirin and downed them with a glass of water. He put on a jockstrap and cup and loose workout pants and pulled a heavy sweatshirt on. He put on his white tennis shoes without socks and laced them tight. He got his bag out of the closet. He walked to the door and turned around and looked at the room. It looked as if no one had ever lived here. He looked at his watch. He had exactly ten minutes. He opened the door and went out.

As he walked, the ICY-HOT began to heat up and work its way into his muscles. The smell of it was strong in his nostrils. Another fifteen minutes, and the aspirin would take effect, loosen his body further. The rain came down hard as steel pellets and washed his hair into his face, but he kept walking, and finally he began to run.

He ran fast until he came to the Anchorinn Restaurant. He slowed there and went around the corner, and there was Jones's fishing boat. He looked at his watch. He was right on time. He walked up to the fishing boat and called out.

Jones appeared on the deck in rain hat and slicker. Water ran off the hat and fell across his face like a beaded curtain. He helped Richard aboard. Jones said, "It's just that I needed the money. I owe on the boat. I don't pay the boat, they're gonna take it away from me."

"Everyone needs something," Richard said. "Take me out, Jones, and listen up. After this, you better hope I go home to Texas. I'm here, walking around, I see you on the dock, anywhere, you better start running. Got me?"

Jones nodded.

"Take me out."

The wind picked up and so did the rain. Richard's stomach began to turn over. He tried to stay in the cabin, but he found that worse. He rushed outside and puked over the side. Finally, he strapped himself into the fighting chair and rode the boat like a carnival ride, taking great waves of water full blast and watching lightning stitch the sky and dip down and touch the ocean in spots, as if God were punishing it.

It wasn't long before the lights of the boat showed land. Jones moved them in slowly to the little island, finally came to a dock and tied them up. When Richard went to get his bag out of the cabin, Jones came down from the wheel and said, "Here, take this. You'll need it for strength, all that pukin' you done."

It was a thick strip of jerky. "No thanks," Richard said.

"You don't like me, and I don't blame you. Take the jerky though. You got to have some kind of energy."

"All right," Richard said, took it and ate. Jones gave him a drink of water in a paper cup. When Richard was finished, he said, "Water and jerky don't change anything."

"I know," Jones said. "I'm going back to St. Croix before it gets worse. I'd rather be docked there. I think it's a little better protected for boats."

"And how do I get back?"

"Good luck," Jones said.

"So that's how it is? You're all through?"

"Soon as you get off the boat." Jones stepped back a step and produced a little .38 from somewhere under his shirt. "It's nothing personal. It's just the money. Margo was pretty convincing too. Peak likes her to be convincing. But it was the money did it. Margo was just a fringe benefit. The money was enough."

"He really wants to fight to the death, doesn't he?"

"I don't ask about much of what he wants. You got to see it from my side, taking big shots out in boats all the time, getting by on their tips. It costs to take out a charter, wear and tear on the boat. I'm thinking about doing something else, going somewhere else. I might hire some goon like me to take me out fishing. I might go somewhere where the biggest pool of water around is in a glass."

"You're that easy for money?"

"You bet. And remember, I didn't make you come. Get off."

Richard went out of the cabin and climbed down to the dock. When he looked up through the driving rain, he could see Jones looking down at him from the boat, the .38 pointed at him.

"You go up the dock there, toward the flagstones. Follow those. They lead around a curve through the rocks and trees. Where you need to go is back there. You'll see it. Now, go on so I can cast off. And good luck. I mean it."

"Yeah, I know. Nothing personal. Well, you know what you can do with your luck." Richard turned and started up the dock.

The directions led him up through a cut in the rocks and around a curve, and there, built into the side of the mountain, was a huge house of great weathered lumber, glass, and stone. The house seemed like part of the island itself. Richard figured, you were inside, standing at one of the great windows, on a good day, you could look out and clearly see fish swimming deep in the clear Caribbean waters, see them some distance off.

He followed the trail, tried to get his mind on what it was he was going to do. He tried to think about Thai boxers and how they fought. He was sure this was how Peak had trained. Peak's shins were a giveaway, but that didn't mean he hadn't done other things. He might like grappling too, ground work. He had to think about all this, but mostly, he had to think about the Thai boxing. Thai boxers were not fancy kickers like Karataka, or Kung Fu people, but they were devastating because of the way they trained. The way they trained was more important than what they knew. They trained hard, for endurance. They trained themselves to take and accept and fuel themselves off pain. They honed their main weapons, their shins, until the best of them could kick through the thick end of a baseball bat. He had to think about that. He had to think that Peak would be in good condition, and that, unlike himself, he hadn't taken off a few years from rigorous training. Oh, he wasn't all washed-up. He practiced the moves and did exercises and his stomach was flat and his reflexes were good, but he hadn't sparred against anyone since that time he had killed a man in the ring. He had to think about all that. He had to not let the bad part of what he was thinking get him down, but he had to know what was bad about himself and what was good. He had to think of some strategy to deal with Peak before Peak threw a punch or kick. He had to think about the fact that Peak might want to kill him. He had to not think too hard about what kind of fool he'd been for coming here. He had to not think about how predictable he had been to Peak. He had to hope that he was not predictable when they fought. He had to realize that he could kill a man if he wanted to, if the opening was there. He'd already done it once, not meaning to. Now he had to mean to.

At the top of the slope there was an overhang porch of stone, and a warm orange light glowed behind the glass positioned in the thick oak door. Before Richard could touch the buzzer, the door opened, and there stood Margo. She had on the dress she had worn earlier. Her hair was pinned up now. She looked at him with those dying cat eyes. The wind and the sea howled behind him.

"Thanks," she said.

Richard stepped past her, inside, dripping water.

The house was tall as a cathedral, furnished in thick wood, leather furniture, and the heads of animals, the bodies of fish. They were everywhere. It looked like a taxidermist's shop.

Margo closed the door against the rain and wind. She said, "He's waiting for you."

"I should hope so," Richard said.

He dripped on the floor as he walked. She took him into a large, lushly furnished bedroom. She went into an adjacent bathroom and came out with a beach towel and a pair of blue workout pants and kicking shoes. "He wants you to wear these. He wants to see you right away, unless you feel you need to rest first."

"I came here to do it," Richard said. "So, the sooner the better." He took the towel and dried, removed his clothes, except for the jock, and, paying Margo no mind, dried again. He put on the pants and shoes.

Margo led him to a gymnasium. It was a wonderful and roomy gym with one wall made of thick glass overlooking rocks and sea; the windows he had seen from the trail. There was little light in there, just illumination from glow strips around the wall. Hugo Peak sat on a stool looking out one of the windows. He was dressed in red workout pants and kicking shoes. His back, turned to Richard, held shadows in the valleys of its muscles.

"He's waiting," Margo said, and faded back into the shadows and leaned against the wall.

Richard turned and looked at her, a shape in the darkness. He said, "I just want you to know, I'm not doing this for you. I'm doing this for me."

"And for the money?" she said.

"That's icing. I get it, that's good. I'll even take you with me, get you away from here, you want to go. But I won't argue with you to go."

"You win, I might go. But ten thousand dollars isn't a lot of money. Not considering the way I can live now."

"You're right. Keep that in mind. Keep in mind that the ten thousand isn't yours. None of it is. I said I'd take you with me, but that means as far as the island, after that, you're on your own. I don't owe you anything."

"I can make a man happy."

"I got to be happy somewhere else besides below the belt."

"It's not fair. You win, I go with you, I don't get any of your money, and I don't get Hugo's.

"Then you better root for Hugo."

Richard left Margo in the shadows, went over and stood near Peak, and looked out the glass. The sea foamed high and dark with whitecaps against the rocks. Richard saw that the dock he had walked along was gone. The sea had picked it up and carried it away. Or most of it. A few boards were broken and twisted on the shore, lodged between rocks. The great windows vibrated slightly.

"There's going to be a hurricane," Peak said, not looking at Richard. "I believe that's appropriate."

"I want you to write the ten-thousand-dollar check now," Richard said. "Let Margo hold it. I lose, she can tear it up. I win, we'll see someone gets us off the island. Jones isn't coming back, so it'll have to be someone else."

"I'll write the check," Peak said, still looking out the window, "but you won't need to worry about getting off the island. This is your last stop, Mr. Young. You see that prominent rock closest to the house, on the left side of the trail."

"Yeah. What about it?"

Peak sat silent for a long time. Not answering. "Did you know, in the Orient, some places like Thailand, India, they have death matches? I studied there. I studied Thai boxing and Bando when I was stationed there in the army. I've fought some tough matches. People brought here from Thailand, champion Thai boxers. They came here to win money, and they went home hurt. Some of them crippled. I never killed anyone though. I've never fought anyone that's killed anyone. You'll be the first. You know I intend for this one to go all the way?"

"What's that got to do with the rock?" Richard said.

"Oh, my mind wandered. At the base of it, Hero is buried. He was my dog. A German shepherd. He understood me. That's something I miss, Mr. Young. Being understood."

"You're certainly breaking my heart."

"I think maybe, since you came here, on some level, you understand me. That's something worth having. Knowing a worthy opponent understands you. There aren't many like you and me left."

"Whatever you say."

"Death, it's nothing. You know what Hemingway said about death, don't you? He called it a gift."

"Yeah, well, I haven't noticed it being such a popular present. Shall we do it, or what? You were so all-fired wanting to do it, so let's do it."

"Warm up, and we shall. While you start, I'll get a check."

Richard began to stretch and Peak came back with the check. He showed it to Richard. Richard said, "How do I know it's good?"

"You don't. But you don't really care. This isn't about money, is it?"

"Give it to Margo to hold."

Peak did that, then he began to stretch. Fifteen minutes later, Peak said, "It's time."

They met in the center of the gym, began to move in a circular fashion, each looking for an opening. Peak stuck out a couple of jabs, and Richard moved his head away from them. He gave Peak a couple with the same results. Then they went together.

Peak threw hard Thai round kicks to the outside of Richard's right thigh, tried to spring off those for higher kicks to the neck, but Richard faded away from those. Thai boxers were famous for breaking the neck, Richard knew that. He was amazed at how hard the kicks were thrown. They were simple and looked almost stiff, but even though he managed to lift his leg to get some give in the strike, they still hurt.

Richard tried a couple of side kicks, and both times Peak blocked them by kneeing Richard's shin as the kicks came in, and the second time Peak blocked, he advanced and swung an elbow and hit Richard on the jaw. It was an elbow strike like the one Richard had used when he killed Martinez. It hit pretty hard, and Richard felt it all the way down to his heels. When he moved back to regroup, he looked at Peak and saw that he was grinning.

Then they really went to it. Richard threw a front kick to get in close, nothing great, just a front kick, more of a forward stomp to the groin, really, and this brought him into Peak's kill zone, and he tried a series of hand attacks, front backfist to the head, reverse punch to the solar plexus, an uppercut up under Peak's arm, solid to the ribs. It was like hitting a hot water heater.

Peak hit him with another elbow shot, jumped, grabbed Richard's hair, jerked his head down, brought his knee up fast and high. Richard turned his head and the knee hit him hard on the shoulder and the pain went all the way down Richard's arm, such pain that Richard couldn't maintain a fist. His hand flew open like a greedy child reaching for candy.

Richard swung his other arm outside and back and broke the grab on his hair, but lost some hair in the process. He kicked Peak in the knee, a glancing blow, but it got him in to use a double swinging elbow on either side of Peak's head, and for a moment, he thought he was in good, but Peak took the shots and did a jumping knee lift, hit Richard on the elbow, and drove him back with a series of fast round kicks and punches.

Richard felt blood gushing from his nose and over his lips and down his chin. He had to be careful not to slip in the blood when it got on the floor. Damn, the man could hit, and he was fast. Richard already felt tired, and he could tell his nose was broken. It was hot and throbbing. He had been a fool to do this. This wasn't any match. There wasn't going to be any bell. He had to finish this or be finished.

Richard kicked twice to Peak's legs. Once off the front leg, followed with a kick off the rear leg. Both landed, but Peak twisted so he took them on his shins. It was like kicking a tree. Richard began to see the outcome of this. He was going to manage to hit Peak a lot, but Peak was going to hit him a lot too, and in the long run, Peak would win because of the conditioning, because he could take full contact blows better to the body and the shins.

Richard faded back a bit, shook his injured arm. It felt a little better. He could make a solid fist again. The storm outside had gotten busy. The windows were starting to shake. The floor beneath them vibrated. Richard began to bob and weave. Peak held his hands up high, Thai boxer style, closed fists palm forward, set that way to throw devastating elbows.

Richard came in with a series of front kicks and punches, snapped his fingers to Peak's eyes. Managed to flick them, make them water. That was his edge, a brief one, but he took it, and suddenly he was in with a grab to Peak's ear. He got hold of it, jerked, heard it rip like rotten canvas. Blood flew all over Richard's face.

Peak screamed and came in with a blitz of knees and elbows. Richard faded clockwise, away from the brunt of the attack. When Peak stopped, breathing hard, Richard opened his fist. He held Peak's ear in his hand. He smiled at Peak. He put the ear between his teeth and held it there. He bobbed and weaved toward Peak. Richard understood something now. Thai boxers trained hard. They had hard bodies, and if you tried to work by their methods, fists and feet, and you weren't in the same condition, they would wear you down, take you.

But that was the advantage that a system like karate had. He was trained to use his fingers, use specific points, not just areas you could slam with kicks and elbows. True, anywhere Peak kicked or hit him hurt, but no matter how tough Peak was, he had soft eyes, ears, and throat. The groin would normally be a soft target, but like himself, Richard figured he had on a cup. That wouldn't make it so good to hit, and there was the fact a trained fighter could actually take a groin shot pretty well, and there was that rush of adrenaline a groin blow could give a foe, a few seconds of fired energy before the pain took over. It was like a shot of speed. Sometimes, that alone could whip you.

Okay, watch yourself, don't get cocky. He can still take you out and finish you with one solid blow. Richard glanced toward Margo. She was just a shape in the shadows.

Richard spit the ear out and they came together again. A flurry. Richard didn't have time to try anything sophisticated. He was too busy minimizing Peak's attack. He tied Peak up, trapped his hands down, but Peak shot his head forward and caught Richard a meaty one in the upper lip. Richard's lip exploded. Richard shifted, twisted his hip into Peak, turned and flipped him. Peak tumbled across the floor and came up on his feet.

And then Richard heard the great windows rattling like knucklebones in a plastic cup. He glanced out of the corner of his eye. The hurricane was raging. It was like the house was in a mixer. The glass cracked open in a couple of spots and rain blew in.

"None of that matters," Peak said. "This is the storm that matters." He moved toward Richard. The side of his head leaking blood, one of his eyes starting to close.

Richard thought. *Okay, I do better when I don't play his game. I'll look as if I'm going to play his game, then I won't.* Then suddenly he remembered the ray. How it had leaped out of the water and flicked its tail. It was an image that came to him, and then he knew what to do. The ray's tail reminded him of a flying reverse heel kick. In a real fight, the jump kick wasn't something you actually used much. No matter what the movies showed, you tried to stay on the ground, and you kicked low, and Peak would know that. He would know it so strongly he might not expect what Richard could do.

Richard threw a low front kick off the front leg, followed with a jab as he closed, followed with a reverse punch, and then he threw his back leg forward, as if about to execute a leaping knee, but he used the knee to launch himself, twisted hard, took to the air, whipped his back leg around into a jump heel kick, whipped it hard and fast the way the ray had whipped its tail.

He caught Peak on the side of the head, above the temple, felt the bones in Peak's skull give way to his heel. Peak fell sideways like a dipping second hand, hit the floor.

As Richard stepped in and kicked Peak with all he had in the throat, the windows blew in and shards of glass hit Richard, and a wall of water took the room and all its occupants, carried them through the other wall as if it were wet cardboard. Richard felt a blow to his head, a timber striking him, and then the water carried him away and everything was dark.

When Richard awoke he was in darkness, and he was choking to death. He was in the sea. Under it. He swam up, hard, but he couldn't seem to make it. The water kept pushing him down. He continued kicking, fighting, and finally, when he thought his lungs would explode, he broke up and got a gulp of air and went under again. But not so far this time. A long, dark, beam of wood hit him in the head, and he got hold of it. It had been an overhead beam in the gym. It was thick, but it floated just fine. He realized the storm had struck and moved on, like a hit-and-run driver, leaving in its wake stormy seas, but an oddly clear sky lit up by a cool, full moon that looked like a smudgy spotlight.

Richard looked down the length of the beam and shuddered. The beam had broken off to a point down there, and the point was stuck through Margo's chest, dead center, had her pinned like an insect to a mounting board. Her head was nodding to one side, and as the water jumped and the wind lashed, her head rolled on her neck as if on a ball bearing, rolled way too far and high to the left, then back to the right. It was like one of those bobbing, toy dog heads you see in the back of cars. Her tongue hung out of her mouth as if trying to lick the last drop of something sweet. He hair was washed back from her bruised face. A shard of glass was punched deep into her cheek. Her arms washed back and forth and up and down, as if she might be frantically signaling.

The beam rolled and Richard rolled with it. When he came out of the water and got a grip on it again, Margo's head was under the waves and her legs were sticking up, spread wide, bent at the knees, flopping, showing her panties to the moonlight.

Richard looked for the island, but didn't see it. The waves were too high and choppy. Maybe the damn island was underwater. Maybe he was washed way away from it. He had probably gone down below and fought his way up a dozen times, but just didn't remember. All reflex action. God, he hated the sea.

And then he saw Peak. Peak was clinging to a door. He was hanging on the door with one hand, gripping the doorknob. The door was tilted toward him, and Peak looked weak. His other arm hung by his side, floated and thrashed in the water, obviously broken. He didn't see Richard. His back was to him. He was about ten feet away. Or he was every few seconds. Waves would wash him a little farther away, then bring him back.

Richard timed it. When the waves washed Peak away, Richard let go of the beam and swam toward him, then when the waves washed him back, Richard was there. He came up behind Peak, slipped an arm around Peak's neck, and used his other to tighten the choke. It was the kind of choke that cut the blood off to the brain, didn't affect the wind.

Peak tried to hang on to the door, but he let go to grab Richard's arm. The waves took them under, but still Richard clung. They washed up into the moonlight and Richard rolled onto his back, keeping Peak on top of him. He held his head out of the water with effort. Peak's hand fluttered weakly against Richard's arm.

"You know what Hemingway said about death," Richard said. "That it's a gift. Well, I give it to you."

In a moment, Peak's hand no longer fluttered, and Richard let him go. Peak went directly beneath the waves and out of sight.

Richard swam, got on top of the door, clung to the knob, and bucked with the waves. He looked for the beam with Margo on it. He spotted it far out, on the rise of a wave, Margo's legs dangling like a broken peace symbol. The beam rolled and Margo's head came up, then it rolled again, went down into a valley of waves and out of sight. Nearby, Richard saw the check Peak had written ride up on a wave like a little flat fish, shine for a moment in the moonlight, then go down, and not come up.

Richard laughed. He no longer felt frightened of the sea, of anything. The waves rolled over him with great pressure, the door cracked and shifted, started to break up, then the knob came away in his hand.

For as long as I can remember, I've been interested in the martial arts. My first exposure to it was through my father. I guess he was in his fifties, and I was ten or so, when we first talked about the art of self-defense. But before this, Dad had introduced me to boxing through televised fights. He loved boxing and he'd lie on the floor in front of the television set, and I'd lean against him and watch with him. He told me what was what and who was who.

But when a few bullies decided to bother me, and I came to my dad for advice, he showed me how to throw the basic boxing punches, some jujitsu (he called it jujitsee) throws and locks he'd picked up here and there, some roughhouse techniques and wrestling moves. My mother later explained to me that Dad had come by all this honestly. He was once considered for a boxing career, but his father would have none of it, and at another time, during the Great Depression, my dad rode the rails and hoboed from one Texas town to the next to fight in carnivals.

These carnival fights were the predecessors of pro wrestling, only unlike modern wrestling, the matches weren't fixed. In these carnival fights, you could box, wrestle, generally brutalize your opponent, and the one that didn't give up, won. Pretty much like Shoot Fighting is today. It was a way to turn a buck, and my dad was very successful at this. Add to this the fact he worked hard and was as strong as a horse because of it, had the constitution of the proverbial ox, and it's not difficult to imagine how formidable an opponent he was. I once saw him put an apple in his palm, then squeeze it to pulp. That doesn't sound like much hearing it, so I suggest you try it some time.

I also know firsthand he knew his business, as I saw him in righteous action a few times, and trust me, he wasn't pretty, but he knew what he was doing.

Anyway, he taught me some stuff, and I read some books on it, and then, while taking Boy Scout lifeguard training at a Tyler, Texas, YMCA, I discovered my swimming instructor taught Judo as assistant instructor.

I discovered, too, that the YMCA also had Hapkido classes, and Tae Kwon Do.

That got me going, and except for a long period while establishing my writing career, I've been in the martial arts ever since, and I currently hold a black belt in Songham Tae Kwon Do and Matsukaze Budo.

But between the time I discovered Judo, and Kenpo, various forms of Kung Fu and Thai boxing, as well as good ole American kickboxing, and many other forms of sport fighting and self-defense.

To make a long story short. I like martial arts and it's been an important and valuable part of my life. It was a pleasure to use martial arts as the background to "Master Of Misery." It was also my chance to write a plain old-fashioned adventure story, something my dad might have liked.

The martial arts do not exist solely for fighting purposes. There is a healing side to them as well. Cheng Man-ch'ing and Koichi Tohei began studying t'ai chi and judo respectively because they were sickly kids and hoped to benefit their health—rather than with the intention of becoming masters. And there is more, even than health or combat skills, to be gained. There is a special mastery in overcoming one's limitations.

ooooo

Eye of the Falcon

Gerald Hausman

I was back. For better or worse. Back to the place where, ten years before, the bus had gone over the cliff into the gorge, and rolled all the way down to the Double Dragon River. Call it an accident, if you want to—I won't, never will. Fate, destiny, anything but accident.

Call it, then, two moments in time that come together, converge. Separate tracks, etched on eternity's great game board. Then, suddenly, who knows why, they intersect.

And the two become one.

How many times, when I was recovering in the hospital in Kingston, did I promise myself that as soon as I got better, I'd leave, never return to the island?

Jamaica. They didn't nickname it Jamdown for nothing.

Only to come back, after all this time; to stand and look down into the chasm where I fell, and lay, helpless as a bug, pinned to an outcropping of bare rock, while the wild river raced all around me.

The hell of it, in retrospect, was the waiting, the long, indeterminate silence, until finally someone should discover a man, a broken shell of a man, lying contorted on a chunk of stone, slowly, dreamily, bleeding to death.

I was on the rock, they told me, eight hours. I wouldn't know, most of them were pure delirium. There are dreams, but never any details. Whatever happened before the crash is sealed off, beyond the brain's computer terminals, beyond access.

So, now I was back. The metal-legged fool was back. And not just to play around, to lie about in the sun and drink daiquiris. I was here on business—no, I was here on an assignment from Fate. In ten years, I'd built myself back into human shape, molded my muscles into working components that did as they were bidden.

I was a competitive runner, a marathon man. And, as Fate would have it, every year I tried out for one major event, The Carib International Triathalon. Every year I came in toward the back of the pack, with the numberless minions.

Why do I do this insane thing, every year?

Why do I elect to suffer, to put myself through such ignominious defeat?

Don't bother to ask. Consider this, though: perhaps I do it, not to win, but to lose. Or, perhaps, to merely remember pain, to feel the icy edge of that blade that hones the comfortable bones of middle age, and makes them quake, once again, with fear, with trembling madness. Perhaps, in the hope of remembering. Yes, that is closer to the truth, to remember. To see the before, and then, to experience the after.

I was two nights on the island, this time, when I met Jan Volta, the sokol master. He, too, was in training for the triathalon. I had no idea who he was, or for that matter, what sokol was. There were a bunch of us staying at the Casa Maria Hotel on the north coast of Jamaica, all of us training for the big event in July.

It was June when Fate put me next to Jan Volta.

The night I met him, I was having a glass of Campari at the bar. There was a white-haired man, drinking a beer beside me.

"I am seventy-five," he told me, for no apparent reason.

"You're not a day over forty," I said, a little embarrassed by his sudden familiarity. However, I wasn't just being polite. The man, except for his hair, was in remarkably good shape. He had a very Slavic face with a sharp, hawklike nose, and the overall appearance of an aristocrat.

"You are looking," he said sardonically, "at one of my country's oldest sokolists, the last of a dying breed."

He sipped his beer, and chuckled.

I took a sip of my Campari.

"What exactly is a sokolist?"

He examined me with his glacial blue eyes. I saw at once that those eyes missed nothing.

"We are—excuse me, I should say, were—members of the army training corps of Czechoslovakia. The Czech infantry recruited us during the war to train men for combat. The training we provided was unusual, but at the same time, highly effective. My assignment was to travel with the Czech brigade in North Africa, then later on, in England, where I became attached to the R.A.F. After the war, I became a teacher at Charles University, in Prague."

"—Teaching this martial art, sokol?"

"Sokol," he repeated. "It means falcon in Czech."

"I'm sorry, but I've never heard of it."

"No need to apologize. What do Americans know, other than football, or basketball?"

I touched his glass with mine, and said, "Touché."

He smiled, "And what do you do?"

"At the moment, like you—I assume—I'm getting ready for the summer triathalon. When not in training, also like you, I teach."

"And what do you teach?"

"Gymnastics."

He grinned and took a large swallow of beer, finishing off the glass.

"We have something in common then," he mused.

Then he trained his blue eyes on me and gave me one hell of an appraisal.

"Why don't you train with me?" he asked. "I doubt you'd find it very demanding, but maybe I could teach you some things."

"I never work out with anyone. Maybe I should, but . . ."

He laughed. "That is an American attitude, if I've ever heard one. The lone wolf syndrome. In Europe, we got over that a long, long time ago. Well, I do sokol every morning at sunup. The rest of the day, I run, swim, and relax. You're welcome to join me anytime."

He moved away from the bar and shook my hand.

That night, in the dream, I saw something. I did not see myself, lying, bleeding on the rock, but I saw through the eyes of that same man, the man that I once was, the man who had been pitched from the bus, the only survivor of the wreck.

In the dream, I saw the sky, a faultless dome of blue. The slate gray feathers circled the sun, blotted it out. I saw the notch of wings, then the bird dropped down low, flew right at me, and I saw the pale belly feathers, the white, unstreaked throat, the fine barring on the buff breast, as it dropped toward my face, talons outstretched.

I woke in a sweat, my heart pounding, knowing that the bird was a falcon.

At sunrise, he was down on the beach, waiting for me.

When I came up to him, he handed me a staff made of green bamboo.

"I cut it for you just before the moon waned," he said. "That way it will be stronger. Here, try it out."

I took the staff, settled it on my shoulders, as he was doing, hanging my arms over it, in the manner of a scarecrow.

"Is this sokol?" I laughed.

"Just follow along," he said with a thin-lipped smile.

The movements were quick, and arclike; and the staff was held in all manner of awkward positions—behind the head, at shoulder height, in front of the chest, straight over the head. Holding the staff like an instrument of war, Jan Volta made all kinds of parrying swings, winging thrusts, and sudden, sidestepping stabs. His quirky footwork, which I couldn't follow easily, recalled—to my mind, anyway—a scene from Robin Hood.

After about a half hour of this, Jan told me to put down the staff and breathe. For a few minutes, we breathed slowly and deeply, from the diaphragm. Then he began to spar with me.

"Our boxing will be done with small, fist-sized, hand weights made of cast iron," Jan explained.

These felt light in the hand, but only at first. Once we began to dance around with them, my arms felt like lead. And Jan moved about swiftly, using precise, clockwork timing that soon had me out of breath, a surprise I hadn't expected—but then, my upper body was out of shape from the long winter of teaching, of showing rather than doing.

Afterward, we cooled off in the sea, which was flat

and calm at that time of the morning. We swam a half mile out to the reef.

"What is the origin of sokol?" I asked him as we were swimming back to the beach.

"It probably came over to Europe with the Mongols. However, these were people, who, in their quest to conquer, picked up a great many European combative skills. The bending and bowing movements in sokol may have come from the East, but the boxing is old Greco-Roman. This is all guesswork, though. Sokol's been with the Czech people for so long that we don't know its origin anymore. In 1948, the Communists tried to abolish sokol, without very much success. In 1956, it was reinstalled—under Communist guidelines, of course."

He laughed at his own wry sense of humor. All of his remarks, I discovered, were somewhat tinged with a sense of the absurd.

"Is sokol available to everyone in your country?" I asked as we reached the shore.

"It was, and still is, though to a lesser degree than before. Frankly, I know of no comparable institution in other countries. Sokol completely erased class lines. Anyone who wanted to learn it could take it up."

"Where would they learn it?"

"From sokol masters, in the gymnasiums. Every town had them."

It happened, as Fate had willed, that from that day on, Jan Volta became my mentor, my sokol trainer. I told him about my leg, that there were plates and pins holding it together. I went into some detail, in fact, telling him what I knew about the bus wreck. All of this he politely listened to, but when I was finished, he shrugged.

"Hitler took away any interest that I once had in people's misfortunes," he replied grimly. "You speak of your injury as if it were tragic. I lost all of my family during the war, my own father I watched commit suicide as the storm troopers entered the village of Lublyana. In

Italy, I lived on a bare rock for several months with nothing to eat, only lichen. And you tell me of a few broken bones . . ."

I was greatly offended by his remarks and told him so.

"I can't help what happened to you, but I did want you to know what happened to me. From my knee to my ankle, there are fourteen splintered pieces of bone, held together with screws and wires. The surgeon who put me back together said that I was lucky just to be able to walk."

Jan shook his head bitterly.

"You don't seem to understand," he said, "that you are alive. Who cares about your handicap? You must turn your injury into something vital, a weapon to cancel the past."

We never spoke of this again, but in our workouts, it seemed that he showed me no mercy whatsoever. Most of what we did was anaerobic threshold. There, Jan Volta showed me plateaus of pain that I had only dreamed existed. It was hard—no, impossible—to believe that Jan Volta was seventy-five years old. His own endurance and tolerance for pain were immeasurable. And, as I said, while progressing in my lessons with him, he showed me no mercy, none at all.

One day he took me beyond the reef into the open sea, and we swam, unaccompanied by a boat, for two and a half miles. Several times I felt the onset of a cramp in my thigh or calf, and Jan showed me how to soothe the knotted muscle by rolling onto my back, and flutter-kicking lightly until it would go away. He knew a great many tricks.

Another time, while swimming toward Cabarita Island, he took me to a place that the native fishermen call the Horns of the Bull. There, the water was cerulean blue with spokes of sunlight penetrating far into the gloom that lay below. The Horns, as they are called, were created by two crescent-shaped reefs that do not quite connect. The depth between the reefs and the open sea beyond created a hell-spout in the middle, a watery weather peculiar to that one place. The swells between the Horns were twelve to fourteen feet high.

"I'm going to make this a bit difficult for you," Jan said as we swam out to the Horns.

He brought a Ziploc bag out of his wetsuit that contained a couple of Jamaican cigars and a Zippo lighter. As we reached the first of the swells, Jan lit a cigar and handed it to me.

"Keep it lit!" was all that he said.

In order to keep the cigar from being doused, I tried, at first, to arch my neck and swim a little above the surface of the swell. But this proved to be exhausting, as well as cramping.

"Lie on your back—like this," he commanded.

And so I reversed my position and suffered the backstroke. This kept the cigar out of the brine. But the tricky part was breathing through the nostrils, while still puffing on the cigar to keep it lit.

When we got to shore, I discovered my cigar had gone out. Jan was still chomping on his, blowing clouds of blue smoke.

"We're not done yet," he grinned, "I have another test for you."

He handed me his canteen and I took a long swallow of water.

"Now take a mouthful of water, and hold it in your mouth without swallowing it," he ordered.

I nodded. If the last "test" made no sense, this one—whatever it was—already seemed idiotic.

Then, taking a swig himself, he started up Firefly Hill along the goat trail that went up the back of the mountain. We were barefoot. I was tired, and annoyed. But I followed him, begrudgingly, wondering why I was unable to say no to these antics. Sokol was one thing, but these lunatic diversions were quite another.

He took the hill at a torturous pace. I could handle it—on a normal day. But not after chewing on a salt-rimed cigar, and swimming two miles out in the Horns.

Now, there was that maddening mouthful of water sloshing around, tempting and teasing and begging me to swallow it. My throat was burning, my back was aching, and now my bare feet were being punished by an assortment of rocks, thorns, and slippery goat shit that I kept sliding on, and which caused me to bang my knee against the cliffside of the mountain.

As we neared the top of Firefly Hill, I was hit with intestinal rebellion—and vomited all over my feet.

I was cursing Jan Volta, hating myself for throwing up that mouthful of water, and, of course, for failing my "test."

But he was unmindful of my suffering. I saw him peeing off the edge of the mountain. Then he walked back to where I was sitting with my head between my knees, feeling sorry for myself.

"May I have a look at the bottoms of your feet?" he inquired.

Nodding, I lifted them up. My feet were bloody.

On the way down the mountain, he explained to me that it wasn't my feet which needed toughening, but rather my mind.

"Your eyes," he said roughly, "lack sight."

"What do my eyes have to do with my feet?" I asked crossly.

"You must see your goal. You must keep your eye on it while you are running."

"What are you talking about? I did that!"

"If you had—and I doubt that you did—you would've seen something."

"What?" I challenged.

"Did you see the way I was running?"

"Naturally, you were in front of me the whole way."

"Have a look," he said, and he lifted up one of his bare feet.

There were no cuts, no broken blisters. His feet looked fine.

"So—" I said petulantly, "what does that prove?"

"It proves that if you'd been seeing properly, you would've noticed that I was running, not to win, but merely to run. The mountain came to me, just like the swells down at the Horns. I let them come, they're bigger than I am. I just let them. But you attack the water the same way you attack the mountain—with a vengeance. That, my friend, must go. Don't you understand? This is all a shadow play, it means nothing. But someday it will mean something, and then, I hope you will be able to see well with your eyes."

The indignity of the run and the pain in my feet made me angry at him. I felt like the kid who has been betrayed by his scoutmaster.

"I ran lightly," I growled.

He guffawed. "If you'd run lightly, letting your feet fall flat, you wouldn't be suffering right now. I saw what you did. You ran with your feet arched like a deer. You attacked the mountain, when you should've floated a couple inches over it."

Though I was furious with him, I knew that he was right. The fact was, I had a hard time accepting that a seventy-five-year-old man could beat me at my own game. I'd gone at it wrong. My poor feet had hammered up that mountain with, yes, a vengeance.

Suddenly, I sat down and began to howl with laughter.

Jan stood by, not saying anything.

My laughter soon exhausted itself and turned into tears.

After a while, I got up and he said, "A stream stays alive by moving, but a man stays alive by thinking."

The next day, while we were sitting on the lawn in

front of the Casa Maria, Jan saw a boy trying to catch a lizard with a palm noose.

"I bet I can catch that lizard without the noose," Jan chuckled.

But the boy said, "No, mon, de noose is what kotch 'im."

Jan stepped up to the pimiento tree where the big green iguana had taken refuge.

The boy said sourly, "You nah go kotch 'im like dat, mon. You haffa use de noose fe kotch dat lizard."

Jan walked boldly up to the lizard and stared into its golden eye. Neither one of them moved. The sun was hot, sweat rolled down Jan's neck, yet he remained as inert as the lizard. Finally, the lizard began to crawl up the tree. Then, like a striking snake, Jan's hand shot out and seized the lizard by the throat. Laughing, he handed it over to the boy, who asked how he had done it.

"Green lizard too fast fe kotch wid de hand," the boy said, holding up his prize, in amazement.

"No," Jan said, "the hand is always quicker than the eye. But with creatures quicker than the hand, you allow them to think that you're not there anymore. Then, when their attention is elsewhere, you take them. That is how I caught the lizard."

I asked him, later, if he had learned that trick from anyone.

He explained that he'd picked it up from his first sokol teacher, a master by the name of Mr. Hoyer.

"We were in the Carpathian Mountains," he said, "and we had caught a small female falcon. My teacher, Mr. Hoyer, told me to sit with the bird, which was tethered to a post in the dirt floor of the barn where we were going to pass the night. 'Whatever you do, don't look away from that falcon's eye,' Mr. Hoyer told me.

"Unfortunately, after several hours of staring mindlessly into the falcon's eye, I got drowsy and fell asleep. When I awoke, Mr. Hoyer was angry with me. 'You have ruined her,' he said, 'now I must start her training all over again.' Then he sat in front of the bird and readied himself for the staring match. Soon the bird and the man were one; they had locked eyes.

"At first, I believed that it was only their eyes which were connected. Then I understood the deeper truth. The two of them were joined—not eye to eye, as I'd supposed—but soul to soul. It was fascinating to watch two creatures of this earth, so different, and yet, because of this strange union, one and the same.

"In the end, somewhere near dawn, the bird finally grew weary. Once, just once, she closed her fiery eye. And Mr. Hoyer's gloved hand folded over the bird's beaked head. She made no move to resist—the stunned falcon was won, her soul now belonged to Mr. Hoyer. Thus do we pass the spirit of that bird, man to man, through the art of sokol."

One week later, we journeyed to the Blue Mountains to climb the cliff known as Jacob's Ladder. Jan said it would be a final test for me. The climb, perhaps because of the condition I was in, was not very strenuous; that is, until we came to the ladder itself.

What lay before us, then, was a promontory of sun-baked clay. Handholds had been carved into it for perhaps twenty yards, then the vertical incline leveled, so that the climber was again on safe ground. The problem the ladder posed was that of a maze. The bright sun played on the faceted footholds, blinding the climber. And the slick clay looked like black porcelain. One lost grip, and the climb would be over.

"Remember," Jan warned, "do not look down. Keep your eye trained on the falcon's eye."

I nodded, then began the ascent.

For better than halfway up, I kept my mind empty, my eye on the clefts of black burning clay. Jan was behind me, placing his hands where I removed my feet. There was no room, no time, for error. We had to climb regularly, breathing in unison, moving steadily upward.

Then, for a fraction of a second, my eye faltered. I saw the crack between my chest and the clay wall. In that crack lay the most beautiful green valley I had ever seen. It was the valley we left behind when we began our ascent. Down there the wind was making the leaves of the coffee trees glitter. I could see the coffee bean pickers, their yellow hats and croker sacks, and I could feel the beauty that was below me, and it never occurred to me that it was the beauty of death.

At the same time I felt the urge to let go, to plummet through that desirable crack in the cloud-mist, I sensed a presence, not Jan, but someone else, pressing me to the bosom of the mountain. The presence, I knew immediately, was female. And then the beautiful valley closed from my sight. The shifting cloud cover wiped it out, and I found my cheek pressed to the hot clay. Again, the presence urged me on my way; I thought of the clear eye of that conquered raptor, and proceeded to climb.

That night we camped in an orchid meadow. The sweet scent of wild Jamaican orchids filled the night with their blooming fragrance, and the pine sticks we burned added to the sweetness. The thin mountain air was cool and refreshing after the arduous day in the sun.

I explained to Jan what had happened to me on Jacob's Ladder.

"Ah," he sighed, "I was afraid so. For a while there, you hardly moved."

"I know that I was dreaming the climber's dream of death, but she brought me back."

Jan stared fixedly at me through the dancing flames.

Finally he spoke, "You just said, 'she' brought you back."

"It was the falcon spirit that I felt. She came to me. The falconess."

For a long time, he said nothing. We both stared at the

flames, the sparks, the gulf of silence between us. Words seemed foolish at such a time. There was the wind, the heady smell of mountain orchids, the impenetrable night as deep as the fathoms that lay below the Horns of the Bull back in the little bay that surrounded Port Maria.

"My friend," Jan said at last, "from now on, you are on your own. I have nothing more to teach you."

"There is one thing that I would like you to tell me."

"Yes?" He looked at me quizzically.

"Once she has blessed you—then what?"

He frowned. "She has not blessed you. Neither has she cursed you. She has merely given you her gaze. Now, the real work begins."

After returning from the Blue Mountains, there were only a couple of days before the triathalon. I mostly spent them on the beach, meditating. Jan came and went, on his various rounds. He was cordial, as ever, but beneath his polite manner he was quite aloof. On the morning of my departure to Kingston, he was nowhere around. I suppose he wanted it that way.

The bus ride from Port Maria to Kingston was on one of those ancient country buses, that have names like Prince Alphonso or King Tubby. They are full of chickens and goats, as well as people, and when the switchbacks on the Junction Road begin, everything inside the bus heaves and rolls chaotically.

Near the little village of Friendship, a beautiful woman got into the bus and sat beside me. The sudden touch of her flesh against mine produced an odd, forgotten sensation—that of sexual arousal. My long absence from any female put me into a kind of decadent daydream, one in which I imagined making love to the woman sitting next to me. And, as the bus pitched forward and aft, I found myself mentally undressing her.

Then we were asprawl, pleasuring ourselves with sex. The bus and its many occupants dimmed and faded. There was only the woman and me, her honey-colored skin melting against mine, as we rolled with the turns of the Junction Road, careening across each curve with passion, aware only of our bodies, our lust.

Just as the two of us spiraled toward orgasm, the bus braked violently, and, failing to make a switchback, suddenly plummeted sideways, crashing down the mountain. Bamboo thickets pounded against the metal sheathing of the bus, and we were thrown about in confusion. Luggage plowed into people's faces; there were shrieks, screams, cries of agony.

Instinctively, I clutched the hand of the beautiful woman next to me. In another moment, the bus went end over end, and crashed into the Double Dragon River. Enmeshed in flailing human forms, I watched as a child was swept by in the floodwater that had now entered the battered bus.

"We've got to get out of here," I shouted at the woman, whose hand was still in mine. Dragging her forcefully, I kicked through an already-splintered window, and, as the green water of the river swallowed us whole, we disappeared, kicking into the gloom. And not a moment too soon, for within a matter of seconds, the bus was gone, and we were fighting for our lives in the tumult of the current.

The Double Dragon is a notoriously treacherous river. Engorged from recent rains, the power of the spray tossed us, smashed us, until, unexpectedly, a hard object slammed into us. It was a steel girder connected to an unfinished bridge. The green water raged past us on all sides. We were pinned, the two of us, to the steel protrusion.

It was then—to my horror—I realized that I'd let go of her hand. She was nowhere to be seen. All around me the wild scales of the Double Dragon flashed in the sun. But the woman was gone, washed away in the flood.

There was nothing left to do but climb up that spike

into the sky, inching my way up, muttering softly as I climbed. I knew that I had gone farther than I had ever gone before, that I was beyond the pale, into the twilight world of non definition, pure sensate truth. Everything glowed like hoarfrost, burned before my eye.

Then I saw Babylon blown away, notes of New Orleans jazz tickling my inner ear. I watched, fascinated, as the mountainous grace of the lion sun slouched toward Bethlehem. The plains of Jericho dynamiting wheat, the watercolors of Atlantis running together, the black clouds hanging over the blue Nile.

I became lost in the wind pines of Lebanon, looking for my name, calling for my love as the children of Auschwitz, listened to Segovia's guitar weeping in the snow.

Then all this whirled away.

Waves of nausea passed through me. I looked at my hand and recognized the crumpled tape, the victory ribbon crushed in my palm. For a hushed second, I was all things: fish, lizard, monkey, man. Then I could hear tumultuous shouting, circling faces. The race was over, I had won. The crowd rioted around me.

I got to my feet, unsteadily, peered into the sky. And even before I saw her wings darkening the sun, I saw the eye of the falcon.

In 1968, after suffering a crippling accident, not unlike the one described in the story, I was challenged to learn the art of sokol from a man who recognized my instability but refused to accept it. He was the master described as Jan Volta. Having seen men gnaw through their wrist bones to free themselves of chains, my teacher had little patience for someone as self-indulgent and weak-willed as myself.

During a period that lasted roughly seven years, he put me through a barrage of personal fitness tests, while teaching me the basic moves of the Czech sokolist. To this day, I have never fully understood how a man of his age was able to put himself through the extreme vicissitudes of mental and physical stress, and always come out smiling. Once, after cross-country skiing for twenty-four miles without stopping, he turned to me and said, "Do you sweat?"

This, in his parlance, meant more than winning, for to sweat was to be alive, and to stay alive meant that you were, as he put it, "always the winner."

Zen or Taoism, depending on whether you are talking to a Japanese or a Chinese practitioner of the martial arts, have given much in the way of attitudes and states of mind which can affect one's philosophy as well as one's body.

ooooo

LISTEN

Joel Richards

Kata.

Cameron looked over the expanse of hardwood floor at the Project's rec center. Though used heavily by the scientists and administrative staff for both basketball and volleyball, the fine-grained wood showed hardly a scuff mark—and without varnish or protective covering of any type. The *temora* tree was a remarkable specimen of this world's flora. A derivative of its bark produced an acetylcholine look-alike that showed promise as a retriever of memory and a reverser of senility. Cameron's research team was working on its synthesis in water soluble form.

But Cameron was not in his professional mode. That aspect of the *temora* tree was for the lab. The polished and unmarked floor was commanding his nowtime attention. He took one step forward, then another, carving his way slowly and fluidly on an unseen path. Each movement flowed from the one before, yet there was no clear line of demarcation between where one left off and the next began. But there was precision.

One step. Two. Turn and pivot.

But no one to throw. Or to throw him.

Cameron switched his mind-set from judo to karate, and wished that he had trained more in that art. He had only a green belt's skill and complexity to work from. Still, a *karateka* could punch and kick at chimeras and feel fulfilled. Judo required an *uke* to offer resistance and a *tori* to counterthrow. There were no other *judokas* on this world.

But somehow, improbably, there was a *karateka*. The air shimmered before Cameron, a heat refraction, perhaps. He looked up to see the serene features of Hideo Nakajima, his old *sensei*, advancing toward him, his faded black belt and its embroidery before him in perfect detail to the smallest thread.

The *sensei* advanced deliberately, with none of the speed that he would produce against a high-ranked opponent in free combat. He launched a series of blows. Cameron blocked, pivoted, and delivered a roundhouse kick. In a movement of grace and economy, the black belt evaded the blow and landed a side kick of his own. Cameron saw his *sensei*'s foot meet his *gi*, but he felt nothing. His mind raced back to that first series of blows he had blocked, his mind registering what it had ignored in the instinctive transition to counter kick. No impact. He had blocked nothing.

He turned to face his partner and found himself alone.

Off to the side stood the Project Manager. Beside him was a visiting Alcaidan, one Cameron had not seen before. Or had he?

The Alcaidan smiled and turned away.

* * *

The Project Manager folded his hands neatly on the desk before him and looked at them. So did Cameron. Those hands were weapons, as lethal as those of any *karateka.* How many forms Mainwaring's hands had shuffled, how many memos they had signed! And how those documents could cut down a career.

But those hands weren't those of a hatchet man now. Mainwaring looked worried himself.

"Peter," Mainwaring said, "it relieves and gratifies me that our hosts have finally extended a social invitation to us. It pains me that it has been extended to you. But so be it."

Cameron waited, but Mainwaring's gaze had once more retreated to his manicured and immobile hands.

"An invitation," Cameron stated, with no interrogatory inflection.

"They invite you to an interview. If you comport yourself satisfactorily—whatever that may mean—you will be invited to a Hunt."

"I see."

"Do you?" Mainwaring raised his eyebrows. "There's a lot I don't see. What these Alcaidans are really like. They're shapeshifters, but what do they really look like when they're not trying to make some sort of impression on us? How do they think? Why do they invent and have us process endless forms and have us carry on to little purpose? My job has involved too much idle paper pushing, even—I'll be frank—by my standards. And I've pushed a lot of meaningless paper in my fight to the top of the tree."

"Very Savoyard," Cameron observed.

"Yes, Peter, I *do* understand my own allusion. It does take some brains to oversee you scientists and free you from the paperwork you all disdain. I'd like to see you do your part and produce some marketable derivatives from these botanical compounds that you seem to think are so unique and promising. It would make my job easier—and yours safer—if you can come up with a pharmaceutical that the company can convert to some value." He paused and frowned. "Meanwhile I've got to deal with these Alcaidans and their whims and ways. And figure out what we can give back to them when they get around to demanding compensation. Perhaps this Hunt will give you some insight." Mainwaring looked at Cameron's expectant face. "Or do you have one already?"

Cameron regarded Mainwaring soberly. "Straw mats and judo *gis*."

Mainwaring's eyes narrowed. He opened his mouth, thought better of it. He silently waved Cameron out.

Ansari Farhal was this year's Master of the Hunt and therefore inheritor of the Alcaidan title of *kir*. Kir—an Earthside drink of cassis and white wine. Very cool and refreshing, as Cameron remembered it. Ansari *kir* looked cool. Refreshing, however, was not the word. Noble was more it. Noble in purpose, not in effete decay.

Ansari's eyes glittered. His clothes glittered. He shimmered as he moved. His motions were economical, smooth, purposeful. Nothing wasted. He used his hands, did not study them. He motioned Cameron to a chair.

"Would you like to join our Hunt?" he asked.

"Yes."

"Do you know what it is, what is its quarry, what it is about?"

"No."

Ansari *kir* turned from his desk to the window and looked out on the forest that began beyond his walls. No tended greensward, no formal gardens to the estate of this nobleman. A local Schwarzwald seemed his estate.

Cameron studied his profile and thought of Roman coins.

Ansari *kir* turned back to look at Cameron full face. "We come to a gorge with an untried bridge over turbulent rapids. Someone must try the bridge—or the quarry escapes. You or a companion of the Hunt. How do you choose?''

Cameron turned and looked about him in studied scrutiny.

''I see no bridge, no rapids, no companions.''

Ansari *kir* nodded. ''You'll do.''

''That answer did it?'' Mainwaring asked.

''Seems so.''

Mainwaring shook his head. ''I don't see that this tells us much. I don't understand the mode of thinking, the allusion. Perhaps that's why I wasn't chosen. But, Peter—would you explain?''

''Explaining spoils it,'' Cameron said, then relented at the sight of Mainwaring's visage. This was no longer the bureaucratic whip cracker that had formerly menaced and plagued him. The Project Manager needed help. ''It's self-referential. The answer is part of the question. And this was an interior joke, acknowledging our own idiom. A bridge that shouldn't be crossed till we get to it. Perhaps we never will.''

Silence from Mainwaring.

''They're telling us to stop making elaborate contingency plans,'' Cameron added gently. ''Stay in the moment.''

The Hunt was gathering in the courtyard when Cameron arrived, but Ansari *kir* disengaged himself from the preparations to meet his offworld guest. Glass in hand and with a lazy camaraderie that transcended noblesse oblige, he placed his arm about Cameron's shoulder and escorted him up the broad steps and into his hall. A great punch bowl of crystal rested on a rough-hewn trestle table covered by a damask cloth. A pleasing set of contrasts. Heaped on silver trays was an array of rolls and loaves, some with warmth rising from them. Several sportsmen busied themselves with cutting the breads and layering them with spreads from nearby bowls. All turned toward the master of the hall and the Hunt as he neared with Cameron in tow, and all raised their glasses in salutation.

"Mr. Peter Cameron," Ansari *kir* announced. He stepped back and raised his glass. "Our new companion of the Hunt!"

All the company swung glasses to lip in graceful parabolic arcs. The nearest took a crystal goblet chased in silver, filled it from the bowl, and extended it to Cameron.

"The Hunt!" Cameron toasted. "And the Field!"

To an approving murmur all drank again. Cameron as well.

"Drink up and eat, gentlemen," Ansari *kir* said. "Our mounts await us."

In fifteen minutes Cameron learned the names to a dozen faces and put down a hunt breakfast that would have done for dinner at many an Earthside inn.

The company turned out again to the courtyard, where it met up with an assemblage of mounts and trackers. Ansari *kir* again detached himself from the general preparations to see Cameron firmly in the saddle of a handsomely turned out *gaffa*, its trappings and harness gay and colorful in the early sun.

"Here," Ansari *kir* handed up a helmet of local design, its utilitarian plastsheen leathered and painted in the amber and green colors of the Hunt. "Wear it and be at one with your mount."

And with the world, he might have said. Cameron pulled the helmet on and found the colors about him jumping at him in augmented brilliance. He heard sounds of forest wildlife beyond the courtyard walls: timid ground rodents; arboreal creatures; raptors soaring. His *gaffa*'s mind was strongest and closest to hand. It awaited not his commands but his impulses, and to course with him as a companion, not as a mere beast of burden. The minds of the trackers, a feeling of all-consuming quest, impinged eagerly. And those of his companions—their swirl and energies flowed about him without words.

Cameron looked about him. If the company felt him, his alienness, they showed no sign. They wore no helmets.

"No need," said/thought Ansari *kir*. "And, yes, they see/feel your presence. With welcome and anticipation."

He waved and the gates folded open. The eager parade flowed out, not into the forest but across a meadow of spring grass and wildflowers. Not at all as Cameron remembered it. He recalled the encroaching forest just outside of every wall. *Every* wall? Were there more outlooks here, more points to the compass than the usual thirty-two?

Another question that held its own answer. It was the best kind. It went unasked.

"Ride!" Ansari *kir* commanded.

Cameron rode.

When Cameron looked back on it later, it seemed a timeless idyll. Perhaps it had been. Perhaps it had all been a nanosecond synaptic flash, a compression beyond words. Words. Words were seldom used. The helmet obviated the need for words, save those that held their own intrinsic and autonomous body and were to be held up and admired as they sparkled. Or words as shorthand for an abstract shard of thought. There were more of these than a morning of coursing through wood and field might be expected to produce.

The Hunt ranged across meadows wet with morning dew, then hot under a noonday sun. Early hour cricket sounds ceased as they rode through the grass, but the small internal hummings carried unabated through the helmet. The insect hummings of midday never stopped.

There were also dark copses of bay and laurel to be traversed, and forest trails that had to be taken at a slower pace and in single file. No matter that the quarry might not choose to hold to wooded paths.

As the day reached its hottest they emerged from the forest coolness to a grassy swale by the river. The sun was at its zenith, but an array of tents, striped with brightness, drew the eye and promised shade. The party dismounted and turned the *gaffas* loose to graze, drink, and dream. The tents were airy, the fabric ending several feet off the ground with only the guy lines to tie them down. Within lay trays of cheeses and breads, drinks in beds of ice, refreshing sorbets. All as if just laid out, though there were no retainers to be seen.

The company looked as if refreshment was in order. Though Cameron was warm, it seemed as nothing compared to Ansari *kir* and the others of the field. Perspiration flowed down their faces, seeming to melt the promontories of their features, flattening them visibly. Ansari *kir*'s aquiline nose seemed to have broadened and spread, appearing almost squashy. Cameron looked closer at his companions. Their clothes, too, though they must have been designed for the Hunt, appeared to be too flimsy for the task. They seemed to be bursting at the seams and rent where twigs and branches had torn and snagged. Beneath appeared patches of mottled skin.

None paid any mind; all addressed themselves to the refreshments. Cameron did as well, till Ansari *kir* called a halt and led them to the largest tent of all. Before his eyes had adjusted to the shadowed light within, Cameron's feet and nose told him that he was in a *dojo*. He felt the firm springiness of *tatami* underfoot. The smell of fresh straw hung in the sun-warmed air. Cameron sat down on the edge of the mat and removed his shoes. When he looked up he saw his companions in a new guise. They were more clearly human again, of varying statures and weights, all attired in judo *gis*. He recognized the faces of old friends and opponents, smelled their body odors around him, felt the rough softness of his often-washed *gi* on his shoulders. A faint breeze stirred the hairs on his naked chest.

"Your *dojo*, your art, Cameron," Ansari *kir* said. He alone kept his features as Cameron remembered them. "Lead us through the stretches and *ukemi*."

The crisp sounds of rollups and arm slaps permeated the air, rebounding off the tent walls. *Uchikomi* followed, as the *judokas* paired off and practiced repetitions of step-ins, taking their lead from Cameron. Cameron's partner was Ansari *kir*, the player on the defensive. Cameron played *tori*, attacking with *ogoshi* in a reverse pivot, spiraling in and down to slam his hips in below his partner's belt. He slid his arm around Ansari *kir*'s waist to pull him onto Cameron's back, and realized something was wrong. He was coming in too high, not breaking his partner's balance. And Cameron's arms were not succeeding in encircling a girth that seemed broader than met the eye.

Instinctively, Cameron pivoted out to stand face-to-face with his partner. Ansari *kir* bowed. "My apologies," he said.

Cameron looked again and saw the squatter and heavier form that Ansari *kir* had presented at the refreshment tent. Only the face remained as before. Cameron nodded in understanding. He took Ansari *kir* through a series of shorter players' moves—hip throws, mainly. The other *judokas* took their cue from the main pair and followed along in the repetitions. In-out; in-out. The air became heavier and moister, overlaid with an exudation subtly different from human sweat.

They were fast learners.

Expectation also hung in the air, as palpable as these other aromas. At last Ansari *kir* voiced the collective desire. "*Randori*?"

Cameron nodded. He stepped to the center of the mat together with Ansari *kir*. They bowed, then grasped each other's lapels and sleeves and began.

Cameron took them in a wheeling counterclockwise shuffle. He tried an ankle block. Ansari *kir* hopped over it. Cameron closed for a left side *osoto gari* and found his opponent pivoting away. They resumed their circling movement. Cameron tried using his tall man's leg reach into a *tai otoshi*, a good throw to use on a short, stocky opponent. He spun on his left foot, shot his right leg out to block Ansari *kir*'s ankle, and tried to wheel him over his extended leg. Again, his opponent hopped over the block, then pivoted into a *kubi nage*, his hips coming in swiftly to break Cameron's balance, his arm going for a headlock. Cameron dropped his hips just in time to get his weight low enough to avoid being doubled over and to slip the encircling arm. Ansari *kir* was fast. Too fast.

They circled again and Cameron thought it over.

And then he had it. He stopped thinking, adopted a state of *no mind*. He let his body think, allowing no premeditation that could be read. When his body found the opening and moved in, it was with a hip throw of his own, unlooked for from a taller man. It was Ansari *kir*'s turn to plant his legs and drop low to block Cameron's *seoi nage*. But as Cameron spun in he reversed his pivot, hooking his opponent's left leg with his right, catching it just below the knee. Cameron slammed his left shoulder into Ansari *kir*'s, driving him back to his left corner. His opponent's right leg was off the ground, and Cameron kept driving, hopping on his left leg and hooking Ansari *kir*'s supporting leg out from under till his opponent fell backward onto his back and slapped the mat hard.

Cameron helped him up. They disengaged to straighten their *gis* and bowed.

"The technique?" Ansari *kir* asked with raised eyebrow.

"*Ouchi gari*. Inside leg hook."

They made way for others to spar. They changed partners and reengaged.

Time passed. The sun lowered till its rays pierced the tent opening, illumining dust motes that danced about them as they sparred.

They were back at the refreshment tent. Cameron regarded his companions over the ices and fruits. They were again in their clothing of the Hunt, and their transmogrification continued. To what end? How much of their reality could he and humankind accept?

What was reality and what illusion? Could they be the same thing, different forms?

Cameron felt a wetness on his bare arm and looked up. A transfigured and no longer patrician Ansari *kir* stood over him, in his hand several pellets of ice. Between his hairy fingers and trickling onto Cameron's arm were droplets of cold water.

Same thing. Different forms.

The ride back was more leisured. The forest itself seemed less sylvan, more brushy and dotted with down wood and dead snags. Cameron watched with interest but no apprehension as the clothes seemed to tear off the huntsmen, leaving only rags to cover mottled skin blotched by almost random tufts of fur. But still the exhilarating mental byplay went on, a stimulating canopy to whatever was corporeal underneath.

There continued a certain nobility of thought. Another had said it before: an ordinary man *is* a Buddha; illusion is salvation. A foolish thought—and we are ordinary, vulgar, stupid. The next enlightened thought—and we are the Buddha.

Ansari *kir* pulled abreast of Cameron, his face a hairy and feral mask. But the mental clarity and fineness were there.

I would have put it differently: a foolish thought—and we are enlightened. An enlightened thought—and we are again ordinary creatures.

Ansari *kir* spurred his mount and pulled ahead. *Enough talk. Enlightenment is an activity, not a state. Let us ride.*

Mainwaring's office was cluttered. Desk drawers open; containers on the floor. Wall hangings were down, leaning against boxes at floor level. Mainwaring's desk was untypically empty, dotted only by a holocube of his family, and a single pad of scratch paper.

"What was it all about?" Mainwaring asked. "This Hunt and its quarry?"

"You can view it as a metaphor. It's what you make of it," Cameron said. "I saw the Hunt as a focusing device. The quarry is what we should be seeing every day, the voices we should be listening to. Sometimes we have to get in motion, out of our ruts to take it in." He paused. "I suppose I was part of the quarry. That and the judo. What I had to say and show them."

Mainwaring nodded. "A valuable insight, no doubt. But I had hoped for something more tangible, something we could run with." He looked at Cameron. "The Alcaidans want me to go, you know. They want you to stay."

Cameron regarded Mainwaring. The Project Manager did not look well. He had undergone his own transformation. The diminishment in power had brought on a distinct loss of bearing.

"I don't understand much of this," Mainwaring went on. "They ask that future teams include zen practitioners. Also martial artists. Karate, judo, the business with the swords—what's the word?"

"Kendo."

"Yes. I gather they're getting all this from you."

"From you, too," Cameron said. "From all of us. Don't plan on keeping any secrets. They keep us happy by talking to us, but they don't have to. They're telepathic."

Mainwaring didn't seem as perturbed by this as Cameron had expected. Perhaps he was more preoccupied with the damage of this assignment to his career.

"What do they want with martial artists?"

"The mind-set mostly," Cameron said. "A way of looking at things. That and the engagement, the sparring—physical and mental. That's what they value in every new culture they encounter, and that's how we earn what we want of them."

Mainwaring was back to the habit of folding and steepling his hands. "I suppose they can adapt to the physicality of our martial arts, being shapeshifters."

"They're not shapeshifters," Cameron said.

Mainwaring looked up.

"That's an assumption our contact party made when observing their artwork and contrasting it with the appearance they presented us," Cameron said. "But it's wrong. They can influence our minds, overlay them with their illusions. They give us a reassuring image, what makes us comfortable."

Including an inventively useless amount of busywork for you. Cameron thought it, didn't say it.

"Do you know what they really look like, then?"

Cameron shook his head. *Hopeless.* "Perhaps. It doesn't matter. Sir. To them that's all illusion."

"Well," Mainwaring said, "I doubt I'll ever understand. But I do try."

"Perhaps you're trying in the wrong way."

"Is there a right way?"

Cameron looked surprised, then nodded his approval. "That's better."

"Do I want to go around asking your kind of questions?" Mainwaring turned to Cameron with the first trace of self-directed humor that Cameron could recall. "And without you to consult, whom do I ask?"

Cameron looked at the lacquered desktop for a moment, then reached across it for the scratch pad. Cameron eyed its thickness, then turned it on edge and rapped the desk sharply with it, producing a crisp wooden sound.

Mainwaring started, then settled back in his chair.

Cameron reached out to return the pad. Mainwaring regarded him with a raised eyebrow, then held out his hand to take it. Cameron turned the pad on edge and rapped Mainwaring's hand smartly. Mainwaring cried out, more in surprise than in pain.

"Why didn't the desk cry out?" Cameron asked.

Mainwaring held his hand and looked at Cameron in bewilderment.

Cameron spoke into the silence.

"Learn to listen, and you can hear it."

Quite a few writers have written stories exploring—sometimes quite provocatively—the offworld exportation of Christianity and Judaism, and their reception among nonhuman races. A lot less attention has been paid to Far Eastern philosophies and religions in this context.

Though Gautama was certainly not a combative figure, the connection between Buddhism and the martial arts mind-set has often been noted. Judo and zen are a discipline and a philosophy grounded in the human experience. I was interested in exploring how they might interact, translate, and transcend with a nonhuman race that knows illusion, and is in fact its master. "Listen" is the result.

One of the two faces of life wears a smile. It is not good to go too long without looking back and laughing at ourselves.

ooooo

True Grits

Jack C. Haldeman II

Bubba Johnson sat on his sagging front porch and looked out past the junked cars and abandoned refrigerators in his front yard to the Georgia scrub pine forest beyond. Rex, his faithful Doberman, snarled contentedly in his sleep; dreaming, no doubt, of ripping the throats out of helpless bunny rabbits. Bubba drained his can of Budweiser, crushed it and tossed it off the porch, where it landed on a pile of about a thousand other crushed Budweiser cans. He belched, scratched his ample belly, and dug into the ice chest for another brew. The ice chest was empty.

No matter. They would be coming soon. Life was good.

Karen sighed and braced herself against the dashboard of the clapped-out VW van as it bounced down the narrow, pothole-infested limerock road. Greg was driving far too fast. He always did when he was on a sacred mission.

Unfortunately, all of life was a sacred mission to Greg, a headlong dash toward some sort of inner perfection. Currently he was heading toward inner perfection at nearly sixty miles an hour on a backwoods Georgia road where he would surely kill them both.

Sanity was not one of Greg's strong points. Karen knew that well, but she loved him deeply and he had many other redeeming qualities, such as inner peace, stubbornness, and a very handsome mustache.

"Watch out for that cow," she cried as an emaciated Hereford ambled across the road in a vain search for something besides wire grass to chew on.

Greg smiled serenely, flicked the steering wheel, and missed creating a few hundred pounds of hamburger by about six inches. The van went into a life-threatening skid, scattering sand and gravel, heading in the general direction of a very large oak tree by the side of the road.

"Far out," said Greg, as he casually brought the vehicle under semicontrol. "It's beautiful when you encounter nature."

"Well, that encounter was a bit too close for me," said Karen, deeply regretting that Greg had abandoned nunjutsu. Even with the bruises, it had been a far simpler time.

Born too late for the sixties, Greg had been playing catch-up all his life. He yearned for the flower power days that were only a secondhand memory from his parents, who had conceived him—according to family legend—in a muddy sleeping bag at Woodstock. He had been raised on a steady diet of high-fiber granola and Beatles music. Greg remembered his childhood with a warm glow, and had adopted as a lifestyle a philosophy that incorporated all of the metaphysical viewpoints of his parents save one.

Passive resistance did not fit in with his chosen profession as a night clerk at the local 7-Eleven.

For Greg truly loved his work, though it was not without danger. He found peace and tranquility in the orderly arrangement of oil cans and cigarette packages. He was in touch with his inner child as he arranged the candy bars and bubble gum. The chance to show lost strangers the given path as they wandered in late at night, dazed from the road and desperately clutching out-of-date maps filled Greg with purpose and direction. He thought of all the branching lifelines he was part of as he made change from the self-serve gas pumps—all those unknown miles to exotic destinations like Atlanta and Waycross and they all were somehow connected to him. He loved the thrill of selling someone a lottery ticket, a chance to radically change their lives and fulfill all their deepest dreams and desires.

Greg kept the coffee black and hot and strong for the all-night truckers and happily cleaned up the sugar they spilled and the little white containers of nondairy creamer that they left scattered on the floor in their wake as they drove off into the Georgia darkness, fulfilling their destiny astride their diesel steeds. He even enjoyed cleaning the rest rooms, marveling at the many faces of love and how that act of emotional bonding could be enhanced by purchasing exotic devices from the machines on the wall. There were even some handy phone numbers written nearby for the lonely. Greg liked the fact that he could meditate at 4:00 A.M. in his brightly lit chambers with no interruptions.

Greg liked everything about his profession except being robbed.

The first three times it happened he simply turned over the money. For his cooperation, he received an interesting and painful assortment of black eyes, bruises, and a first-class bump on the head. The fourth time, he pulled out a baseball bat and ended up in the emergency room at Northside Regional. Greg was no Ted Williams.

He had lots of time for meditation in the hospital while they patched him up. He also watched a lot of TV. On Channel Five he discovered enlightenment.

In a Darvon-induced fog that fateful night in the hospital he watched a made-for-TV movie about a gentle man who came into a crime-ridden town and wiped out about a hundred bad guys with his bare hands and a whole bunch of well-placed kicks. The hero also had every good-looking chick in town falling all over him.

The martial arts sounded very appealing to Greg. Thus his quest began.

The paths to enlightenment were not easy to find in his hometown, which was not much more than a stoplight, a feed store, two churches, three bars, and a 7-Eleven. That's when he bought the VW van. It expanded his options and got good gas mileage.

In a neighboring town he started with kung fu. To his surprise, he found he had a natural talent for it. Not only did he have an innate sense of balance and self-preservation, but the philosophical aspects of the activity meshed well with his personality. He advanced rapidly and stayed with the group for over a year before he got bored, which was some kind of a record for him.

He then moved over to karate, discovering that he actually liked delivering powerful hand blows and kicking people. He studied under a variety of instructors and fared best under the hardest ones. Then he shifted over to judo and threw and grappled in the dojo with the best of them. Something was still missing, though. He had not yet found the center.

Jujitsu seemed the answer for a time, then aikido. Yet every time he took another step to the integration of mind and body there seemed to be something missing. He kept looking.

The answer was not found in t'ai chi, nor kendo

(though he did like whacking people with sticks). He drifted aimlessly from group to group, trying on and shedding philosophies and techniques as he went. He joined up with a small band of other dissatisfied souls. Together they continued a seemingly fruitless journey for enlightenment. It was on one of their many quests that their karma converged with the front bumper of Bubba Johnson's pickup truck at a rural intersection.

Bubba ran the stop sign. That much was clear. What confused Greg and the others was the way he jumped screaming from his pickup truck and tossed a Budweiser can against the passenger door of the VW van. Their first thought was that the man had not found his center, and was clearly not in harmony. How wrong they had been.

Bubba was abusive, kicking the van and calling them hippies. Finally George, who was six-four, got out and faced the angry man. He towered over Bubba, who backed up to his pickup truck, which was leaking steam from a busted radiator. George raised his hands and struck a classic pose.

"Kung fu," he said gently, in an even and quiet voice that held great power. He had never had to do more than that, being an impressive hunk of a man.

Bubba reached inside the truck. "Tire iron," he said and took out George with a swift clunk to the side of his head with an oversize lug wrench.

Greg was stunned. He had never seen such quick and decisive action. There was grace and beauty here, hidden behind the clever facade of a redneck farmer. The application of maximum force with minimum effort was magnificent in execution, clearly the result of a lifetime of study. He stood in awe.

At last he had found, in this unlikely place, what he had been seeking for years. Enlightenment.

Greg looked at his friends around him. Bert had a look of sheer amazement plastered over his face. Sam radiated respect and wonder. Jimmy was simply overwhelmed.

"Tire iron," they whispered together, having shared the vision. "Tire iron."

Thus the students started their long apprenticeship at the feet of the master.

"Do I have to?" asked Karen as the VW skidded through a patch of loose sand. "I hate these caps."

Greg smiled gently at her and touched the brim of his John Deere cap. Her own cap said Purina Feed across the front. It all meant something, but exactly what was not real clear to Karen. And that in itself, she knew, meant that she would never qualify for a John Deere cap. "I liked the belts better," she said, and it was true. "At least you know where you stand with a belt."

Karen had teamed up with Greg somewhere between karate and kendo. From the first time they'd hit the mat together she had been hopelessly in love.

The gate to Bubba's place was open, and the dirt path leading up to the house was littered with empty beer cans and discarded fast-food hamburger containers. Greg admired the stark and purposeful maleness of that carefully planned action. It was not unlike the alpha wolf in a pack lifting his leg to mark and define his territory. The leaving of spoor had a long and honored tradition.

The old wooden house looked as if a strong wind would blow it away. Its boards were weathered and rotten, patched at irregular intervals with scraps of plywood nailed at haphazard angles. Several broken windowpanes were covered with cardboard. It sat precariously on cinder blocks, leaning sharply to the left.

Surrounded by almost two acres of junked cars, the shack was a statement of Bubba's rejection of every traditional materialistic value known to Western man. Although the master claimed proudly that he had never crossed a state line in his life, his life clearly had been painted with a Zen brush and touched up here and there with the essence of Taoism.

They were late. The others had already started. Greg

placed his six-pack offering in Bubba's ice chest and they joined Sam, who was hard at work under the crumpled hood of a blue Oldsmobile Cutlass convertible.

"Fuel pump," said Sam without looking up.

"Fuel pump," echoed Greg, pulling an adjustable wrench from his back pocket. Karen climbed inside and started disconnecting wires at random under the dashboard. You could never have too many wires.

Nearby, Bert was struggling with the rear bumper of a black Oldsmobile Cutlass convertible with a stoved-in side. Jimmy and George were pulling the cylinder heads off a green Oldsmobile Cutlass convertible with a cracked block and busted rear quarter panel.

All of the 173 junked cars that surrounded Bubba's abode were Oldsmobile Cutlass convertibles. At one time Bubba had started painting numbers on their trunks, but after a few beers he found himself duplicating some numbers and skipping others, so now he simply painted the number 87 on every new old car he towed onto his property. It made things a lot simpler.

Simplicity and order were two concepts that Greg immediately grasped, just as he intuitively understood that they could not simply walk up and have the master show them how to manipulate a tire iron. Not only were there layers upon layers of subtle nuances and technique in that deceptively simple action, but one must first attain harmony and balance through apprenticeship. It was a rule.

Apparently Bubba's apprenticeship program involved Oldsmobile Cutlass convertibles.

Somewhere among all the scattered and assorted parts of the 173 clapped-out Oldsmobile Cutlass convertibles were the makings of the One True Car. Or maybe not.

All it would take was to find the proper combination of parts. Or maybe not.

If they did, Bubba was going to paint it red.

So it came to pass that Greg and his fellow seekers of light toiled long and hard every Saturday under the blazing sun and the watchful eye of Bubba, suffering mosquitoes and chiggers, dodging scorpions and snakes as they moved rusted and potentially useless parts from one Oldsmobile Cutlass convertible to another in search of the One True Car.

Or maybe not.

Yes, that was the part that appealed to Greg, the point where he realized that he had found his true path. For the goal might or might not exist; the possible, impossible; light and dark, yin and yang. He could accept that and hold it close.

Meanwhile Bubba eyeballed the activity from his porch, deep in contemplation and Budweiser beer. When his inner voice said that sufficient time had passed he rose slowly and majestically, took a whizz off the side of the porch and sat back down. Three times he did this and when he sat for the final time the acolytes, sweaty and covered with grease and oil, gathered, as always, at the foot of the porch to hear the master's words.

They sat so quietly and respectfully it was possible to hear Rex pass wind in his sleep. Their concentration was that deep.

"You know you have found enlightenment," said Bubba, cracking another beer, "when your belt buckle weighs more than three pounds."

The group nodded thoughtfully.

Greg frowned. This was a hard one. But, of course, there were no easy ones.

He considered last week's proverb: "You have achieved enlightenment when your father walks to school with you because you are both in the same grade." Analysis: *We are all but students in the study of life.*

The week before: "You have achieved enlightenment when you have a rag for a gas cap." Analysis: *Consider function over form; disregard convention for expediency.*

Or the one previous: "You have achieved enlightenment when you go to a family reunion to pick up girls."

Analysis: *We all belong to the extended family of mankind.* This was closely related to the one concerning your family tree being a straight line. Yes, a thought to ponder indeed.

Or that biggie last month: "You have achieved enlightenment when your dog and your wallet are both on chains." Analysis: *Keep things of value close.* It was a deep enough thought to tempt Greg into getting a dog. And some chains.

Bubba, of course, would never acknowledge that there was a single interpretation to these weekly sayings. The first few times a student expressed an impression, Bubba simply laughed that powerful, rolling belly laugh of his and collapsed into a coughing fit befitting a master amused at the naïveté of his students.

Belt buckle. Heavy. Near the navel, the essence of creation and being. Greg figured it must have something to do with finding one's center and keeping your pants up. This would take a lot of thought. He looked over at Karen, who also appeared to be confused. Yes, this was a tough one.

A Jeep bounced into the yard, careening off of a couple of Oldsmobile Cutlass convertibles. The door flew open and a man wearing camouflage fatigues jumped out. He appeared to be upset.

"I catch your dog around my chickens again and you're dead meat," he shouted. "Damn worthless hound."

Bubba reached down, grabbed his tire iron, and rose from his chair. A collective gasp came from the students, who backed away to give the two combatants room to maneuver and to catch a good view of the master's technique.

"Watch what you say about Rex," said Bubba, coming down the steps and swinging the tire iron with grace. "Rex is a killer dog."

Rex the killer dog opened one eye, wagged his tail, passed wind, and went back to sleep.

"Only thing that dog's got going for him is that he smells a lot better than you do," said the stranger.

Bubba swung the tire iron behind his head and Greg was watching the windup so closely he almost missed the stranger dip down and pull a tiny gun from his boot. There was no mistaking, however, the smart snap of the shot nor the loud bellow of pain as Bubba simultaneously lost the tire iron and part of a finger.

Greg was stunned. The man had been so quick! Such discipline to react that way in the face of a master! It must have taken years of training. A path to small-caliber enlightenment was opening before his eyes.

"Derringer," whispered George in a hushed voice full of awe. Sam's jaw was hanging open: he couldn't believe what he had just seen.

"Derringer," echoed Greg, as he took off his John Deere cap and dropped it in the dirt. "Derringer."

As she gratefully tossed away her Purina Feed cap, Karen wondered how she was going to look in camouflage fatigues.

Jack Haldeman lives on a 40 acre farm in rural Florida with nine dogs, none of them named Rex. He drives a 1974 VW van and a clapped-out pickup truck. A 1968 Oldsmobile Cutlass convertible sits on cinder blocks behind the barn. Jack works out by crushing beer cans.

Walter Jon Williams outdid himself on this one. It is bright and flashy and quirky, reminding one of an updated Chinese legend. Some playwrights come up with the damnedest titles. . . .

OOOOO

BROADWAY JOHNNY

Walter Jon Williams

The joint was jumping as I strolled in from Lockhart Road. The band was jazzing away on ''Skid-Dat-De-Dat,'' the clientele was expending world-class quantities of vim in dancing the black bottom, and the bar seemed to be doing enough business to suggest there had been a twelve-year drought ended only just that afternoon.

I doffed my silk topper and ambled up to the bar, seeing in its wavy deco mirror a picture—all modesty brushed firmly to the side—of soigné elegance. I was in evening dress, my tie a perfect butterfly shape, my white silk scarf floating casually off my shoulders. In one impeccably white-gloved hand was a silver-topped cane. One had to admit that my shoulders were rather broader than the proper Vernon Castle ideal, and my neck thicker; but on the whole Art substituted rather well for what

Nature had not provided. I removed one glove, draped it elegantly over the rim of my topper, and signaled with a faultlessly manicured hand to Old Nails, the bartender.

"What ho, o son of toil," I said. "My customary grasshopper, if you please."

"Right, boss."

I lit a cigaret and inhaled. All, I couldn't help but feel, was well with the world. The horizon seemed cloudless. No cares were reflected in my countenance.

Then I glanced down the bar and saw an immortal, and the heart's blood ran chill.

Probably no one else observed that this prune-faced geezer sitting at the bar was anyone out of the ordinary. But if you've been around immortals enough, you recognize the signs at first glance.

Old Nails swanned up with my cocktail, and as I sipped it I found myself wishing I'd ordered a double bourbon.

"Who's the undertaker down the bar?" I asked.

"He's been sitting there all night," Nails said. "He said he wanted to talk to you."

"I'll just bet he did," I muttered, and took another swig.

"Only bought one drink," Nails said. "No tip."

I tugged on my cuffs to cover the profusion of hair on my wrists—my worst feature, I've always thought. Then I put on my best smile, summoned such bonhomie as remained, and sauntered toward my visitor.

"I understand you wanted to see me?" I said.

The prune raised an eyebrow and looked at me. "I do if you're Chan Kung-hao," he said.

"Call me Johnny if you like."

"I'll call you Mr. Chan, if it's all the same."

I adjusted my silk scarf. "Suits me," I said.

"My name is Ho. I'm one of the Ho Ho Erh Hsien."

You may have heard of the Ho Ho Erh Hsien, known otherwise as the Two Gods Named Ho. If you haven't,

I imagine they'll serve well enough as an introduction to the intricacies of Chinese legend.

One of the immortals in question is a fellow named Ho Ho, famous for having traveled ten thousand *li* in a single day to pay a call on his brother. Another of the twain is a disreputable monk named Han Shan, who made rude noises during meditation, cursed and kicked the abbot, and eventually got biffed out of the monastery to live as a hermit. And a third is a chappie named Shih-teh, who worked in the kitchen of this selfsame monastery and fed Han Shan on kitchen scraps. Because Ho means Harmony in Chinese, they're all celebrated as immortals of compatible union.

If you've been paying strict attention here, you may note a discrepancy or two in the accounting. Firstly—*bereshith*, as it were—the Two Gods Named Ho are actually three. Secondly, only one of them is actually named Ho, and he's named Ho twice. Nextly, one of these immortals celebrated for his utter and sublime mateyness was, by all accounts, an utter misanthrope, incapable of holding civil converse with man or beast.

These sad contradictions, I'm sorry to report, are perfectly in accord with Chinese cosmology. The inhabitants of the Middle Kingdom appear to have taken to heart Emerson's dictum that consistency is the hobgoblin of little minds—taken the dictum, that is, flogged it within an inch of its life, and then booted the remainder right through the goalposts. Nothing in Chinese legend makes any kind of sense, especially once you've met a few of the principals involved. Take my word for it.

This particular Ho was a tall, spare, disdainful bird, dressed in a long silk Chinese gown and skullcap—elegant enough, but not often the sort of thing seen in my nightclub. His pinky fingernails were about five inches long and protected by silver caps. He carried a two-foot-long iron tobacco pipe with which he probably clouted disrespectful pedicab drivers and unruly children. His expression suggested he'd just choked on a plum pit.

As I eyed him I wondered which of the chummy threesome he represented. Ho Ho, the one who traveled ten thousand *li*, seemed a useful sort of bimbo to have around, particularly if you fancied a quick vacation or needed a fast trip out of town. Shih-teh, the cook, seemed pretty goopy, but at least he might have picked up a few recipes in his years in the kitchens. But knowing the way that Fate has of flinging me in the soup, I was certainly prepared for the worst, which meant Han Shan.

"Do you actually *like* this hideous din?" the immortal demanded. "I've been sitting here for hours!"

"I take it," I replied, "that you aren't a jazz baby conversant with the syncopated rhythm and the hot-cha-cha?" I gazed with pride at my house band, Chinese made up in blackface to help provide the proper *Vieux Carré* atmosphere. "The Ace Rhythm Kings provide the heppest sound this side of Basin Street," I said.

"The Ace Rhythm Kings can retire at once to Bad Dog Village in the Infernal Regions," my guest griped. A pretty crude thing to say, which only confirmed my worst surmise.

"Han Shan, I take it?" I said.

"Correct."

"Would you like to go to my private office?"

"And get out of this hell of imitation foreigners?" he said. "Lead the way!"

As I took the prune-faced god of concord aside I cast a wistful glance in the direction of the band singer, Betsy Wong, who was about to launch into her rendition of "I'm a Little Blackbird Looking for a Bluebird," my personal favorite among her repertoire.

I led Han Shan into my office and put my hat and cane on their respective racks.

"Can I get you something to drink?" I asked.

He gave a sniff. "Do you have anything Chinese in this place?"

"Will mao tai do? I have a particularly potent vintage in my possession."

"If it's the real thing."

Ignoring this slur on my oeniphilic discrimination, I unlocked my private cabinet and poured my guest a drink. "I think you'll find it possesses a fine bouquet," I remarked, "hearty and challenging but without pretention." I offered it to him, then picked up my grasshopper. "Skin off your nose."

We drank. He looked suspicious as he raised his glass, perhaps worried that for mischief's sake I'd try to slip him a Château Latour '03 or some other inferior vintage. But after the first sip came another, and then he tossed down the whole glass, and by the time I'd refilled it he looked somewhat less the twenty-minute egg. He actually managed a thin smile.

"Thank you, Mr. Chan. I see you haven't been completely contaminated by foreign tastes."

"Sorry to have kept you waiting," I remarked. "I was at the Lyceum for the Asian Road Company premiere of *Music Box Review,* the new Irving Berlin musical. Then I went out to the clubs with some of my pals and the girls from the show."

Han Shan looked as if he wanted to retract his last appraisal. I smiled at him.

"Seeing as it's late and I've kept you waiting," I went on, perhaps we should play the last waltz, as it were, and see the cotillion to its conclusion."

"If I take your meaning, which is difficult due to your insistence on marring good Cantonese with bizarre foreign idiom, then I find your suggestion agreeable. I have a condition, however: what I tell you may not go past these doors."

"Of course," I said, "I have no desire to attract attention to myself by exposing my dealings with immortals."

"Very good." He knocked down his third drink and poured himself a fourth. "Are you familiar with the golden swords Kan Chiang and Mo Yeh?"

"I believe I've heard a legend or two."

Kan Chiang and Mo Yeh are swords named after the smiths who made them, a chummy married couple who owned their own swordsmithing shop on Shih Ming Mountain. They died on the job, as it were, by chucking themselves into their own furnace in order to provide the necessary *matériel* for turning a couple of magic gold nuggets into swords. Perhaps, I have thought, their charcoal delivery was late.

"The two golden swords," the Ho said, "are mighty items of great power. They contain nothing less than the martial fortune of the Chinese people."

"They don't seem to have done us much good the last few centuries, what?" I said.

Han Shan looked sore as a gumboil. "That's because of a certain immortal named Wu Meng."

"Wu Meng? The filial piety chap?"

"Yes. The same."

"Hmm."

Chinese, as you may know, are very big on a quality called *hsiao,* which gets translated into English as "filial piety," though on reflection I could think of a few other words for it. Wu Meng was an immortal famous for being filled to the bunghole with *hsiao,* which probably meant that he probably spent his days giving the old oil to his grandparents in hopes of getting an extra slice of inheritance. Maybe he got it and maybe he didn't, but he got immortality, which in the long run is probably better.

As you may have gathered by now, I'm about the least filial Chinese you'll ever meet. You may consider this is a great sin, but then you haven't met my family. Try having your doting parents sell you into slavery at the age of eight, and see if it doesn't provide a whole new perspective on this *hsiao* business.

If Wu Meng's family had sold him into slavery, he probably would have sent them half his gruel.

"So what did Wu Meng do?" I asked. "Did he let the swords get rusty or something?"

"No. Wu Meng had nothing to do with the swords. He was the guardian of another great token of power, the Five Tiger Fan. The nation that possessed the Five Tiger Fan was guaranteed to have a great spirit of enterprise, originality, and genius. Due to our possession of the fan, China became the greatest nation in the world, the envy of all. But during the Ming dynasty, Wu Meng lost the fan in a dice game with a Portuguese merchant named Pires de Andrade."

"I see. And as a result, the spirit of enterprise has fled the Middle Kingdom?"

"Correct. Our decline as a nation can be traced to that unfortunate dice game. We can't originate anymore: we can only repeat the patterns of the past. And the martial valor guaranteed by possession of the golden swords is of much less value without a spirit of genius and enterprise among the soldiers."

Well, that was two strikes against Wu Meng as far as I was concerned. First the filial piety business, then losing the spirit of originality for the whole bally country. And the Five Tiger Fan strife affected me personally—as fine musicians as the Ace Rhythm Kings may be, they never sound any different from the recordings I play for them on my gramophone. "Improvisation," I keep telling them, "is the keystone of jazz." But all they do is nod and agree and then play "Dippermouth Blues" exactly the way King Oliver's band did five years ago.

"And how did the Portuguese do?" I asked.

"He got rich trading and went home to Portugal."

"Which," I mused, "judging from history, lost the fan shortly thereafter."

"If you say so. You're the expert on foreigners."

"And how about Wu Meng? How did the Jade Emperor and the other gods feel about him losing the fan? I imagine they dished him good and proper."

"I'm not here about the fan!" Han Shan snarled, and banged on my desk with his glass. "To hell with the Five Tiger Fan!"

I reflected the mao tai seemed to be hitting him pretty hard. He was the one who brought the fan up, after all.

"Right ho," I said. "All thoughts of the Five Tiger Fan are hereby consigned to perdition." I took a last puff on my cigaret, then stubbed it out in my Baccarat ashtray. "Why did you say you were here, exactly?"

The immortal banged down another round of mao tai. "It is my honor to be the appointed guardian of the golden swords."

I considered that if I gave him a bit of the old soft soap, he'd get to the point a little quicker. "They couldn't have been entrusted to a better fellow," I said.

"The swords lie concealed beneath the waters of a fountain."

"So your lodgings have a water view, I take it? Couldn't be better. But don't the swords rust?"

"They do not rust," he said, "because they are so sharp they cut the water in half."

"Excellent swords, then," I said.

"The finest swords in all history!" he shouted, banging his glass once more. And then, to my amazement, he began to weep. "And they're gone!" he sobbed. "I lost them!"

I leaned across the desk and handed Han Shan my handkerchief with one hand while I refilled his glass with the other. Baleful harbingers of dread were beginning to cloud my personal horizon. My part in all this was becoming ominously clear.

"Perhaps you remember where you were that day?" I suggested. "Have you checked the left luggage office?"

"I know precisely where I was!" he wept.

"Well, jolly good," I said. "That should make finding them easier, what?"

"I was gambling with a kami and I lost them!"

"You were gambling with a communist?" I asked.

He glared at me. "Not a commie, a kami! A Japanese god."

"Ah."

Gambling, I might observe, is the curse of the immortal class. They get bored, I suppose, hanging out on their mountains, meditating endlessly in their shrines, or standing guard over their treasure troves—to name three favorite immortal occupations—and they don't have the prospect of death to focus the mind and quicken the pulse the way it does for the rest of us, so after a few centuries of glassy-eyed boredom they take themselves to the city and risk everything on a throw or two of the dice. Entire empires have been known to change hands as a result of a couple immortals wanting to relieve their ennui with a few brisk rounds of mah-jongg.

It's the sort of thing that results in disillusionment, once you discover how these things really work. Results, in fact, in chaps like me.

"Some sort of immortals' convention, was it?" I said. "Best dry your eyes and tell me the whole story."

He dabbed his cheeks, then honked his beezer and went on. "Well, we were playing fan-tan at a club in Shanghai, and I kept losing—oh, it was really unfair! You shouldn't be able to lose *that much* at fan-tan—not with a fifty-fifty chance at every throw!" He snarled. "It's all Wu Meng's fault!" he snapped.

"How so?"

"If there were any reward for enterprise left in this benighted country, I would have won."

"Not necessarily. The game was probably rigged."

He stared at me. "How do you mean?"

I lit a cigaret. "Well, you put the beans in a dish, right?

And then bet even or odd—all you have to do to change the outcome is palm a bean, you know. Easiest thing in the world. And if you want to make absolutely certain, you can carry loads of beans up your sleeve, and then add the palmed bean or not, depending on how people are betting."

Han Shan's eyes widened with belated understanding. He howled and stamped on the floor. "That rat! That fixer! That's how he must have won!"

"Indubitably. Now who was this Japanese bimbo exactly?"

"His name was Teruo Shokan No Kami Minamoto No Tadaoki." His face contorted with anger. " 'Call me Teruo,' he said. 'Come into the club, have a drink, have a little fun. Meet some girls. We immortals should get together more often!' " His expression darkened. "I should have known he was after something."

Indeed. It was obvious enough that anyone who actually invited a wet smack like Han Shan to share some raucous good fun was in pursuit of something other than a jolly fine time.

"So I gather," I said, "you would like to commission me to gaff this Teruo bloke and chuck him off your lakeside property."

He looked a little crafty. "Well," he said, "in a manner of speaking."

"Why? Where's the fountain?"

"It's in Tsingtao."

I frowned. "Tsingtao is under Japanese occupation."

"Well," he admitted, "yes."

"So how am I going to kick Teruo off the land if he can just call in the marines and jump your claim all over again?"

"It's not as bad as all that," he said hastily. "The fountain is actually in an amulet."

I must have looked a little blank. "The fountain's inscribed on an amulet?"

"No, it's *in* an amulet."

I took a firmer grip on my cocktail glass. "I understand how swords can be in a fountain, I suppose, but how can a fountain be in an amulet?"

"It's a metaphysical fountain," he said simply. "It can be anywhere it likes."

I suppose this made as much sense as anything else immortals ever get up to. "Fine," I said. "Spifferino. What's the amulet look like?"

"It's made of two colors of gold, red and white back-to-back. It's about the size of a copper *cash*, it's covered with writing on one side and a picture of the Door Gods on the other."

"So why don't the Door Gods guard the fountain?"

"I don't know. I don't make the rules."

"And where in Tsingtao is the amulet?"

"Around the pirate's neck, I imagine. I wore it around mine."

I tapped cigaret ash into the Baccarat ashtray. "And where in Tsingtao is this Teruo geezer?"

"I don't know where he lives, but I've done a little discreet checking, and I've discovered that he's the personal kami of the 142nd Military Police Battalion based in Tsingtao, so I imagine he can be found in the vicinity of the barracks."

"Yipes!" I took a swig of my grasshopper and wished, not for the last time, that I'd thought to order bourbon.

"Well," I said, "it was a pleasure meeting you. I believe you know the way out."

His face fell about fourteen inches. "You're not going to help me?" he whimpered.

"It's bad enough you want me to take on an immortal," I said. "Immortals have long memories—not that they can help it, I suppose. But an immortal with his own private battalion of Imperial Japanese plug-uglies—now that takes the cake!"

"But, Mr. Chan—it's your patriotic duty—you owe it to your homeland!"

"Tell it to the marines," I said. "If you have a hang about patriotism and the homeland, you wouldn't have wagered the amulet in the first place."

Han Shan turned haughty. "Your maternal grandfather would have undertaken this quest at once."

I self-consciously tugged my cuffs back over my hairy wrists. The grandfather in question is an unpredictable egomaniac with a big stick, and in my estimation stands about as high as the rest of my family, concerning whom I believe you have already been informed.

"Fine," I said. "You can approach him, then, if you like."

"But—where is he to be found?"

I shrugged and took a puff off my gasper. "I'm afraid I don't know. We seem to have lost touch."

Which, I'm pleased to report, was perfectly true.

Tears came to the Ho's eyes once again. "Please, Mr. Chan! You must help! If I don't get the swords back before long, the other immortals will find out!"

"And then you'll really be in the cart, eh?"

He sobbed and took another swig of mao tai. "If only I hadn't been so hard on Wu Meng during his trial!"

"Ah? Really?"

Tears were beginning to stain his gown. "Yes!" he moaned. "I insisted he be punished severely for the betrayal of his trust."

I was beginning to sense why he'd insisted on changing the subject when the matter of Wu Meng's fate had come up. "How do you punish an immortal, anyway?" I asked. "You can't kill him."

"No." He gulped. "But you can chain him for four hundred years in the Hell of Having Your Entrails Eaten by Dogs and Wild Pigs."

"Sounds gruesome, all right," I said. "But I guess old Wu Meng should be getting out of stir anytime now." I grinned at my guest. "Perhaps he'll be out soon enough to sit on *your* jury."

Han Shan began to wail. "Won't you get the swords back, Mr. Chan? I don't know what to do—I'm not a fighter or a thief!"

"Neither am I," I said, "if I can help it." I waved a hand. "It's true that in my wayward youth, I undertook various commissions on behalf of certain prominent personalities. But I've given it up, and I've opened Broadway Johnny's here and commenced a very successful career as a man-about-town. Surely an upright person such as yourself will appreciate the values of my reformation."

He snarled at me. "I'll curse you!" he said. "I'm an immortal! I can make your life a misery!"

I tugged at my cuffs again. I was onto his curves by now. "Oh, come now," I said. "If you do, I'll know who did it. A little word in the right celestial ear, and it's Entrail Heaven for the hogs."

He began to tremble. He took a swig of mao tai from the bottle. "I'll give you money!" he said.

"Didn't you gamble it all away?"

"I lost everything I had with me. But I'm an immortal, and I've been around a long time—I know where there are hidden treasure troves."

I examined my nails while I considered my finances. Though the club was doing well enough, it could always stand a few improvements. A band composed of genuine jazz artists, say, imported from Basin Street. A line of chorus girls in sequined flapper garb and Josephine Baker bobs. Perhaps a talented mixologist imported from the States—since Prohibition started over there, bartenders were probably easy enough to come by.

And if I could wring enough of the ready out of this bozo, perhaps I could even embark on a career I'd only dreamed of, that of theater impresario. With a trip to New

York and London every year, to see the new shows and decide which to bring back to the East.

"Treasure troves?" I said. "Probably just old strings of cash buried by frugal peasants."

"No! Real treasure! Silver ingots! Ancient bronze and porcelain! Gold! Gems!"

"It better be a lot," I said. "If I do this for you, I'll need a bankroll before I ever set out."

"Why? I can pay you when you're done, after you steal the—"

"I'm *not* going to steal the swords back," I said, and before the old monk's chin began to tremble I added, "That would be foolish in the extreme, with the target surrounded by a battalion of cops. I'm going to get the amulet the same way Teruo did—I'll win it gambling. And for that, I'll need a stake."

He looked at me eagerly. "You'll do it, then, Mr. Chan?"

I frowned deliberately. "Possibly," I said, "but you'll have to make it really worth my while."

I'll spare you the details of the agreement, save that, as I ushered Han Shan out of the club, there was a smile on my face and a puzzled frown on his. He really ought to stick to minding his fountain and leave money matters alone. Finance is not, as the saying goes, his forte.

Still, my smile faded the second I turned and walked back into the club, and not even Betsy Wong's rendition of "Cakewalking Babies From Home" could set me right. So I sat in with the band and tickled the ivories for a couple sets, hoping that "Texas Moaner Blues" might set things right; but it didn't, so I went to the bar and ordered another grasshopper and brooded.

Grasshoppers aren't precisely the sort of drink that traditionally accompanies brooding; but I've always felt that, with sufficient dedication and attention to detail, these sorts of handicaps can be overcome.

After the club closed I collected the receipts and had the Hispano-Suiza brought round to the Lockhart Road entrance. Betsy Wong looked at me expectantly, probably wondering if I'd ask her over for a nightcap, but the blues had set in good and proper, and I just kissed her good-night, hopped in the Hispano, and buzzed off into the night.

I was cautious on approaching the bank night depository. There was a general dock strike in progress up and down the Chinese coasts, and people had been thrown out of work. Some of them were desperate enough to turn to robbery. But there were no suspicious lurkers around the bank, and I dropped off the receipts and buzzed off home.

I'd got my apartment cheap because it was haunted. Ghosts, I've found, daunt most people, but after my life of dealing with immortals and my crazy grandfather, a collection of spirits was a trivial annoyance at best. The ghosts were busy as I arrived, sitting at a corner table and making a lot of racket playing mah-jongg. A rough lot they looked, too, with their scars and tattoos—they were gangsters who had been sitting at the table gambling when an acquaintance paid a call. Unfortunately for the gamblers, their acquaintance had first thought to provide himself with a Browning automatic rifle.

If you looked closely at the wall, you could see the patches in the plasterwork where the bullet holes used to be.

I wasn't in the mood for the company of surly dead people, so I walked straight up to their table and began to spit at them. The ghosts looked at me resentfully for a few baleful seconds, then faded, along with their mah-jongg tiles.

Most Chinese hold the belief that human saliva is somehow toxic to ghosts. This may be true, but I'm inclined to the belief that ghosts leave because they're annoyed they can't spit back.

I poured myself a snifter of brandy and sat in my easy chair and continued my pout. Immortals were entering my life once more, like thunderclouds on a beautiful springtime day, and it hardly seemed fair. I had built a pleasant life away from all of that, and I disliked being dragged back into my past. I felt, as the poet said, like a "jazzbo looking for a rainbow."

Oh well. At least there was hard cash involved.

Fate, I decided, was at least furnishing a few compensations.

After Han Shan provided the promised funds I took a ferry across the bay and from thence a cab to the Kowloon Walled City. The Walled City is a part of Kowloon which, through a technicality, still belongs to China rather than the British Crown. Since the Chinese government pays no attention to the place, and as the British can't enter, the Walled City has become a den of criminals, fugitives, political extremists, and refugees from the mainland. It is a decidedly unsafe place to be at the best of times, and these were not the best of times, with the dock strike increasing the city's population of desperate people—indeed, I could not get my cab driver to drive through the crumbling gate.

I paid him off and walked through, my cane tapping the ground at every other step. My pockets were laden with jingling coin, a certain temptation to the wicked inhabitants of the place, but I wasn't worried about robbery. I knew that the luck I had temporarily acquired would not permit accidents.

And indeed it didn't. A pickpocket who moved in my direction stumbled on a heretofore unseen crack in the street and went down with a crash, breaking his nose on the curb. A hatchet man let fly from a dark alley, only to bury his hatchet in the skull of his partner, who had just lunged at me from behind a barrel. A gang of surly youths in red turbans, swaggering toward me with the obvious intention of exacting a heavy toll for my trespass on their territory, suddenly found themselves the objects of profound attention on the part of another surly gang of youths, these in yellow turbans, who charged out of an alley, knives and hatchets gleaming bright as the homicidal glint I believe I detected in their eyes.

In each case, I was able to amble on unmolested, smoking my cigaret and enjoying the sights.

I knew this would be the case, for I was about to visit the luckiest man in the world.

His name was Ping, though he was also known as the Great Sage of the Chinese City, as the Walled City is also called. Since I was about to give Ping money, I knew that his luck, or joss as it's called here, would not permit me to suffer any indignities while I was en route to his dwelling.

It was what would happen to me after the visit that concerned me. Once I'd given the Great Sage his coin, he'd have no further use for me, and getting out of the Walled City was going to be less easy than getting in.

Ping's house was an eccentric place, a three-story structure partly of stone, partly of brick, and partly braced with metal. Cockeyed gables, balconies, and odd-shaped windows were distributed more or less randomly over its surface, like warts on the back of a toad. The design of the house was dictated by Ping's eccentric theories of geomancy, or feng shui—he had designed his house to attract luck and repel evil. And such, remarkably enough, it seemed to do.

I often wondered why Ping chose to live in the Walled City, but it since occurred to me that he probably chose the district because it's the only place in the world that would permit him to build a house of this description.

Most fortune-tellers are mountebanks, of course—after my tumultuous departure from the Golden Nation Opera Company of Shanghai, I traveled with such a mountebank for a time—but very rarely, perhaps one time out of ten thousand, you encounter a seer who's right on the money. Such a one was Ping.

He received me in a room shaped like an elongated hexagon, one of your auspicious room shapes in feng shui. In the corners of the room were objects colored white, red, yellow, green, blue, and black, which stood for the Six True Words of Buddhism. The trigrams of the Pa K'ua were seen in the floor tiles. Various subtle marks in the room Traced the Nine Stars and indicated the spokes of the Eight-Door Wheel. Plants in pots composed of different materials were placed in careful relation to one another, and oddly angled mirrors were set here and there, while rudely shaped bits of quartz hung off the ceiling on the ends of strings. . . .

If you didn't know the fellow was a true sage, you'd think he'd gone right off his coconut.

"What ho, Mr. Ping," I said as I toddled in. "I seem to be in need of a bit of luck."

"How fortunate it is that you've come here instead of someplace else," said the sage. "Please sit down and have some tea."

And a servant with tea and some snacks walked in right at that instant—Ping being so lucky, you see, he'd had a hankering to order the stuff before I even arrived.

Ping looked more or less as you'd expect a sage to look—he had long white eyebrows that hung down to his jawline, and a wispy white beard, and rather a mischievous glint in his eye. I'd never been able to figure out whether or not he was an immortal—usually I can tell, but Ping's quarters were so charged with powerful vibrations that I could never be certain which came from him and which came from the setting. Certainly he'd been there a very long time, but perhaps that was because he was so lucky that Death lost his address, or gaffed the wrong bird by mistake, or simply got knocked on the head and had his pockets emptied by the gangs that loiter about the Walled City.

"I'm afraid it's all rather a complicated rannygazoo," I said.

"In that case, Mr. Chan, you'd best begin at the beginning, and proceed straight through to the end." Which, if you've not met one, is how sages talk.

So I described the afflicted god of concord, his loss of the mystical swords to some kind of Japanese police god, and my decision to fetch them back. I tried to stress the patriotic nature of my quest, along with all the sacrifices I was undertaking on behalf of the motherland—in hopes, of course, of getting a price break.

"Your love of country is a fine thing," Ping said, smiling, "A splendid example of *hsiao*. Such a one as I can only stand back in admiration. I'm sure you will be richly rewarded in your next incarnation."

So much for the price break. Ping lit up a pipe, and I a cigaret, while he considered.

"Your joss will need to be mobile," he said, "as you do not know where you will encounter this foreign immortal. And it must be inconspicuous, as otherwise it would be discovered." He blew a smoke ring that immediately resolved itself into the trigram Gen, which stands for knowledge. "Right," he said. "I think I know just what you need."

He whipped out a piece of paper and a small calligraphy brush, made some ink into which he sprinkled a few metallic-looking powders from pockets in his wide sleeves, and then—mumbling a little inaudible charm—he wrote quickly on the piece of paper, covering it all with characters and diagrams and odd little drawings. He then produced a straight edge and some scissors, cut a small square out of the center of the paper, and crumpled the rest. He pushed the little square toward me.

"If you have $822 American, plus one silver dime, I would be obliged."

This was a request as eccentric as his taste in architecture. For some reason not acquainted with the rational mind, the most common currency in China at this time were Mexican dollars, but I didn't have even that. "I'm afraid I only have old Chinese coin," I said. "Silver boats."

"I suppose I shouldn't have expected my good luck to quite stretch *that* far." He scratched his wispy mustache with the end of his pen. "Han Shan dug up an old treasure trove, did he? Too bad—American dollars will be auspicious for the next hour or so. I'm afraid I'll have to charge you more if you can't pay American."

I looked at the little square of paper, in form a common paper amulet. "But wasn't the charm on the larger sheet? Didn't you throw most of it away?"

"The large implies the small, and the small the large," he said. Which, as I believe I may already have told you, is how sages talk.

"How does it work?"

"Carry it where it won't get wet," he said. "Inside your cigaret case, perhaps. When you need good joss, lick the amulet, then paste it on your skin such that the ink imprints on your flesh. After that, you'll have staggeringly good luck."

"Splendid," I said.

"But it won't last. At some point afterward, your joss will turn bad, and you'll have to transfer the bad luck to someone else by repeating the process."

"I'll have to lick the amulet and stick it on someone else?"

"Correct. Or suffer catastrophic luck yourself."

"But why do I have to have bad joss at all?"

Ping blew a smoke ring that resolved itself into a revolving mandala. "That's the way it works," he said. "Into every yang a little yin must fall."

"How will I know when my joss shifts?"

"You won't be able to tell," Ping said. "It depends on how much luck is drawn from the amulet in the course of its use. If you don't need much luck to begin with, the amulet will last a long time. And if you make high demands on the available luck, it may be used up quickly—say within a day."

"Any other drawbacks?"

He considered for a moment. "The amulet's luck is very good, but it won't protect you against what I might call cosmic bad joss."

"Such as?"

"The amulet won't prevent an earthquake from happening in the district you're in, for example, although it might prevent roof tiles from falling on you if an earthquake occurs. And it won't keep something like a war from breaking out if a war is scheduled to break out anyway, though it might keep any bullets from your immediate vicinity."

"Unless the luck shifts, in which case I become a lodestone for lead."

He nodded. "You have applied the needle and seen blood immediately," he quoted. By which he meant I'd hit the nail on the head.

"I wish you wouldn't mention blood," I said.

"Perhaps," he said, "I should speak instead of silver."

So I paid him, which actually took some time. It wasn't a matter of shoving the ready across the desk, but rather of placing money in little piles around the room in whatever locations he deemed auspicious. Old Chinese silver ingots are in the shape of little boats, so you can stack them one atop the other, and by the time I was through old Ping looked as if he were surrounded by a silver armada, circling him like cinematic Red Indians ogling a wagon train.

Then I thanked him, took my amulet, and said farewell. By way of a warm-up I did a few deep knee bends in the hall before I stepped out, because I knew that my return journey through the Walled City wouldn't be covered by Ping's luck, and I didn't want to use the amulet yet. I was planning a brisk skedaddle straight to the nearest gate, and then a hop into the first available cab.

The first fellow I encountered was a pickpocket who intended to run into me as if by accident, lifting something in the course of the collision; but I got my elbow in first, heard a couple of ribs crack, and saw his eyes go wide. "Apologies," I said, and tipped my fedora as I glided away.

Have I mentioned that I am quite large and strong? I suppose not, as it has not been relevant till now, and I'm somewhat reluctant to admit that I do not quite fit my own ideal of physical perfection, which tends toward the Rudolph Valentino model. I do not imagine Valentino has to tug his cuffs down over his hairy wrists, or buy extra large collars. Alas, we must all live with the features bequeathed us by our ancestors, or in my case my grandfather.

Next I was mobbed by children, about a dozen, who swarmed up and started sticking grubby fingers in my pockets. I was familiar with their type, urchins who trusted to their marks' reluctance to smash in their adorable little faces just long enough to pick them clean. I was myself disinclined to damage them overmuch, so I managed to hold them at bay long enough to spot their manager or Fagin, a fat oily type who loitered in a doorway and watched his charges with an expression of paternal avarice. I bounded over the heads of the children, seized the fat fellow, and ran him through the barred window on a nearby house. As the bars were not proportioned to someone of his girth, I imagine this caused him some discomfort. At any rate, he began loudly to voice his dismay, and his apprentices abandoned their efforts to rob me and went to his succor, an event that permitted me to continue my stroll.

The next street corner brought three surly youths in yellow turbans, ruffians who had apparently just vanquished their red-turbaned foes and turned their attention to collecting the rewards that accompany an expansion of the tax base. The first, before he had quite grunted out his demands, got my cane thrust *à la épée* between his eyes, which sat him down in the street; the second got my boot where it wasn't wanted; and the third I dropped onto the first with a low sweep of my cane.

At this point the threesome commenced to call loudly for help, which, unfortunately, was at hand. At the sight of a horde of yellow turbans swarming out of the local gin mills, knives and hatchets at the ready, I found it expedient to leg it for the wall pronto, without, as it were, leaving my card. By dint of perseverence I managed to get a good half block lead, which is as good as a mile in a narrow street choked with pedestrians, bullock carts, and street vendors.

The turban salesman must have cleaned up in this district, because after sprinting a couple of blocks I found myself approaching another street corner occupied by yet another gang of surly youths, this lot in green turbans. These seemed not to be actuated by a spirit of brotherhood and bonhomie, for at the sight of the yellow turbans they immediately drew their weapons and began screaming for reinforcements. These proved ready to hand, and soon the two sides were advancing toward one another at full speed, while I, caught in the middle, felt a bit like Buster Keaton, trapped in an alley while swarms of cops thunder toward him from either direction.

I must admit that for a brief moment I thought of deploying the amulet. But then reason took hold, and I considered that perhaps, in the urgency and heat of the moment, the two gangs might well overlook my existence if I were not around to remind them of it; so I grabbed hold of an awning and swung up into its hammocky embrace just as, below me, the two hosts came together with a meaty sound not unlike that of the New York Giants front line encountering that of the Oorang Indians.

I clamped my cane in my teeth and used the bounce

of the awning to get me to a barred window overlooking the street. "Thief!" screamed a high-pitched voice from the window. "Get away, vile creature!" I ignored the advice and climbed to the top of the bars, which unfortunately provoked the old lady within into jabbing at me with a broom. I tried to bat the thing away but failed, then reached overhead for the roof overhang and found it. "Monster!" the old lady yelled. "Ape!"

"Lady, it's not my fault what I look like!" I mumbled past my cane. I let go of the bars and swung out over the street as I dangled one-handed from the overhang.

"Gorilla-strength demon!" she shrieked, then lunged.

The broom caught me a solid one in the ribs, and then a hatchet whirred past, demonstrating that not every thug below had neglected his original priorities. Muttering what I believe the better writers are pleased to call "vile oaths," I hauled myself up to the red-tiled roof. Once there, I paused to chuck a few loose tiles at the hooligans below—it helped relieve my feelings—and then I did a joyful buck-and-wing over the roof pole. The lanes of the Chinese City were very narrow, and even in my unsuitable Western boots I managed to leap from one roof to another, agile as the siamang of faraway Sumatra, before returning to terra firma near the gate, where I whistled "God Save the King" as I crossed back to the jurisdiction of good King George, Fifth of that name, sovereign of the realm on which, I am assured, the sun never sets, and whose arms, by that point, I was willing to bless forever.

It wasn't easy to get to Tsingtao. The general strike on the docks had paralyzed shipping, and there was trouble along the railway line. In the area around Peking, workers had been agitating in the district controlled by a powerful warlord, General Wu P'ei-fu. Worker agitation wasn't normally the sort of thing one did in the domain of a warlord, but General Wu was well thought of, as he'd chucked out the corrupt politicians, all in the pay of the Japanese, who had run the area previously. As a result of this splendid action Wu was thought to be a progressive sort who would be sympathetic to the notion of paying his workers much larger salaries than were other warlords, perhaps even a sum approaching a living wage. To the surprise, perhaps, of no one but the agitators, Wu proved reluctant in this regard, and he commenced the activity warlords know best, shooting and beheading with fine abandon.

The result of this botheration was that I had to make several lengthy detours, traveling by branch rail lines, a bullock cart, a rented Ford automobile, and at one point a motor barge on the Grand Canal. Mr. Phileas Fogg would doubtless have been pleased, not only at the itinerary, but at the splendid pace: I managed to reach Tsingtao in a mere four days.

I rode the last stage in a first-class railway carriage, carefully dressed in a spotless Western suit of grey flannel, with pleated high-rise trousers, a short-waisted waistcoat, and a carefully knotted scarf. I possessed the intimidating amount of luggage, all fine hand-stitched calfskin, with which people of means were expected to travel. I blush to admit that I wore a grey derby hat, which is not the sort of thing a sporting gentleman such as myself normally permits on his head, but unfortunately I was supposed to be a businessman and was forced to confine myself strictly to my adopted *rôle*. At least the pearl grey derby matched the spats I wore on my black calf oxfords. As I suffered pangs of mortification beneath the derby I found myself longing for my hep threads, my oxford bags and colorful cravats and the daring double-breasted jacket of the style only recently imported from America and called the "tuxedo," and I considered that Han Shan and Teruo between them had a great deal to answer for.

As Tsingtao was under occupation, I had to clear Japanese customs, something for which I was prepared. From Hong Kong's finest gang of forgers I had acquired a British passport under the name of Yin Lo Fo, who, as it happens was a real person, a minor Hong Kong textile merchant who had never been out of the colony in his life, and who, if my luck held, was not about to start now.

We passengers were compelled to leave the train and have our luggage carried to the customs shed. Japanese citizens were waved through with little formality, and Westerners had their documents examined, but the Chinese were forced to wait till last, and then have our luggage ransacked by a swarm of the local uniformed locusts, hirsute Korean peasants conscripted into the Japanese army, men who cared neither a jot nor tittle for the laws of man and who lived entirely for loot.

I was, however, prepared for this. I looked for the officer in charge, who turned out to be typical of the type Japan was sending abroad in those days—very young, with a nascent mustache and a sword bigger than he was, probably hailing from an impoverished, provincial samurai family, raised on shabby gentility and bushido, and now ripe cannon fodder ready to have his untutored head turned by the ruthless gang of plunderers and militarists who had sent him here.

"Instruct your men to take care with that package!" I bellowed, roaring in Japanese and pointing with my cane. "It contains an ancient Shang bronze, a priceless gift for General Hiroshi Fujimoto of the Tsingtao Garrison!"

In certain cultures, certainly that of authoritarian military adventurism, it is presumed that he who shouts must possess the status and authority to do so. Certainly the youth was not prepared to contradict appearances, not when a brawny fellow like myself was doing the bellowing. He looked startled, then saluted—which amused me—and directed his soldiery to put my luggage on a cart and have it delivered to my train compartment forthwith. He didn't even glance at my carefully forged passport.

Where, the discerning reader might wonder, did I get a Shang bronze? Han Shan's treasure troves contained several, as it happens, but they were so pitiful, so corroded and homely, that I'd ended up giving another commission to Hong Kong's finest forgers, and they'd produced a bronze tripod much more pleasing in form and appearance.

Once the train pulled into the central station I checked into the Hotel Bayern, a relic of the city's German occupation, and then arranged to send the forged bronze and Yin Lo Fo's card with compliments to the fellow who was pumpkins in this bailiwick, one General Fujimoto. I idled away a few hours in the beer garden, sipping a fine lager, listening to a German band and learning the lyrics to "Ein Prosit," and then an arrogant young subaltern, immaculate in dress uniform and sword, came to summon me to the general's presence.

General Fujimoto and I got along like a house afire. I understood him, and I gave him to understand that he understood me. He was a stout old chap, large of belly and of mustache, with an office crammed with Chinese bronze and porcelain that he'd looted or extorted or otherwise screwed out of the population. On my arrival he produced a bottle of brandy and toasted my health. Over drinks and cigars I told him that I was a textile manufacturer from Hong Kong who had become alarmed by the general strike, and that, as the Japanese had such a splendid way of dealing with strikers, I was thinking of relocating my plant to Tsingtao.

"Strikers!" A bit of fire entered his bloodshot eyes. "Curse them anyway! I have my men shooting and bayoneting them every day, and still they march and demonstrate and carry on!"

I assured him that I thought shooting and bayoneting strikers was just the cat's pajamas, and that this should be done early and oft, mixed perhaps with a little beheading when the soldiers got bored. The general slapped his knee and said I was a good chap and understood the way of the world.

I reluctantly concede that this was one occasion in which my appearance stood me in good stead. If I hadn't looked like a thick-necked brigand crammed into an English-tailored suit, perhaps the general wouldn't have treated me as one and welcomed me, as it were, to the fold.

Over the third drink I mentioned a game of cards I'd played on the train, wherein I'd lost five hundred Mexican dollars, and he perked up and asked if I played auction bridge, which as it happens I did. He then asked if I'd care to join him that evening at the Japan Services Club for a rubber or two, and I replied that I had no other engagements to impede me.

That evening I thankfully traded in my grey bowler for a black silk topper and headed for the club. Once there I poured brandy down my starched shirtfront, poured a great deal more down my throat, and wagered Han Shan's money with a degree of recklessness that my partners probably found staggering. I didn't use Ping's amulet, as it didn't matter to me whether I won or not—if I lost, I planned to win it all back once I met Teruo. I was more interested in studying the other players rather than concentrating on the game.

One of the players was a businessman named Yamash'ta, a thin wand of a man with gold-rimmed spectacles and a greying Douglas Fairbanks mustache. He drank nothing but cold tea, and he was a precise player with a prodigious memory. He was an official of the railway the Japanese were building across Manchuria, a concession granted by the previous Chinese government, and this fact alone caused me to suspect him of being a spy. This suspicion narrowed to a certainty once I was introduced to his companion, a Chinese named Sung, who, despite his Western evening dress, proved to be a Mandarin of the First Rank, With Twin-Eyed Peacock Feather and Ruby Button, and an emissary from China's former emperor, the faintly ridiculous Pu Yi.

Pu Yi had been emperor twice now, first as a puppet of the former empress, Hsiao-ting, and then, for a couple weeks, as a puppet of a general named Chang Hsün. Although he had no part in Chinese government, Pu Yi was still ensconced in his palace in Peking, with all his ranks and privileges and a handsome subsidy, and the fact that his emissary was here playing cards with a character like Yamash'ta suggested to me that, now that General Wu had chucked out the pro-Japanese government in Peking, Pu Yi was hanging out his strings for a third puppetship, this time with Japan as a sponsor.

None of which, I supposed, was a concern of mine, other than to suggest a few of the dirty deals that might soon occur in Chinese politics. We were playing for twenty Mexican dollars a point, which gradually increased to fifty as the evening wore on. I'd lost about eight hundred simoleons, to the despair of my first partner Fujimoto and to the apparent delight of his successor Sung, who, as an Imperial official, was playing with his own money no more than I was.

My next partner was Yamash'ta, and I told myself to look sharp. If anyone here was capable of penetrating my disguise, it was he. So I took the trouble of slopping some more brandy down my shirtfront and drunkenly suggested raising the stakes. My opponents loudly agreed, but Yamash'ta merely narrowed his eyes, called for more cold tea, and stroked his delicate little mustache. I could tell he was calculating whether his own machine-like play stood any chance against his partner's recklessness, and apparently he decided in the affirmative, for he nodded and reached for the bridge block.

His calculations were on the money. Though our opponents won the first game, we scored higher in honors. We won the second game, though it was a squeaker. And the third game went all our way, ending with a little slam in no-trump, doubled no less, and while I played dummy and spilled brandy into my lap, Yamash'ta went on to steamroller our opponents, getting fifty honors points for the little slam, ninety points because he held four trump honors while I held the fifth, and then another fifty points because the contract was doubled.

Yamash'ta then apologized to our opponents for beating them so badly, saying it was mere luck, after which the two of us filled our pockets with Mexican dollars till we jingled with every move.

"The luck was certainly ours tonight!" I said as I lit a cigar.

"I am delighted that your first visit to Tsingtao should be so occasioned with fortune," Yamash'ta said. He examined his stogie without lighting it. "Perhaps you would care to join us tomorrow night for another of our little evenings. Do you play American poker? We meet regularly every Wednesday night."

"We do?" blurted old General Fujimoto.

"Of course we do," Yamash'ta said. "Every Wednesday."

"Oh!" the general cried, suddenly up to speed in re plundering the newcomer. "Beg pardon! Is it Tuesday already? My mistake!"

I understood why they wanted to shift to poker. Poker, you see, would permit them all to play against me at once, and if my reckless betting held true, at least some of them could count on walking away from the table with a small fortune, perhaps even a textile factory or two in Hong Kong.

"Poker, eh?" I said. "I've played it, but you'll have to refresh my memory concerning the rules. Is it a straight that beats a flush, or the other way around?"

After that remark, I believe the others were ready to become my friends for life.

General Fujimoto dropped me off at my hotel that night, and promised to pick me up the next evening promptly at nine. I whiled away the next day reading a mystery novel—a Reggie Fortune, as I recollect—and then made a special trip to the railroad yards to make a few little arrangements of my own. Then I donned evening dress, brushed my topper, and waited for the general to arrive.

When I arrived at the Japan Services Club I discovered my companions of the previous evening had been joined by two others. One, I knew at once, was an immortal—a powerfully built man with prominent eyes, whose hair gleamed with brilliantine and who wore a plain military tunic with no rank or insignia. I permitted my eyes to graze him briefly and then turned to the other man, who in full dress, epaulets and all, looked like Mrs. Astor's doorman, but turned out to be Colonel Arakaki of the 142nd Military Police Battalion. It was Arakaki who turned to the immortal and offered introductions.

"This is Captain Kobayashi of my battalion," he said briefly.

"Honored," I said, and bowed. I was disinclined to think it was possible that the 142nd could contain *two* immortals, so I was fairly certain that Kobayashi was a pseudonym of Teruo Minamoto, the immortal who'd won Han Shan's amulet. Well, I thought, we'll soon find out.

"Shall I order brandy?" offered a smiling General Fujimoto. I smiled back at him.

"If you promise not to let me drink too much," I said. "I'm afraid I had quite a bad head this morning."

I wasn't afraid of getting skunked and losing—the amulet would take care of that—but rather of what might happen after the game. I wanted to be clearheaded enough to make my getaway.

So I sipped at the brandy and played poker for an hour

or so, plunging on every bet. At the start I often won simply because my reckless bluffing intimidated players with better hands and drove them out of the game, but once they caught on I began to lose heavily.

I did observe one important thing. All the Japanese were exceedingly deferent to Captain Kobayashi, even those who supposedly outranked him. They apologized to him when they won, they bobbed little obeisant bows in his direction when he spoke to them, they offered to light his cigarets. A mere captain would hardly merit such attention. So I knew not only that Kobayashi was a kami, but that the others knew it, too.

And after a few hands I began to see Kobayashi's prominent eyes begin to glow. A twitchy little grin settled onto his lips each time cards were shuffled. He began to smoke continuously, lighting each cigaret with its predecessor. His words were cut to monosyllables, and he reached for each new card as if it were his heart's desire.

He was a gambler, all right, one of the immortals who couldn't stay away from games of chance. Perhaps Yamash'ta and Fujimoto made it their business to line up suckers for him before he got involved with a real sharp and started betting the Japanese Imperial Regalia. After the first hour I didn't think Kobayashi would notice anything but the cards, so I thought perhaps it was time to deploy some magic.

I lost three hundred dollars on a single card at stud, then excused myself and made a beeline for the gents', where I withdrew Ping's amulet out of my cigaret case, licked it, and stuck it to the inside of my left wrist, over the pulse point in hopes it would get to work faster. I waited for a moment to see if anything was going to happen, but I didn't feel any different. I glanced in the mirror, just to see if something was happening, like my ears going pointed or my eyes beginning to glow with hidden power, but it wasn't on, so I put the amulet back in my cigaret case and rejoined the game.

My first hand drew a flush, and I knew Ping's amulet was the real Tabasco.

I didn't alter my style of play one whit and continued to plunge. I pretended to be more snootered than I was, for which I thank my training at the Golden Nation Opera Company of Shanghai, in which—between beatings and intermittent starvation—I was drilled thoroughly in the Seven Mannerisms of the Drunkard. My cards were phenomenal, with straights, big dogs and tigers, flushes, and fours-of-a-kind coming one after another. And consistently it was Kobayashi who had the second-best hand, who bet against me longer than the others and lost the largest sums. General Fujimoto, amazed at his bad joss, pleaded poverty and dropped out with an apologetic bow to the kami, but the others played on and on. Yamash'ta grew very quiet and still, his eyes flicking from me to Kobayashi, tracking each card as if he were trying to work something out in his head.

"Big tiger," said Kobayashi, and laid down his hand, K-J-10-9-8.

"How interesting!" I said. "I have a big tiger, too!" And then I laid it down, K-Q-J-9-8, and gave a drunken laugh.

Kobayashi sat back in his chair and eyed me coldly as I raked the gelt toward my end of the table. Yamash'ta looked as if he were trying to figure out how I'd done it, but he knew I couldn't have rigged the cards, because he'd dealt them himself. "Perhaps," he said, "you gentlemen are growing tired of poker. Shall we change pace with a round or two of fan-tan?"

Ah, I thought, fan-tan. Han Shan's downfall. "Suits me!" I said cheerfully, and we adjourned to the fan-tan table. Yamash'ta said that he would preside if we gave him a moment to refresh himself: he went to his apartments upstairs and came down, I noticed, wearing an evening jacket of slightly different cut, no doubt with loads stowed up the sleeves. He obtained a bowl, a chopstick, and a handful of small white stones, then joined us at the table.

He used the chopstick as a stage magician uses his wand—not to furnish a distraction, which is what most people think, but to provide an excuse for the hand to be in an unnatural position, in this case because he would shortly dump a load of stones into his palm. He called for our attention by knocking the chopstick against the upraised bowl, then grabbed a handful of stones, dumped them in the bowl, and inverted the bowl on the table. What I wasn't supposed to observe was that the stones that went into the bowl actually came from his sleeve, and that the original stones stayed in his palm. Once he inverted the bowl on the table, he slipped his hand into his pocket to dispose of the stones. He was really very good, and didn't need the chopstick at all—I never would have seen the move if I hadn't been looking for it.

"Odd!" I announced, and shoved out a fistful of Mexican silver.

"Even!" Kobayashi said promptly. I looked for the palmed stone being added but didn't see it, so I suspect the number of stones was even to begin with.

I watched Kobayashi as Yamash'ta lifted the bowl and counted out the stones with his chopstick, two by two. Kobayashi's bug eyes glittered, his color was high, and the pulse beat prominently in his temples. He had the fever, all right—even though he knew the game was rigged he was still in a sweat over it, perhaps more excited by the certainty of his victory than he would have been by an honest game.

I lost. Sung commented that perhaps my luck was changing. I allowed the possibility, and planned to bet odd next time to force Yamash'ta to use a palmed stone. But I never got the chance—as Yamash'ta lifted the hand with the chopstick to commence the next round, a load of stones flew out of his sleeve and scattered all over the table.

Yamash'ta turned pale. Fujimoto's jaw dropped, and so did Sung's. I played stupid and stared at the fallen stones.

"Say," I said, "I've never seen that happen before!"

Kobayashi stared at Yamash'ta with cold fury, a little muscle twitching in his jaw. "I'm terribly sorry!" Yamash'ta gasped. "I don't know how such a thing could have happened! Please excuse me—it's late and I should go to bed."

"Could've happened to anyone, old chap," I said soothingly, still pretending I didn't understand what had happened.

Then Kobayashi spoke to Yamash'ta. In Japanese, which he probably thought I didn't understand—though it is possible he didn't care a hang whether I did or no. He spoke in mild tones, as if he were chatting on the phone to someone who bored him mildly, but his words were vicious and cutting, and the faces of the other Japanese turned to stone as they pretended they weren't hearing Yamash'ta's being verbally cut to pieces right in front of them. I could tell that Sung understood because he turned pale and began to fidget.

The hell of it was, Yamash'ta was only doing his job—keeping Kobayashi, or Teruo as I thought he was, from betting the Empire in a game of chance. But Kobayashi reviled him in terms I would not use to address a dog, or even Pu Yi. And Yamash'ta just sat there and took it, face stoic, eyes on the table. When Kobayashi was finished, Yamash'ta begged to be excused again, swept up the stones, and walked quietly away.

It occurred to me that I didn't like Captain Kobayashi. I didn't like the way he treated the people whose job it was to look after him, I didn't like his greedy, drooling way of anticipating the outcome of a fixed game, and, far as that went, I didn't think much of his overreliance on brilliantine, either.

Even if he wasn't Teruo, I thought, I was going to enjoy clipping him for his potatoes.

Even someone as stupid as Yin Fo Lo was supposed to be couldn't miss the undercurrents here, and I tried to look as if I were trying to work out what was making everyone so uncomfortable.

"Perhaps another game," Kobayashi said.

I tried to look relieved at the suggestion. "Certainly," I said.

"Do you perhaps know shogi?"

"Most sorry, but I don't." Shogi is a type of Japanese chess, and there's no luck involved: I was afraid that Ping's amulet wouldn't help me there.

"Mah-jongg?" This was Colonel Arakaki, trying to be helpful.

"Splendid!" I said. "Absolutely the bee's knees, as we say in Hong Kong."

Kobayashi gave a thin, superior smile. "No skill involved, of course," he said, "but I don't mind a game."

I knew I was really going to enjoy this next part.

We had one of the club's staff prepare the table while we hammered out the rules. There are thousands of ways of scoring mah-jongg, and we had to decide how many points to give for what hand, and what the limit would be. Arakaki suggested ten thousand, and I said, what the devil, let's make it twenty. After all this was committed to paper, we began.

My luck wasn't quite as pronounced this time, which was probably better in the long run, as it lulled my opponents into a false sense of security. I lost a few games to Kobayashi, though I never scored less than second or a close third, which meant I actually made money, since in mah-jongg you don't just pay the winner, but everyone who scored higher than you—so when I came in second, Arakaki and Sung had to pay both me and Kobayashi, and though I paid him, too, my winnings from the others usually kept me ahead of the game.

I had piled up a modest profit on the counting sticks when we had a no-win game, with no one getting mah-jongg. Prevailing wind shifted from East, who was Kobayashi, to me, playing South. I drew a three of bamboo from the tile wall, then discarded it, and Kobayashi pounced on it like a drowning man reaching for a life preserver. "Mah-jongg!" he cried, and grinned wide.

The grin faded when it turned out that I'd actually pointed higher, since I had a Bouquet of Flowers, three Green Dragons, and three of my own West Wind, all of which meant my score was doubled no less than seven times, while Kobayashi's mah-jongg was doubled only once, for Three Small Scholars.

Kobayashi leaned back in his chair and reached for his cigarets. The prominence of his eyes assured that his pupils were surrounded entirely by white, and his stare was quite eerie. "You're very lucky tonight, Mr. Yin," he said coldly.

"You said it yourself," I laughed, "no skill at this game! Only luck!"

"Hmmm," he said, and stroked a cigaret with his fingers as if it were a dagger he was planning on plunging into my liver.

"My apologies," said Colonel Arakaki as he added up his losses, "but I'm afraid I've reached my limit. I should be in bed. Please continue without me."

We all said good-bye, except Kobayashi, who just kept stroking his cigaret and staring at me. I began to feel nervous. Immortals live a long time, and you never know what sort of abilities they may pick up along the way. Could he know I was using the magic of luck?

Whatever he knew or suspected, it didn't stop him from eagerly setting up the tiles for another game. We both racked up honors and were only a few tiles from victory—assuming, of course, we could get the right ones. I drew a Season, which I displayed, then drew a loose tile from the top of the tile wall. It was five of dots,

I just realized, which completed my hand, and then I dropped the tile in my surprise.

"Mah-jongg!" I said. "And look—I've drawn Plum Blossom on the Roof!"

"A limit hand!" gaped Sung. "Twenty thousand points!"

We were playing for a dollar a point, I should add. And, because both losers had to pay me in full, I was owed a full forty thousand dollars.

Sung turned pale. He'd been spending freely all night, but an extra twenty thousand smackeroos on the old expense account was probably more than the Imperial Exchequer would willingly fork over.

Oh, well. He'd probably make up the difference by selling a state secret or two.

I confess I could not care overmuch for the dilemma of this palace flunky—my attention was on Kobayashi, who was staring at me again with those goggle eyes of his. The little twitch had returned to his jaw. He ground out his cigaret with a determined twist of his fingers.

"Did we mention Plum Blossom on the Roof when we began?" he said. He began reaching for the list of scores we'd hammered out before starting. "If not, my apologies, but—"

I smoothly plucked the sheet of paper from beneath his outstretched fingers. "Oh yes," I said. "I remember distinctly. Plum Blossom is right—" I pointed. "Right here."

Sung looked at the list, sighed, and nodded sadly. "I hope you will take my note of hand," he said.

I looked at him and screwed up my face in imitation of a drunken man trying to decide if he was offended or not. "Beg pardon," I said, "but do you mean to say you came to this game unprepared to make good your losses?"

"Well," he said apologetically, "a limit hand—twenty thousand points! How often does it happen?"

"Often enough," I said. I gave an inane little drunken giggle. "I'm sure that Captain Kobayashi is prepared to pay at once, or give security."

Which put the kami smack-dab in the vise, and didn't the little weasel know it! He glared at me with those peculiar eyes, and I believe for a second or two I could hear his teeth grinding. Then he pushed all his money across the table at me. "There's almost two thousand here," he said.

"That's a start," I said.

"And—" He glared at me defiantly for a long moment, and then his hands reluctantly rose to the collar of his tunic. "Here's something for security."

He unbuttoned his collar and reluctantly drew out an amulet on a chain. I reached out for it, and almost snatched my fingers back at the touch—the thing was loaded with power that snapped through the air like a charge of electricity. Still, I forced myself to pick up the thing, and then I held it before my face and looked at it skeptically.

"At least it's gold," I conceded. "But it's not worth anything like twenty thousand."

"It's a family heirloom," he said. "I daren't return to Japan without it."

I rather hoped, on reflection, this was true.

"Is that old Chinese writing on it?" I said. "What does it say—I can't quite make it out—" The amulet was quite old, because the writing was in an obsolete style, with rounded characters instead of the squared-off ones used today.

"Yes," Kobayashi said. "It's quite ancient."

I looked at the other side. "Are those the Door Gods?" I asked. I frowned and looked at him. "This amulet is Chinese!" I said. "How can it be an heirloom of the Kobayashi family?"

He ground his teeth again at the thought of having to make up some degrading lie in order to oil up a man he believed to be a miserable Chinese bourgeois. I could see the blood pressure building up behind his pop eyes. Another notch or two and I fully expected his eyeballs to come hurtling at me across the table, propelled by jets of steam.

"My family has had business in China for generations," he said.

"Well," I muttered, "if it's all you've got." I stowed the thing in my jacket pocket. "I suppose an army captain doesn't get paid all that much."

I found myself faintly surprised the eyeballs didn't come shooting across the table right on the bally instant. I turned to Sung, who to his embarassment had nothing to offer but his note of hand and a pair of platinum cuff links. (I still have the cuff links, by the way. The note I laundered through a number of brokers and eventually got about twenty cents on the dollar, which shows you what Imperial officials are worth.)

"You must all come to my hotel tomorrow night," I said, rising, "and I'll give you a chance to win it all back." And then I turned and found, to my surprise, that Arakaki and Yamash'ta were standing in the doorway, lounging a bit yet blocking my path.

"Hullo!" I said. "I thought you'd gone to bed!"

"I couldn't sleep," Yamash'ta said, "knowing that you had to face that long journey back to your hotel."

"Oh, it's not so long," I said cheerfully.

"But your ride has left, and the strikes have made the streets dangerous at night," Yamash'ta went on, "so I arranged for you to have a room here at the club, as my guest."

"You're too kind, but you shouldn't have gone to all that trouble," I said, and tried to wedge my way between them. Over Arakaki's shoulder I caught a glimpse of men in uniform standing in the front hall. Members of the 142nd Police Battalion, no doubt, called up by Yamash'ta and Arakaki as soon as they figured out which way the Prevailing Wind was blowing at the mah-jongg table.

Arakaki put a fatherly hand on my shoulder. "It's past four in the morning," he said. "The banks will be open in a few hours, and you can breakfast here and then accompany Mr. Sung and Captain Kobayashi to the bank in order to collect your winnings."

I misliked the thought of having to fight my way out of the club. Police units, unlike most members of the military, actually get to make practical use of their training in the regular course of their peacetime duties, what with having to subdue drunks and felons and the odd hatchet fiend; and the 142nd, I'm sure, had been burnishing their skills to a fine amber glow over the last weeks skirmishing with strikers. All of them, no doubt, had been trained in one of those dreadful Japanese arts with "gentle" in its name, as in "Gentle Art," or "Gentle Art of Beheading," or "Gentle Art of Disembowelling Your Enemy and Strangling Him With His Own Intestines."

It was clear enough I'd been laid a stymie. So I let myself be escorted upstairs, where one of the guest rooms had been thoughtfully provisioned with a snifter, a bottle of brandy, and a pair of pyjamas with the club emblem handsomely embroidered on the pocket. Perhaps, I thought as I hefted the brandy bottle, I was expected to drink myself into insensibility.

Well, I considered, perhaps I ought. If I just played along with Yamash'ta, I'd be forty thousand to the good in just a few hours. Forty grand would buy a whole chain of New Orleans–style clubs throughout the East, or indeed in the Flower Kingdom itself, the USA.

I looked at the brandy bottle, then decided I had other plans for it. Tempting though it was to submit to the dictates of Fate, and disinclined though I was to worry overmuch about the martial fortunes of the Chinese people, the fact remained that I didn't like Teruo much, or his gang of pirates, and that after trying to rob me, then cheat me, they'd now stuck me in chokey, and even though an upstairs room at the Japan Services Club wasn't bad as dungeons go, still I'd much rather be somewhere else than stuck in the cooler by a couple of bad losers.

Besides, Teruo and company might decide to save themselves the money and kill me as I slept.

I determined, as the poet says, to "look for the silver lining." I glanced out the window and saw a half dozen military policemen stationed in and about the club drive. No silver lining there. I closed the curtains. I would have to work out something else.

It was but the work of an instant to dump my winnings into a pillowcase, undo my collar and tie, put the amulet around my neck under my shirt, locate a couple of bath towels, and then glide to the door, where I listened for a long moment. I heard no one in the corridor, so I opened the door and nipped out.

A sentry jumped to his feet, knocking back the cane chair in which he was sitting. Displaying a minimum of six of the Seven Mannerisms of the Drunkard, I swayed up to him and, in a voice slurred by drink, asked him for directions to the bathroom. He couldn't quite make out my words and leaned closer, at which point I slapped him in the throat with the back of my left hand. Not hard enough to cause him permanent injury, but certainly with enough force to cause him to make gasping sounds, clasp both hands about his neck, and—rather more importantly—to refrain from crying an alarm. At which point I whanged him behind the left ear with the brandy bottle, which I'd concealed in a towel, and then dragged his unconscious form back to my room.

I scouted the upper floor a bit and found an unused guest room which enabled me to get a view of the back. There was a kind of zen garden there, gravel with a few interestingly shaped rocks and bits of driftwood strewn about, and a high wall over an alley, and about half a dozen military gumshoes standing in the shadows and pretending to look alert.

No more promising than the front, really, but at least it was darker, and I hoped I could still count on Mr. Ping's luck. So I stripped the spread off the bed, tied it to a bedpost, and let myself out the window.

I suppose even phenomenally good joss can only stretch so far in preventing sentries from seeing a large man in full evening dress descending from a window on a bedspread while carrying a pillowcase full of silver. Certainly, in the better fiction, gentlemen burglars like Raffles seem to escape the consequences of such behavior with a generous regularity. But the fact of the matter is that my feet had barely touched ground before the first cry rang out and I was obliged to leg it for the wall.

There were three guards in a position to block me. I discovered Mr. Ping's amulet hadn't yinned out on me when one of them tripped over one of the rocks in the zen garden and fell on his face. The second guard planted himself in my path and dropped into some kind of classic Oriental boxing stance—unfortunate for him, as I had no intention of doing any classical Oriental boxing. As I dashed past him I wound up like Ty Cobb standing at the plate and swung the weighted pillowcase at his head. He dropped and I charged on without breaking stride.

The third one was their officer, a young fellow with a uniform too big for him. He rightly judged he didn't quite have time to draw his sword, so he jumped in front of the wall with his arms outstretched, planning on tackling me and hanging on until the rest of his troops arrived. I jumped at him and planted the toe of my right foot in his groin, the toe of my left in his solar plexus, the heel of my right foot on his collarbone, the ball of my left on the bridge of his nose, and then the heel of my right foot on top of his head, from whence I sprang to the top of the wall while my improvised ladder crumpled silently behind me.

Once in the alley behind the wall I was home free. Avoiding the military cops who were driving up and down the streets in cars and motorbikes, I made a beeline for the rail yard, which I'd visited that morning, and headed for the engine house. I was going to have to abandon all my belongings at the Hotel Bayern, but I wouldn't miss any of them except for the luggage. I'd always had a fondness for hand-stitched calfskin.

I'd thought ahead, you see. The docks were closed by strikes, the roads were patrolled, and if I'd waited for the first passenger train out in the morning, the Japanese would already have sealed off the station. Instead, I'd visited the rail yard that morning and commissioned a special, one that would have its steam up and be ready at an instant's notice to flee the Japanese Concession. And I'd paid the engineer to bring another set of work clothes with him, so I could look like one of the train crew if we were stopped.

But when I arrived I found the engine house empty, all the locomotives standing silent and dark and exuding a faint odor of grease and bituminous coal. There was a faint light in the back, and I ran for it, my pillowcase jingling. There, beneath a lantern, I found my engineer lying on a bedroll, an oil lantern by one elbow.

"What's going on?" I demanded. "Where's my train?"

The engineer woke slowly, propped himself up on one elbow, and scratched his head. "Oh, Mr. Yin," he said. "I had given you up."

"What about the train?"

He shook his head. "Canceled. All trains are canceled."

"In heaven's name why?"

"We're on strike—all the railroad workers. We're protesting General Wu's actions against the strikers on his rail line. Hey!'' he said, alarmed at the changes in my appearance, ''don't blame me! It wasn't my idea!''

''Money!'' I said. I opened my pillowcase and pulled out a fistful of silver. ''I can give you money!''

The engineer looked wistful. ''I'm sorry, Mr. Yin. I'd like to oblige you. But I can't run a railroad by myself—we need switchmen and people in the control tower and so on, and they're on strike, too. In fact, I came here to return your money to you.''

I'm afraid I lost control for a moment. I stomped around in a little circle, cursing General Wu, the railroad workers, Kobayashi, Han Shan, Yamash'ta, and eventually Mr. Ping, whose amulet had finally let me down—though, after I'd had a chance to think about it, I remembered his warning about ''cosmic bad joss,'' the kind the amulet couldn't do anything about. Apparently railroad strikes were on a par with earthquakes, floods, and warfare.

''Well,'' I said, calming down a bit. ''Did you at least bring me a change of clothes?''

''I'm sorry, no,'' he blinked. ''We weren't going anywhere, so I didn't bring them.''

''We'll exchange clothes, then.''

''Are you sure? Those clothes of yours are pretty nice.''

I held up the handful of silver again.

The engineer's clothing was a bit tight across the chest, and short in the legs and arms, but it would enable me to disappear among the population of Tsingtao much better than would evening dress. As I slipped out of the railroad yard, I realized that I was stranded in a town where I knew no one, from which there was no practical exit, and where powerful enemies were doubtless looking for my head.

Well, it wasn't the first time. So I headed for the oldest cemetery I could find.

I believe I mentioned earlier that I was once apprenticed to a mountebank, a Mr. Piao, who was a member of the Vagabond Sect. The Vagabonds hire themselves out in wartime as spies and assassins, but in peacetime they live as wandering con men, fortune-tellers, and traveling players, the latter a natural occupation for my fifteen-year-old self, at the time a refugee from the tyranny and oppression of the Golden Nation Opera Company of Shanghai.

Mr. Piao's crowning achievement was his attempt to convince Yuan Shih-kai, a rather unscrupulous Imperial general who had betrayed the Republican movement to the Empress Dowager and then been exiled for his ambition, that his political misfortunes were the result of a curse from his mother, to whom he had behaved in life with insufficient *hsiao.* One of the elements of Mr. Piao's charade was that Yuan's mother actually show up to haunt him—and this was my job, which involved sneaking into General Yuan's quarters to appear dramatically, dressed as a woman in the white of mourning, and to howl curses and imprecations at the unfilial Yuan.

It was Mr. Piao's bad luck that some of his apparatus—a kind of magic lantern designed to project ghostly images on the walls of General Yuan's home—malfunctioned at the wrong moment and betrayed the plot. That was the last of Mr. Piao, who was marched out and shot; and I found myself on the run, in a strange town, and furthermore dressed as a female ghost, the sort of costume that causes a fellow to be noticed.

Fortunately I bethought myself of the cemetery. People are perfectly prepared to see ghosts in a graveyard, and for that reason hardly ever venture there—and when they do visit they often leave food offerings, off which any lurking ghost can make an excellent meal. The only disadvantage of living in a cemetery, in case you're ever in a jam and are inclined to try it, is that graveyards are chock-full of yin—it's all the dead people, you see—and if you want to keep feeling yeasty, you should try to get a lot of yang-heavy foods in your diet.

So from the rail yard I hastened to the cemetery, located an old Manchurian tomb that, from inscriptions, hadn't been used in the last couple generations, and broke in. The original occupants seemed to have been returned to their ancestral tombs in Manchuria, and the place was empty. After sunrise, I hid my winnings save for a few silver pieces, then ventured out to purchase some better-fitting clothes of the common laboring sort and some yang-heavy food.

When I returned, I took the amulet from around my neck and gazed at it. The old-style characters were a bit difficult, but I finally made out the words "Noble Heart Nine Golden Apertures." The heart of a wise man, it was said, had nine apertures, whereas the rest of us made do with a lesser number, but what this had to do with the Golden Swords was more than I could say.

I held the amulet before me and concentrated on it, reciting the inscription to myself, first in Cantonese and then in the Peking dialect, and then—quite instantaneously—I was in another location altogether.

Han Shan had described the place as a "fountain," but it looked more like a small lake, a cold deep body of water of the sort fed by natural springs, surrounded by wild grasses and overhanging willows. The lake itself was in a small valley, surrounded on all sides by ice-capped mountains. Above was a very blue sky, and the only sound was that of wind sighing through the willows. It was the sort of place where a chap might want to bring a girl, a bottle of wine, and a portable gramophone, but unfortunately I had none of these available, so I circled the lake, looking for sign of the swords and finding none. So I peered into the wind-ripped waters, which were crystal clear and very deep, in hopes of finding something useful, and indeed saw a faint golden glow deep in the depths.

I disrobed and dived in. The sensation was curious—there was the shock of cold, but no real sensation of moisture or pressure, and my dive continued without cease, heading straight for the bottom. I tried blowing a few bubbles in passing, but no bubbles appeared. I discovered, after a few cautious attempts, that there was no need to hold my breath because I could in fact breathe the water, or whatever it was, perfectly well.

I reached the bottom of the fountain and there they were, two swords lying on a table crudely carved out of the rocky bottom. The swords were both unblemished, gleaming gold. It rather surprised me that the blades were of two different styles—Kan Chiang was a powerful broadsword of the type called a dau, with a heavy single-edged blade. Mo Yeh was a lighter blade of the type called a female sword, with a narrow, double-edged, pointed blade. Of course, this female sword actually *was* was a female, at least if you credit the story of how the blade came to be forged.

Well, I had no use for swords at present, and they were illegal to carry around, so I just bowed politely in their direction and then sprang for the surface, which I reached without effort. I rose from the fountain perfectly dry, and wishing I owned the patent on whatever type of water I'd just been in—I'd had all the refreshment and fun of swimming, with none of the danger or inconvenience.

Once I'd put on my clothes I recited the words "Noble Heart Nine Golden Apertures" again, and there I was, back in the old Manchu's tomb. And there I continued for three more days, during which I grew a heavy beard to assist my disguise—fast beard generation is the only advantage I can think of to being as hirsute as I. And then, as I slipped out of the cemetery one morning to get my breakfast noodles, I saw a part of my past walk by me in the street, and I knew that Mr. Ping's amulet hadn't quit on me yet.

"Yu-lan!" I called. She turned at once and her jaw dropped as she recognized me.

"Wu-k'ung!"

We embraced, an act which I enjoyed to the full. Years ago, when we both suffered under the vile despotism of the Golden Nation Opera Company of Shanghai, Yu-lan had been quite a stunner, and I had been thoroughly smitten by her charms, but now that she had grown to maturity I found myself staggered by her wide brown eyes, her gleaming black hair, her glowing complexion, her coral lips—during our years apart she had become nothing less than a pippin of the first water.

"How extraordinary!" Yu-lan said. "What are you doing in Tsingtao?"

"Hiding from the Japanese," I said.

"What an odd place to do it," she said. "Still, I might have known. You haven't changed much in the last few years, have you?"

"Whereas you have only grown more beautiful," I said. "Are you still with the Golden Nation?"

"Oh, not at all," she said. "After you beat up all the teachers and left, the company went from bad to worse. Director Wang died, and Mr. Hsü became the new director—"

"That idiot!" I exclaimed. "I'm glad I stuffed his quilt with fireworks and set it on fire one night!"

"It *was* you who did that!" she said, delighted. "You were so angry when they punished you."

"They never had a jot of evidence," I said, "but they pinned the rap on me anyway. I ask you, is that justice?"

"Well," Yu-lan said, "who else would it have been?"

I was compelled to concede the justice of this remark. "If I know Hsü," I said, "he drank away the profits within the first year."

"Indeed he did. And then he proposed to sell us apprentices to the Splendid Opera Company of Ningpo to make up the losses. . . ."

"I hope you beat him within an inch of his life," I snarled.

"No need to make fists," Yu-lan said, and I realized I was doing just that. "We got him drunk, then escaped in the dead of night."

"Ah," I said, pleased, "following my example, what?"

"Minus the broken heads and ribs, yes."

I believe, in the course of my earlier remarks on filial piety, I may have alluded to the fact that, when my parents desired to emigrate to the Golden Mountain, which is what they called San Francisco, they concluded on scanty evidence—the ceaseless complaints of prejudiced neighbors and vicious local tradesmen among them—that their eldest son would be too much trouble on the journey, and accordingly sold me at the age of eight to the Golden Nation Opera Company of Shanghai—a ten-year apprenticeship contract that amounted to slavery. And so, when my parents—and, I might add, my three younger sibs—were prospering mightily in the Land of Opportunity as worthy, hardworking members of the food service industry, I was being beaten, starved, and tortured by a gang of professional sadists under the direction of the aforementioned Hsü. My maternal grandfather—you know, the homicidal maniac—was supposed to look in on me from time to time to see how I was faring, but by age fifteen I'd seen him only twice, and he'd had to leave early both times because the police were after him. My only regret was that, when I went, I hadn't been able to persuade Yu-lan to run off with me—well, that and missing the opportunity to kick Teacher Yang in the pants a second or third time. The whole business was what one might call a defining experience.

It certainly served to define filial piety for *me*, at any rate.

"And how are you faring now?" I asked.

She brightened. "I'm working for the Yellow River

Floating Opera Company," she said, "under Master Chiang and his son, Com—ah, Young Master Chiang."

They were pleasant people to work for, she said, and the young master had been educated at university and had all sorts of new ideas. Including, as it happened, packing up the whole opera company and moving it from place to place on a river barge, an ideal situation in a time of civil disorder, when a fast exit from town was oft a consummation devoutly to be wished. When they put on performances, they either rented a theater or simply built their sets right on the barge and performed on the riverside.

"And you—you're in trouble again," she said. "Why are the Japanese pursuing you?"

I calculated how much of the truth I dared let slip, and decided it was easier merely to lie. "I have information they want suppressed," I said. "I need to get it south."

Her eyes widened. "Are you working for the revolutionary government in Canton?"

"I can't say," I said cagily. "But I need to travel in that direction." Canton, where Dr. Sun Yat-sen had established his government, was just upriver from Hong Kong. Close enough for my purposes.

"What sort of information is it?"

"There's an Imperial envoy in town named Sung," I said. "He's here to negotiate an agreement for an Imperial restoration, with Japanese money and troops backing Pu Yi. I've got all the details of the treaty." It was an improvisation, but a reasonable one, and for all I knew true.

"Do you need money?" she asked.

"I have plenty of money," I said. "What I need is a place to hide and a way out of the Japanese Concessions. Perhaps your Master Chiang knows someone who owns a boat and could get me to Chinese territory."

"Can you still do opera?" Yu-lan asked. "Do you remember all the old routines?"

These selfsame routines had been beaten into me by vicious old men armed with bamboo whips, and I allowed as how they, and the whips, were still fresh in my mind.

"Come with me at once." Yu-lan seized my hand, which was the occasion for a thrill to run up the old spine, and led me firmly toward the waterfront to introduce me to her boss.

Master Chiang proved to be a cheerful old stick, bald as an egg, who, once the situation was explained to him, was perfectly willing to shelter me as long as necessary, particularly as I would be able to work, as it were, my passage.

"In what parts did you specialize?" Master Chiang asked.

"Wu-k'ung was a wonderful Monkey King!" Yu-lan said, before I could speak.

"Indeed?" said the master. "Please let me see it!"

I gave Yu-lan a resentful look—this was hardly my favorite part—but I obliged old Chiang with an excerpt from *The Handsome Monkey King versus the Demon of Golden Helmet Cave*, which is one of oodles of operas featuring the Monkey King, all based on stories from the popular if rather lengthy novel *Journey to the West.* The audition piece I chose featured a lot of fighting and yelling and tumbling around, and by the time I finished the commotion had attracted a number of other performers, all of whom applauded vigorously when I was done.

"That was splendid!" Mr. Chiang said. "We'll have to add that play to our repertoire! Your interpretation of the Monkey King was the finest I've ever seen—why, you might be the son of the Monkey King himself!"

"Not quite," I muttered. But still, my audition had got me a berth in the company, and from that point on I sang and danced and battled demons nightly. And, since we all performed masked, I didn't have to worry about being spotted. Unfortunately it appeared that the Yellow River

Floating Opera Company was booked for a lengthy run here in Tsingtao, and so I wouldn't be leaving the Japanese Concession anytime soon. But I was in a safe enough place, and happy to get closer to Yu-lan, and so I was content enough with my lot. Aside from some pocket money, I left my Mexican silver buried in the graveyard, which I concluded was the safest place.

And, as I grew chummier with my fellow thespians, I observed that certain of them, Yu-lan included, would ofttimes slip away during the day, and return just in time for our evening performance. After this pattern was repeated a few days in a row, I found Yu-lan strolling about the deck and asked her what was up.

"Well," she said slowly, "Young Master Chiang told me not to tell you."

"Come now," I said, and patted her hand. "We're old friends. There's nothing I wouldn't do for you. Any secret is safe with me."

"It's clear enough you're not working for the Japanese," Yu-lan said. "I don't see why you shouldn't be informed. We're going off in the daytime to perform revolutionary drama for the strikers."

"Oh, really?"

"Yes. Com—I mean, Young Master Chiang says that we must educate the workers in their proper role in the revolution."

I must confess I did not like the soft glow in Yu-lan's eye when she mentioned Young Master Chiang—or, as she'd almost called him twice now, Comrade Chiang. Perhaps she was fond of the overeducated, broad-shouldered, slim-waisted, handsome-looking sheikish sort of bloke—many women are, much to my loss.

"Splendid task," I said, "inspiring the workers and all. Where did you say Young Master Chiang received his college education?"

"Moscow, of course," she said.

"Natch." It occurred to me how useful it would be

for a Comintern agent to move up and down China's rivers on a barge, gathering intelligence and organizing revolutionary cells, or whatever it was that Comintern agents did.

"And where does he get these plays?" I asked.

"He writes them himself. He's quite a dialectician, you know."

The glow in Yu-lan's eyes was getting a little too luminous for my taste. It had wormed its way into my vitals and was commencing to set fire to some of my more significant organs, chiefly, I think, the spleen. "Ahh—" I said. "You haven't mentioned to him the reason I was hiding from the Japanese, have you?"

"None of the details, no." She blushed a little. "If you're working for the Canton government—well, I thought it best he didn't know."

The Canton government and the Communists were working for similar goals but weren't formal allies, and the competition between them wasn't always gentlemanly. It was more than possible that Yu-lan's reticence had kept me from being interrogated by Chekhist goons.

"Thank you for your loyalty," I said, quite sincerely. Perhaps, I considered, it was time to dish out some ideologically correct action. "I think it's absolutely spiff what you're doing," I said. "You couldn't slip me copies of these glorious works of revolutionary art, could you?"

She did, and when I read them my sympathy for the strikers' plight increased a hundredfold. It was bad enough they had to face Japanese swords and bayonets every day, without asking them to sit through plays along the lines of *Comrade Ng Discovers Dialectical Materialism* and *Laborers Vigilant Against Capital Accumulation.* The dialog was full of absolute corkers like, "I'm fascinated! Please elucidate further on the subject of Labor Value Theory," and, "Why, Comrade Chou, this Condition of Alienation of yours describes my situation exactly!"

"Do you know," I told Yu-lan later, "I think I might try my hand at writing a revolutionary drama myself."

"Do you think you could?" A little glimmer, perhaps too tenuous at this stage to be called a glow, kindled in her wide brown eyes.

"I'm sure I could!" I said, promptly inspired. "And I want it to be absolutely grand—workers and peasants, you know, singing and dancing their hearts out to music as revolutionary as their sympathies."

"Singing and dancing?" Doubt fluttered across her face. "Why would they sing and dance? That's so old-fashioned."

"All *real* workers and peasants sing and dance," I pointed out.

"Oh—well, if it's realism, then."

"Only thing is—do you suppose Old Master Chiang will object if I buy a piano and move it onto the boat?"

Well, buy it I did, and then suffered the tortures of the damned as I banged out chords and mumbled lyrics to myself and scribbled things down on sheets of paper. Never having written a musical play before, I hadn't realized the sort of agony I was letting myself in for. Problems of translation affected me particularly—I found I composed in English, and then had to translate my sentiments into Northern Chinese. I kept Yu-lan informed of my progress, and sang some of the songs for her, and she was enthusiastic. I recalled some stuff I'd seen in the musicals that had toured the East, and I threw in some business I'd learned from Jerome Kern and Guy Bolton and Eubie Blake. At the end, I reckoned I had something to be proud of—better than Chiang the Younger's turgid stuff, anyway. So I called in my fellow revolutionaries for a run-through.

I seated myself at the piano and warmed the digits running through a few snatches of melody. "The title," I said, "is *Call Me Comrade.*" Young Chiang looked at me skeptically and rolled a cigaret. "Our story opens,"

I continued, "with a mixed chorus of male dockworkers and female textile workers. They sing as follows:

The Mandate of Heaven has gone away,
Looks like bad times are here to stay—
Our situation's frightful, the bosses are so spiteful,
And the Mandate of Heaven has gone
a-waaaaaay.

"What is this reference to the Mandate of Heaven!" demanded Young Chiang. "That's just a ridiculous superstition the feudal classes use to justify their centuries of misrule!"

"It can also be used by revolutionaries to justify their attempts to change the government," I pointed out.

"Absolutely!" Yu-lan said. I basked in her approval for a moment, then finished the song.

"Now here's where the hero comes in," I said. "His name is Plain Chou, and he's a dockworker. By way of introduction, he does his solo dance. A little buck-and-wing, over the tops, over the trenches . . . Something flashy to get the audience involved."

"Over the tops," demanded Young Chiang. "Over the trenches! What kind of steps are these?"

"A new sort, quite revolutionary," I said. "Invented by oppressed classes in the States. Perhaps I ought to take this part myself, since I'm familiar with them. Anyway, Plain Chou is in the dumps because Old Moneybags, his boss, isn't paying him enough, and he can't marry Miss Chong, the girl of his dreams."

"Dancing!" Chiang carped. "Love stories! What kind of foolishness is this? What does any of this have to do with the inevitable progression of history?"

In spite of this kind of heckling I managed to get Plain Chou and Miss Chong through their first love duet.

"This is absurd!" cried Chiang. "There's no ideological content at all in this story!"

"Ah, well," I said, "we're about to get to all of that. Up to this point all we've been doing is providing characters that our proletarian audiences can understand and care about. But now Chan the Union Man enters. He's a brilliant young Moscow-educated intellectual, here to organize the dockworkers." I feigned indecision. "Who do you suppose will play him?"

"Hmmm," he said suspiciously.

"Here's his song," I said.

The world is in trouble, we all agree
Filled with vice and villainy
But life isn't very nearly such a mystery
Once you know the view—
(the truly scientific view)
—the scientific view of his-to-ry

"Hmmm," said Chiang again, stroking his chin.

I won him over by giving the Union Man all the good arguments, which was what Chiang considered most important; and I gave myself and Yu-lan all the love duets, which was what *I* thought the whole point of the exercise. By the end of the story, the dockyards had been unionized, Old Moneybags humiliated, and Plain Chou and Miss Chong were chirping away happily in each other's arms.

We went into rehearsals right away, and were ready for the premiere in jig time. That's the advantage to working with a Chinese company: they're all cross-trained in everything, singing, dancing, mime, acting, and music, and they're accustomed to learning quickly by rote, so they can get their lines and steps down faster than you can say Bill Robinson.

For the premiere, which was held in a rented godown or warehouse, empty on account of the strike, we had a smallish audience on our rented folding chairs, a hard core of dedicated Union types who attended Young

Chiang's dramatic efforts, I'd guess, in order to test their capacity for enduring torture at the hands of the Japanese. I suffered through the usual opening night jitters, and wished I'd had the Ace Rhythm Kings to provide the music instead of the band we'd acquired, whose usual job was to play at funerals. But from the moment I stepped out onto the stage I knew all was well, and from the gasps of the audience as I went over the tops and the trenches I gathered I'd made an impression, and by the time I took Yu-lan's hands in mine and began our first duet, I was confident things were going swimmingly.

It was a socko, in short. The audience went wild with enthusiasm, we were called out for fifteen encores, and at the end of the evening Yu-lan kissed me in a fashion that suggested all the clinches we'd rehearsed so diligently had not been in vain.

The play went on from success to success, our audiences growing larger, enthusiasm overflowing all bounds. They brought their parents, their children, their relatives from out of town. The strike was spreading, with the textile workers, miners, and factory workers joining in, and with nothing else to do they came trooping in their thousands. They brought picnic lunches and bottles of wine. Some came so many times they learned all the lyrics and started singing along with the cast. After my first glimpse of five hundred people harmonizing away about the Scientific View of His-to-ry, I was inclined to wonder, like that Frankenstein bird in the flickers, just what it was I'd wrought.

But I had little inclination to think about such things, as every instant I spent away from the stage was spent with Yu-lan. And though I will draw what I believe the finer writers call "a tactful veil" over the particulars, I think that I can safely remark that our private love duets continued long after our final curtain calls, and that I left my little sleeping cabin untenanted for days at a time.

It was, to be sure, a heady and intoxicating experience.

First, it was my first triumph on the stage, and, far from last, I was able to spend my private hours with Yu-lan and I, sitting on the piano bench, me gazing into what the better writers would refer to as her "goo-goo eyes," and practicing sentimental ditties like "Tea for Two" and "Deep in My Heart, Dear." I taught her the goopier songs from *Rose Marie,* as a result of which, at five in the morning, the haunting warble of the "Indian Love Call" was heard floating above the silent, and no doubt to some degree surprised, Tsingtao dockyard.

All idylls, alas, must end, and this one was a victim of its own success. Any play that preaches sedition, and that attracts ever-increasing audiences of thousands of striking workers intent on chucking out their overlords, is bound to become of interest to the selfsame overlords. I suppose I should have foreseen it, had I not been so besotted with Yu-lan and with my own success. And so, one fine matinee, as I was kicking up the dust in my opening solo, there came the booming crash of the go-down's main doors being thrown open, and then in poured a brown river of my old friends the 142nd Military Police Battalion, all brandishing weapons.

"This performance is canceled!" some Chinese collaborator bellowed into a megaphone. "Everyone here is under arrest!"

They had picked the wrong thing to say, or at any rate the wrong audience to say it to. These people had been fighting with the Japanese and their Chinese puppets for weeks, and they weren't about to go down quietly. The audience rose as one, and in an instant the intruders were buried beneath a perfect blizzard of missiles, teapots and plates and bowls of rice and dumplings and sausages and anything else the audience had to hand, a volley that was followed by a barrage of folding chairs—and once the Japanese had been stunned by what must have seemed like the entire contents of the warehouse being flung at them, the audience members hurled themselves into the fray, drove the enemy from the godown, and slammed the doors in their face.

A bit slow on the old uptake, I still found myself onstage, staggered by what appeared to be the sight of the last act taking place a couple hours early. And then, as the sound of rifle butts hammering on the godown's doors began to clang out, Yu-lan stepped out onstage and called out in her clear soprano, "Barricade the doors! Don't let them in!"

As the cast and audience busied themselves with piling furniture and set flats against the doors, I gave the matter some thought. Barricading the doors was all very well for the moment, I considered, but in locking the Japanese out we were also locking ourselves in. And if the cops brought in reinforcements—an armored car or two, say—I feared to think of the hideous massacre that could all too easily take place. So I nipped around to where Yu-lan was directing operations and took her by the arm.

"We're safe for the moment, but we're trapped in here!" I said. "Is there any way out?"

She blinked at me, not having quite thought this one out. "I don't know."

"Then we'd better find one!"

A search was undertaken, but the godown was unconnected to any other structure, and though I had high hopes for the sewers, these were dashed when the drains proved to be too small for anyone but a child to negotiate. By the time we'd discovered this the Japanese had given up trying to break down the doors, and an ominous silence now reigned in our improvised theater.

"We've got to make a break for it!" I declared. "Now, while the Japanese are still trying to figure out what to do!" We sent lookouts to the roof to see where the Japanese cordon was weakest, and on their report we laid our plans.

Strategy-wise, I decided to take a leaf or two from the book of Jim Thorpe. "A flying wedge of actors first," I said, "with me in the lead. We'll break through the line, and then everyone else will follow. Once we're past the cordon, we all split up and make a run for it."

You may think it odd that, with hundreds of brawny dockworkers about, I should choose a pack of actors for my elite squad. But there's a lot of combat in Chinese opera, and actors are taught from the cradle how to fight. They use a theatrical version of a boxing style called Northern Long Fist, or Chang Ch'üan. The training includes the use of weapons, so I was able to equip my chorus with the weapons they used in the play to overthrow Old Moneybags, spears and clubs and blunt-edged stage swords of light metal, which didn't have the bite of a real weapon but were better than nothing. Unfortunately there was no time to fetch Kan Chiang and Mo Yeh from the bottom of their pond, so I stuck a couple of the stage swords in the old belt and then further armed myself with a long chunk of wood I tore off one of the sets. I then ordered one of the doors be silently unbarricaded.

While this was being done, I slipped up to Yu-lan. "Stick close to me," I said. "And in the event that we get separated, head for the graveyard near where we first met. Do you remember?"

"Yes," she said. "But shouldn't we go back to the barge?"

"That depends on whether the Japanese have connected us with the Yellow River Floating Opera Company," I said. "If they have, the barge will be their next target—if they're not already there, that is."

The barricade over the door had been dismantled, so I quietly arrayed my forces, explained once more the plan of action, and commanded the doors be thrown open.

The second the hinges commenced their squeal I headed for the nearest barricade at a modest trot, knowing that it would take time for my troops to pass the door and then fill in the flying wedge behind me. I didn't want to take too much time ordering my formation, because I didn't want the Japanese, if they were in a shooting mood, to have time for more than one volley. All I could do was hope my troops weren't running straight into the yellow winking eye of a Maxim gun.

We had caught them a bit off guard, standing about smoking and leaning on their rifles, and it took them a few moments to array themselves behind their barricade of sawhorses. By this time I judged I had enough force behind me, and I increased my speed to a dead run as I waved my whangee over my head and bellowed the ancient battle cry of the Chan family, something that translates out of Cantonese as something like, "O Lord, why dost thou so afflict us?" or, perhaps more to the point, "Why me?"

The enemy got off a ragged volley, which went mostly over our heads, and then I launched myself into a flying kick, aimed not at any of the foe but at the long sawhorse they were standing behind. The sawhorse went over, taking with it the first rank of police, and what should have ensued was the grand sight of yours truly leading my brave troops into the disorganized enemy, windmilling about me in the classic heroic style, as for example Charlie Chaplin beset by welfare agents in *The Kid*, but what happened instead was that my foot got tangled in the sawhorse and I went down flat on my face, and then the chorus line behind me zealously performed an extended tap dance on my kidneys as they charged over my sprawled body to come to grips with the foe.

I was up as soon as the circs permitted, wondering if these sorts of things ever happened to my maternal grandfather, the bloodthirsty maniac, who had been through more fights than God, I believe, made chickens. As far as I could determine things were pretty much a katzenjammer. I was being hauled to and fro in the press, and my head, which had been kicked about a dozen times, was hurting like sixty, but it appeared that my wedge of troops had driven the foe back, by sheer weight if nothing else, and there was nothing for it but for me to add my poundage to the general mass hurling themselves in the general direction of freedom.

Perhaps our front line, who were running straight onto Japanese bayonets, would have preferred to reconsider the whole business of pressing on, but the mass in the rear didn't give them any choice, and in one breathless mass we lurched onward. Eventually, as our mob gained weight and determination, the cops were faced with the decision of either running for it or being trampled, and like sensible chaps they decided to take it on the lam, at which point there was a lurch, and suddenly we were all running free, streaming down the waterfront street like those marathon coves in the last Olympics. There were still a few Japanese among us, either crazed with lust for battle or deprived of the opportunity to flee, and I was able to take a few swipes at them in passing with my bit of lumber, which promptly broke in half.

I looked for Yu-lan but couldn't see her in the mob, but our opposition seemed to have evaporated and I thus concluded that I should bend my efforts to eluding the coppers, so I nipped off down a side street only to run smack into a Japanese officer, sword drawn, leading a squad of reinforcements to battle. The young fellow looked familiar, and he had a broken nose and one of those plaster cast thingummies on his left arm, the kind where the elbow sticks out to the side. He gaped at me.

"You!" he said, and at that moment I recalled using him as a ladder as I made my exit from the Japan Services Club. Apparently I had inadvertently damaged him that night, and in so doing had rather made an impression, because he recognized me in spite of my bushy beard.

He seemed in no mood for receiving my apologies, and cocked his sword arm to cut me in half, at which point I thrust my busted bit of lumber up under his nose and smote him decisively on the mazard.

Later I would conclude from this encounter that the benefits of the point are not stressed in Japanese fencing schools. At the time, however, I was too busy in grabbing his throat with my left hand, and seizing him rather farther down with my right, and then hoisting the poor chump off his feet to use him as a weapon against his own troops. I knocked a few coppers sprawling with the plaster cast, and in his flailing, ineffectual attempts to slash me with his sword the officer managed to chop a few of his own men, and the rest, too wary of damaging their commander to really press their attack, let me charge through to safety. I knocked the sword out of my captive's hand, which I hadn't had the time to do till that moment, and then hoisted him over my shoulder as a shield and ran for it. I really had no intention of letting him go, as he'd recognized me, but I hadn't got as far as deciding where to stash him.

I broke out into the clear between some buildings and there was General Fujimoto, standing up in his staff car, which had the roof folded back and Japanese flags on the fenders. He was brandishing a riding crop and directing a whole company of troops toward the fray, but he stopped in mid-gesture, stared at me with an open-mouthed expression that was growing all too familiar, and pointed with the crop and said, "You!" and then he pointed a bit lower and said "The swords!" and then he turned to his troops and cried, "Kill him!"

Bootless it would have been to point out that the swords stuck in my belt were the merest of stage props, so I concluded to run for it instead. As I dashed down the nearest alley I considered that my luck seemed to have turned rather decisively: I'd been jumped by a whole battalion of troops, I'd been used for a hurdles course by my own side, and I'd run into the two officers in all of Tsingtao who could recognize me. Mr. Ping's amulet, I judged, had swung to the yin side of things rather decisively, so as I ran I reached into my pocket, pulled out my cigaret case, and managed one-handed to remove the amulet. I licked it, yanked down the puttee on one of my captive's hairy legs, and pasted the paper in place.

There was the tramp of hobnailed boots right behind me, and I concluded that my prisoner was only slowing me down, so I let him fall and put on a burst of speed. As he hit the pavement I heard him cry, "*Otodokoi!*" which is Japanese for something along the lines of, "Whoops, I'm about to take a fall which will cause others to laugh endlessly at my expense!" I would have felt sorry for him if I hadn't been so busy feeling sorry for myself.

Once I'd dropped my shield, I heard the sound of snicking rifle bolts, which served only as further impetus to my flight. And then I heard the young officer's voice again, calling attention to the dubious status of my antecedents—something that, in all honesty, I could not dispute—but a rifle shot cut the voice off in mid-tirade, and I concluded that he'd stood up at the wrong moment, just as one of his men drew a bead on me, and I'd dropped my bad joss just in time. Some more bullets whizzed past, and then I came to a corner and executed a proper Charlie Chaplin turn, hopping on one foot while clinging to a drainpipe, after which, with a clear field ahead, I legged it to freedom.

I caught up with Yu-lan around sunset. She was waiting in the graveyard with a few of the actors, all of whom looked like the subjects of an heroic painting, standing nervously on guard clutching their weapons and glaring into the gloom with eyes that gleamed with lofty majesty from beneath bandaged brows . . . or so they seemed to me, anyway. Even Young Chiang was there, looking somewhat less the ass than usual.

"You're safe!" Yu-lan said, and we fell into a relieved embrace.

"How's the barge?" I asked, and kissed her.

"The barge is fine, and so is Master Chiang," she said, after extricating her lips. "We've shifted our mooring, and after the moon sets we're going to try to slip out of the harbor on the tide, without running lights."

"When does the moon set?" I asked, and scanned the sky as if I knew what to look for—other than a moon nearing the horizon, that is.

"In around three hours."

"I'll try to create a distraction just before that time," I said, and she stared up at me.

"You're not coming along?"

"I can't."

This was the point where, if this were the cinema, I would puff out my chest like Wallace Wood and point emphatically at the ground, while a title read, "My place is here!" but what happened is that Yu-lan's chin began to wobble and then I sort of fell to pieces, and I recall saying that, if they were caught without me, they might be able to talk their way out of their jam, whereas if they were caught with me, we'd all be tortured and killed, and I couldn't bear the thought of anyone hurting her. And she said, in that case, she'd join me in creating a diversion, and I said no, it would be too dangerous, and she retorted that, if we were to die, it was best we die together, and I said she ought not to talk bally rot, and the upshot of it was that we had a wretched little weep there in the cemetery, and her comrades looked away and shuffled their feet and pretended they weren't hearing every word.

After we pulled ourselves together somewhat, I took her out of earshot and told her that I had a place in Hong Kong called Broadway Johnny's, where I was known by the name of Chan Kung-hao, and that if she could ever tear herself away from the Chiangs, there was a place for her there. She sniffled. "After the revolution," she said. "The way things are going, it can't be *too* far away."

"You must write as soon as you make your escape," I said, and then I led her away to where I'd buried my pillowcase full of silver and dug it up. I put a few handfuls in my pockets and then gave her the rest. "You might have to bribe your way out of a jam," I said. "It's enough to buy a whole potful of river barges."

"But you might need to bribe an official yourself," she said.

"The kind of jam I plan to get in," I said grimly, "no amount of bribery will settle."

So she kissed me, and we embraced, and had another depressing wail together. By the time I sent her back to her comrades I was about wept out, so I just sat on a tombstone and stared angrily at the gathering dusk until, echoing among the tombstones and willows, I heard, receding in the distance, the haunting cry of "Indian Love Call." I tried to answer it, but I'm afraid the weeping business had left the old vocal cords a little clogged, and the best I could manage was a kind of croak, which did not improve my temper.

A couple hours later, when I marched out of the cemetery, I carried the two golden swords in my hands. I was in a perfectly bloody-minded mood, having lost my girl, my money, and my dreams of theatrical success all in the course of an afternoon, and I was perfectly ready to take my disappointment out on the first enemy to come within my ken.

I had wondered if there would be any pyrotechnics when I actually touched the swords, any sudden, dramatic burst of symphonic music emanating from an invisible orchestra pit, or perhaps a few enigmatic words of warning called out in a harsh, croaking voice . . . but nothing of the sort happened.

The swords were very fine work indeed, balanced wonderfully, and much lighter than I'd suspected. I'd done some practice with them in the graveyard, a bit of hopping and chopping, and it went like nobody's business. Kan Chiang, carried in my right hand, was a heavy blade, good for power attacks and suitable to my big shoulders and long arms, and Mo Yeh, in my left hand, was a splendid little fencing sword, light and agile, with a deadly waspish sting. With the swords came a feeling of quiet confidence, mixed with a *soupçon* or so of somber purpose, that served to fortify me for the evening better than a splash of brandy and soda.

You might think that someone walking down the streets of a major city carrying a pair of swords would have no difficulty getting in trouble, but in my case you'd be wrong. The escape from the godown and the Japanese that afternoon had sent hundreds of revolutionaries dashing off into all parts of the city, where they'd all located their friends and gone out looking for a spot of vengeance. There was a full-scale riot in progress, complete with looting and arson, and the Japanese authorities were nowhere to be seen. So I tossed a brick through the window of a tailor shop and got myself some clothing—normally I don't hold much with off-the-rack suits, but this was an emergency—and once I looked like a respectable bourgeoise again, I headed for the Japan Services Club.

Here I found the enemy preparing for the worst. A group of soldiers was digging a sandbagged bunker on the front lawn, for all the world as if they were planning on refighting the Battle of Ypres. One rather dim-witted-looking recruit was standing by the gate guarding them from any rioters, none of whom were to be seen, of course, since they knew better than to attack a well-guarded site. I stuck the swords down my trousers in back, and walked a bit stiff-legged toward the club, as if I were a businessman seeking shelter from the riot. As I strode through the gate I was pleased to see that the guard had decorated his chest with a couple grenades, and was furthermore delighted to discover General Fujimoto's staff car in the drive.

I stuck a cigaret in my mug, then patted my pockets as if I were looking for matches. This bit of pantomime convinced the guard I was looking for a light when I approached him. As soon as I got within arm's length I socked him in the beezer, then snatched one of the grenades off his chest, yanked the pin, and tossed it into the bunker. I then grabbed the guard and tossed him in likewise. The ensuing explosion, I am pleased to report, accounted for the whole Ypres Salient in one fell swoop. I then drew my swords and charged the building.

The first fellow I skewered turned out to be the Chinese footman, for which I suppose I ought to be sorry, but it serves him right for toad-eating the Japanese anyway. From the hall I roared into the front parlor, and found there General Fujimoto, standing on the far side of an open coffin. He gaped at me for half an instant, saw the golden swords at the ends of my long arms, and fled straight into an office, slammed the door, and locked it. I ran my shoulder into the door, but it proved a stout bit of woodwork and I bounced off. At this point a couple more officers came in, and I had to deal with them. There is a Japanese art of drawing the sword and cutting with a single move, but it appeared neither of these two had learned it, because I dropped them both in their tracks before they got their blades out.

I have to give a certain amount of credit to my Kan Chiang and Mo Yeh. They seemed to do more damage than their weight would account for, and they never twisted awkwardly in my hands or ended in an unbalanced position. Amazing how much the right tools will help a chap in his trade.

At this point I glanced at the coffin and its occupant, who proved none other than my old friend Lieutenant Chump, somewhat the worse for wear. I should have recognized him earlier, as he didn't quite fit his box, what with the plaster arm-and-shoulder cast that had to be propped up on the coffin's edge. I supposed he must have been a member of the club. Perhaps a touching memorial service was planned for the next day. I'd try to see that the good lieutenant wasn't sent to the beyond all on his own.

I took another run at General Fujimoto's door, and was rewarded by a splintering groan that meant the frame was on the point of giving way, but then a young fellow in naval rig jumped into the room with what I believe the better writers call a "John Roscoe," .38 caliber I believe, and I had to do a hasty somersault that put Lieutenant Chump's coffin between myself and the bullets that began, at that point, to be spent rather freely. Nothing came near me, though I'm afraid the coffin suffered badly. Eventually the sailor ran out of either bullets or nerve and made a break for the doorway that led into the back hall, so I popped up from behind the coffin and tossed Mo Yeh, the lighter of my two swords, right through the blighter's spleen.

I came up out of my crouch and began to move toward the body to retrieve the sword, but I was distracted by a file of soldiers who, having just arrived in a lorry, now came charging up to do battle. Japanese soldiers are trained to attack at all costs, which can be intimidating if you're facing them on a fair and open field, but I was encountering them indoors, and I must say that, brave as they were and able, their doctrine rather let them down this time. All I had to do was station myself inside the front hallway door and chop the brave saps down one by one as they came in. By the time I'd finished and was able to return to the parlor to fetch the lighter sword, I found Yamash'ta, the spy, standing over the body of the naval officer with Mo Yeh in his hand.

Yamash'ta was a very inconvenient man, I was discovering.

I hurled myself at him forthwith, and he dropped into

a fencing stance and met my attack. He was a tall, thin wand of a fellow, you remember, and the light weight and darting style of the female sword suited him well. With its sharp point, edge, and double-handed hilt, it was perfectly adaptable to Japanese fencing techniques. I came at him like fury, slashing away with Kan Chiang, and though Yamash'ta was obliged to retreat, he held me off and even forced me now and again to pay attention to his counterattacks. I kept hoping to corner him—it wasn't a very large room—but his footwork was nimble enough to escape me.

At this point a couple more Japanese officers showed up, drew their swords, and prepared to charge into the melee, so I hopped over Lieutenant Chump's coffin to gain a little space on Yamash'ta, played lumberjack for a few well-placed strokes, and then hopped over the coffin again once the newcomers fell like unto the stately fir of British Columbia.

I felt more like Douglas Fairbanks every minute.

Yamash'ta dropped into stance again and we slashed away. The fight went much as it had before, me charging and hewing, Yamash'ta retreating, parrying, and venturing the occasional thrust. It occurred to me he was playing for time: sooner or later someone might show up with a gun, and finish me off while I was occupied. So I stepped back, and let my guard fall a bit. His guard, I observed, fell too.

That's the problem with people who learn fighting in academies, I've found. They practice in rounds, attacking and defending in turns, or fighting in flurries and relaxing in between, and they learn little pieces of timing that are wrong for when Fate dishes up a genuine fight. I had just stepped back and dropped my guard, which signaled to Yamash'ta that he could relax, so he did.

"Better hope you've got something more clever up your sleeve this time than a bag of lousy rocks," I said.

You can tell when a fellow is thinking—his eyes go

all abstract—so while he was chewing on my little witticism and working perhaps on a devastating reply I somersaulted forward, rolled under his guard, and rose slashing.

Timing, I've discovered, is everything.

I retrieved Mo Yeh from Yamash'ta's body, cleaned the slippery blood off the hilt, then applied my shoulder to General Fujimoto's door again. It crashed inward with an admirable rending sound, revealing the general himself on the telephone, calling no doubt for reinforcements.

"I surrender!" he said promptly. "Don't hurt me!" Which was rather letting down the old side in terms of Japanese tactical doctrine, I thought. I dropped his sword and pistol to the ground and marched him out.

"I've come here to liberate Tsingtao!" I snarled at him. "I'm not going to quit until the Japanese are driven into the sea!" Whereupon having (I hoped) given him cause to concentrate his forces on defending Tsingtao rather than preventing the escape of a certain bargeload of refugees, I picked him up by his collar and the seat of his trousers and flung him through the front window. I believe, regarding his expression as I hoisted him up, that he went more thankfully than not.

I dusted my hands, turned, and discovered none other than Captain Kobayashi, or the kami Teruo, politely waiting for me. He was dressed in formal Japanese style, with a kimono and trousers and split-toed shoes, he had the wide sleeves of his jacket tied back with the kind of harness swordsmen use, and he had a sword in either hand, the Japanese long sword in the right, and the smaller short sword in the left. Both swords seemed impressively sharp, gleaming like the brilliantine in Teruo's hair.

In short, he was here for a fight. I must confess that I misliked the very sight of him, and drew my swords at once.

"Why's everyone here?" I demanded. "Did I come on poker night or something?"

"Perhaps we could step outside," Teruo said. "I could order the soldiers not to shoot."

I reflected that he could just as well order the soldiers to volley away the second they drew a bead. "I'd just as soon fight in here, if it's all the same," I said.

He walked straight up, a thoughtful look in his protuberant eyes, and commenced an attack without any more preliminaries, moving with an unpleasant sort of unearthly tranquility that I found decidedly unnerving. I parried his strike with Mo Yeh while slashing with Kan Chiang, and the most extraordinary thing happened—the swords began to snarl like a couple of cats. And not just mine, but his as well.

I must admit I found it more than a little shuddersome. A fellow doesn't want constant reminders, amid the clang and fury of battle, that the weapons he is wielding are living beings, with perhaps wills of their own, who might decide on a whim to stop being swords and become instead, say, a bouquet or two of daisies.

Not that I was particularly worried about flowery transformations in this instance, because it seemed my swords had a grudge and were only expressing it. Teruo's swords were howling as well—they had a lower, bass viol sort of cry—and it was clear enough they were stuffed as full of power as my own, and as determined as mine to triumph over their rivals.

The shock of discovery must have made me hesitate, because he lunged straight at me with his long sword, and I parried only at the last second. That lunge was a move from Western fencing, not Japanese at all, and it was looking as if I were going to have to keep my wits about me. I didn't know how many lifetimes this character had had to perfect his swordsmanship, and I was glad I didn't know because I had a feeling the knowledge would be certain to depress me.

So I retreated while trying to gain the Teruo's measure, and the result was even more discouraging—he was damned good, and very tricky, and perfectly calm about the whole business, as if he had nothing to worry about—and since he was an immortal who couldn't be killed, he probably didn't, at least in the long run.

I rolled under the coffin to gain a little space to think, and we battled back and forth over Lieutenant Chump's form, and with four weapons flailing out at once—not to mention all the bullets that had been fired into the coffin earlier—his body began to suffer from all the attention. It seemed that his bad joss was pursuing him past his actual departure from the planet, which served only to confirm my suspicions about how the universe actually works.

It was rapidly becoming clear that Teruo was a better swordsman than I, and that I wasn't going to beat him in a straight-up fight. I was going to have to think of something extremely clever, and do it soon.

Unfortunately nothing came to mind, so, to give myself space, I disengaged, and maneuvered around the coffin. "Nice couple of swords you've got there," I said, and dropped my guard a bit, hoping he'd take the hint.

Teruo smiled pleasantly and kept his guard steady, which caused a lengthy round of curses to chase each other round the interior of my skull.

"Muramasa swords, quenched in the blood of a prince," he said. A smug look entered his pop eyes. "Some people think that Muramasa swords are cursed, but I have always found them perfectly congenial."

"How lucky for you," I said. "Of course, my swords have been around a lot longer than yours, so I expect they know quite a few more tricks."

"They have not displayed such knowledge so far," he observed.

"We've just been taking your measure," I said. "Take

my word for it, from this point forward, you're up to your neck in the *bouillabaisse*."

I was hoping that he'd stick on the word *bouillabaisse*, and take at least a few seconds to decipher it, but he didn't change expression, so I launched myself at him anyway, a full-bore assault just on the off chance. Apparently he was at least a little surprised, because he gave way, and I backed him up, but he counterattacked and locked my blades up with his own, and then we were *corps-à-corps*, like Jack Pickford glaring at Erich von Stroheim over crossed sabers, except that on this particular occasion the swords themselves were howling like banshees. The proper behavior at this point is to exchange witticisms, or at least give a devil-may-care laugh, and I am pleased to report that I was on form.

"Swords are all very well," I said, "but as it happens, I've got some additional magic that's going to make this fight a cinch."

"Oh really?" At least he was doing me the courtesy of taking a polite interest.

"The magic of twenty-three," I said.

"And what is that?" he asked.

"Twenty-three skiddoo," I said, and while he was chewing that over I kicked him in the crotch and ran for it.

I made it partway across the lawn before the first shots rang out, and then a few paces later I was able to use General Fujimoto's staff car for cover. The old fellow had had the sense to purchase a Daimler, which was practically bulletproof. I tossed the chauffeur out and got behind the wheel, then jammed the thing in gear and put my foot to the accelerator. I am pleased to report that the guards at the gate scattered at my approach, led in their retreat by General Fujimoto himself, who, it appears, I'd trained well.

Once in the road outside I had to make a couple turns to point myself in the direction I wanted—which was west and a long way from Japanese territory—and I was just shifting out of second gear when a motorcycle roared out of an alley and banged right into the fender, and something jumped from the saddle and plastered itself to the far side of the car. My swords, lying on the seat next to me, gave a howl of recognition. I saw a flash of blade and a glare of pop eyes and the old heart gave a jump straight into my throat. It was Teruo, and he was standing on the running board and trying to find a way into the car. Fortunately the windows were closed on that side, and the doors locked, and I made the task difficult for him by feeding gasoline to the supercharged in-line eight and throwing the wheel from side to side.

"Coward!" he yelled. "Honorless ape!"

"Sticks and stones, old chap," I reminded him.

There was an alarming rip as he drove one of his swords through the canvas top of the car, the better to provide an anchor. "You're going to pay for that treacherous blow, monster!" he shouted. He seemed to have taken that little kick of mine to heart, or somewhere else vital anyway.

Apparently the demonstrated vulnerability of the canvas top gave him an idea, and he commenced flailing away, chopping at the roof to get to me, but fortunately the Daimler's canvas was as stout as the rest of the car and his efforts were not crowned by conspicuous success. Persistence would have told eventually, but fortunately at this point I saw a telegraph pole coming up and took instant advantage—I swung the wheel and scraped the pole along the Daimler's flank, and there was another rip from the canvas over my head and Teruo was flung off. As the car lurched away I saw him in the road behind, rising to a crouch in a cloud of dust and showing every readiness to pursue, on foot if necessary, so I slammed the car into reverse and gunned the motor and came lunging back out of the dust cloud to pin Teruo's knees between the rear bumper and the telegraph pole, after which

I switched gears again and roared away. Triumph sang an Act III finale in my veins as I saw him crumpled at the telegraph pole's base, shaking his fist—immortal he may have been, but he was going to have a hard time chasing me on a pair of broken legs.

Still, I took no chances. As soon as I got onto the highway I climbed a pole and cut the telegraph wires so as to prevent any alarms from reaching the outlying garrisons. With the Japanese flags flying on the general's staff car serving as my passport, I drove unmolested through every checkpoint until I left the Japanese Concessions, and then all the way to Nanking without stopping save for fuel. There I sold the car to a Hui merchant, and it was only then that I discovered Teruo's short sword still stuck in the car's canvas top.

It appeared that China had come out of this exchange one magic sword to the good. I don't know whether the sword contained a slice of anything so grand as the martial fortunes of the Japanese people, but still it was a handy little trophy of the adventure, and worthy of respect. Still, according to some people all Muramasa blades were cursed or otherwise afflicted with unwholesome vibrations, so I'd have to take special care with it. Perhaps I'd stow it safely in a temple somewhere.

I returned Kan Chiang and Mo Yeh to the bottom of their fountain, then bought a special case for Teruo's sword, some fresh clothing, and a ticket on a train back to Kowloon. It seemed that the strikes in Hong Kong had been settled in favor of the strikers, and now Hong Kong's example was being followed all up and down the coast, and the situation was returning, in Mr. Harding's winning phrase, to normalcy. The trains were running again, at least south from Nanking, so I took an entire first-class compartment for myself, slept most of the way, and when I crossed the harbor back to Hong Kong went straight to my apartment and found it inhabited by a dozen ghosts, all of whom seemed to have made free with the place while I was away. I glared at them, and they decided they were clearly facing a two-fisted hombre who would stick at nothing to clean up this one-horse town, and they all wisely faded.

After a long, hot bath and a nap, I donned my evening duds and biffed off to Broadway Johnny's, where I discovered a couple of plug-uglies from the Triads making an extortion demand on Old Nails. The Triads and I had made an agreement re protection money some time ago, and I was disturbed to see the agreement apparently being subjected to some kind of unilateral amendment. So disturbed, in fact, that I was compelled to inflict severe physical injury on the two gangsters, and then to drag them to their clubhouse, where I spoke with some heat to their bosses and all their bodyguards and anyone else loitering about the place, all of which helped to relieve my growing sense of ennui and no doubt vastly increased the profits of the local Chinese hospital. Straightening my lapels, I returned to the club, signaled Old Nails for a grasshopper, and asked Betsy Wong to sing me the blues.

Feel free to correct me in this surmise, but I concluded I had earned a moment or two of pensive self-indulgence.

The letter from Yu-lan arrived next day. The company had succeeded in escaping Tsingtao and were now cruising up the Yellow River. When they found a venue they were going to go back into repertory, Chinese classics at night and, as soon as safety permitted, *Call Me Comrade* in the afternoons. My money, Yu-lan informed me, was being devoted to worthy causes along the way.

Well, I seemed to have got Marxism off to a roaring start in China, for whatever that was worth.

Yu-lan didn't know when she would be in South China—as soon as the revolution occurred or business permitted, whatever came first. But she had little doubt that she would see me soon. Much less doubt than I, as it happened.

I went to the piano and let the digits take a few passes

through. "I'm Going Away to Wear You Off My Mind"—not, of course, that I did any such thing. And then I went in search of Han Shan.

He had put up at a temple in Hong Kong—he *was* a monk, after all—but I discovered he was no longer in residence, and he'd left a message urging me to contact him at 151 Rua Felicidade, all the way down the coast in Macao. I wondered if the local priests had responded to his unique brand of charm by chucking him out on his ear, but the chap I talked to wasn't very informative, so I toddled off and hired a cab to get me to the ferry terminal. Macao was a rather lengthy boat ride away, and I wanted to be back by evening.

As I sat on the ferry and watched the coastal islands sail by, it seemed as if the gold amulet around my neck was heavier than usual. It occurred to me being the possessor of the martial fortunes of China might have its rewards.

Counting the Muramasa blade, I had in my possession no less than three tokens of power. There were others around, and presumably I could make an effort to collect them. Broadway Johnny Chan could, if he set his mind to it, become something of a center of power himself.

It wasn't as if my country didn't need it. The Canton government controlled only one city, the rest of the country was divided between warlords, foreign powers had taken advantage of our weakness, Japan was annexing us piece by piece, and, as if that weren't bad enough, it looked as if they were also going to attempt the restoration of the Manchus, who more than anyone had created the mess in the first place.

Perhaps, it occurred to me, it wasn't too late to set things right again. A fellow with luck and enterprise, who'd seen a bit of the world and who wasn't afraid of innovation and improvisation, could go pretty far these days. And, if he gained sufficient power, he could begin setting things right. Clearing out the warlords and the corruption, adjusting the treaties with the foreigners, bringing in progress that would benefit the population.

The fly in the ointment was that I wasn't sure whether I could see myself in this role. It's one thing to have a cocktail or two and tell your buddies, "Hey, given the chance I could run this country better than any of those coves that are doing it now," but how many people would actually leap at the chance were it offered them? I had got used to thinking of myself as a *boulevardier,* with ambitions no higher than a string of nightclubs and a flutter at producing a show now and again, and now I was contemplating becoming the Chinese answer to Napoleon.

We Chinese had our own Napoleon, of course. Shih Huang Ti, the first emperor, the chap who built the Wall and standardized the currency and the weights and the roads and the writing, the chap who dug the canals and burned the books. And do you know what? For all the good he did, his memory is loathed by every schoolchild in the country, because he was also the first in a long series of tyrants.

So it was with a heavy tread that Johnny Chan left the ferry terminal and began my search for Han Shan. I couldn't decide what Fate was demanding of me.

Rua Felicidade, I knew, was in a rum sort of neighborhood, but I reckoned there had to be a temple or monastery there somewhere, a last bastion of virtue in a district devoted to vice. To my surprise 151 turned out to be a fairly plush sort of gambling den of the kind in which Macao excels. I asked for Han Shan and was shown to the manager's office, where I was offered a cigar and a brandy. I puffed away for a while, trying to picture the prune-faced monk amid all of this, and then the padded door opened and in walked Han Shan himself, smoking a custom-rolled cigaret in a jade holder and dressed in splendid Western clothes, complete with a braided waistcoat of gleaming extravagance. Gone was the silk gown, the skullcap, the five-inch nails. In the old monk's place was a prosperous businessman with a wafer-thin wristwatch and a diamond stickpin.

"Johnny!" he said with a grin. "I had about given you up! I was afraid I was going to have to hire someone else."

"Your appearance surprises me, Monk Han," I said.

"Have a seat and I will procure some luncheon," he said.

He ordered, refreshed my brandy, and then put his feet up on the manager's desk and flexed his handmade oxfords.

"You seem to be doing rather well for yourself," I said. "Did you hit a lucky streak at the tables?" In which case, I knew, he'd be wagering the martial fortunes of China the second I handed them over to him.

"Better than that," he said. "As it happens, the tables outside are my property." He blew smoke at the ceiling. "The world seems to have really moved along since I went off to meditate in my little hermitage. Back in my day we couldn't think of anything better to do with wealth than hoard it in temples or bury it in treasure troves. But now, with this spiffy capitalism philosophy we've imported from the West, I can actually make my money work for me. After you left, I dug up a couple more treasure troves and invested in this little club. Now I can gamble any time I like, and the house rules favor me. Any profits get invested in the stock market. It's almost risk-free." He gave me a wink. "Extraordinary how things change, you know. Once upon a time, that amulet of mine would have been considered an everyday sort of thing, and a telephone would have been thought magic. Now it's the other way around. The world is spinning pretty fast, eh?"

"So I hear," I said.

"Now, I believe you were going to give me something?"

Well, the moment of truth had certainly come. I could either give the amulet to this reborn capitalist and merchant of vice, or keep it, become Napoleon, rescue my country, deal out justice left and right, and endure a legacy of hatred from every succeeding generation.

"Perhaps you would like to try your luck at the tables?" the monk suggested. "I can pay you in gambling chips."

"Silver," I said. "Great stacks of it. Now."

He winked again. "Can't blame a fellow for trying."

He emptied his safe of money, and in a tick I forked over his property.

Outside, as I headed for the ferry terminal, I began to whistle.

I believe, though I could not swear to it, that the tune was "Alligator Hop."

Okay, so I like kung fu flicks.

Not so much the dreary revenge dramas that seem to constitute the majority of the genre, but rather those with a lighter, imaginative touch, such as Jackie Chan's *Police Force* or *Project A,* with their wild action, incredible stunts, and whacked-out humor; or the wonderful fantasies of Tsui Hark, like *Warriors of the Magic Mountain* or *Chinese Ghost Story*, which are probably the best sword-and-sorcery movies ever made.

Broadway Johnny is an outline for a kung fu film, complete with the scene at the end where the hero takes on all the bad guys at once. Johnny is named after his inspiration, Jackie Chan, and shares a bit of Jackie's biography—both were sold to an opera company at an early age, but managed to rise above it.

I've been accused of having too Chinese a sense of humor (whatever that means), and I've been exposed to a degree of Asian culture through the martial arts and elsewhere, but (sense of humor to the contrary) I was a bit hesitant of my ability to write from the point of view of a Chinese. But a Chinese who was fascinated by Western popular culture was something I thought I could handle. And so the grandson of the Monkey King, a martial artist who would on the whole rather be Fred Astaire, was born.

So why set the story in the twenties? That's a mystery to me, too, except that Johnny's character, as he began his preliminary chats from his perch somewhere in my skull, began to speak in some kind of hybrid hepster slang that seemed a cross between Damon Runyon and P. G. Wodehouse. So in the end I just let Johnny speak on, and wrote the words down.

Kerry Li once said to me, "The spirit of all the martial arts is the same, from the hard-ass kick-punch to the softest push hands. They are all taking you to the same place, if you are willing to follow. . . ."

ooooo

The Seventh Martial Art

Jane Lindskold

A minute and forty-five seconds was a long time. Oddly, Grandmother had never thought this until her daughter had installed the microwave in Grandmother's kitchenette. Satoko had insisted that the machine would make her life easier, but Grandmother rarely used it, preferring instead her old blackened pots, the fat rice steamer, and the little copper teakettle with the bird on the spout.

Today, though, she had awakened from a drowsy revery of her youngest days in old Kyoto to find the digital clock's red eyes accusingly informing her that it was 3:27 and that the children would be home momentarily to find no cocoa waiting to banish the chill of a winter's afternoon. Anxiously, she had put the mugs of milk in the microwave, hoping to make things right.

There was so little she felt she did right anymore.

The microwave shrilled as the apartment door went "click! click! snap! bang!" and the children stormed in, bringing with them the scents of cold and, more faintly, of the charcoal smoke from the hot pretzel and chestnut vender's cart on the sidewalk below.

With an arthritic hand, Grandmother pressed the pad that released the microwave's door and lifted the mugs out. The milk was barely lukewarm—certainly not suitable for cocoa.

Puzzled, she looked at Yukari, who was peeling herself out of her lucky red winter coat. Static made the girl's black hair stand out from her head after she pulled off her stocking cap. Grandmother forestalled smoothing the girl's hair. Yukari or Carey, as she was insisting on being called these days, was ten and getting sassy. Instead, Grandmother held the two mugs out in confusion.

"They are barely warm," she said, "but I put them in for the time that your mother told me."

"Oh, Grandmother," Yukari's bossy expression softened into something quite sweet when she realized that Grandmother was genuinely upset, "Grandmother, that was for one cup of milk. When you put in two you need to set the timer for longer, otherwise there isn't enough power."

"Ah, I see," Grandmother answered, though truly she did not, "A saucepan is simpler. Can you and Ryu wait for your drinks?"

She looked down the hallway, realizing for the first time that her grandson was not there.

"Where is Ryu?" She glanced to where a neatly written schedule hung beside the children's artwork on her refrigerator, "This is not one of his late days. Is he in trouble again?"

Yukari hesitated, "Ronny had to meet some boys from school. He'll be here very soon."

Studying her granddaughter, Grandmother shook her head. She might be too old for almost everything as Satoko saw it, but she was not stupid. Gently but firmly, she steered Yukari into the kitchenette.

"You make the cocoa, Granddaughter," she commanded, reaching for her heavy winter coat and a head scarf, "I will go and find your brother. Where is he meeting these boys?"

"By the library," Yukari answered reluctantly. "I'll go for you."

"No, stay in and start your homework. I won't be long."

Closing the apartment door behind her, Grandmother heard the locks being reset, then, more faintly, the pingping of the microwave. Leaning on the handrail, her cane under her arm, she carefully made her way down the dark, muddy stairs. When she reached the ground floor, she breathed deeply the spicy scents from the Tiger's Claw restaurant, where she still worked on weekends or when things became busy. Then she wasn't too old; then they still needed her. Most days the irony stung her, but today she was too busy concentrating on finding Ryu and bringing him home.

The air was bitingly cold, the remains of the morning's snow already blackened and icy along the curbs and gutters. Thankfully, the sidewalk was shoveled clear. Turning left, she waved to the pretzel vender and started toward the city library, her cane tapping the pavement with each step.

She was a block away from the library when the unease that had driven her from the warm apartment, although Yukari could have run the three blocks in the time Grandmother took to descend the stairs, came to settle. She remembered—the library was closed today, just as it was every Wednesday since the latest round of budget cuts. Ryu was certainly not there to study; he had no good reason for a meeting there at all.

Her cane tapped more quickly as she hurried her swollen feet along. When the library was in sight, she tucked her cane under her arm and went along silently in her soft-soled boots.

No one was in front of the small, glass-fronted building. Only one light shone behind the rainbow of public announcements taped to the window, but Grandmother remembered that there was a sheltered courtyard behind the building. In warmer months it was an oasis for old men with newspapers and women with little children. Now, however, it should be deserted, a place to invite mischief.

Fine. Mischief did not belong only to the young.

Peering around the corner, she saw Ryu, twelve years old, his dark, glossy hair shaved high on the sides, shoulders hunched within a battered leather jacket with a battling dragon and tiger embroidered on the back. He sheltered something rounded and white in his hand. The smoke that drifted from it smelled sweet, like but not the scent of the herbs that her acupuncturist burned on his moxibustion needles.

Ryu was the smallest boy in the group, the youngest, too, she thought, with a pang for him, remembering what it was to be young and hurrying to grow up and prove yourself.

Picking up a newspaper the wind had wedged beside a bench, she tottered around the corner, weaving more than she must, an old woman seeking a place to read. She would save face for the boy this once, even at the loss of her own.

The boys saw her. There were six of them, stomping their feet against the freezing slush. Ryu was the only Oriental. Two were black, two Hispanic, the last a gangly redhead with freckles. None were older than fourteen.

When Grandmother picked her way around the corner,

the boys pretended not to see her, but their chatter grew more rapid. When she began sweeping crusty snow from a bench with wild swings of her cane, they could no longer ignore her. One of the black boys left. The remaining boys began to giggle, all but Ryu, who could only manage a forced smile.

"Hey, Ronny," she heard the red-haired boy say. "You know the crazy lady?"

"Where, Pat?" Ryu asked, making a show of turning.

For a long moment he studied her, the white smoke burning to ash in his not-quite-chubby hand. She pretended not to hear them, beating the ice away, a far deeper chill soaking into her at the thought that Ryu would deny her.

"She's a friend of my mother's," Ryu not quite lied after a pause. "I guess I'd better take her home."

He crunched across the snow to her; she felt his hand grasp her arm through the thickness of her sleeve.

"Later, guys," he called to the boys. Then she let him steer her from the courtyard.

They did not speak until they had returned to the apartment and Yukari had pressed a cup of steaming tea into her hands, cocoa into Ryu's.

"You can't stop me," Ryu said as if they had been arguing for hours. "No way you can stop me. You're too old to chase me and if you tell Mama I'm not coming home, all she'll do is sign me and Carey up for some after-school programs and you'll never see us anymore."

He took a deep drink of his cocoa and tried to look tough; that he succeeded with a thin marshmallow mustache said something about how determined he was. Even Yukari couldn't manage a giggle.

"I'm just too old to sit around with a baby-sitter," Ryu continued, "I'm bored here. I need action and real company."

Grandmother sipped her tea, wrapping her fingers around the china cup's belly. The tea smelled like her memories, fragrant and welcoming. Why was she bothering to deal with this Americanized brat? So much better to fade away.

Yet, finding nothing to push against, nothing to strike, Ryu's anger and indignation were vanishing. Grandmother looked at him sadly.

"There are more ways of stopping you than by telling my daughter about your behavior," she said slowly, "just as there are more ways of fighting than by blows and weapons."

She let the words hang, remembering both the power of an unfinished threat and something else that she had nearly forgotten. Ryu studied her and then slouched over to pick up his book bag. Yukari followed him into the dining alcove with her own homework.

That night, after Satoko had picked up the children, Grandmother sat wrapped in thought. Remembering.

Grandmother had not always been Grandmother; once she had been a little girl named Ayumi and had herself called someone Grandmother. Ayumi's grandmother was an artist and a devotee of Shinto. Buddhism, she said, was good only for funerals. Long ago, in old Kyoto, Ayumi had sat at Grandmother's feet as Grandmother did her sumi-e—brief, brush stroke paintings that suggested rather than realistically portrayed an image.

"The many," Grandmother's grandmother had said, "will do their katas or caress their katanas. The few forget the forms and practice the art that underlies them. The rarest of all are those who forget form and practice and art and to these the kami will listen."

She had put her brush with its bamboo handle and sable tip into Ayumi's hand, "You have the gift to go beyond form, practice, art, and to find the kami at the center of each thing. Were you a boy, I might have sent you to learn kendo or kyudo; were the age an older one, I might have taught you naginata-do. But for you the seventh art will serve best."

So many years, oceans of time ago, those lessons had been given. Although her grandmother had found the power in sumi-e, what served Ayumi best was the formal calligraphy based on elegant renditions of the kanji characters the Japanese had borrowed from the Chinese. Something awoke in her as she shaped them, especially the simplest ones, in which ideographic suggestions of the word were clearest.

For Ayumi's grandmother had been right; the gift had been there, stirred to life after many lessons. But Ayumi had let it slide away as husband and children, war and removal had claimed her attention. Now, now that she needed it, would the gift still be with her?

She took her memories into sleep with her and in the morning dragged a stepladder over to the storage closet and climbed to the topmost step so that she could reach the box stored at the back of the shelf. The box was covered thickly with dust. Her nose itched against sneezing and her knees trembled from the weight as she climbed down.

To re-create the mood of her childhood, she brewed some green tea and lit a block of the jasmine incense that her grandmother had liked. Grandmother's head ached as she breathed in the pungent scent. Still, the tea was hot and as she opened the black-lacquered lid of the box the years and the headache slipped away together.

The inner lid of the box held seven brushes with a variety of handle types and tips. Her favorite bamboo and sable leaned slightly forward in its cloth strap. The box's deep bottom section held an ink stone worn into a gentle oval curve in its center and sheets of eggshell white cotton paper. Those on top bore a series of characters—baby, home, man, mountain, money--reflecting the concerns of nearly sixty years ago. The sheets on the bottom were empty of all but potential.

What should she paint? Anxious lest she should fail, Grandmother ground the ink, made certain her chosen brush was pristine, and meticulously centered her paper on the table.

She needed to stop Ryu's interest in experimenting with drugs, not just delay or harry him. What kami would convince a boy who wanted to be a man that drugs were not the path? What would attract him to her, not drive him farther away?

Her first attempts were terrible; palsied hands could not control the brush. Even a simple character like "mountain" was surrounded by spatters of ink when she finished, so that the mountain's three peaks seemed under rainfall. This, however, gave her an inspiration.

With a flourish of confidence, she painted the character for "little" and followed it with the character for "wind." On the last downstroke, Grandmother felt the air stir and swirl. The pool of ink rose in tiny wavelets. No matter what artists show in their paintings, there is no way to see the wind. Grandmother addressed the turbulent air.

"You will help me?" she said, her old voice's quaver making the words a question rather than a command as she had intended.

"I will?" came the breathy voice, responding to her weakness as well as her words.

Grandmother steadied herself with her love for Ryu, her desire to take his feet from the road he would walk.

"You will, little kami," she said, her lips a pale rosebud smile. "I have a game for you."

And the air stilled as the kami listened.

That afternoon, Yukari came home alone again. Grandmother could see in the set of the girl's little shoulders, in the defiant twitch she gave her glossy ponytail, that brother and sister must have argued. Wisely she ignored the signs nor did she comment on Ryu's absence. Instead, she gave the little girl her drink.

Yukari looked up from the steaming green tea with a startled expression.

"What is this?" she asked, sniffing the fragrant liquid with apprehension tinged by appreciation.

"Tea, just like my grandmother used to make for me when I was a girl in Kyoto," Grandmother answered. "I thought that you might enjoy it."

Yukari sipped, wrinkling her nose at the clear, almost bitter taste, so different from American cocoa. Then she took another taste.

"Your grandmother made you this?" she asked. "What else did you do with her?"

Grandmother sipped her own tea. "She told me stories, played games with me, and taught me cooking and martial arts."

"Martial arts?" Yukari tilted her head to the side. "I didn't know that you could do those. Ronny said . . ."

She stopped, at last aware that Grandmother had not commented on the boy's absence.

"Ryu said what?" Grandmother coaxed.

"That you were old and couldn't do anything," the little girl whispered.

"I am old," Grandmother agreed, squeezing Yukari's hand, "but I can still do some things. Would you like to see my art? It is Japanese painting, nothing like the American painting you do at school."

"Aren't you going to go and look for Ronny?" Yukari asked. "He's gone out again with those boys, not to the library, to the big park."

"Are you worried?" Grandmother asked.

"No . . ." Yukari stopped herself. "Yes, but he won't listen to me. He says I'm a dumb kid and a girl."

"Come here, Yukari," Grandmother said. "I will show you the martial art my grandmother taught me. I'll even show you how we can use it to bring back your stubborn brother."

Yukari hesitated but let herself be guided into the dining alcove, where brushes and paints and ink and paper waited. Stiffly, Grandmother got into her chair, while Yukari bounced up next to her.

"Now," Grandmother said, "I have told you before that the kanji letters we took from the Chinese are meant to be pictures—not like hiragana, which is an alphabet."

Yukari nodded. "Some aren't very good pictures."

"Maybe not," Grandmother dipped her brush in the ink. "Here is the word 'son'—Can't you see a boy in that?"

Yukari squinted at the black lines, something like a three with a line below the middle dart. She tugged her ponytail then giggled.

"No."

Grandmother grinned, "No matter, let me follow the kanji for 'son' with the hiragana for 'Ryu' and then the kanji for 'window.' Tell me what you see now."

Yukari's giggling stilled. "Grandmother! There, through the window! I see Ryu! He's in the park with that awful McDonnel boy."

Grandmother put a finger to her lips, "Shush, let's see what happens now."

Yukari's ponytail bobbed; together gray head and dark bent over the white paper, which now showed Ryu and the freckled McDonnel boy rolling joints beneath the shelter of a bare oak tree. Pat McDonnel lit his from a plastic lighter with green-and-yellow leopard spots and tossed the lighter to Ryu.

"Here, Ronny."

"Thanks," Ryu snagged the lighter with two fingers and spurred the rowel. Obediently, a flame emerged, but before Ryu could raise it to the joint he held loosely between his lips it flickered out.

"Shit!" Ryu muttered, flicking the flame to life again. This time he almost had it to the white tip before it was blown out. The small wind skated through the oak's tattered leaves with a sound like dry laughter.

By the third failure, Pat was watching him, his own

smoldering joint pinched expertly between two fingers. He giggled and Ryu flushed.

"Got a problem, Pat?"

"Uh-uh, you got one?" Pat snickered again.

"You got a cruddy lighter," Ryu said, dropping it to the dirt and fishing in his pocket.

The book of matches he pulled out bore the logo of the Tiger Claw restaurant. They were good matches, but he couldn't get even one to stay lit. The burnt ends tumbled around his feet, caught in a tiny whirlwind.

Pat was too stoned to giggle anymore, his joint sucked down to a smoldering end, his pale blue eyes wide and unfocused. He was so absorbed in watching the dancing matchsticks that he didn't even see Ryu grab the roach from his fingers.

The wind kami did and Grandmother heard Yukari giggle as it was swept away to burn out in midair.

"Shit!" Ryu cursed again. "I'm going home, Pat."

Pat waved vaguely and Ryu stuck his hands in his pockets and stomped away. Behind him, the wind stirred puffs of dust like snorts of laughter.

The bird perched on the kettle's spout whistled merrily as the water came to a boil. After pouring it over the tea leaves, Grandmother glanced up at the clock. The children were late. The weather was bad; the buses could be late. Still, it had been weeks since either Ryu or Yukari had failed to hurry home from school.

Anxiously, she walked over to the table, where the brushes and ink and paper awaited the children's lesson. Yukari was showing a talent for sumi-e; Ryu, like his grandmother, preferred the kanji. Still, a long period of training must be undergone before either of them would be able to call upon the kami. Had they grown bored?

Impulsively, she picked up her own bamboo-handled brush and dipped it into the pool of ink she had prepared. On each out breath she drew a line until she had a boy, a girl, a cart (for the bus), and a window to see them through.

The kami were kind and the black lines stirred into a battered yellow bus struggling through congested streets. Grandmother recognized the corner nearest to the apartment, saw the bus stop and Ryu and Yukari climbing down. She was letting the picture fade when she caught a scrap of conversation.

"Ronny, want to come and hang out for a while?" the McDonnel boy was asking. He pinched an imaginary joint enticingly. "I got some new stuff."

Ryu shook his head, "No way, Pat, I don't have time for that shit. My grandmother's teaching me martial arts."

"The Seventh Martial Art" owes a great deal to page one hundred in Michael Random's book *The Martial Arts*. On this page he takes a break from discussing the kicking, cutting, throwing, and shooting techniques used in such fine arts as karate, kendo, aikido, and kyudo to comment calligraphy is considered by most martial arts masters to be the seventh martial art: "For is not the ability to make the stroke flow naturally, to let the brush move freely across a thin piece of paper, also a superior struggle of the most testing kind?"

This story also owes something intangible to my meeting the Japanese brush artist Kazuaki Tanahashi during the summer of 1992 and later reading his book *Brush Mind**—a fine collection of one–brush stroke paintings

---

*Published by Parallax Press, Box 7355, Berkeley, California 94707.

accompanied by short anecdotes and free verse poems. Kazuaki Tanahashi studied martial arts with Morihei Uyeshiba, the man who created aikido, and feels that his painting and Uyeshiba's martial art both share an awareness of the power of breath. Breath, some might say, is life. And life, of course, is magic.

My story also owes a great deal to Ayumi, Satoko, Yukiko, Yukari, Yumiko, Shizue, and Mami, who were my students over the past several years. Through the essays they have written for my classes I have learned about contemporary Japan, Japanese tradition, and something of the hearts and minds of these fine young ladies. They have learned something of grammar, organization, and spelling from me. Somehow, I think I have gotten the better portion from our time together.

Finally, this story is indebted to the minute and forty-five seconds that a cup of refrigerated coffee takes to heat in my microwave. This gave me my opening line and from that point the story took over on its own.

Dave Smeds queried me when he heard of this book, saying that he had a terrific story idea. He was right.

OOOOO

FEARLESS

Dave Smeds

I knew the Peruvian would be trouble from the moment he appeared on the tournament floor. He seemed to hover an inch above the polished hardwood, coiled and ready to spring. He was heavily muscled, dark, hairy—the quintessential kick-ass karate player.

Armando Ruiz. Mongo, his enemies called him, though never to his face.

I wasn't likely to spar him until at least the quarterfinals. A lot could happen between now and then, but the way things looked, Mongo was the competitor most likely to steal my shot at the trophy.

I'd already defeated my first opponent; my second match was half an hour away. I had an opportunity to devote full attention to Ruiz as he stepped into the ring and exchanged bows with a sturdy, Nordic Shito-ryu player.

He scored a kill in eight seconds.

The match consumed so little time I had to replay it in my head to fully grasp it. Mongo had charged forward, punches flying one after the other, erasing the Viking's powerful defense as if it had been made of smoke. Three, four, five potent impacts to the face and the Viking logged off, leaving empty floor behind.

The referee raised Ruiz's arm and declared him the winner. The audience roared. The Peruvian waved at the bleachers, seemingly intoxicated by the noise. The stadium bulged to overflowing, attesting to the increasing popularity of VR combat arts. And why not? Not since the days of gladiators had sport combat been to the "death," and there was no such thing as a poor seat. Though the figures I saw seemed to extend up to the rafters, every spectator experienced the tournament as if from front row center.

Mongo strutted out of the ring, joining the contingent from South America. After the mandatory sixty-second delay, the loser logged back on in a fresh surrogate. The Viking, though now whole and uninjured, shook his head as if dazed and wandered off to the end of the tournament hall, where the consolation rounds would begin. The crowd mocked him.

Beside me, Mr. Callahan ran his fingers through his mop of intensely black hair. "First boxer I've seen at a WUKO event this season," he commented dryly.

At tournaments sanctioned by the newly reestablished World Union of Karate Organizations, contestants were supposed to be *karateka*, testing their skill against others of their kind. Ensuring that had been a problem long before the advent of full-scale virtual reality conferencing. Now it was worse. All sorts of opportunists were flocking to bask in the glory and prize money, including those who had scarcely seen the inside of a *dojo*.

I'd studied Ruiz's record after the contestant list had been issued—just as he no doubt had checked mine. The Peruvian did have a black belt, but it was a hastily awarded *sho dan* from some backwater South American kenpo school known for its loose standards. Winner of dozens of boxing matches, the man had ridden the karate tournament circuit less than two months, just long enough to qualify for single-A class. Now he'd come up to northern California thinking to walk over the players accessing the prestigious San Francisco VR node.

Mongo was a fake. A cheat. He diminished us all.

"Think you can beat him?" Callahan asked.

The grandmaster could answer that better than I. I figured it had to be a trick question, a teacher-to-student moment.

"I don't know."

Callahan smiled. Apparently that was the correct reply. He leaned close and said conspiratorially, "Think of it . . . as a challenge."

I won the remaining elimination rounds. I'd figured I would. The players who faced me were good, but their moves were transparent. The important thing was not to think about Mongo while I was in the ring with others, and I succeeded. I'd always been able to focus during a match.

Ruiz won as well. He backed one opponent up against the perimeter of the ring. The invisible wall, uncrossable to contestants during a match, served as his ally. Despite all the running away the other guy did, Mongo took a mere twenty-seven seconds for the kill. The next competitor's fighting technique bought him two solid kicks, but in the end he lasted no longer.

Three opponents out in less than thirty seconds each. I'd never done that well. Ruiz was radiating self-confidence. But I didn't tremble as I entered the ring.

"Go get 'im, Fearless," called my *dojo*-mate, Keith Nakayama.

"Fearless! Fearless! Fearless!" shouted the crowd. I appreciated the support, but I made myself ignore them all. It was time to concentrate. Mongo swaggered into position. We bowed.

"*Hajime!*" the referee shouted, backpedaling out of the way.

Ruiz charged forward, cocking his fist at his right side, left hand extending to brush away any block I might raise in his way. It was the same attack that had overwhelmed his previous opponents.

Sidestepping, I planted a roundhouse kick to his solar plexus. He grunted, momentarily dropping his guard. I took the opening to his face. Blood exploded from his nose as my fist landed, staining both our *gi*s as well as the referee's shirt.

He staggered back. I chased him. Wrong move. He surprised me with a right hook.

Stars flickered across my field of vision. My ears rang. Suddenly I knew what I was up against. Nobody should have been that fast or hard with their fists. I resisted the urge to close in—my normal inclination. I circled, keeping him at kicking distance.

He wanted none of it. Blood pouring from his nose, he sucked air through his mouth and moved in, trying to put a stop to me before I got lucky. His knuckles battered against the bones of my arms.

Escaping to the left, I slammed a side kick into his lower thigh. He cried out and pitched to the ground. Good enough. I'd missed the knee I'd been aiming for, but the muscles of Ruiz's leg were spasming so much from the impact, he couldn't stand.

I swept forward, raising my foot to crush his throat.

Too slow.

His good leg lashed out. Instantly I felt as if I'd landed on a spear. My groin and then my entire abdomen clenched. I folded up and tried to roll away—anything to dismiss the pain.

Ruiz tripped me. I fell to my hands and knees, and

somehow a moment later he was crouching over me. He landed a hammer-strike on my left kidney.

My diaphragm muscles locked up, taking my wind. The Peruvian slammed his fist down again. The pain sharpened to an unbelievable level—

And suddenly I was no longer in the arena.

The pain vanished. Time held motionless. Around me loomed the familiar walls of my room at home. A view of the tournament filled the videoscreen on my desk. I saw my surrogate on hands and knees, Ruiz raising his fist for a third blow. The referee leaned over us, his expression a study in concentration.

The neural jack at the back of my neck itched. A warning light on my virtual reality deck was flashing: I had one point three seconds to reengage the link to my surrogate or it would dissolve.

I gripped the arms of my wheelchair and thumbed the switch—

Back in my VR body, a malicious agony greeted me, but I couldn't give in to it. If I permitted Ruiz to land the third hammer-strike, the pain would once again surpass the safety threshold and drive me out. I rolled—

His fist glanced off my side. I kept twisting my body, wrapping my legs around Mongo's hips: Scissor throw. We ended up tangled together. I grabbed his arms and the match degenerated into a wrestling contest. That gave me some of the recovery time I needed.

"*Yame!*" shouted the referee. "Start over."

Mongo seemed reluctant to disengage, but he wiped the torrent of blood from his upper lip and stalked back to his starting place.

I got up slowly, partly to earn even more of a respite, and partly because I was incapable of rising quickly. My breath came in rapid snatches—that was all the fierce tightness in my midsection allowed. Judging from the burn in my groin, at least one of my testicles was herniated.

I dared not delay too much. The referee would disqualify me. I straightened as much as possible, facing Ruiz at regulation distance.

The time clock loomed huge in the background. Eighty-seven seconds left in the match. Ruiz glared, daring me to fight hard. If neither of us killed or drove the other from his surrogate in the remaining time, we'd both be declared losers and be ineligible to continue to the next round. I guess he figured that in my condition I might play defensively, ruining his chances out of spite. The Peruvian wanted his victory.

"Rei!" the referee cried. We bowed to each other once again.

"Hajime!"

Ruiz hurtled forward, eager to seal his triumph. I maintained a squinting, defeated expression until he was committed to his attack.

I kicked. This time I didn't miss his knee. Bone gave way beneath my foot. The jagged end of Ruiz's femur, broken just above the joint, jutted through skin and pant leg.

As Ruiz collapsed, I staggered back. Loose, rocky objects rolled in my mouth and it dawned on me that while I'd kicked him, he'd punched me. I spit the teeth out and moved in. Mongo was vulnerable *now*, occupied with the pain of his destroyed limb, perhaps even driven out of his VR body altogether. I wasn't going to let the opportunity slip away.

I shaped my thumb and forefinger into a pincer shape—*koko*, or tiger-mouth—and struck, capturing the Peruvian's larynx and ripping it from his throat.

He gurgled. His body spasmed. Blood gushed from the hole between his jaw and clavicle. Then he vanished as the software logged him off.

Alone in the ring with the referee, I straightened up. All I had to do to cement my victory was stride to my starting place and allow my arm to be raised. But the room was spinning. My head felt swollen to five times normal size. Mongo's earlier blow had done more than liberate teeth. It was threatening to become a knockout punch after the fact. The anguish from my groin and kidney area also demanded that I give up.

Hell with that. I staggered across the distance. My arm went up. The applause from the gallery began. "Log off and reboot," I sighed gratefully.

My VR deck accepted the cue. My battered surrogate dissolved. For an instant I was back in my wheelchair at home, then I rematerialized at the tournament. Gone was the pain, the blood, the exhaustion.

The cheering reached a crescendo. I must admit it felt good. But I waved to the spectators strictly for the sake of form. Tonight there was only one person whose approval mattered.

I headed for the group from my *dojo*, who stood dressed in *gis* at the periphery of the floor.

"Congratulations, Fearless," they called.

"On to the semifinals!" added Keith.

I nodded, smiling, and turned apprehensively to Mr. Callahan, who waited slightly apart from the others, hands folded across his chest.

"Block your face, block your face, block your face," the grandmaster stated as if reciting a mantra. He was interrupted by a torrent of boos from the crowd. We turned to see Mongo, logged into a fresh surrogate, standing on the ring. He was staring at me as if I were some kind of Inca king somehow resurrected from the dead. Whirling, he stalked off toward the South American contingent.

"Still can't believe he lost," Keith chirped.

I laughed. Soon I forgot the incident entirely as *sensei* began advising me regarding my next match. A warm, satisfied glow suffused like liquor through my body. Though Callahan's comments might sound like criticism, I knew better. I hoped I wasn't grinning like a fool.

* * *

Hours later I won my category, clearing the way for advancement to double-A level. I was walking on air by that time. I lingered as long as possible, enjoying the congratulations, and left with the stragglers.

It was always difficult to abandon the VR environment. Had the deck not been hardwired to prevent constant use, and were the access fees not quite so high, I might have spent ninety percent of my waking hours ambling around in my surrogate. You would, too, if your real body were like mine.

A miasma of aromas cascaded into my nostrils as my sense of smell, held in abeyance while in the virtuality, regained its natural place in my perceptions. The faded traces of fried onions drifted from the kitchen, the redolence of unflushed toilet from down the hall, and closer to home my terry cloth sweat suit reminded me that I needed to throw it in the laundry basket soon. I stretched muscles grown stiff from my long sit in the wheelchair, released the restraining straps and neural jack, and wheeled into the bathroom for an overdue draining of my bladder. I didn't waste time with the reflection in the bathroom mirror.

I rolled down the long hallway toward the kitchen and living room. "Dad?" I called.

Silence. I searched for a note on the fridge. Nothing.

"I won, Dad," I said to the air.

Oh, well. All in all, I didn't have it so bad. Dad might not have approved of my interest in combat arts—"blood sports," he called them—but at least he let me pursue them, and had even before I'd turned eighteen.

He'd never been that indulgent with my older brother Bennett, but Bennett wasn't a double amputee. Especially not a double amputee as a result of Dad's drunk driving.

After a snack, I returned to my room and ordered my VR deck to replay my last match. On the videoscreen a lean, mean, fighting-machine version of myself took on

Ruiz. My moves looked worse in playback than they'd seemed to me at the time. Mongo's looked better, especially the punch that had scattered my teeth.

Ruiz had done it so effortlessly. He hadn't even thrown a full karate-style strike, but simply extended his hand forward ten or twelve inches at hyperspeed.

It fascinated me. I should have been a good boy and exercised my real body on my physical therapy equipment, but I kept studying the video, trying to devise strategies that would help me out next time I faced a skilled boxer. I couldn't afford weaknesses. I was on my way. Thomas Callahan himself was watching me. Thomas Callahan, reigning champion of the Tokyo International Tournament of Karate Masters in the unrestricted category. The big cheese of the big event. He wasn't just tolerating my presence in his classes, he wasn't just humoring me. He was paying attention. Two of his senior students had even told me that he was grooming me as a successor. It wouldn't be too many more years before he'd have to retire. No one, naturally, would ever beat him in the ring, but after all, he was eighty-two years of age. What better way to go out than have one of your own students assume your place?

I wasn't there yet, but I would be. Double-A play next season, then triple-A, then the master's circuit. A lot of players stood in my way, but I knew I could beat them eventually.

The front door opened. "I'm in here, Dad," I called. Engrossed in my big plans with my eyes pegged on a slow-motion version of the match, I barely paid attention to the footsteps coming down the hallway.

And then my head was spinning, my cheek swelling, and blood was trickling down to my chin. My wheelchair spun around.

Mongo loomed over me, teeth bared, his real body as intimidating as his surrogate. "No cripple makes a fool out of me," he said in Spanish, and struck.

My head slammed into the chair's headrest. Teeth—real teeth—bounced off my tongue and palate.

My reflexes, conditioned by my VR fights, kicked in. I threw up a block as Ruiz's second punch came in. My technique and timing were perfect, and my real-life arm was nearly as strong as that of my surrogate, but it didn't mean much. Without legs, I couldn't back off, couldn't veer enough. I blocked two punches, missed, blocked the fourth, and then my focus was gone.

Boom—there went my nose. The spray blinded me. A groan spilled out of my mouth; I couldn't help it.

I kept expecting the safety feature to log me off. All I could feel was pain, pain, pain. Overriding it came the stench and taste of blood, reminding me that this was no virtuality. There was no escape.

"How does it feel, cripple?" Ruiz hissed. "Think you can win this one?"

Still he battered me. My hands fell limp—I'd lost the power to keep them raised. There was a spiked ball bearing slamming back and forth on the inside of my skull.

He wasn't going to stop, I realized. Mongo had left the rational world behind. He meant to kill me. He was holding back his strength, prolonging my suffering, but he was going to keep punching until I died.

I don't know how many times his fists crashed into me after I came to understand just what kind of danger I was in. Adrenaline alone was maintaining what little shred of consciousness I had left. I felt myself sinking down a funnel. Following me was the echo of my own sobbing and a distinct blast very much like a gunshot.

I woke up slowly, through a haze of pain. The odor of antiseptic and bleached bed linens wormed through the gauze and bandages covering my nose. My bloated tongue pressed uncomfortably against the stumps of my teeth. I recognized the pinch of an IV tube feeding into my left arm. Wires held my lower jaw together.

I opened my eyes. Dad rose from a chair beside the hospital bed and leaned over me. In the far corner sat a pasty-skinned, gray-haired man I didn't recognize.

"Kaiser Hospital," my father explained. "You've been unconscious about eighteen hours."

I squeezed my eyes shut. The woozy feeling had to be from the painkillers, I decided. Whatever they had me on, it wasn't enough.

"Mongo?" I mumbled. Between the wired jaw, the swollen lips, and mashed tongue, I sounded like Jabba the Hutt without subtitles. The old man was first to understand.

"Your father was napping in his bedroom. The noise woke him," the stranger said. His voice tickled my memory. Maybe one of the hoarse old senior citizens from the physical therapy clinic?

"I shot him in the ass," Dad said.

I blinked, wondering if this was the same man who had raised me. "*You* had a gun?"

"I've had one since Desert Storm. I never said violence didn't have a purpose."

Live and learn. "He's . . . alive?" I mumbled. I wasn't sure how I felt about that.

"Of course," Dad replied. "In jail, booked for assault, battery, and attempted murder. You won't have to worry about him. He'll serve time, then he'll be deported back to Peru. He'll never be local enough to do this again."

"And WUKO has already banned him from tournament play forever, upon my prompting," said the old man.

Now I knew where I'd heard the man's voice before. *"Sensei?"*

"Yes." Mr. Callahan climbed laboriously out of his chair, straightening up with arthritic awkwardness.

It was really him. He'd come all the way from San Francisco to my Sacramento home. I didn't know which to feel: I was startled to see just how old and bent his real body was, even though I'd heard about it from veteran students. And I was damn proud that I mattered enough to deserve a bedside visit.

"Looks like I still have to work on that upper block," I tried to joke.

The grandmaster smiled, reached out a gnarled hand, and squeezed my elbow. "Just get back into the tournament circuit as soon as you can. Think of this incident . . . as a challenge."

His usual advice. I tried to grin. *"Hai . . . sensei . . ."* I murmured, and sank back into a morphine haze.

Mr. Callahan had left by the time I next awoke. I didn't hear from him during the weeks that followed. By the end of my convalescence, the memory of the visit had paled, vividness drained behind the ordeal of pain and drugs. It resembled more a dream than something that had actually happened.

When my surrogate finally materialized at his headquarters *dojo*, the grandmaster just pointed to my regular place in the line, as if I were just another student who had been attending all along. During warm-ups, basic exercises, and partner drills, he focused on other pupils. There were, after all, plenty of them to focus on. As usual, the night's class filled the room; in fact the walls had been expanded to accommodate a heavy attendance. Thomas Callahan's reputation drew hundreds, perhaps thousands of potential students. Not only was VR karate a big prize money affair these days, but VR *dojo*s eliminated the constrictions of classroom size and the hassles of commuting. A student still needed to live within the radius of the local node to participate in partner exercises such as sparring, because bouncing data off satellites introduced too much delay into reaction times, but others who were content to restrict themselves to observation and individual exercise could attend from anywhere in the hemisphere. Callahan kept the group at a manageable size only by restricting attendance to the cream of the crop recommended by lesser instructors. That's how I'd gotten in, back when I was fifteen.

I had never felt so invisible. Sure, there were a lot of people, but this night of all others, I had expected a word or two, a nod, a "Welcome back." The other students expected it as well. They cast sideways glances from me to *sensei* and back, anticipating interaction. None came. Finally the class completed a long session of kata and sat down to rest.

Callahan was pretending to be an inscrutable Oriental. It was a role he played regularly. His surrogate body was as freckled and redheaded as his Irish surname would indicate, but like many of the original generation of great American players from the 1960s, he wore the legacy of his direct study under traditional Japanese and Okinawan experts. Those old farts never gave anyone a break. They marched like God in front of their students, all aloofness, hardness, and discipline, even if they liked you. Maybe especially if they liked you. Right then, I didn't know what was lurking inside the grandmaster's head.

"Jiyu kumite," Callahan announced, signaling the beginning of the sparring section of class. Tonight's session would be freestyle combat. Unlike *shiai*—competitive sparring—there would be no declared winners or losers, no points taken. The object was to show off a diversity of karate technique. The best performance was that which demonstrated artistry and a balanced repertoire.

Yet because the venue was an integrated virtuality, contact would still be hard. Killing and maiming might occur. This possibility kept us on our toes. It gave us the attitude Callahan wanted us to have—gave us an opportunity to practice *bushido*, the way of the warrior.

I submerged into that alertness. I kept my breathing steady, synchronized with my heartbeat. Warmth radiated from my skin, stoked by the fires in the muscles beneath. Rivulets of sweat traveled down my torso. Except for the lack of odor, my surrogate felt more like me than my real body. At times, while at rest, I could feel featheriness in my legs as if my real body's somatic sensations were written atop the simulation as on a palimpsest. But not tonight. Tonight I was *there.*

Mr. Callahan looked down the long line of practitioners local enough to spar. Often during freestyle, he would simply divide these students in two equal groups and everyone would fight simultaneously. Tonight he selected his favorite alternative: He picked just one pair at a time, leaving the rest of us to serve as an audience.

I licked my lips as two of my *dojo*-mates faced each other. I wanted to be out there.

The pair danced around for most of their session, coming away intact save for bruised forearms. The second match followed just the opposite pattern—one partner got the drop on the other immediately, and proceeded to batter him severely, though Callahan had them pause twice and restart. The third pair charged at each other so enthusiastically they both were logged off by the pain threshold override.

Abruptly the crowd vanished from my view. The moment I'd been waiting for had arrived. The only figures I could see on the floor were Mr. Callahan and, facing me, an opponent. I couldn't identify the latter—his appearance was a composite of average Caucasian features, which was probably how I looked to him.

The headquarters *dojo* master program had temporarily disguised us. Callahan believed that students would have difficulty attacking friends and classmates with proper vigor unless identities were secret. Only the grandmaster and the audience saw who was who, and the latter, invisible and inaudible, could only reveal what they knew after the *kumite* session had ended. I didn't yet know whether I was facing, for example, my pal Keith Nakayama or that asshole *ni dan* from Oakland.

The grandmaster gave the commands. At last.

As always, I seized the initiative. My opponent faded back, avoiding a front kick, so I drew back my hand to strike—

The other guy started to cock his own fist. Without intending to, I hurried my punch. It glanced off the player's chin, rendered meaningless by my overreaction. Simultaneously, his counterstrike hit me hard in the ribs.

I backed away. My opponent pressed, narrowly missing with a roundhouse kick, partially connecting with a face punch, and landing a stout kick to my midsection that I handled only because I tensed my abdomen correctly at the last moment.

My momentum was gone. I fought hard and made my partner earn every gain, but the match felt wrong. I should've been dominant. I should've been shaping the give-and-take. I always did that. All too soon Callahan yelled, *"Yame!"*

I limped to my starting place, nursing a swollen cheek, sore ribs, and a lacerated shin. My opponent was bleeding a little from one nostril, but seemed otherwise untouched.

The grandmaster excused us. The *dojo* master program cycled us off. Reappearing two seconds later in a refreshed surrogate along the sidelines, I saw from the reaction of my *dojo*-mates that my opponent had been Mark Evanoff, a player I barely knew. The man was an undistinguished student who competed at C level in tournaments—a good *karateka*, but not the sort I had ever had problems with before.

I hadn't "lost." That term didn't apply to freestyle. Nor did I regret that Evanoff had done so well; he'd earned it. Yet I had never come away from a match so devastated.

I turned to Callahan. The grandmaster met my glance with a neutral expression that could have meant anything, then called up the next pair of partners. Back to the routine of the class.

I put on a mask of indifference, acting by rote until

the last sparring session was done and everyone lined up to bow to the *Shomen*, to the grandmaster, and to each other. As was his habit, Callahan logged off as soon as the closing ceremony was over. As soon as was practical, I followed suit.

The yellow and green status lights of my VR deck and the stale odor of the cologne I'd put on that morning greeted me as I became aware of my all-too-real bedroom. I remained in my chair, straps snug, neural jack connected, staring out my tiny window that *almost* allowed me to see the state capitol.

Almost was the key word. I could almost walk normally. I could almost get by without people directing their stares at my empty pant legs.

And now, in the one place where I had still been as complete and perfect as anyone else, I no longer measured up.

"I can't help you," said Dr. Lavin. "The condition has nothing to do with the surrogate or the interface. The reflex is buried in your brain and in your spinal trunk nerves."

I'd expected as much, but I'd wanted to hear it from a VR specialist. By this point, no straw was too thin to grasp. Nothing had improved since that first workout. Whenever I sparred, I flinched.

I wasn't afraid to step out on the floor. I still had all the courage I'd ever had. The problem was below the level of conscious manipulation. As Dr. Lavin had so depressingly confirmed, my neurons remembered the beating Mongo had given me. I couldn't just shake off that psychic legacy the way I could repair a wiped-out surrogate.

"We're able to erase fatigue or pain or tissue damage in a surrogate because those experiences are entirely part of the simulation. The programming automatically negates those parts of the construct each time you log off."

Behind his bottle-bottom glasses Lavin's eyes blinked exuberantly. The man was one of those intense, wiry engineering types who, once given a start on his favorite subject, could hold forth for hours. "Of course, the surrogate does learn. Your deck performs an ongoing analysis of data in order to preserve gains. That's how you develop stamina and coordination and strength. *If* this reflex of yours was a flaw recorded somewhere in the heuristic net, I could probably find and purge it. At the very least, we could reconfigure the surrogate as it was the day before the attack. You'd lose some of its accumulated customization, but you'd still have everything up to that point."

He sighed. "I work in an industry that seems to make anything possible. That's a chimera, my boy. We can send all sorts of input along an existing nervous system, we can trick the brain into establishing a whole second set of somatic feedback loops in order to operate a surrogate—as long as the simulated body is a close analog of the real one—but we can't re-create the nervous system itself. If we could do that, you wouldn't be tied to that wheelchair and VR deck. We'd be able to fashion you into a cyborg with legs as good as any you were ever born with."

The technical details obviously fascinated Lavin. Lost in his expounding, he didn't understand what all this meant in human terms, what it meant to me. This slight effect, this involuntary tic, changed everything.

Fearless, they had nicknamed me. And it had been true. I'd always attacked full-out. It was reckless, maybe, but it allowed me to dominate players of better technical skill. My boneheaded confidence was my secret weapon. So what if a surrogate was obliterated? I could be back a minute later, ready to go again. My subconscious had accepted that.

Now when a partner made a move against me, flashbacks of Mongo's fists would pop up—not so much the actual image as my reaction, my recollection of cringing. With that sort of handicap, I could never win tournaments. At my level of expertise, there was no room for distraction. My competitive career had just been aborted.

"You're awfully quiet. Have you been following all this okay?"

"Fine," I said, staring at his Far Side desk calendar. "Just wondering what I'm going to do now."

"It's manageable, I would think," persisted the specialist. "Over time the symptom may extinguish itself. Meanwhile, there are plenty of VR sports that where a slight hesitation won't matter. Tennis, perhaps. Certainly bowling. Have you tried golf?"

"Log on," I order my VR deck, and listed the code for Mr. Callahan's headquarters *dojo*.

"Password?" asked the deck in its pleasant, motherly voice.

I was surprised when it accepted the one I gave. I hadn't tried it in eight months. I'd expected Callahan to have dropped me from the roster of those who had clearance into his VR conference address.

The headquarters *dojo* foyer materialized around me. Out on the floor several players were loosening up. Mr. Callahan was not there; he would make his appearance precisely at the hour, if he followed his habit. Six minutes to go.

I felt like a damn fool. I avoided the glances of *dojo*-mates who recognized me. I didn't need their pity. I'd been a player who counted. A player who was going places. Now I wasn't. Everyone knew that. That knowledge had kept me away the better part of a year.

Yet retirement hadn't worked. Karate-do had written too many chapters in my book. Call it an addiction, maybe. In any event, I'd decided I'd rather be able to add a page or two to the narrative once in a while than let the work lie totally fallow.

For six minutes I paced the foyer. Right on time, Mr. Callahan winked in on his dais of honor. He raised an eyebrow at me and gestured at the workout floor, where everyone was lining up for the opening ceremony. I took my place with the others of my rank. Callahan continued in silence to the front of the room.

I blew out a pent-up breath. First hurdle crossed. I was allowed to resume training.

The class knelt and bowed. Warm-ups began. I fell into the familiar routine. With each calisthenic, and later with each move of *kihon*—basics—I relaxed more and more. This was what I needed. I belonged here.

Finally we wrapped up a choreographed attack drill and lined up for sparring. Callahan had not taken much note of me—just a slight posture adjustment during *kata* practice—but I didn't let what he did or did not do affect me. I was here simply to run the paces. I'd worked out as hard as possible. Harder, even, in that I'd set my surrogate's default so that "I" was just a bit out of shape. Normally, like most VR players, I maintained my body's programming at the prime level of strength, agility, youth, and flexibility possible for my morph. Some players complained that they wanted to be able to switch back and forth to an array of differently configured surrogates—larger and more powerful I would assume. But I was happy with what VR hardware and brain physiology allowed. It gave me my body as it would have existed had my legs never been pulverized and were it possible to remain age twenty, perfectly toned, and completely fresh. The challenge was not to forget to work on the stuff technology couldn't cover. Tonight the extra strain kept me focused. I needed that if I were to face an opponent.

Mr. Callahan called up a dozen members of the class and matched them up with partners. He skipped me. I sat twitching as my colleagues were set free to test their skills, as I wanted to do.

Or rather as I had to do, even if I came away as unhappy and defeated as before.

The first group sat down. Mr. Callahan looked straight at me. My heart rate sped up. To my frustration he selected a combination of sparring partners that left me out.

And so it went. He called up a total of seven rounds of players. Some of my buddies got to spar three or four times. Aside from me, the only students he left out were the ones he always left out, chiefly those players who were by nature or philosophy opposed to the active combat portion of the discipline. The rabbits, the jerk from Oakland called them.

"Time to close class," the grandmaster said. It was over. He hadn't given me an opportunity to prove myself. I'd been relegated to the list of those who required special handling. He might as well have hung up one of those blue-and-white placards you see all the time on the best parking places.

I logged off the instant we finished the closing ceremony.

"How was class?" Dad asked as I rumbled across the hallway to the bathroom.

"Chickenshit," I said.

Though attending the next workout gave me as much pleasure as eating sawdust, I went. Again, Callahan didn't allow me to spar. Nor did he the next few times.

I could've gone elsewhere to train. The Sacramento-based martial arts virtuality where I'd started out years before would have been delighted to take me back. But I'd practiced with the best. Accepting anything else would have been another kind of surrender.

I also could've asked *sensei* why he was treating me as he was. I didn't. Traditional *dojo* etiquette precluded a student from questioning his master's style of instruction. Call it a silly custom, but to me ritual is the essence of karate. Callahan would accept me by the book, or not at all. I could be just as Japanese as he.

After six weeks, I did speak with Keith Nakayama. We were lingering after a class, refining a *kata* after the other students had winked out. "Is he ever going to let me spar again?"

"Does it matter?" Keith asked.

I cocked my head to the side. "What do you mean?"

"Sparring is a late addition to karate-do," Keith reminded me. "Gogen Yamaguchi introduced it in 1935. You don't have to spar to be a legitimate *karateka.* Mr. Callahan himself stopped sparring forty years ago, and didn't begin again until the VR renaissance. All through his middle years he practiced only kata and drills, until the arthritis made him give up that, too. Nobody ever stopped calling him a master. He went from seventh to tenth *dan* in that time."

"Not the same," I said. "That was his choice."

"Oh?"

Keith sounded like a learned grandpa. And come to think of it, that was exactly right. Nakayama was one of Callahan's *sempai*—his senior students. No matter how young he might look standing there in front of me, he had to be at least seventy years old. To him, I was an infant.

What was he saying? Clearly, he was serious that giving up sparring altogether seemed to him an honorable option, one that he felt completely comfortable with and had at one point chosen for himself. Even now, in VR mode, he rarely entered tournaments, though he participated regularly in freestyle within the context of the class. He was a damn good fighter, but I strongly suspected that when middle age had hit him and he'd cut back on *kumite*, he hadn't felt it to be a great loss.

But Callahan? He'd taken his first major title at age eighteen. Men like him didn't just gracefully accept being put out to pasture. That's why he was world champion in his weight class now.

"If . . ." I stammered, "if *sensei* understands what it's like for me right now, why is he doing this to me? Shouldn't he be pushing me to spar, instead of cutting me off?"

Keith waved his hands vaguely. "I don't know what he's up to, but I trust him. Why not give it some time, and see what happens?"

"How much time?" I asked. Too much had already passed.

Keith smiled strangely, and shrugged.

I wasn't sure I had as much faith in Mr. Callahan as Keith did. On the other hand, I didn't have any solutions of my own. I kept working out. Callahan maintained the moratorium on my sparring. Three months passed before I began to notice a change.

My partner that night was a very quick player named Tim Bromage. We were engaged in *yakusoku kumite*—prearranged sparring drills. This was not a circumstance I enjoyed. Tim wasn't a problem for me during unrestricted freestyle. Quick as he was, I knew ways to ruin his balance and break his concentration. But in *yakusoku kumite*, it was a different story. Every move was predetermined. One side was the attacker, one the defender, and neither partner could throw in unrehearsed techniques. Much of the practice was by Mr. Callahan's count. This left me no opportunity to use intimidation, fakes, alternate angles of attack, or superior pacing. Form was everything. With my repertoire stifled, Tim had a way of getting his front kick in on me before I could step back and block. He was simply too fast for me. It was frustrating as hell.

But not tonight. Every time Tim kicked, I caught him. Every damn time.

"Good," said Mr. Callahan as he passed by. It was

the first comment he'd directed at me, other than routine instructions, since the day at the hospital.

A few workouts later, the class was again immersed in a session of *yakusoku kumite*. This time my partner was a wide, very powerful *san dan*. His punches were slow. In freestyle, I could find a million openings on him thanks to his ponderosity, but if he ever landed one, it was bad news. That night, of course, the nature of the practice didn't allow me to get out of the way, and though he was supposed to pull his punches, I expected to be bruised.

Instead, I blocked him. Powerful as he was I succeeded, thirty times out of thirty, in performing the defensive technique so precisely, so well-timed, that his fists never once struck their target.

"Good," Mr. Callahan said again.

I got the idea. *Sensei* had been emphasizing defense more than usual. Not in an obvious way, but with such regularity that I couldn't help but improve that part of my repertoire. I'd never cared much whether I perfected my blocks—"a good offense is the best defense" was my motto. He was steering me toward a new personal style.

All right, you fucker, I thought. I don't know why you don't just say it aloud, but if those are the dues you're asking me to pay, I'll become the best damn blocker in the universe.

For nine more months, I honed countermoves to every type of offensive technique—even those that attackers never used. By the end of that time there were still players better at blocks than I, but I was closing the gap.

One night Mr. Callahan announced at the beginning of the freestyle section of class, "We're going to do an exercise I haven't brought out for the past few years. Mr. Nakayama and Mr. Titelman will demonstrate."

The two men, the highest-ranked players there that night other than Callahan himself, rose and faced each other. "Mr. Titelman may use only offensive techniques. Mr. Nakayama may only defend."

The grandmaster gave the command to engage. The two *hachi dan*s merged in a flurry of technique. Accustomed as I was to high-level play, my mouth still dropped open. They were awesome. Titelman's combinations blended one into the next, minus the hesitation that came from worrying about counterattacks. Deft, compact, and quick, he radiated such a command of his movements he seemed unstoppable.

Yet Keith thwarted him. With inhuman precision my pal deflected, avoided, and battered his opponent's fists and feet out of the way. He didn't look *at all* like a defender. As Titelman kicked, Keith caught him by the ankle and swept him off his feet. As Titelman swung a *furi uchi*—a whiplike strike—to Keith's temple, the latter ducked under it and shoved his attacker far back out of range. Titelman spent more time on the floor than the guy who should, by rights, have been a complete victim. It took him half the match to land a single blow.

They bowed to each other and sat down. Callahan pointed to me, "You will be the defender. Mr. Siddens will attack."

At last. Though not true sparring, the exercise was the removal of a tether. I hopped up quickly.

As we faced one another, the *dojo* reprogrammed our appearances. Siddens's rugged features dissolved into those of a generic opponent. Yet for once I did know who I was up against. Siddens was an ex-Marine, a dedicated *ni dan* with a fighting style as aggressive as mine had been.

"Hajime!" cried the grandmaster.

I hesitated, wanting to leap forward as Keith had done, but Siddens raced in and my cringing reflex kicked in strong as ever. But I had time to fade back. My hips twisted, removing my groin—his target—from the line of fire. I snagged his foot with my palm and guided it away. It was a classic move known as *sukui uke*—scooping block. I'd practiced it a million times that year.

He punched. I danced aside and leaped forward, turning him so that I ended up behind him, my body tight against his. He tried to whirl, lashing out with his elbows and heels, but I had a good grip on his *gi*, and for five glorious seconds, he couldn't touch me. A snarl of frustration leaked from his throat, and my mood climbed to a height it hadn't seen in nearly two years.

Good things don't last. Siddens broke free of my grip. His elbow connected with my ear. I staggered back, leaving way too much of an opening. Blocking furiously, I managed to hold on for about thirty seconds before he knocked me down and killed me with a kick to the back of my neck.

Yet as I logged back on in an uninjured surrogate, I didn't feel defeated. Keith, seeing my glow, winked at me as I returned to my place in the line. He and I both knew that if I'd had to spar a player like Siddens a year earlier, without being able to punch or kick, I would have been wiped out in half the time. A warm river of satisfaction percolated through my system.

One thing would have made it better. I had still quailed at the moment of attack. But for the first time, I looked forward to what Mr. Callahan might have up those white cotton sleeves. He had already turned to the next set of freestyle partners, seemingly absorbed in them, but I knew he had a plan just for me.

For the next six months, the grandmaster let me spar nearly every class in the modified way he'd introduced. I was always the defender. A sense of anticipation mounted among the *dojo* regulars. They knew, as I did, that sooner or later I'd be set free.

That moment came in a way I never expected. It was an ordinary workout in every other respect, until Mr. Callahan called me to the center of the room . . .

And stood across from me.

"Tonight, you will spar normally. *Jiyu kumite.*"

All the moisture vanished from my mouth. The grandmaster. The *ju dan.* The *hanshi.* He had not sparred one of his own students in years. He saved his sorcery for tournament opponents. Outsiders. Enemies.

I stared him straight in the eyes and tried not to soil my *gi* pants.

Keith handled the commands. As he shouted, I sprang into the most defensive position I knew.

I didn't even see most of the techniques Callahan threw at me. Fists, feet, elbows flew all around me. Abruptly I was in my wheelchair at home. My VR deck cheerfully informed me that the match had lasted fifteen seconds. It had seemed like one.

I rematerialized at the *dojo.* Callahan nodded and said, "Again."

Shaking, I took my place. We engaged. And this time, something awakened in me, something that had been developing for a long time. Call it the state of mind a doe calls up to defend her fawn against a mountain lion. My rising block redirected the fist racing toward my face. My body twisted away from the kick arcing toward my belly. I lifted my leg out of the way of *sensei*'s stomp at my knee joint.

He took me out with a roundhouse kick to my head. I hadn't lasted any longer than before. But everything had been clearer. I'd seen what most of the techniques coming at me were.

I rematerialized. "Again," said Mr. Callahan.

Oh, God, I thought. He charged. I retreated as fast as I could, frantically defending myself.

And this time, in the midst of all the yielding, pumped up with fright, I saw a brief opening.

I struck. My fist tapped *sensei*'s chin. Not as strongly as I might have liked, but enough to make him blink, enough that jawbone kissed my knuckles.

A few moments later he killed me again. I'd lasted twenty-three seconds.

But I'd gotten a punch in on him. A punch on *him.* When I logged back on, I found him smiling at me. A drop of blood hung from his split lip.

"Perhaps we'll have the chance to spar again one day," he said, and gestured for me to return to my place.

The next three months—during which I sparred every class—confirmed what had ignited that night. I had a new ability. Though I still couldn't leap in undaunted as I had before Mongo, I now knew how to wait, letting my opponent commit to his movement, and on a good night, when I was sharp, I could turn the tables on any number of players. It was not as easy as bowling them over with an unbridled attack, but it gave me a goal to reach for, virgin territory to explore. As Fearless, I'd never have been able to score a hit on the grandmaster. Only someone capable of being truly intimidated could ever be a master of defense.

I'd just finished an invigorating workout and was staying late, polishing a little *kata* to wind down, when a voice from the foyer startled me.

"Did you enjoy yourself tonight?"

I jumped and turned around. Mr. Callahan strode onto the floor.

"Yes," I replied, trying to seem as casual as he. "Yes, I enjoyed myself a great deal."

His lips curved into a Mona Lisa pose. "I've heard you've signed up for the Riverside Invitationals."

"Just C level," I replied. "To test my wings. It's a start."

"Yes. It is. How do you feel about it?"

"I . . ." I coughed. "It's never going to go away, is it? I'm going to flinch for the rest of my martial arts career."

"Quite possibly." He scratched his chin. "Does it matter?"

Not the way it had. The bitterness was leaching out, the sense of being a victim was fading. But . . .

"I still want to win," I said. "When I was Fearless, I knew I'd make it to the top. I don't know if the new me ever will."

He smiled fully. Turning to the mirror, he pointed at the reflection of my lean, perpetually healthy surrogate. "You've got fifty, sixty, maybe seventy years left. Who can say what you'll be able to do in all that time?"

His arm dropped to his side. Though the move was graceful, it seemed to carry the weight of eight decades. How many obstacles, how many disappointments, I wondered, had this man weathered on the way to becoming a karate megastar? I wasn't sure if I'd ever be in his league. At the moment, though, that wasn't as important as this: Thomas Callahan was envious of me. The obstacles I faced might be too much for me, but then again, they might not. I had hope. He, no matter how well his brain and spinal cord had been preserved to this point, was up against a handicap that no amount of resistance could conquer.

"Guess I'll just have to try," I said. I understood now that my attempt mattered as much to him as it did to me.

He nodded. "Think of it," he said softly, "as a challenge."

By the time I sold my first story in February of 1979, I was already a black belt instructor of goju-ryu karate-do. Yet in all the years between then and the assembling of this anthology, the only fiction I produced that could be labeled a martial arts piece was a vignette in *Far Frontiers 6* about a null-gravity karate tournament held in Earth orbit. People who knew of my karate credentials would ask why I didn't do more.

It's simple, really. I'm a science fiction and fantasy author. I create works of imaginary pasts and futures. Things beyond my experience. Often, in fact, beyond the very possibility of my experience. Money and readership aside, the reward of creating a piece of fiction is the way it expands my universe just a little more, makes me more complete. Novels and stories bring to me aspects of existence that I would never otherwise sample.

Karate, however, is with me three times a week, fifty-two weeks a year. My parents have long since thrown out the television set on which I used to watch David Carradine walk through walls on "Kung Fu" and Bruce Lee shape himself into a legend on "Green Hornet" and "Longstreet" (the movies came later). Back then, I could believe the myth that ninety-pound weaklings could master enough secret arts in a few weeks to wipe the floor with the hirsute, muscular bullies who'd been persecuting them. Though I wasn't exactly a weakling (I was, in fact, well on the way to becoming not only hirsute and muscular, but a great deal more than ninety pounds), I'd been a victim of bullying. My martial arts power fantasies would've filled a dozen anthologies.

Not anymore. Karate is part of my real world. I know the potentials of a punch. I've sweated through bouts with opponents who are bigger, stronger, faster, more confident. To do a story now, I can't simply insert whatever sounds most dramatic. I'd like to. It would do wonders for my nostalgic side. But I know now just what a martial artist can and cannot do. To write "Fearless," I had to sift through a maze of accumulated experience, searching for scenes that jibed with what I've encountered in my martial arts career. Though I managed to insert a fair amount of fantastical material, the ambiance of the dojo and methods of the sensei are straight from life (though not, I hasten to add, a depiction of any living person or actual place).

It was a hell of a lot easier when I could just make things up.

I have long admired the things Dick Lupoff can do in the way of atmosphere and characterization, in any sort of story—dark or light. I'm happy he wrote me one to include here.

OOOOO

EASY LIVING

Richard A. Lupoff

Four o'clock in the damned morning. Pitch-black and freezing out even in Hollywood, and the old Pontiac wouldn't start. Banger ground the starter until the battery started to get weak; the grinding faded to a feeble moan. Then Banger gave up. He leaned his head against the steering wheel.

But only for a minute.

He ran back upstairs, bypassing the elevator. His bifocals were steamed up and he wiped them with his shirttail. He must be falling apart, couldn't see a damned thing without cheaters. They would have laughed him out of the gym if he'd showed up wearing specs in his prime. But of course in his prime he hadn't needed specs.

At Chim's apartment door he fumbled until he found the key Chim had loaned him and let himself back in. He scurried past the couch that he'd carefully made up after a night's restless tossing and paused outside Chim's bedroom.

Had Chim got lucky? Had some lonesome barfly ex-groupie hung around after the Tiger's Den closed last night, and come home to spend the night with the good-looking bass player?

Banger tapped gently on Chim's door. On the second try he heard Chim moan.

Banger said, "Chim, I gotta talk to you."

Chim mumbled something that Banger couldn't make out. There was a stirring, then Chim opened the door a crack. Banger could make out only a vague grayness behind Chim, maybe the suggestion of a rounded hip under a draped sheet on the bed.

"Jesus, what time is it? What's the matter?"

Banger said, "My car won't start."

Chim opened a bleary eye from quarter-to half-mast. "What the hell time is it?"

"Pushing four-thirty, Chim."

"In the God damned *morning*?"

"Yeah. Chim, my car's dead. I gotta get to the set. Chim, can I borrow the Honda?"

Chim leaned his head on the doorjamb. He was wearing a pair of bikini underpants. His hair was sticking out in all directions and somehow Banger could see how women chased him all the time.

"Can I borrow the Honda, Chim? I wouldn't ask but you know I really . . ."

"Banger, I only been home a couple hours. I got—" He looked back over his shoulder, shook his head, stepped out into the narrow hallway. "Man, it's cold. I wanna get back in the sack. I need my rest."

"I know, Chim. I'm sorry. Look, I had a call last night. From the casting director. Katie. I gotta get out to the set, Chim."

"Why'd she call you?" He padded into the living room, pulled a quilted jacket off the back of a chair, shoved his arms into the sleeves. "That's better." He turned the chair around and leaned his arms on its back. "You told me you had the work anyhow. Why'd this Katie call you here?"

"I gave 'em this number. You don't mind, Chim. They have to be able to reach me. You know it's only for a little while."

"You bet it is."

"See, that's what's so great. She called me cause they need me to play Slam Shaughnessy. He's Cole's opponent in the big match. It's a real part, Chim. It's a week's pay at scale. As an actor, not an extra. And billing. I'll get billing."

"That's great, Banger." Chim didn't sound enthusiastic. "I'm going back to bed. Congratulations."

"Wait. Chim." Banger grabbed Chim by the elbow. "My car won't start. There isn't time to do anything about it. I can't afford a cab. Dunno if I could find one now anyhow. Chim, please, let me take the Honda. I have to be ready for makeup at five and they're shooting way out in Pasadena. Please, Chim."

Chim reached for his pocket, discovered that he was wearing only underpants under the quilted jacket. "I need the car tonight, Banger. I'll be around most of the day, maybe walk around the neighborhood, maybe have lunch out. I think, Thai. Yeah. She said she likes Thai. But I need the car tonight. I can't lug a bass on the bus."

He started back toward the bedroom.

"I promise, Chim. The set closes at seven-thirty. I'll head straight back here. It's after rush hour. I'll be here by eight."

"I have to be at the club by eight-thirty." Chim was waking up. Behind him, through the fourth-floor apartment's broad windows, the sky was beginning to lighten. "Eight o'clock, that's cutting it awfully close."

"I'll be on time, Chim. If I'm not, I'll pay for a cab.

Don't wait for me. Take a cab. A week at scale, Chim, I'll spring for a cab."

Chim shook his head. "Wayne is pretty uptight about punctuality. Imagine me standing on Hollywood Boulevard in a tux with a double bass and hailing a cab." He disappeared into the bedroom. Shuffling and bumping noises came from the room. Then a feminine sound, half a moan and half a question that drove a knife into Banger's heart. Then the door opened again, just a crack, and Chim handed Banger the keys to the Honda. "I don't wanna take no cab. Be on time."

Banger pulled into the parking lot. He remembered to turn off the Honda's headlights. The sky was light. The air was still cold. He sprinted across the parking lot and past the trailers. He slapped his pockets until he found his production ID. At least he had that.

An assistant assistant director stood at the square doorway with a clipboard. He looked about eleven years old. Banger waved his pass at the AAD. The pass had a logo of a boxing glove and a stylized atom sign. In block letters it said, *Neutron Kid—Set Pass.*

The AAD ignored the pass. He nodded at Banger and made a mark on his clipboard. He jerked his head. "Better see Katie. She's waiting in Makeup. You're late."

Banger grunted, sprinted across the huge, shadowy room. He could feel the cold concrete floor through his sneakers and heavy socks.

Katie was waiting at Makeup.

She said, "Thanks for coming in, Banger."

"I gotta thank you, Katie. You don't know how—well, what happened to the other guy, whatsizname?"

"Yeah. He got a chance to do a commercial in Maui. A lot more than we were paying him. Saturday morning, I get a phone call. 'I'm on the red-eye,' he says, 'I'm calling from a 767. Back in a week. Can you shoot around me?' "

"You couldn't." Banger wasn't asking. What happened was obvious. It was a windfall for him. He'd been on line to get extra work, be a face in the ringside crowd for the big Mark Cole–Slam Shaughnessy bout. Now he was Shaughnessy, or he would be as soon as Makeup got through with him.

Katie said, "When I finish talking to that bum's agent he'll think he lost a *real* prizefight. Okay. You can't wear those glasses for this part. You have a set of contacts?"

Banger shook his head. "I'll be okay. I just wear these to drive."

"All right."

A Makeup tech pushed Banger into a chair. "You better take off your shirt. I want to blend the face pancake into your shoulders. They're just shooting you in the dressing room today, and walking to the ring. Once the fight starts we're going to slime you up a little for sweat. Later on we'll do some nice blood and bruises. Slam cuts up Cole but Cole bleeds all over Slam."

"Yeah. Unnerstand." He took off his shirt. He could feel his skin start to pucker in the cold, but he knew he'd be hot under the lights.

Katie was walking away. Banger had put his glasses in his shirt pocket and Katie looked fuzzy. He yelled after her. "There lines I got to study?"

She turned and walked back into focus. She had a thin face, red hair, pale green eyes. The shadows in the big room were fading. She had a clipboard, too. Seemed like they all had clipboards. She looked at it, said, "No. You'll have a few lines, we'll feed 'em to you. We'll talk to Jerry and Hugh about it. Just so you can hit your mark."

"Hit my mark. Mark Cole?"

Katie laughed and walked away. He must have made a joke.

The technician finished him up and he ran by Wardrobe and got outfitted with a pair of trunks and boots and a robe. The robe was imitation satin. On the back it had his character's name in comic book letters surrounded by sequined stars.

They set up the first scene in his dressing room. It wasn't his picture, he knew that. He hadn't seen the script, only heard scuttlebutt in coffee shops, read about it in the trade papers. That, plus what Katie Healy had told him when she phoned to offer him the part of Shaughnessy. Still, she'd told him that he'd get a scene in his—Shaughnessy's—dressing room, and the walk to the ring, and then the fight itself, and then another scene after the fight. They'd intercut that with Mark Cole's scenes. The loser and the winner.

He didn't know the actors around him. He'd had to leave his glasses in his shirt in his locker. Everybody was a little fuzzy and he could feel his heart racing the way it used to before a bout. He'd never been a headline boxer, either, but he remembered the feeling, the mixture of terror and eagerness to get in the ring and get started. The waiting was always the worst.

His manager was there, wearing a suit, a chippie hanging on his arm, cooing in his ear. She reached over and pushed a long red fingernail into Shaughnessy's biceps. She was wearing a diamond ring with a stone the size of an egg and a bracelet that flashed under the bright lights. She made a little squeal and pulled away.

His trainer was a squatty guy in a gray sweatshirt. He had a fringe of black hair around his bald scalp. A cigar hung from his mouth. He was talking, giving Banger instructions, talking about his opponent. The guy was a pushover, a pansy, a perfessor. He din't know nothing about the fight racket. Just wade in and crunch him up, don't try nothin' fancy.

Banger nodded, made grunting noises, "Yeah, yeah, gotcha, yeah, kill him, I'll kill him."

This was the brightest dressing room Banger had ever

used. Jeez, the lights were strong. Hot, too. There was some kind of machine over there, too. He ignored it.

Jerry Valdez said, "Okay, one more dry run."

His manager's chippie poked him with her red fingernail, squealed, pulled away. The lights flashed on her diamonds.

His trainer started his spiel again. The guy was a pushover, a pansy, didn't know nothing, just wade in and crunch him up. Shaughnessy nodded, grunted. "Yeah, yeah, gotcha."

Valdez was a shadowy figure and a voice from behind the light. He said, "Okay, good. Let's get ready for a take."

Somebody came at Shaughnessy and dabbed at his face. It couldn't be his cut man, he hadn't even been in the ring yet. In fact it was a woman. She dabbed something on his face, nodded, turned away, disappeared behind the lights.

People were hollering. Shaughnessy wondered if they were reporters, cops, hangers-on. He could hear them clearly enough even if the things they said didn't make much sense.

"Sound."

"Speed."

"Rolling."

A man stepped in front of the training table. Slam was sitting on the edge of the table, his robe over his shoulders, his hands bandaged, ready for his trainer to slip the gloves on him. The man had his back to him, some kind of square thing in his hands. He said, "*Neutron Kid*, scene 238, take one." He did something to it and it made a sound almost like a pistol shot.

His manager's chippie poked his arm, squealed, pulled away.

His trainer started in again.

He nodded, grunted.

How many times did it happen? The shot, the chippie, the trainer.

Jerry Valdez yelled, "Print it. Okay."

An assistant director yelled, "Clear the set." The bright lights went off. The room was darker now. Banger Barnes jumped off the training table. His jump was kind of off, he hit the floor a little harder than he'd meant to and he felt the jolt up to his hips but he was okay.

Somebody from Props pulled his gloves off his hands. An AD said, "You can take the tape off if you want to. It won't show in the walk scene."

Another AD said, "Take a lunch break. Set up for 239, Slam's walk-to-the-ring, in ninety minutes."

People swirled around. Banger slipped his arms into the sleeves of his robe. He found his locker and got his bifocals out of his shirt. Everything came back into focus.

Katie came over, put her hand on his arm. She still carried her clipboard in her other hand. "Nice job, Banger." She looked up at him and smiled. What a nice smile. She said, "That isn't your actual name, is it? Banger Barnes?"

He said, "Barnes is real. Banger was for fighting. Sounded nice. The sportswriters liked it. I got so used to it, I kept it when I retired."

Katie said, "Catering truck's outside. You sure you want to keep that robe on? Don't spill anything on it. You'll need it for the next scene."

Banger said, "I'll be careful."

He stood in line at the catering truck, behind a couple of technicians who were studying a morning LA *Times*. They were pointing to a photo of a bloody crime scene, handing the paper back and forth, talking about the increase in drive-by shootings, gang wars, strong-arm crime in the metropolitan area.

Banger handed his tray up to the window, got a piece of chicken and some broccoli stalks, filled a cardboard cup with coffee, and looked for a seat at one of the long lunch tables.

All of the extras were sitting at one table. They didn't mix with the actors or the crew. Banger carried his tray past them. Some of them looked away. A couple smiled at him. He could read their minds. Why Barnes? Why not me? What's it take to get out of the crowd scene and get a part, even a bit, even a walk-on? Why Barnes?

An actor gestured him over. He put his tray on the table and pulled out a folding chair. He was sitting with his trainer, his manager, his manager's chippie.

Why Barnes, he asked himself. Because he was a real fighter. There was no substitute for the real thing. He'd been there, he knew the footwork, he knew the moves. He knew the feel of your fist thudding into an opponent's ribs. He knew the feel of hard leather crushing your nose. He knew the joy of dancing around the ring while thousands of people cheered for you. He knew the baffled despair of lying on your back, trying to focus on the referee's fingers, squinting against the glare of the ring lights while the crowd cheered for the other fighter.

His trainer introduced himself, shook Banger's hand. "Nice job this morning. Healy says you used to be a real boxer."

Banger said, "Yeah."

His trainer introduced him to the other actors, to the man who played his manager and the woman who played the chippie. They both shook his hand.

The chippie said, "You really never acted before?"

Banger said, "Only extra work. It isn't much but it sure beats dishwashing or janitor work."

"But you can do better than that. I mean—and all the money you made fighting."

Banger laughed bitterly. He had to take a swallow of coffee before he answered her. The coffee was hot and strong. One thing about movie work, even extra work, they had good coffee on the set. It was a long hard day and if they didn't have coffee to keep them going, they'd use other things. That was more extra scuttlebutt. Who was on pep pills, who was on speed, who was on cocaine. They didn't do it for fun, they did it to get up as high as they had to, to work, and to work a ten-, twelve-, fourteen-hour day. And then they needed booze to get them unwired at night. Booze or grass or Valium or horse.

It was an occupational hazard.

He put down his cardboard cup.

"You ought to know better than that. Your boyfriend there takes his bite of every purse." He pointed a chicken bone at his trainer, said, "He gets another piece." He glared at the chippie. "I must have paid for those sparklers you like to flash. What did they cost? How many jabs did I have to throw, how many hooks did I have to take to pay for your fancy bracelets?"

She looked puzzled. She said, "Those aren't mine. Look, I had to give them back to Props." She held her hands toward him. The long, polished fingernails were still there but the diamond ring, the diamond bracelet were gone.

His trainer said, "They're only props anyhow, Banger. Paste. You don't think they'd use real jewelry, do you?"

Banger shook his head. "No." He managed a feeble laugh. "No, I just—sorry. I kind of . . ."

His manager said, "It can happen, don't be embarrassed. You get into a role, you kind of stay in character sometimes. The role takes you over. Can happen to anybody."

Banger said, "Yeah."

"Especially since you were a real boxer. Say, I used to follow boxing a little. I remember you. You were ranked, weren't you?"

"Not very high."

"Even so." His manager made a sweeping gesture. "You were somebody. You know, you counted. They wrote about you in the boxing magazines. People knew who you were."

Banger said, "Yeah."

His trainer looked at his watch. He said, "Still a little time. It's nice out. I'm going to have a stroll before we go back to work."

He carried his tray away from the table. The others followed suit. Banger, too. He scraped the chicken bones and the rest of his trash into a barrel and left the tray for the caterers. Then he went looking for the set for the afternoon's shooting.

He felt a hand on his arm and knew without turning around that it was Katie Healy. She said, "Okay, this is a long tracking shot, Banger. You don't have any lines. It's just you walking to the ring with your entourage."

He said, "What entourage?"

She consulted her clipboard. "Your manager, trainer, cut man, bodyguards, boxing groupies."

"All I do is walk to the ring?"

"That's all."

"Okay."

Katie said, "You looked good this morning. Jerry's pleased."

Banger didn't say anything.

Katie said, "You're a member of the guild, aren't you?"

"Since they merged with the extras."

"You never know, you might get some more work."

"I can use it."

The set was like a real arena. The ring was in the middle with a huge light fixture above it. The canvas and ropes looked real, the iron steps leading up to the apron. The timekeeper's table and the press tables were in place, vacant, waiting for officials in fancy dress and reporters in shirtsleeves to take their places.

There were only a few rows of seats on two sides of the ring, and a few seats on either side of the long pathway that led to the ring. On the far side were cameras and lights.

Nobody blew a whistle or sounded a bell or hollered when it was time to work. People appeared, lighting technicians and sound engineers, camera operators and assistant camera operators and focus pullers and assistant directors and property masters and costumers and makeup technicians.

The extras filed in. Each of them had a slip of paper. Each of them found the right seat in the mock auditorium.

Suddenly the timekeeper was in his place and the reporters were in theirs. The referee was in the center of the ring and Slam fidgeted at the head of the runway, surrounded by his entourage.

Still photogs aimed their Leicas and Ektars. One veteran even hefted a massive, ancient Speed Graphic.

A pair of metal guides like railroad tracks ran down the center of the runway. The Paniflex was mounted on a sitting dolly with a cameraman behind the eyepiece. A boom mike hung over the actors.

An AD hit the clapboard.

Slam Shaughnessy and his entourage started forward. His handlers were pawing him, urging advice on him. Women reached for him, wanting to touch the hem of his robe, wanting to feel his glove, his face before he climbed into the ring. His bodyguards shoved them away.

He nodded agreement to everything his handlers told him. He grinned and waved to the crowd. The extras waved back at him. Some of them cheered. More of them booed, hurled angry comments. Clearly, it was Mark Cole's crowd.

Somebody held up a sign and waved it. It read, *Mark Cole—Neutron Kid—New Champ.* Somebody started a chant and in seconds the crowd had taken it up. *New-Tron! New-Tron! New-Tron!*

The dolly was rolling backward along its metal guides. The lights half blinded Banger. He started to reach for his glasses, then remembered they were back in his locker. And he couldn't wear them on-camera anyhow. He tried to remember what Valdez had told him. Valdez himself, the director, not Katie Healy or any other AD.

Hit your marks. They're red tape. Ignore the green tape, that's Hugh Keating's marks. And ignore the black tape. That's for the referee.

Who was Hugh Keating? The crowd was roaring and he hadn't even reached the ring yet. Keating, right, he was the star. The top male star. He was Mark Cole, the Neutron Kid. And Banger Barnes was Slam Shaughnessy, the reigning champ, the bad guy.

He was the champ. That meant that the challenger had to be in the ring already. He tried to see past the lights, past the rolling dolly. He could make out a couple of figures in the ring now. At first when he looked it had been only the referee in his black pants and white shirt and little bow tie. Now he could see the Neutron Kid, too, in his radioactive green robe, bouncing around the ring, waving to the reporters and the crowd, to the bit players and the extras, waiting for the champ to arrive.

Slam arrived at ringside.

Jerry Valdez yelled, "Cut."

Slam started up the iron steps.

Valdez yelled again, "I said, Cut."

Slam felt an AD's hand on his shoulder. "Din' you hear Jerry?" Banger blinked. The AD was pretty close. Slam could see his face. He looked annoyed.

"Sorry. Sorry. I was just into the scene."

"Yeah. Hunnert-fiddy people on the set. You know what that costs per minute? This is *The Neutron Kid*, not *Rocky*."

"I'm sorry."

Banger turned and started back up the runway. He bounced off Jerry Valdez, who was studying a videotape of the scene. Banger said, "I'm sorry."

Valdez huddled with a couple of ADs and the cinematographer. Banger stood with his entourage at the top of the runway. He tried to get a look at the extras lining the runway but they were only a parti-colored blur.

The Valdez group broke up and ADs rearranged Slam's entourage. Now there was a woman in a low-cut red dress on one side and his trainer in his gray sweatshirt on the other. The woman in the red dress wore sparkling gems. A couple of burly bodyguards flanked the trio. A woman from Makeup darted into the group and sprayed glycerine on the bodyguards' bald skulls.

Valdez said, "Okay, we're going to run through it again. On video only."

They repeated the roll. Valdez was happier.

By late afternoon they had a take. By the time they had four takes, Valdez called a coffee-and-relief break. Banger had to get a prop master to take his gloves off for him. He had to go something fierce, and barely made it to the bathroom in time.

The producer had rented a huge building for the shoot, an abandoned computer factory that hadn't found a new permanent tenant, and there were lavatories galore. Slam Shaughnessy's dressing room set was some onetime executive's office. The arena itself had been set up in an area that must have been a main assembly room for the computer plant, and the cafeteria must once have been a shipping dock.

Banger drank a cup of coffee standing at the table in front of the huge urn, then took another cup and a donut and sat down. One of the extras sat with him. There was one set of rules for mealtime, another for breaks. Banger wondered if this was the same extra who'd waved the Neutron Kid sign. Banger didn't have his glasses and he couldn't be sure.

The extra shook his hand and introduced himself. He said, "Everybody envies you."

Banger said, "I was lucky. And I know boxing."

The extra said, "You know the story line?"

Banger said, "I just show up when they call me. This is about boxing, right?"

The extra said, "You ought to stop in the production office and look at the script. Hey, now that you're a real actor, they might even give you a copy."

Banger started to answer but an AD was hollering and shepherding people back onto the arena set.

Jerry Valdez stood near the iron steps outside the ring. He said, "We're doing fine, everyone. We're going to bring this thing on time and budget. The company and the network will love us for that. But we have to keep pushing. There's time for another scene today. We're going to do this with three cameras, so everybody be on your toes. All right?"

Banger looked around. Everybody was nodding and pledging his all to the success of *The Neutron Kid*.

Valdez said, "Now, Mark Cole, Slam, ring announcer, initial positions please. I can't emphasize the importance of hitting your marks too much. With three cameras, we have to stay in focus and we can't block each other off. No prima donnas here, I know that. We're all professionals, right?"

Everybody agreed.

Banger stood with his hands up while Valdez gave his pep talk. A prop master fitted his gloves back on. Banger dropped to one knee for a second and found his first mark. A good broad strip of red tape on the canvas.

He stood back up and looked at the mark. It was fuzzy but he could make it out. He stood with one toe on the mark. A focus puller stuck a measuring tape against his nose and said, "Hold this." Banger managed to grasp the tape between the thumb and body of his glove. The focus puller got back to his camera and said, "Okay, thanks." Banger let go.

The ring announcer took his place and Hugh Keating took his, and they walked through the scene a few times.

Then Valdez ordered a take, studied the video rush

with a couple of ADs, then conferred with somebody who might have been the writer. They held a conference with the ring announcer, then tried another dry run. The ring announcer's lines were shorter.

Between takes Banger scanned the ringside seats. He spotted a remembered face in the front row, sitting between a couple of mock celebrities. She had shimmering honey-colored hair and wore a sexy emerald-colored dress. Without his glasses, Banger couldn't see any more detail but he knew she was Helen Silver, the female lead in the film.

Extra scuttlebutt said that her former name was Ellie Silverstein. It took a nose job to get her into the movies. Her habit of powdering her nose from the inside out had got her into a series of legal scrapes and rehab programs and very nearly ended her career. Now she was trying for her umpteenth comeback, making a TV movie-of-the-week and hoping to get back onto the big screen.

By the time they finished the ring announcement shoot it was seven-thirty. Valdez called for a five-thirty start the next day. Technicians started shutting down the set while the cast and extras scattered.

Katie Healy caught up with Banger on his way to the Honda. He'd dressed without showering. He was hustling between the trailers when Katie reached out of the studio trailer and pulled him in by the shoulder.

She was sitting with a gray-haired man in a tweed jacket and button-down shirt and tie. The gray-haired man shook Banger's hand. ''Meldrum Cornell,'' he said.

Banger started to give his own name.

Cornell said, ''I know who you are. Just wanted to thank you for stepping in at the last moment. Katie told you what happened with your predecessor in the role. You know we have to run a tight ship here. *Neutron Kid* isn't *Rocky*.'' He paused. ''Or *Heaven's Gate*.''

Cornell and Healy laughed. Banger joined in. He'd heard it before.

Katie Healy handed him a fat script, multicolored pages held together with brass clips. She said, "You can take this home and study it, Banger. It's a numbered copy. Make sure it gets back here with you. We're shooting 171 through 199 tomorrow. Read those. See you in the morning."

He knew he'd been dismissed. He trotted toward the Honda. It was a squareback model, a funny kind of mini–station wagon. That was why Chim Hughes had bought it. It had room for his string bass in the rear compartment. It was cheap, too. The rusted-out body and the smoking exhaust that would never pass an honest smog check accounted for that.

Banger pushed the Honda as fast as he dared on the freeway, checked the cheap digital clock taped to the dashboard, and saw that it was a quarter after eight by the time he passed Chim's apartment. No way that Chim would still be in Hollywood. Banger headed for Santa Monica.

He pulled into the Tiger's Den parking lot fronting on Olympic. On a Monday night the Tiger's Den was mostly empty and business would be dead. But the Wayne Masters Trio needed every nickel they could earn and the owner of the Den let them play for tips and a tiny cut of the Den's receipts.

A couple of black-and-whites were pulled up in front of the nudie bar across Olympic. Banger took off his glasses and cleaned them, feeling crusty and stale after his day's work. He really needed a long, hot shower, but he'd wanted to get to the Den, let Chim know that he'd brought the Honda, and would make good for Chim's cab fare.

Whatever had happened at the nudie bar must just have happened because there hadn't even been time for a crowd to gather on the sidewalk. Banger could see somebody lying in front of the bar, a cop standing over him with his revolver to the suspect's head. The poor sap on the sidewalk looked like a junior high school student. He wore a baseball cap with the bill turned backward.

Another youngster came running out of the nudie bar waving a gun. He wore the same kind of cap, and had a huge scar on one cheek. The cop standing on the sidewalk jerked his arm up to point his weapon at the newcomer.

The prone figure swung a fist awkwardly. It had to be awkward with him lying on his face, but it was good enough to jolt against the cop's wrist. The man running from the bar fired once and the cop fell. The two men sprinted away, disappearing around the corner. More cops came pouring from the bar and jumped into the black-and-whites. They took off in full flashers-and-siren mode.

The door of the the Tiger's Den swung open and a couple emerged onto the sidewalk, quarreling. Banger slipped inside and let his eyes adjust from the darkness outside to the deeper darkness inside.

The trio were on their low bandstand playing a schmaltzy version of some standard. Banger recognized "Body and Soul." There were barflies on about half the stools and diners at a third of the tables. Dorothy was holding down the hostess station.

She wore a tawny angora sweater and a gold-and-cloisonné tiger pin. Her glasses hung on her chest by a neck cord.

"Banger, how are you?"

He said, "I'm good, Dorothy. I'm pretty tired but I'm good."

"Chim says you been working."

"Yeah. Playing a boxer."

She laughed. "Chim was pissed."

Banger said, "About the car. I know."

"You owe him."

"I know."

"You want a table?"

Banger shook his head. "I'll get a snack at the bar. I'll leave the keys for Chim. I'll catch a bus back."

Dorothy said, "Better not. Chim wants to see you. Hang around, talk to him at the break. Besides, Wayne's got a new kid trying out for the band. Supposed to sound like Chet Baker. You ought to listen to him."

Banger hoisted himself onto a barstool. On one side a drunk was crying softly between slugs of rye. He had a fedora on the back of his head, like somebody out of a late-night movie. On the other side a sharp-faced woman smoked furiously and scribbled numbers on a yellow pad, not looking up when she reached for a rickey glass between deep drags on her cigarette.

The bartender gave Banger a cup of coffee, straight no chaser. A waitress brought him a T-bone and a baked potato.

Wayne Masters introduced the kid who was supposed to sound like Chet Baker. The kid looked like a high school sophomore. He wore his hair in a pompadour and a sports jacket and a shirt with a rolled collar and a narrow tie. He might have fallen into the Den through a time warp. He was pure 1950.

He signaled to Chim with his trumpet and Chim started a slow walk on his bass that sounded like a heart beating. Wayne Masters sat at the piano and Mike Le Conte sat behind his drum kit and they watched.

The kid put his trumpet to his lips and started playing, so softly at first that Banger couldn't even hear him. Then the kid came on, never rushing, never playing very loud, playing "My Funny Valentine."

The drunk to Banger's right dropped his face onto his arms and started crying seriously. The woman on Banger's left jammed her pad and pencil into her purse and swung around on her stool, watching the kid play.

After the set Banger swiveled through diners' tables and handed Chim the keys to the Honda. "You saved my life, Chim. I owe you one, buddy."

Chim was holding a glass of water. He slipped the keys into his tuxedo trousers and handed another set back to Banger. "You bet. Big time. I figured, if your Pontiac's dead you're just gonna hit me up to use the Honda again tomorrow, so I called my friend Benny Mechanic and had him take a look at it. Your fuel pump was shot. He installed a recon'd unit and put a charge on your battery. You're all set."

Banger held his head. "That's gonna cost. Where's the Pontiac now?"

"In back. I'm surprised you didn't see it when you came into the Den."

"Too much distraction. Some kind of upset across the street."

Chim took a sip of water, then put the glass down on a coaster on top of Wayne's piano. He said, "Did you hear that kid? Too good for us by far. Wayne will hire him for a while, then he'll be gone." He picked up his glass. "I'm going in back, put my feet up for a little. You gonna stay?"

Banger said, "I gotta clean up, get a few hours shut-eye. Early call tomorrow."

The temperature had dropped outside the Den, and the nudie bar across the street was closed off with yellow police tape.

The Pontiac ran like a watch.

Makeup took longer this morning. The technician said, "We have to put on a good base. Jerry wants to get the whole fight in the can today. I don't see how he can do it. This is a twenty-three-day shoot. That's four minutes a day for a TV feature. The fight is supposed to run something like twelve minutes. I don't see how he can do it in one day, but I guess that's why Cornell hired him."

Katie Healy came by and asked if Banger had read the script.

He said, "I soaked in the tub with it. I didn't have time to read the whole thing, I just read the fight."

Katie said, "That's okay. You don't need to know the rest of it."

"Calls for a pretty tough fight."

"Meldrum insisted. He likes to push the network as far as he can. He strike you as a refined gentleman?"

"I guess so."

"Well he is. He's also bloodthirsty. He gets what he wants. He cultivates that tweedy look. He's a shark. They're all sharks." She narrowed her eyes, gave Banger an odd look. "Me included." The technician took Banger's glasses, handed them to him to put in his pocket. Katie said, "Just remember to hit your marks."

Glasses in his pocket, the Makeup tech working on him, Banger couldn't make out Katie's expression.

Jerry Valdez said, "We don't have time to do all the shots separately on this sequence. We're going with three cameras again. This is a twelve-round bout, two-minute rounds and one minute rests, that would be thirty-five minutes in real time. We're going twelve minutes screen time. We'll shoot silent and add wild sound. We'll have ADs to coach you through this. We'll shoot the corners tomorrow and cut them in between rounds. And keep your mouthpieces in. They change the shape of your face. If you lose 'em, the audience will spot it. Everybody ready? Walk through round one."

It was tougher than half of Banger's real bouts had been. Both fighters started clean and dry. Whenever Valdez yelled "Freeze!" Makeup techs would run out and spray glycerine for sweat. They used water for the referee's shirt. After a couple of rounds the ring lights got so hot that Banger and Hugh Keating were sweating under their own power.

In the third round Slam Shaughnessy was supposed to open a cut in the Neutron Kid's eyebrow. A technician took care of that. A trickle of blood ran into Keating's eye, then down the edge of his nose.

In the fifth round Mark Cole raised a mouse above Shaughnessy's eye. Cole's cut man had closed up his eyebrow with a stapler and put Vaseline on it. In the sixth round, Shaughnessy reopened the cut. It bled heavily. The eye was closing, but the mouse over Shaughnessy's eye was puffing up and Cole opened a cut on the bridge of Shaughnessy's nose and the blood was running into both his eyes.

The referee checked both fighters in their corners after the sixth round, then let them continue.

In the ninth, Shaughnessy staggered Cole with a series of hooks to the body. He nearly had him finished, aimed a hard cross to the jaw but missed. Cole hung on until the bell. Shaughnessy shoved him off and watched him stumble back to his corner.

Shaughnessy slumped into his stool, took a mouthful of water from the ladle, and spit it into a cup. His handlers were all over him, giving instructions, urging him on. He heard the bell for the start of round ten. His trainer slipped Shaughnessy's mouthpiece between his teeth and boosted him toward Cole.

He heard somebody yelling advice to him, squinted through puffy eyes, trying to keep up with the younger Kid. Slam Shaughnessy was the old champ, out to crunch up the young challenger. He should have finished Cole earlier but he hadn't been able to put him away. Now he knew he couldn't but he was ahead on points. If he could look good for a couple of rounds he'd still be the winner, the judges hated to take the crown from a champ on points.

Round eleven. He was almost blind but he thought the Kid wasn't in much better shape. Slam threw a couple of roundhouse rights. The Kid danced away. Slam lost his balance, went to one knee. He looked up. The referee signaled no knockdown, but when Slam struggled to his feet the ref looked into his face, trying to see his eyes.

Slam said, "I'm okay. I slipped." He didn't know if the ref could understand him. He spit out his mouthpiece, said it again.

The ref signaled Slam and the Kid to go at it, but the bell sounded almost before they could move.

Between rounds one of Slam's handlers retrieved his mouthpiece and shoved it between his teeth. Some woman got into the ring and told Slam what to do in the twelfth round. He couldn't remember who she was. He blinked, trying to see the color of her dress through the blood running into his eyes. She looked familiar but he couldn't identify her.

The bell sounded. He started for the center of the ring but his legs were rubbery and his fists each weighed a thousand pounds. The Neutron Kid was a faint blur, moving around him like a wolf circling a lamb. Slam turned, turned, trying to keep the Kid in his sights.

He lost him for a moment. He blinked, trying to clear his head, trying to see his opponent.

Somehow the Kid had circled around, sneaked up and blindsided him. He saw the punch coming but he couldn't move. He felt it connect, felt himself swimming slowly through hot, moist air, heard the thump as he hit the canvas, facedown. He heard the referee counting, heard the crowd cheering. But they were supposed to be shooting MOS—silent—and add the sound later.

Then he was in the first aid room. A nurse was dabbing at him and Katie Healy and Jerry Valdez were there.

The nurse said, "This man isn't injured at all. Look, all of these bruises and injuries are makeup. He's just exhausted. He just needs a little rest."

Valdez said, "Will he be able to work tomorrow? We got the fight. God, Katie, you wouldn't believe it. It's going to make this thing a hit. Cornell is going to love us all. You remember Kirk Douglas in *Champion*? Do you think he'll be able—what's his name?''

Katie said, ''Barnes.''

''Able to work tomorrow? We can shoot around him, move up 282 through 304. Do the cut-ins end of the week, even Monday if we have to. We don't wrap 'til next Friday.''

Banger closed his eyes.

He heard Valdez say, ''Take a day off. Take two days off. Get back here Friday, we'll do the cut-ins, Barnes. That'll finish your scenes. You did good, old tiger.''

Banger grunted some kind of thank-you.

He pulled the Pontiac in behind the Tiger's Den, feeling a thousand percent better. A whole day in bed—or on the couch. A few solid meals. A couple of good hot soaks.

Across Olympic from the Den, the yellow tape was gone from the nudie bar and the establishment was back in business.

The Den was almost full tonight. Dorothy met him at the door wearing a tailored jacket and blouse over a dark skirt. She had transferred the tiger pin from her sweater to the lapel of the jacket. She said, ''You're looking good, Banger. I could almost marry you again.''

He raised his eyebrows. Even in the dark Den he knew she could see his face by the reflected light of the lamp on the hostess station.

She said, ''Just kidding.''

He slid into the last vacant barstool in the place. He ordered his usual steak and coffee. It wouldn't keep him up tonight. He felt too good. He would finish his week on *The Neutron Kid*, collect a nice paycheck, look for a place of his own so he could get off Chim's couch and start to have a life again.

He stayed through the first set and into the second. Dorothy came over and put her arm around his shoulders and they listened to the kid play "All the Things You Are."

The Den was almost empty now. The late crowds only came on weekends. Other nights it was an early to mid-evening house.

The door swung open and somebody shouted. Banger swung around on his stool. Two youngsters stood near the doorway, shouting confusing instructions. They both wore baseball caps, their bills turned backward. One had a huge scar on his cheek. They were waving machine pistols. Customers were diving for the floor. The bartender disappeared. The Wayne Masters Trio dropped their instruments, all except for the kid with the trumpet. He stood with his eyes closed, still playing the corny "All the Things You Are."

One gunman ran halfway across the restaurant, pointed his machine pistol at the trumpeter and cut him in half with a short burst of bullets. The second gunman pointed his machine pistol at the bar and raked the backbar mirror and the bottles standing beneath it.

Banger launched himself off his barstool, away from Dorothy, straight at the nearer gunman. He knocked the gunman's weapon aside with his right hand, landed a solid left to the gunman's face. He felt the satisfying crunch of knuckles against jawbone.

The second gunman turned back from the bandstand and cut his partner and Banger in half with the same volley.

Somehow I keep encountering the notion that I am an accomplished pugilist. Or at least that I was in my youth. Some years ago, Piers Anthony wrote a piece in which he referred to me as "a real heavyweight." On another occasion Roger Zelazny phoned and asked if I hadn't been a Golden Gloves boxer, once upon a time.

In fact, I *was* an amateur boxer briefly, when I was in my teens, although nowhere near Golden Gloves caliber. I was a strong kid, I packed a real wallop, and I was tough. Like the great Jake LaMotta I could boast that I had never been knocked off my feet.

But unlike LaMotta, I could never develop what are known in the trade as "fast hands." And as for footwork—forget it. I gave the term *stumblebum* new meaning. Consequently, while I could hit hard, I didn't land many punches. And while I could absorb punishment—well, who wants a career as a human punching bag?

So I got out of the racket very quickly. But in an odd way, I did enjoy it. Whenever anybody asks, *But didn't it hurt, getting punched like that*, I answer that, Yes, it did hurt. But somehow that pain was appropriate, and being appropriate, it was somehow all right, far more acceptable than it would have been under other conditions.

So I don't regret my brief career in the Sweet Sport, but I also don't regret moving on to other amusements.

As for the movie-making aspect of "Easy Living," I once again drew on real-life experience.

It's a quirk of fate that, in all my years as a writer, with dozens of novels and scores of short stories to my credit, I've seen my work adapted for the screen just three times—and all three times, it was the same story.

In 1973 *The Magazine of Fantasy and Science Fiction* ran my short story "12:01 PM." It's a slightly tongue-in-cheek piece about a middle-aged, middle-class office worker who gets stuck in a sort of time warp (or "time bounce") and relives one day's lunch hour, over and over and over and over.

In 1989 "12:01 PM" became a thirty-minute featurette by a brilliant young screenwriter-director named Jonathan Heap. The little movie was so good that it was nominated for an Academy Award.

If you ever get a chance to see this film, look for me. I'm an extra in it, and you may spot me crossing the street, wearing a gray tweed jacket, a lime green shirt, and a stolid expression.

In 1993 the same story was plagiarized for a big-budget, multimillion-dollar-grossing theatrical feature. Was I outraged by this piece of literary-cinematic larceny? You bet I was.

And even as that Hollywood outrage was raking in box office lucre (and critical raves for the crooked screenwriters who slavishly copied Jonathan Heap's vision of my original story), an authorized version was being filmed as a Fox TV feature. The title was shortened to "12:01." Again I was called upon to appear as an extra. Director Jack Sholder even offered to let me act in one scene—if I could produce a convincing sneeze on command.

We had a run-through, I sneezed on cue, Jack shook his head and said, "Too big. Give me a smaller sneeze."

We tried it again and Jack said, "Still too big. Try again."

This time the sneeze was too *small.*

Once more, but still my sneeze wasn't quite right. So I lost the job to another extra, and he's the one who sneezes in the film. Next time the long version of "12:01" pops up on TV or in your video store, and you notice that fellow sneezing, you might remember that I was almost The Man Who Sneezed. But not quite.

But you might still catch a glimpse of me if you are eagle-eyed and on your toes. After firing me from the role of Designated Sneezer, Jack Sholder took pity on my poor shattered ego and gave me a walk-through in another scene. Keep an eye out for me, wandering through a cafeteria with a lunch tray in my hand.

Let's see: My boxer's host Chim is based on novelist

Michael Kurland, who kindly offered me couch space during my stay in Hollywood. And he didn't just lend me his Honda, he actually chauffeured me to and from the set for each day's shoot. Such hospitality goes above and beyond the call of duty, and answers to the higher and nobler name of friendship.

These experiences, as onetime boxer and as movie extra—plus an occasional evening spent in various establishments in West Los Angeles and Santa Monica—provided the raw material for "Easy Living." In fact, there's so much reportage and so little invention in the piece, I wonder if it's fiction at all. Maybe autobiography would be a more accurate description.

Except for the final scene, of course.

Fast, brief, and to the point. What more can I say?

ooooo

Blood Duty

Michael A. Stackpole

The night was as black as blindness. I only saw him because he was blacker than that, a void. Dark and cold, an obsidian statue moving through the night, he padded silently across the tiled roof overhanging the courtyard. He moved fluidly through the night, as if he were as inexorable and invincible as the death he brought with him.

He paused as the wind changed, waiting for it to carry to him a scent, a sound, a clue to the identity of the one who waited for him. He knew someone was there, someone *had* to be there. Lord Kusunoki would not be unprotected. He would slay the one who waited, then slay the Lord. Then his treachery would be complete.

He crouched and moved to the roof's edge. Another watcher would have lost him without the night sky to offer contrast, but I did not. I knew where to look. I knew where he would move. I knew him better than he knew himself.

He jumped down to the courtyard floor. Soft leather tabi allowed his toes to grip the stones while his powerful legs absorbed the impact of the drop. His left hand reached out and touch the ground to balance him. His right hand bore a fire-blackened katana. Again he searched the courtyard for the guardian.

I let him see me. I did not move from the shadows or draw my weapon. I made no sound to challenge him. I just let him see me.

He gave no outward evidence of the shock—shock at having missed the guardian before, shock at learning who it was. He rose to his full height and bowed to me. "The others honor me by setting you out for my capture." His tone mocked me.

I returned his bow. He thought I could not read his face, hidden as it was by the cloth mask. He believed he was closed to me, but I read his eyes and his stance, even his breathing. He was surprised, pleased, and confident. He saw me as no impediment, merely a fillip to enrich his legend.

I narrowed my eyes. "The others decided you would not dare approach this way and are waiting for you by the south wall."

His mask tightened across his face revealing a hidden smile. More confidence and contempt. "Woman, you have no part of this. Leave and I will spare your life." His words were reassuring, offering me an escape. It was the silence between the hisses of a snake.

I shook my head. "Leave and dishonor my clan as you have? I would sooner slit my throat. You owe a debt to me and my clan. I will collect it." His smile faded. "I will collect it now."

His eyes narrowed, a conscious effort to fight his true feelings. Disbelief filled them, backed by memories. Then the coldness, the black void of his life, sucked all but hatred from his eyes. "Can you collect that debt, woman? It is not too much for you to bear?"

I refused to join his game of pettiness, of blaming others for acts he had committed, fully cognizant of the consequences for him and for me. "The debt is vast. My husband's life, taken by his own hand. The shame of Lord Kusunoki refusing me the same surcease. The dishonor my clan has felt since your betrayal. It is a great debt, one that must be collected before you inflate it. But it is not for me to carry. It is yours to bear."

His smile returned, power shook his frame. "I will kill you, woman, and you cannot kill me. You know that."

I felt my stomach tighten. "We love each other . . ."

"You love me. I have no more love . . . none for you in any event."

"Your lack of love is obvious by your actions here and in the past." I concentrated on my breathing, purging myself of fury and hurt. "If you had love, you would kill yourself now to repair some of the damage you have done." I calmed myself more. My action was of love, and therefore could have no anger or hatred in it. "Would you take tea with me first?"

His body shook with the laughter he could not voice. "I have wasted enough time. Come and I will kill you."

I stepped from the shadow and faced him. We were similarly attired, from tabi and hakama up to quilted jacket, gloves, and hooded mask. Our clothing was black—the clan crests on my kimono blacked out, his cut away. My katana, like his, was smoke-kissed. Our blades were invisible in the darkness.

We bowed to each other, his bow a fraction deeper than mine. Not out of respect, out of habit. His mind rebelled, but his body performed as it had many times before. We straightened five paces apart, and each struck a guard.

Both hands on my sword's hilt, I held the weapon cocked high by my right ear. My stance was low and wide. My left leg was nearest him, my left side was open.

His blade almost vanished within his body's silhouette.

His stance was good, his legs wide enough apart and tensed to spring. His sword was held before him, hilt to tip, protecting him groin to eyes.

We waited.

It was an eternity that passed without notice. We were both alive and dead. An attack would take centuries to reach the opponent, but the counterstrike would take less than a heartbeat. It was a game of waiting, where time could not be noticed, for if time entered the game, impatience would come with it.

In the game of waiting, impatience is death.

Stars shot through the heavens, omens to be read by wizards and soothsayers. That one there or this new one might mean my death, or his death. Were the gods mocking us with skysparks like those that would fly when our blades met?

If our blades met.

In an instant, an infinite moment, it began and was finished. In our black clothing surrounded by darkness, wielding razor-edged steel that could not be seen, we were shadow within shadow. Like tendrils of oily smoke we drew together, twisted about each other, passed through each other. In that instant, as it had been before, we were one.

This time there was a difference. Before, life and creation was our concern. Now death and corruption was the fruit of our labors.

Beyond him I turned, and likewise he turned. Then he stopped turning. His knees buckled, his sword flew. His hands fell to his stomach and tried to stem the tide of entrails abandoning him. He stared at me, eyes now wide. His body, his eyes, said he was afraid.

He did not voice his fear. Like his laughter, it was for no one but himself.

I watched him die, the man I'd killed. The man who had betrayed my clan and wished to assassinate my lord.

I watched him with remorse and grief, for when love dies that is all there can be.

And when he was dead, I buried my son.

I first heard of Zen art in a botany course at the University of Vermont. I found the idea of completing a work in seconds, yet having it be perfect very intriguing. I never truly *understood* the concept until years later driving down Indian School Road in Phoenix when "Blood Duty" came to me. I raced home and the story flowed out in just over an hour. It had just been there, and felt right, and it left me feeling more like a conduit than a writer. Mind you, it's far from perfect, but then I'm not a Zen master and I sincerely doubt I ever could be.

Time to smile again.

OOOOO

Doing the Angry Centipede

Karen Haber

At ten after four on a rainy Monday afternoon two weeks past Christmas, in a well-heeled suburb of Seattle, the regulars of the low-impact aerobics class at Butt Out straggled into the white and shiny health club for their forty-five minutes of pain.

They threaded their way down dank, malodorous "Sweat Alley": a corridor of mirrors and bulky machinery that, at first glance, resembled a medieval torture chamber more than a modern temple of health. Inched past the rows of sweating weight lifters and body-sculptors, who had eyes only for their own reflections, and emerged into the relative fresh air and open space by the entrance to the aerobics studio.

Only when they had passed through the white door with its chicken wire–impregnated glass window and were inside the white room with its spinning ceiling fans and polyurethaned wooden floor upon which the soles of their aerobics shoes—too expensive to be called sneakers—squeaked, did they see the sign taped on the mirror, hastily written in red pen, with one misspelling: *Monday Afternoon Low Impact: Chuck can't make it. Sorry. Guest instructer: Ricky Kravitz.*

''Who's he?'' Sharon Taylor asked. She pushed a fugitive strand of curly black hair out of her eyes and hiked up her raspberry leotard where it was binding her, just below her right buttock, and scratched vigorously.

Felice Covino, neat in blond braids and green leggings, shrugged, pulled off her purple sweatshirt, and folded it carefully. ''Hope he's as good as Chuck.''

Anna Marie Chow waddled into the room wearing a hot pink bodysuit. She was munching on a candy bar and her brown eyes were wide with distress. ''Charles isn't coming? But he's so spiritual. So giving.'' Clamping her lips around the last uneaten bit of chocolate, she pulled back her mane of long brown hair, fastened it atop her head with a hot pink rubber band, and finished off the bar. ''I don't know how I'll get through this session without Charles. He's so-o-o-o inspirational.''

''Yes, ma'am,'' Sharon said. ''Especially around the buns.''

Anna Marie looked stricken. ''You shouldn't say that about him—he's gay.''

''So what? I admire him the same way I admire a piece of fine artwork. A sculpture.''

''Only this sculpture just happens to sweat,'' Felice said. Her dimples were showing. ''And wears short shorts. I don't think Michelangelo's *David* sweats.''

Sharon sighed reverently. ''Never underestimate the motivating power of a good pair of short shorts.''

A trim, muscular young man with olive skin and short dark hair entered the studio and strode, like a panther, to the front of the room. He was dressed in a tight black spandex unitard which clung to every curve and bulge of his impressive musculature. He had a tense aura about him, a sense of barely contained force. With a cold and practiced eye he surveyed the three women and obviously found them wanting.

A bit sternly he said, "Good afternoon. I'm Ricky. I'll be taking Chuck's class today."

Without another word, he leaned over and turned on the stereo tape player. A popular song with a strong, driving beat filled the air.

Bomp-bada-bomp-bada-bomp-bomp-bomp.

Ricky nodded in time to the beat, flexed a perfect bicep, and shouted, "Okay! Let's warm up with a few stretches."

Reaching right, then left, Sharon, Felice, and Anna Marie fell into step obediently. A moment later, they were joined in their squat thrusts by Olivia Watson, Moira Skulnik, and Mattie Christopher. The Monday crew was nearly all present, wrapped in spandex, and accounted for.

"Where's Jenny Matthews?" Felice whispered.

"Who knows?" Sharon said. "I haven't seen her here in at least a week."

"Less talking over there," Ricky said. His voice had a drill sergeant snap to it. "Pay attention, ladies. I want you to watch these next moves carefully. They're the basis for everything we'll be doing today."

Sharon rolled her eyes at Felice. Chuck's substitute seemed to be a real martinet.

Ricky squatted, leaned to one side, and thrust his right leg out, heel first, in a savage kick. "Hah!" he cried. A moment later he repeated the move, this time with the left foot.

Next, he lunged, still squatting, and thrust his right hand forward, chopping the air, followed by the left. He moved swiftly, with an intensity that verged on being downright frightening. Right, chop! Left, chop! "Okay," he called. "Let's go!"

Bomp-bada-bomp!

They chopped right and left, squatting, side to side.

"Now lift those feet!"

Sharon struggled to match his leg extensions.

"Higher!"

She imagined him in black leather, coaching the S.S. before a big raid. One more kick like before and she thought that her hips would come right out of their sockets.

"Now," Ricky called. "After me. Let's travel!"

Back and forth they went across the room, lunging and punching, kicking and chopping the air, feeling faintly ridiculous, as Ricky marched up and down, barking orders. "Faster. Harder. Come on, ladies. No wimping allowed here. I want strong kicks. You couldn't knock down a shadow with those moves. Attitude. Give me some attitude!"

I'll give you some attitude, Sharon thought. *Just as soon as I get back some breath.*

Bomp-bada-bomp-bomp-bomp!

Moira called out from the back line, "Hey, isn't this like karate or something? All these kicks?"

Ricky nodded and his eyes gleamed with fanatic joy. "You got it."

"But this is supposed to be a low-impact aerobics class."

"That's precisely what it is. We're not jumping up and down, are we? No, we're just thrusting and punching. We're keeping our center of gravity low. Getting those heart rates up. Now punch out as though you're punching a mugger. Come on, I want to see some intensity."

They punched with intensity. It wasn't good enough for him. Not nearly.

"Like you mean it!"

They kicked their way across the floor, backed him against the mirror, and they meant it.

"Reverse!" he yelled. "Faster. I want to see those feet move, move, move."

"Jesus," Sharon panted to Felice. "where did they find him? Parris Island?"

"Heart rate check. Fingers on your pulses, everybody!"

"There *is* a God," Felice said, and reached for her purple water bottle.

Sharon checked herself in the mirror. Her hair was a flat, matted mess and her shining face was bright pink. Sweat was pouring down her body, turning her leotard from raspberry to maroon. She saw that the other members of the class were all mopping their faces and leaning against the wall, gasping, or sucking down water as fast as they could. The break was more than welcome. He had worn them out already and the class had barely begun.

But their relief was brief. Whereas good old dependable Chuck would have gone on to talk about the importance of centering and knowing where your chakras are—Chuck was very big on staying in touch with your chakras—Ricky called everyone back to order immediately.

"Now," he said. "Ladies, listen up. We're going to do the Enraged Centipede. It's a terrific defensive traveling move which we've been working on at my dojo all week."

Dojo?

Sharon and Felice stared at one another in horror. They were in the hands of a training fanatic, one who obviously regarded aerobics as just another branch of martial arts. Alarmed, but still too out of breath to protest, they peered hopefully at their fellow campaigners. No luck. Despite the red faces and heaving chests, nobody else seemed ready to complain, and neither Felice nor Sharon wanted to look like a wimp. Especially in front of people like Anna Marie Chow.

"Watch closely."

Ricky was a blur of black spandex flying through the

air across the studio, kicking, twisting, punching, scissoring his legs, waving his arms, pivoting, rolling, and jumping to his feet with a triumphant shout of "Hey! Yah!" He paused, gazed around the room, and said, "Got that?"

Before Sharon could say something sarcastic, Felice Spoke up. "Could we see that one more time, please?"

Ricky frowned. "All right. But pay attention, now. I don't want to spend the entire class demonstrating moves."

He kicked with such ferocity that he might have separated someone's head from their body. He punched, jumped, spun, bounced, twisted, pivoted sharply, dropped to the floor, rolled, and bounded to his feet. "Okay?"

Sharon shrugged. *What the hell,* she thought. *Let's try it. It sure looks aerobic.*

"Get focused, everyone," Ricky commanded. "Now, one, two, three, and kick."

They kicked, they twisted, they bounced. They spun, they punched and they scissored their legs. The sound of spandex meeting spandex filled the room.

Anna Marie Chow tripped and fell down.

They marched around her and went gamely on. They waved their arms, they pivoted sharply, they yelled, they rolled, they jumped, and, pop!, just like that, Felice vanished.

For a moment, Sharon thought that, perhaps, her friend had just left the room when she wasn't looking, gone for a quick whizz. But the moment passed and Felice didn't return. "Ricky?" Sharon said. "Ricky, did you see what happened to Felice?"

"No, I didn't," Ricky said, not sounding very interested. "Keep those heart rates up! Move those feet and maintain that focus. No distractions."

"But—"

"Now kick, bounce, punch, twist . . ."

On the next roll-and-pivot, Moira disappeared. Olivia and Mattie went right after her.

"Ricky?" Sharon said. The studio was beginning to seem disturbingly empty.

Anna Marie tripped again.

Ricky ignored her. "Kick harder!" he yelled. "Come on, stop wimping!"

Sharon kicked. She kicked as hard as she could. She twisted, she bounced, she lunged, she waved her arms, she pivoted and rolled, and . . .

. . . she felt the air shift around her as though it were boxing her in, making a neat package, lifting her up, and flinging her down, unwrapped, upon orange sand. Right next to the rest of the aerobics class.

She stood up. Her head was spinning. The orange sand seemed to stretch from horizon to horizon, without a break. It had an odd glassy texture. The sky above was white, flat, featureless. There were small blue-green clouds arranged in a straight line high overhead. Directly below the clouds were a line of orange-red mountains with flat tops, as though a giant knife had come flying through the air and neatly cut the peaks off, chop, chop, chop. This place looked like nowhere on Earth that Sharon could think of. Certainly not Seattle. Probably not even Cleveland.

"What's going on?" she said. "Where are we?"

Felice hugged herself unhappily. "I don't know. I thought that maybe I was going crazy."

"Look at it," Mattie said. "It's a wasteland. Terrible." She sounded as though she were on the verge of tears.

"Well," Moira said. "We're obviously *somewhere*. Maybe we should look around for a house or bus stop. A gas station. Some sign of civilization."

Olivia nodded. "Yeah. And we should definitely sue."

"Great idea," Felice said. "Better look for a lawyer and a telephone, while you're at it. You've got about as much of a chance of finding them out here as you do a gas station or house. Namely, zilch."

They stared at each other in confusion. They began to murmur to each other in apprehensive tones. Gradually the unthinkable realization was sinking in that something very, very peculiar had taken place, something that was almost impossible to comprehend and extremely difficult to adapt to, and that they were in very, very big trouble.

Sharon said, "What the hell are we going to—"

Pop!

Ricky appeared, still kicking. He hovered for a moment in midair, a couple of feet up, and dropped lightly to the ground without missing a beat. He paused, shook his head, and looked around at the alien scenery.

"Weird," he said. He shrugged, turned with military precision, and saw the women standing scattered around him in a loose semicircle.

"C'mon," he said. "No goldbricking."

"What about the studio?" Felice demanded.

"Ricky," Sharon said. "What happened? Where are we?"

He didn't seem to be listening. His eyes had the glazed look of the true and ruthless exercise fiend. "Let's go," he cried. "Can't you feel that buzz? Don't let down now. One and two and three and four. Kick. Punch. Bounce-bounce-bounce. Kick, punch, bounce-bounce-bounce."

On his fifth bounce, Ricky was intercepted by a large grey creature the size and approximate shape of a school bus but with scales, wattles, and talons instead of tires. It sprang up out of the sand as though jet-propelled, and caught the instructor in its mouth.

The mouth would have suited a shark, if there were any sand-dwelling sharks the size of school buses. Its hide was crisscrossed by what appeared to be green mold. It had one huge orange eye and a curved tusk directly above it.

Everybody screamed. The monster glared at them but

hesitated nonetheless. It seemed to be debating whether just to chew Ricky up with its serrated teeth and bolt him down, or throw him back upon the sand and, perhaps, tenderize him with a nice bit of trampling, first.

Dazed, Sharon stared at the monster and said, "Thank God for endorphins. Otherwise, I'd be really scared."

Felice's endorphins didn't seem to be working properly. She was pale and shivering with terror. "Omigod," she whispered. "We've got to do something."

"Yeah, right," Sharon said. "After you, please. I say, let it eat him. Those damned kicks and bounces got us here in the first place, didn't they?"

"You really think so?" Olivia said.

"Sure," Sharon said. "What else could have done it? That stupid karate freak. I say he gets what he deserves."

"No!" Felice grabbed her arm. "We can't just let it eat him, don't you see? We need him."

"I don't."

"Stop kidding around, Sharon. He's the one who taught us the moves that got us here. We need him to get back. Absolutely, we do. He's the only hope in hell that we have of ever finding a way out of here."

Sharon made a rueful face at her friend. "Okay. I guess I see your point. He's got to lead us through a reverse set of exercises, or something."

"Help!" Ricky cried. The monster was still pondering him. "Don't just stand there."

Felice turned to the rest of the class. "He's right. We've got to save him, or else we may never get back to the studio. Come on, let's see if we can do those kicks he showed us. Maybe we can scare that thing into dropping him."

Moira stared at her, shoulders trembling. "You've got to be kidding. Us against that thing? It's bigger than my father-in-law's RV."

"Look at those teeth," someone groaned.

"If we let it have Ricky, we might all get a closer look at those teeth," Sharon said. "Much closer."

"Besides, this isn't nearly as bad as what my five-year-old watches on Saturday morning television," Mattie babbled. "Now *that's* scary. Not to mention disgusting."

Olivia cocked a dark eyebrow at her. "You actually allow Joshua to watch Saturday morning television?

"Well, only one show—"

"Hey," Sharon yelled. "Do we want to rescue Ricky or not? Let's go!"

"Heee-yah!" cried the women of the Monday afternoon low aerobics class. The orange sand rasped under their feet as they kicked, lunged, and kicked again. They chopped the air, they pivoted and jumped, they thrust, and they punched.

The grey thing stopped chewing on Ricky and watched them, seemingly fascinated.

"Hah!" The women yelled. They bounce-bounce-bounced, and kicked some more. They rolled and screamed. They made nasty faces and rude gestures.

The monster snorted. Its grey and scaly hide shifted convulsively. Triangular hackles lifted, vibrating, upon each monstrous limb.

Sharon and Felice lunged.

The thing fell back a step.

Moira, Mattie, and Olivia scissored their legs.

The beast snorted again, rolled its single orange eye, and dropped the aerobics instructor.

The women chopped the air ferociously. "Yah!" they yelled. "Yah! Yah! Yah!"

The thing glared at them.

The women glared back.

The beast seemed a bit troubled.

Adrenaline surging, the women screamed their war cry one more time and fearlessly leaped forward, kicking, punching, lunging, and spinning.

With a sort of choked snort, the monster gave them one more look and beat a hasty retreat beneath the sand.

The women turned to Ricky.

Bruised and a little bit bloody, he sat, eyes closed, hands cradling his nose. For perhaps a minute he didn't move. Then he got to his feet.

"Nice job," he said.

"Never mind that," Felice cried. "Hurry! Let's get out of here."

"What do you expect me to do?" Ricky said. "I don't know how we got here to begin with."

"It was that Angry Caterpillar thing," Felice said.

Ricky smiled mockingly, in obvious disbelief. "You mean the Enraged Centipede?"

"Yeah," Sharon said. "Felice is right. Show us how to do it again and maybe we'll get out of here in one piece."

"Forgive me, ladies. It's just hard for me to take you seriously about this."

"Well, we're here aren't we?" Olivia said. "Wherever *here* may be."

Mattie nodded vehemently. "Yeah, and we were right in the middle of that special big-deal move you were showing us when we got landed here."

"It's worth a try," Felice said.

Ricky shrugged. "Okay. If it'll make you happy. Line up, ladies. After me."

He took a deep breath, then another. He cracked his knuckles, loudly.

"One, two, three," Ricky chanted, and, with a leap, began once again the steps of the Enraged Centipede. The women were right behind him, copying every move he made.

Kick. Twist. Lunge. Punch. Yell. Scissor. Wave. Pivot. Roll. Jump.

Pop!

Moira disappeared.

The others cheered.

Pop! Olivia vanished.

The air around Sharon contracted, enfolding her, lifting and carrying her, right up, away, and into the aerobics studio. She landed in a heap on the hard wooden floor. For a moment she lay there, scarcely daring to believe she was back. Finally, she opened her eyes.

Anna Marie Chow sat atop a pile of plastic steps, sipping from a can of diet soda, and staring at her. In the background, the aerobics tape continued to emit its primal beat.

Bomp-bada-bomp!

Thank all the gods of karate, Sharon thought. *Real or imaginary. I'm back. Really, really back.* She scrambled to her feet, and bounced in time to the rhythm, as, one after another, Mattie, Felice, and Ricky reappeared.

"What happened?" Anna Marie said. "Where'd you go? I blinked or something, and you were all gone. I don't understand."

"Don't worry," Felice said. "You wouldn't believe it."

Sharon nodded. "And don't try that pissed-off centipede move, either, whatever you do."

"It should be illegal," Olivia said. "I'll bet it is in California."

"Let's all keep our heart rates up," Ricky called. "Come on, everybody, stay focused. We still have time to learn one more routine."

Sharon looked at Felice. Felice looked at Moira. Moira looked at Olivia. Olivia looked at Mattie, who nodded. No one looked at Anna Marie.

As one, they advanced upon Ricky, chopping the air, lunging and kicking. "Hee-yah!" they screamed. Bounce. Thrust. Kick. Jump. Punch. Their kicks alone would have separated a healthy man's head from his body.

Ricky took one look at their faces, started to say something, thought better of it, and bolted from the room.

As the door closed behind him, the class members smiled at one another with giddy satisfaction. Moira and Mattie hugged, whooping in delight.

"We did it!" Olivia cried. "Good riddance!"

Sharon and Felice exchanged exultant high-five slaps with both hands.

But as they were toweling off, their euphoria faded. The women dressed in silence, quickly and efficiently, without looking at one another.

Felice, neat once again in her purple sweatshirt, sidled up to Sharon.

"Do you really think we should have done that?" she asked. Her blue eyes were cloudy, her expression troubled.

Sharon shrugged. "Hell, yes. Otherwise, someday he might substitute for Chuck again, and who knows where we could all end up? Better that we chase him away, now."

"But what if he goes back to wherever it was that we were and gets that terrible critter, and somehow manages to bring it back here?" Moira said.

Mattie frowned pensively. "He could. You never know. I think a fanatic like that is capable of anything."

"In that case," Sharon said, "I suggest we all adjourn to the nearest coffee bar for double low-fat cappuccinos. As soon as possible."

"Yeah," said Felice. "If he brings that monster back, let the weight lifters deal with it."

"Or their lawyers," Olivia said.

Anna Marie looked stricken. "I still don't understand what's going on."

"Never mind," Sharon told her. "Who's driving?"

I am not, by nature, an exercise fan. My idea of a good time is sitting still and watching somebody else sweat. However, I regularly (at least three times a week) abandon all common sense, pull on some turquoise spandex, and hurry down to my local aerobics studio to run slowly around the room in time to a pulsing beat.

This may be a damning admission, but there is something about the silly, superficial aerobics scene that I find compelling and even comfortable. Maybe it's the color and relentless rhythm, or the absolutely nonintellectual nature of the activities. I don't have to think. All I have to do is bop with my buddies. The ritual movements repeated en masse remind me of a line dance at a postmodern bar mitzvah. It's almost tribal. Perhaps that's another factor: friendship. The loneliness of the long-distance writer can be exorcised through exercise. Aerobics is my defense, a martial art designed to ward off the blues.

So, yes, I become God's own little goose-stepper as soon as I hear that rap beat and see a honed male body in tight purple shorts leap up to lead the class through a syncopated cancan.

I admit that I have, occasionally, encountered an instructor whom I would gladly have sent to another dimension if all it took was a couple of spins, bounces, and kicks. But that has been the exception to a mostly benign experience.

Yang down mean streets, and good men are often taken in evil times when they shall suddenly come upon them.

OOOOO

GUARDIAN ANGEL

Victor Milán

August sun turned every link of the zipper stitched into the tall young man's forehead into a white-hot branding iron. And that was as it should be. Zipperhead was cruising his urban-village domain, showing his face and claiming his place. He breathed deep, filling his lungs with the morning smells of horseshit and sewage and hot asphalt. His world was as good as it got.

Down the 900 block of Forrester near California he spotted a pair of citizens on lawn chairs in front of an apartment building that was only half–fallen in. An eleven-year-old girl with a basketball belly and walking-stick legs was dancing around in the street in front of them, calling to the passersby and tossing her burlap bag smock up over her head. She wasn't wearing anything beneath.

The drabs spotted him and the two soldiers from his Community Assistance Group, Katana and monalisa.

They yelped for the kiddo and tried to scuttle inside. Too late.

"What we got here?" Zipperhead said, giving them a big wide grin. "You ain't trying to *sell* that little girl, are you?"

The girl giggled and flashed him again. Most of her adult teeth had come and gone.

Her father was tall and kind of sunk-in, with hunted eyes. "Oh, no," he said in a rush. "That would be exploiting you as well as her."

His wife smiled at Zipperhead. She had long matted hair of indeterminate color parted in the middle to frame a big round face. She wore a pendant with a little brass cutout of Earth, and "Love Your Mother" spelled out in wire. That and her heft convinced Zipperhead that these two needed to increase their contribution to their Community.

"The truth is," she said, "Mia is so loving by nature that she has a *great deal* to share. Even with strangers."

"And nobody's *really* a stranger in Island America," the man interrupted. She gave him a glare.

"Of course," she continued, "if she shares all that love with others, it's only Communal for them to share with her, isn't it?"

Zipperhead smiled bigger. He agreed to settle for fifty percent of the take and swung on down the street. That was the cool thing about running a CAG: You weren't just above the law, you *were* the law.

He hadn't gotten far when the watch in the pocket of his leather jacket bonged. He hauled it out. It was a big shiny fob job with hands, not one of those digital things foreigners would be trying to foist on people if it weren't for the Wall Around America. He was the only Zip who could tell time by it.

"Shit," he said. "Gotta see my social worker. You two finish the tour, and don't let nobody show you attitude. Got that?" Katana and monalisa nodded, and off he went.

"What we got here?" Katana asked, emulating his boss. He took an age-wrinkled fruit baseball from a crate in the bare-dirt front yard of a ranch house and tossed it in the palm of his grubby hand.

"What the sign says," said the stoop-shouldered man in a grey undershirt that might have been white a decade or so ago. "ORANGES." Actually, the sign, hand-lettered on water-warped cardboard, read ORNJS.

monalisa gave him a slit-eyed look. "Didn't grow that in the backyard."

"Uh-*huh*." Katana mashed the fruit. Yellow pulp oozed between his fingers. "Smugglers, are we?"

The man moistened his lips with a tongue like a grub. "They just come from Delano."

"Foreigners begin the next block over," monalisa reminded him.

His wife bustled out of the house holding a sheaf of papers. "Here. We got the paperwork. Licenses, environmental impact statements, everything done up right."

Licking his fingers, Katana accepted the documents. "These don't look like they prove you're employed by a recognized, American-owned concern," he said, squinting at them upside down.

"You know what that means," monalisa said, weasel eagerness glinting in her eyes. "You're *entrepreneurs.*" It came out "enter-preeners."

"And that means," Katana said, grabbing undershirt, "we're gonna have to *mess you up* some."

Rotten fabric tore. The shirt held enough together to drag the man into range of the fist Katana cocked.

Somebody grabbed his wrist from behind.

* * *

"Bolton," Zipperhead said, breezing into the office in the fortified Courthouse Complex on Chester with his hand outstretched for five, all styling. "My *man.*"

"Sit the fuck down and shut the fuck up," his Proactive Welfare officer growled.

And that was what was uncool about running a CAG: You might be above the law, but you were never above the Man. Cherished street wisdom said the pigs couldn't put all the CAGs down: that was how they got recognized as Community Assistance Groups, whether they started as Crips, Act Up!, PETA, or Right to Life.

But if the pigs couldn't beat you, they could make you join them. Zipperhead sat the fuck down and shut the fuck up.

"Your ville's not comin' across with enough blood donations," Bolton said. "You need to do something. *Now.* I'm getting heat."

Zipperhead blinked. "What? You want me to line 'em up for the Bloodmobile?"

He could never tell whether Bolton was fat or not. Bolton had a big head with curly brown hair sweat-plastered across the bald spot—Public Servants rated AC, but his wasn't working today—and the palest skin the CAG boss had ever seen.

"Don't give a rat's ass how you do it. Hang 'em up and bleed 'em into tubs if you want. Just make sure you don't get no hep cases, and get the goods refrigerated fast."

The office was so tight Zipperhead could barely move without scraping elbows on the posters on the walls—which, like the humidity-gummed paper piles on Bolton's metal desk, he couldn't read. It hurt to think that a pig with the power of life and death over him and all his Zips should rate such a narrow little asscrack of an office.

"Look, Mr. Bolton." Didn't hurt to use grease every now and again. "I'm trying to like, *build* something with these people. They rely on me to protect 'em from CAGs without the social conscience I got, like Patriot Park. And I figure, the more they build, the more they got to share. As in, with me *and* you.''

Bolton leaned forward onto his arms. They looked like albino sausages, squeezing out of his short sleeves. The hairs on them were so pale they looked transparent.

''You could be replaced, dipshit,'' he said.

''Hey, man!'' Zipperhead exclaimed in tones of practiced outrage. ''You can't lean on me. I represent the community—the people all downtrodden and exploited by the White male–dominated system.''

''We got a culturally diverse community here, Zipperhead. Maybe you don't represent such a wide enough *spectrum,* you know? We could turn over any rock in Bakersfield and find replacements for you scurrying to get out of the light.''

Zipperhead sucked a long breath in on top of his rage, to tamp it down. He nodded, convulsively, as if his puppeteer didn't quite have the hang of controlling him.

''You want blood,'' he croaked, ''you got it. What you do with all that shit, anyway? Drink it?''

Bolton's face became a chubby fist. ''Don't crack wise with me, dickmouth.''

Zipperhead swayed back, holding up placatory palms. The social worker sighed.

''It's for the kids. You watch the teevee, don't you?''

''Oh, yes, sir. Helps formulate shared national values.''

''Yeah. We outlawed guns, weapons of all sort, even knowing how to use them. But still we get a million homicides a year, one percent of the population, thanks to smugglers and hoarders and wetbacks and other selfish elements. National Health's runnin' to keep up.''

He leaned back and stared at Zipperhead with eyes like blue marbles. ''Just make sure you do your part for all them poor bleeding kids. Or I install another zipper in your neck and forget to fucking close it.''

* * *

Katana was so astonished that he turned to face the interloper before wrenching his hand free.

The puke didn't look like much. He was maybe eight centimeters shorter than Katana, not much taller than monalisa, not much meat on his bones. He wore ratty canvas trousers with a rope belt and a jute bag vest. He was handsome in a dark way. Katana could fix that.

"You just bought yourself a ticket to the world of hurt, shitbag," Katana said. He looped a punch toward the prettyboy face.

The Assistants were seasoned gangbangers. But they weren't in combat mode. They were out to push beaten-down drabs around.

The dark kid slipped the punch. He just ducked his upper body back and then straightened, looking at Katana calm as you please.

The Zip glared. A citizen fighting back: this could not happen. It was time to put the social order back in order.

"That's it for you," he snarled, and whipped his namesake sword from the sheath across his back.

Ricky Angel glided two steps back, glancing at the young woman. She had kneed the citizen in the groin and stood with her boot on his neck, waiting to be entertained.

Ricky pulled out the two half-meter sticks, *garrotes,* he carried concealed in the leg of his trousers, held them up before him.

"You gonna fight me with a pussy-ass pair of sticks?" Katana laughed. "I have a *sword,* man. You lose."

"Maybe," Ricky said.

"*Oh,* yeah." Katana stomped forward, slashing horizontal. Ricky danced back into the street, out of the sword's gleaming arc. He dodged the return cut the same way.

His sandaled foot came down on a chunk of cement

crumbled from the curb. His ankle twisted. He dropped to one knee.

Howling triumph, Katana charged, sword upraised for a two-hand killing stroke. As the blade whistled down Ricky's right-hand stick stuck its side with a clack. It pushed the blade a fraction off-line and slipped behind it, guiding it in a harmless rush past Ricky's shoulder to embed itself in sun-softened asphalt.

Katana had put everything he had into the blow. When it didn't connect he overbalanced. Ricky's left stick slammed backhand against the base of his skull, aiding his forward progress. He hit blacktop with his face, lay still.

Laziness and desire to be amused had kept monalisa out of the fight, not fair play. It took a beat to register that the impossible had happened: this skinny-ass kid had put Katana on his snout with his sticks. Then she unlimbered twin knives in glittering brass butterfly spins, just to show the shit what he was up against.

"Don't you know it's illegal for a citizen to bear arms, shitbag?" she asked.

"I can't afford a shirt with sleeves," Ricky said.

She scowled, not getting the joke. She had shiny steel studs inset in a diamond pattern in one cheek. She advanced, holding the left knife withdrawn, the right weaving before her, cobralike. That was supposed to intimidate him, he guessed.

He'd felt concern when she produced the knives; *balisongs* were used in his own art, *escrima,* though he'd never practiced with one himself. Camp security had been good enough to keep metal weapons out of the prisoners' hands, if not much else. If there was one thing that worked in Island America, at least outside the air-conditioned pillboxes in which the Public Servants devoted selfless lives to the community, it was metal detectors.

But her opening twirls, however fancy, had been mere

juggling. Her moves betrayed her as just another street slasher.

That didn't mean he was safe. She'd obviously cut people with those knives before. She sliced air in curlicues. Sun glittered on a blade that was the only clean thing about her.

"*Draw the fangs,*" *Guro* had told him, "*and the snake cannot bite.*"

He slide-stepped toward her. Her hand flicked for his throat. He sidestepped outside the cut and brought his right stick whistling down. It cracked across the backs of fingers. The knife fell with a ringing sound, skittered across the hot blacktop like a frightened animal.

—He was caught from behind in a sudden full nelson. "Cut the fucker." Foul breath hissed hot on his neck. "*Cut* him."

Shaking her wounded hand, monalisa stalked forward. "You want his balls for earrings?"

"Cut off his dick," Katana said, "so I can shove it up his—"

Ricky couldn't get much power, clapping the sticks simultaneously against his attacker's temples. But the supple strength countless hours of twirling exercises had given his wrists served to generate some speed. Katana yowled, relaxed his grasp.

Ricky held arms straight over his head and dropped. Cement impact on his coccyx sent sparks shooting red up his spine and into his brain.

monalisa's remaining knife flashed for his face. Rattan sticks whined to converge on the hand that held it.

monalisa screamed and dropped the knife. Ricky jumped up, wheeling. Katana had a right-hand haymaker bound for his head. Ricky rapped the inside of his forearm with the stick in his left hand, what *escrimadores* called the "alive" hand. His right stick backed up the block, striking the inside of the Community Assistant's elbow.

Rebound energy helped Ricky snap the *garrote* into Katana's face and break his nose.

Katana sat down and began to scream and bleed through his fingers. "You son of a bitch!" monalisa raged. "You busted my hands!"

Ricky grinned. He advanced on her, twirling his sticks in a fluid double-*sinawalli* to weave sinister butterfly wings to either side of him.

"Leave," he suggested.

monalisa grabbed her fellow Community Assistant by the back of his jacket with her right hand, which wasn't really broken. The two went pelting off down the street in the loose-jointed scramble of the shit-scared.

Ricky's brain did a sudden buck-and-wing. He sat down hard on the curb. It was his first real fight since *Guro* Santistevan had begun training him. And he'd actually won.

The two householders were all over Ricky, hugging him, calling him their hero.

He wondered if that was true.

"He's bad karma," Mia's mother said. "Bad news. Anyway, it's our communal duty to turn him in. He's *violent*."

The thirty-odd residents of Forrester 900 had gathered in the fetid dimness of the ville's Community Hall, which had been somebody's house before the Feds communitized it. There was graffiti on the walls and human shit in the corner; since nobody owned it, there was nobody to look out for it. But it served.

Even Cardboard Katie was there, sitting well to the side with her knees drawn up. A purple H was tattooed on one sunken cheek to show she had Hepatitis E. The government TV, which was all the teevee there was, said Hep E wasn't infectious. The government always told the truth. Just the same, people stayed clear.

"You just want to suck up to the Zips because they're

protecting your scam now," said a bowlegged man with a balding head and a dark beard. "Nobody'll dare shop you for peddling your little girl's butt."

"Zipperhead takes an interest in our community," Mia's dad said defensively. "We could have a worse Chief Assistant looking after us."

"How could it be worse?" asked the man who'd been selling oranges. His name was Jason. His wife was Tracy. "His goons beat us up and steal what little we've got."

Boss of the ville was Tolson. He was a dusty freckled man with faded carrot hair, from whom body fat and hope had long been burned. He had the air of a man who knows that the only change is for the worse.

He rubbed his chin and nodded. "Fact is, Zipperhead doesn't seem to be keeping control too well."

"You can't be thinking of letting that horrid young creature stay!!!" Mia's mother exclaimed. "What about our communal duty?"

"I'm block chairman, all legal and official," Tolson said, giving her a hard eye. "I decide what's duty and what's diddly."

He rubbed the bristle on his cheek. "Might be a nice change to have somebody fighting for *us,* rather'n just to keep hold of his turf."

"We can't risk—" Mia's father began.

"We can always turn him over to the proper authorities," Tolson said, "if things don't work out."

Tracy scrubbed her hands nervously in her skirt. "How will we get him to stay?"

"Fortunately, we got something better than eleven-year-olds on tap." Tolson turned his head and yelled, "Patty, front and center!"

A young woman with lank blond hair slunk in. She was pretty in an undernourished way. Her blue eyes were big, if not bright. She wore ragged cast-off cutoffs faded white and a greyed man's undershirt; small, pointed breasts showed a tendency to poke unheeded out the armholes. The men eyed her with frank hunger. She ignored them.

"Girl," the block chairman said, "time to serve your neighborhood."

The dull eyes got narrow and crafty. "What?"

"You know the stranger kid just blew in, sent a couple Zips packing?"

"Yeah, He's kinda cute. What about him?"

Tolson laid a hand on her shoulder. "You gotta make sure he wants to stick around."

Her face clenched. "*Dad!* Why do *I* have to do it?"

"Cause I don't think I'm his type, girl. He ain't wearing Flaming Faggot colors."

She knotted her arms across her sternum and turned away. "This is sexual exploitation. You could go to jail."

"Yeah," Tolson said with a grin that seemed to start slipping off his face the instant it appeared. "And they'd turn you over to the Twisted Sisters for consciousness-raising."

He grabbed her cheeks with one hardscrabble hand, made her face him. "And you know what the Sister's say? They'd say that pretty little face was an enticement to men an' a betrayal of your gender. And they'd take care of *that* in a hurry."

She jerked away. "All right. But he better be clean."

Tolson laughed. "I'd say he's cleaner than you, hon. Boy looks like he's been in the Camps. You get sick there, you don't last long."

The smell of human sweat just managed to make itself known above the syrupy stench of old grease and mildewed cloth that filled Tolson's garage. Lying on his back on a lumpy mattress with the buttons poking into his back, Ricky gazed drowsily at the nude form beside him, upturned buttocks zebra-striped by silver bars of moonlight dropped between the slats nailed over the window, and decided he liked this hero business.

He didn't have much by way of role models. TV heroes were kids or pastel animals who sniffed out hoarders and sinister foreigners nonviolently and turned them over to smiling Public Servants for their attitudes benignly to be adjusted. That didn't square with any reality Ricky knew, street or Camp.

"*You're* juramentado, *now, boy,*" his teacher had told him, the night before he died under the guards' lasers. "*A man on a mission.*"

"*What kind of mission?*"

"*To free the people.*"

Ricky couldn't quite grasp that. "*How do I do that,* Guro?"

Guro Santistevan sat in the blacked-out barracks gazing at him, wise, brown, and wizened. He grinned through his perpetual cloud of illegal cigarette smoke. "*First, free yourself.*"

It was all the old man would tell him.

It seemed to Ricky that *Guro* had freed him, distracting the guards while Ricky eeled through the miniature arroyo eroded beneath the wire. That meant he could get on with the rest of his mission. Once he figured out exactly how.

He kept his grief for the old man bottled within, not knowing where to put it. It was not the only such bottle on the shelves of his spirit.

Bakersfield was the nearest concentration of people who might need freeing. He walked in from the south, paralleling 99, dodging government work gangs out either repairing the road or tearing it up, depending whether they came from Infrastructure or EPA. He didn't have the internal passport to let him ride on one of the steam-powered public buses that occasionally rumbled by, belching smoke from their stacks, and the farmers riding in horse-drawn wagons made from halves of long-defunct cars refused to so much as look at him when he tried to flag them down for a ride with their bug- and bird-chewed produce.

Mainly he tried to stay out of sight. He was a fugitive from justice, and he risked being taken for a foreigner. Dark, lean, and not real big, he could pass for Anglo or Chicano, but he was mostly Filipino, like so many in the Agro Camps. Racism was illegal, but suspicion of foreigners was mandatory. They might be import-pushers or wetback job-grabbers—though in his seventeen years Ricky had never met anyone who'd crossed the ten-meter Wall which surrounded the entire continental United States, legally or otherwise.

Also, trashing Asians was a culturally correct expression of rage for Black CAGs. He had to be careful.

But when he saw the spiky kids about to pound the citizens, his sense of mission kicked in.

He gazed at Patty, who slept drooling onto her rag bundle pillow, and felt the pangs of puppy love. He felt something else, too. He put a fingertip between her shoulder blades, ran it with the slow fascination of the recent virgin down her spine. When he reached her tailbone, she stirred, murmured something half-drowsy and half-peevish, and rolled over to give him another installment on his reward.

Screams woke him. He jumped up to see orange light dancing on the wall of the house next door to Tolson's.

"Shit!"

A rooster crowed hysterically. Ricky leaped up, stumbled over Patty as she started to sit up, grabbed his pants and tried to climb into them. They stuck at half-mast. He hopped around with one leg stuck out before him, his heart jumping around in his chest like a frightened frog. "Shit, shit, *shit.*"

"Whassamatter?" Patty inquired sleepily. He finally

got his pants on. She draped her moth-holed blanket over her shoulders and followed him out into the night.

Jason and Tracy's place was all lit up like a Public Servant's digs for a party. Of course, as citizens, the couple didn't rate electricity for light or heat.

What they did rate was fire. They had a lot of that. If you looked real close through the picture windows, whose cardboard-and-plywood covering had already been eaten out by the blaze, you could see them in there in the midst of it, hanging head down from the ceiling. Rich barbecue smell filled the air. Guilt slapped Ricky for salivating.

"It was Zipperhead and his people," said Cardboard Katie, standing apart from the crowd before the burning house. "I saw it all."

Tolson's scrowled and scratched his bare chest. "Why didn't you warn somebody?"

"I got scared and hid."

Ricky felt eyes on him. "You were supposed to *protect* us!" somebody yelled. Another somebody made a snorting sound, spat. Something wet hit Ricky's cheek.

"Some fucking hero."

But now he wasn't a hero at all. He was a scared seventeen-year-old adding his dinner of beans, tortillas, and half-ripe backyard tomatoes to the refuse already crowding the gutter. An overwhelming sense of failure and loss gaped inside him like an unbridgeable chasm.

He turned and raced back to Tolson's garage. Jeers pelted his bare brown shoulders like stones.

The hero business wasn't turning out like he'd planned. He had not protected anyone. He'd screwed and slept while they got killed.

But anger had begun to consume his shame. Anger and determination.

They'd see he was a hero after all.

* * *

Zipperhead didn't rate a fancy base like a former shopping mall or the old Metro Recreation Center; his Zips weren't many or mean enough. He had to make do with the husk of a Von's supermarket, sickened by regulations that proliferated and mutated by the hour like some demon retrovirus, killed off by the collapse of the nation's transportation/distribution system, and looted bare long before Zipperhead or any of his minions were born. Tolson had told Ricky where to find it that night over dinner. It wasn't a secret; Zipperhead kept an open door, he claimed, so his people would feel free to come to him with their problems.

The Zips had had a good night. The dozen who accompanied Zipperhead on his little errand had gotten to hurt some people. They were wired and wanting to talk about it. The envious rest wanted to hear. Booze, chocolate, tobacco, and other proscribed substances were consumed in abundance around oil drum fires in the parking lot.

All those mind alterants didn't help anyone's alertness. Neither did gazing into fires improve night vision. Ricky ghosted past on callused soles, flowing with the rhythms of the party, moving in darkness when the raucous talk and laughter peaked, freezing when it ebbed.

The guards in back of the store were busy watching the action out front and loudly resenting that they couldn't partake. Ricky slipped past them too.

The solid metal rear door had long been scavenged for scrap. The CAG had nailed scrap wood over the opening. It wouldn't keep out a serious intruder, but was impossible to get through quietly.

Ricky didn't try. Behind the supermarket a half-height cinder block wall had been built to screen the Dumpster from view. It was taller than Ricky. He jumped, pulled himself up onto it.

Breathing hard, he stood, balanced, gathered himself and leaped. His fingers caught the roof edge. Grit rasped fingertips as he began to slide backward. He moaned and flung himself over the parapet by sheer force of will.

He lay gasping, winded not so much by exertion as the conviction he had made too much noise. He listened to his breathing and the hearty partying from out front. No change in its tone, no shouts of alarm.

He scrambled across the roof in a monkey crouch. The rooftop cooling unit had gone the way of the back door. This hole was covered with a sheet of black mylar, cross-linked to brittleness by the sun, held down by a random scatter of two-by-fours and cinder blocks. Lower lip gripped in teeth, Ricky eased the blockage away.

His veins ran with fire. Rage and fear and the need to rush headlong into a future he could no longer stand to anticipate made him vibrate like a fresh-struck tuning fork.

But neither could he stand to fail again. If he rushed, if he made too much racket, if he overbalanced and went tumbling down to bust his leg, he could never atone for failing to protect the ville. To work deliberately took all the discipline acquired in endless illicit sessions in the fields, the willpower to practice twirling and footwork and *sinawalli* when too much work on too little food had already pushed him past the point of exhaustion.

Guro Santistevan had never threatened him to get him to keep at it, never cajoled him. He just stood watching. *''You wanna quit anytime, boy, you go ahead. The choice is yours. The road of* escrima *ain't easy to walk, and there's never any guarantees.''*

Maybe that was why Ricky found the will to continue. He had lacked control over almost all his life, he was literally the property of a State-owned plantation, but *Guro* offered the chance to do something for *himself.* Ricky could surrender, get with the program the caring State held forth, forgoing individuality and striving and care. Or he could face the terrifying risks of choice.

He had chosen to choose. Now he forced himself to live with its consequences.

He cleared an opening sufficient for his frame. He slipped over the edge and down into blackness.

Zipperhead occupied what had been the manager's office. As was customary for CAG bosses he stuffed it with a magpie hoard of the finer loot trolled in by his minions: the gaudiest and least age-stiffened clothing, pillows with still some softness to them, knickknacks. His passion was toys: miniature cars and trucks and planes, action figures, even dolls. Most were antiques; their production, sale, and even possession had long been outlawed, as promoting violence, as promoting stereotypes, as promoting the selfishness of play. His troops had only been upholding the law when they confiscated them.

Sometimes, with the door locked and his squeeze of the moment sent packing, he liked to take them down from the warped shelves and pretend that they were real people, real vehicles. He made them act out little scenes from his mind. At such times he felt calm, remote from his own pain.

He came awake feeling hardness poking into the base of his throat and the warmth of human presence pressing unmistakably down on him. In the dark his toys' faces were ghostly blobs.

"Whoever you are," he said calmly, sitting up against the pressure, "you've picked an uncomfortable way to die."

"Maybe," Ricky Angel said, letting him rise.

"What do you want?"

Ricky blinked in darkness. He had grown up with little exposure to toys. Being surrounded by tiny humanoid figures was prickling the hairs on the back of his neck. Zipperhead's question took him aback; he'd expected the CAG boss to demand his identity first. But Zipperhead kept his eye on the bottom line.

"To kill you," Ricky said. That sounded inadequate. "For the people in the ville."

"But you didn't kill me," the CAG boss said, scooting backward. Ricky didn't try to stop him. "You're talking instead. What's the matter? Not feeling so sure of yourself?"

"Why didn't you kill me?" Ricky asked.

"So you're the vigilante punk the drabs sweet-talked into taking the heat for them." Zipperhead chuckled. "I wanted to show 'em you didn't *count,* boy."

Ricky's cheeks burned like a sheet tin roof in the south California sun. "Stand up," he hissed.

"Why? Afraid to off me sitting down? Or do you just want to be able to tell yourself it wasn't murder?"

"You murdered those people. You're the criminal."

"*They* were the criminals, kid. I'm the law."

"Then the law sucks."

Zipperhead laughed hugely. "No. The law is great. It lets people like me exist. It gives me *scope,* man. Maybe someday I'll be a Public Servant, get blow jobs in the back of my air-conditioned limo, taste *real* power runnin' wild in my veins."

"Never happen," Ricky said. "You're just property to them, just another renewable resource. You're as big a fucking victim as those people you torched tonight."

Zipperhead launched himself at Ricky's legs. Taken by surprise, Ricky sprang reflexively back out the door into the open receiving area. The CAG boss caught him by the shins, slammed him down so hard the back of his head bounced off the pavement and filled his brain with a brief spark maelstrom.

But Zipperhead had not caught enough of him to pin with greater mass and strength. Ricky kicked blind. His foot connected with yielding solidity. Zipperhead grunted. His grip loosened.

Ricky came to his feet weaving sticks *sinawalli* before him and beneath his arms in interlinking figures of eight.

Just enough light bled in from outside to let him see the big man standing light on the balls of his feet. He had been sleeping in boots, trousers, and dark undershirt.

Zipperhead crouched, hiking up the legs of his pants. Ricky lunged, but Zipperhead snapped back erect with knives twirling in his hands, deft as an *escrimador*.

He settled into a shallow boxerlike stance not much different from Ricky's, left leg advanced. That probably meant he was right-handed; unlike *escrimadores*, most fighters kept their weak hands forward. His weapons were bowie knives with twenty-five-centimeter blades. He held them reversed, blades along forearms, metal pommels to.

Guro Santistevan had told him fighters who held their knives so were either fools or very, very good. Ricky reckoned Zipperhead held rank by fighting skill—his conversation showed surprising intelligence, but Ricky doubted intellect cut much ice with the savage kids who ruled the streets as viceroys of the welfare state.

Zipperhead began to circle. Ricky pivoted to face him, watchful lest the bigger man try to crowd him against a wall or some obstruction. *Guro's* teachings emphasized the defensive, first as a moral posture—he was supposed never to be the aggressor, which gave him a twinge—and also as tactics. *More fights are lost than won, boy, Guro* liked to say. *Give the other dude the chance to lose first.*

Ricky tried to focus. Long training had done much to keep the fight-or-flight reflex, that hot red adrenaline rush, from turning him into an animal in combat. But his mind was spinning free, trying to assimilate more than he could. . . .

Zipperhead cut right-handed at his eyes. Ricky snapped a *garrote* for his knuckles, following with the other in case his counterstroke missed. The riposte struck blade; Zipperhead had rotated his wrist inward to block.

Ricky snapped his alive stick against the blade to control it momentarily—freeing his right to parry the left-hand slash to the belly Zipperhead already had in motion. Another clatter of rattan on steel, and each fell back a step.

"Not bad," Zipperhead said. "But my kids warned me you go for the hands, stickfighter."

Ricky watched him, waiting. It occurred to him that his opponent had centimeters of reach and at least fifteen kilos on him. Worse, torchlight and startled voices flared from the front of the store. Community Assistants began to pour in.

Zipperhead smiled ruefully. "Got me on the spot, kid," he said. "I can't order my people to take you down without losing face. So I gotta do you myself."

He launched a whirling attack, left and right, striking high, not extending far enough to permit Ricky a hand shot or a trap. It was all Ricky could do to keep blocking without being overwhelmed.

Zipperhead kicked him in the crotch.

Ricky just managed to twist hips and take the shot on a buttock. The thrust-kick threw him sprawling back into a pile of decaying boxes stuffed with shabby plunder.

Zipperhead loomed over him. He didn't drop to grapple, or bend down with his knives. He kicked Ricky in the side with brutal simplicity.

Ricky gasped. Pain like a stab wound shot through him. The boot had broken ribs.

"Stomp him, Zipperhead!" the boys and girls were yelling. Grinning joylessly, Zipperhead raised his foot to do just that.

Ricky made an X of his sticks, thrust upward to catch the raised boot in its fork. He put his left foot beside Zipperhead's down ankle, crossed right leg over left, and scissored fiercely.

Zipperhead toppled sideways. He tucked a shoulder, rolled, came up with ready knives.

Ricky was already on his feet, trying not to hunch too

much around the pain. *Guru* used to whack him at random, stinging-hard with his *garrote*, to teach him to control the fight/flight impulse, and that pain wouldn't kill him. He could endure, though each breath was a spear in his side.

"Finish him, Zipperhead!" the Community Assistants yelled. "Show us some blood."

"First lesson in leadership," Zipperhead told him. "Give the people what they want."

He charged, reversed blades spinning like dust devils.

Ricky parried left hand to right, moved *into* Zipperhead, past him to his left, jamming the left-handed stroke before it could develop power. He slid his right stick over Zipperhead's arm, around, beneath, out between blade and wrist. "*Snake draws the fangs,*" *Guro* called this maneuver.

He followed stick with hand, spiraling the *garrote* around Zipperhead's arm, keeping Zipperhead's powerful body between him and the other knife. A twist, and the stick's leverage popped the bowie free.

Zipperhead bellowed outrage and surprise, reversed grip on his other blade and hooked it towards Rick's ribs. Ricky blocked it with left stick held vertical, cracked the other hard against the CAG leader's wrist. A second knife sang desolation on cement.

Zipperhead's elbow smashed into Ricky's temple.

Ricky had forgotten that while an *escrimador*'s first tactic was the disarm, he always fought the man, not the weapon. Stunned, half-blind, he got his sticks in front of his face. Zipperhead slammed a knee roundhouse into already-broken ribs.

Ricky sagged. Zipperhead crowded between his *garrotes*, piling blows into him with fists and elbows. Feebly, Ricky tried to defend. The CAG leader got a foot behind his and swept him to the floor.

Zipperhead dropped astride him. He slugged Ricky in

the face, knocked the sticks from his hands. Then he locked fists around Ricky's throat and began to strangle him.

Ricky clawed at relentless hands, trying to pry loose a finger to break. Zipperhead had them tucked between Ricky's neck and concrete, impossible to get.

This isn't how it's supposed to end, Ricky thought as the circle of hooting firelit faces began to revolve around him. *I'm supposed to be a hero. I can't die like this.*

He saw *Guro's* calm brown face again, wreathed in smoke and a sardonic smile. *Being a hero's not easy like you thought, is it,* hijo?

He felt his eyes start from their sockets. His chest was about to implode from sucking for air that would not come.

I've lost my sticks! he thought wildly.

An escrimador *fights with what's to hand*, came the response in his mind. The old man took a drag on his outlaw smoke. *And weapons are where you find them, you know?*

Ricky stared at his opponent. The big face was set in a grin of demonic determination. Sweat sheened the high forehead, glinted in torchlight like rubies set into the shiny silver zipper.

Ricky reached up and grabbed the zipper. With the strength of hysteria he tore it out of the CAG leader's head.

Blood cascaded over both their faces. Zipperhead reared back screaming. He didn't let go, but Ricky worked his left little finger up and broke it. The sound was like a twig snapping. Even in his madness of fear and sudden hope it sickened Ricky.

He slithered out from between Zipperhead's legs, skittered quadruped across the floor. Zipperhead came after, face a crimson mask that seemed to snarl through two mouths. His good hand caught Ricky's belt from behind.

Ricky spun and jammed one of the dropped bowies to the hilt in Zipperhead's belly, just above the belt.

Zipperhead howled and clutched himself. Not having been exposed to action movies and teevee shows, Ricky had no expectation that a single stab wound, however severe, would down a man; he knew better firsthand. He instantly began casting about for another weapon. He saw one of his *garrotes* lying in shadow dance by a wall, dived for it, snatched it up.

When he turned Zipperhead hung over him like a skyscraper, arms outspread, knife hilt jutting from him like a mutant phallus, as if he were intent on rape.

Screaming, Ricky rammed the tip of his stick into the CAG leader's throat.

The cartilage of Zipperhead's trachea buckled into his airway. He reeled back holding his ruined throat. Charged silence filled the store.

He tried to speak, through lips going blue, from a face that had begun to go black beneath the red. Cautiously, *garrote* at the ready, Ricky approached.

Zipperhead could produce no sound. But it seemed to Ricky his lips shaped the words, *I thought I could change the world, too.*

The struggle to stay upright overpowered the big man. He fell heavily, lay writhing on his back, kicking at blood-slimed cement with his heels.

Ricky caught the glimmer of the other knife by the boxes he'd been kicked into. Keeping wary distance from the spectator circle, he retrieved it and his second stick.

He slashed Zipperhead's throat. It seemed a kinder death than choking. He could not make himself look into the pale eyes as he cut.

He let the knife fall, stood facing the Zips, ready to bolt or go berserk, as circumstances warranted. The Community Assistants looked at each other.

"I guess that's it," one said. "What do you want us to do?"

It took a moment for Ricky, dazed with adrenaline aftermath and the experience of taking life for the first time, to realize the boy was talking to him. "What?" he asked, thick-tongued.

"You beat Zipperhead. You're our leader now."

"You got the power," a girl said, smiling invitation.

Power. It opened to him like a beautiful vista to a traveler cresting a hill: his own young army, ready-made to carry out the mission *Guro* had laid upon him. The power to reform—the power to change the world.

Then he looked at Zipperhead, lying at his feet in a pool of blood and the stink of his own shit. He heard the last words Zipperhead could not voice.

Vision turned to a glimpse down Abyss, a bottomless blackness—and that blackness was his soul.

He tried to say, "no," but sour vomit filled his mouth and slopped over his lip. He stumbled through the silent expectant circle and out into the darkness. No one tried to stop him.

He spent the night huddled somewhere dark and close. By chance no CAGs or ravers or police found him. He returned to the ville with grey dawn curdling the air around him.

At some preconscious level he was expecting the people to turn out and give him a hero's welcome. He had fought for them and triumphed and slain the evil. What it had cost him, he reckoned, was the price of playing the hero.

Indeed they were all turned out when he strode onto the block. But not to greet him. The residents of Forrester 900 lay along the sidewalks, pallid, graceless, and dead.

As if through half-congealed air, he moved from body to body. Mia's parents lay side by side, and next to them Mia herself. Tolson, bare-chested still, head gone from the jaw up: a laser had flash-boiled his brain fluids and exploded his skull. Patty—he turned away and dry-heaved in the gutter.

Their hands had been secured behind their backs by

quick professional twists of blue polymer tape. Some's throats had been slit; others showed no sign of violence but bruises on their arms, just inside the elbow. All looked unnaturally pale, and little blood had puddled beneath them.

"You came back."

He wheeled, sticks in hand. Cardboard Katie stood there in her ragged foul smock, sunken eyes big and round as pits.

"What—?" Words solidified in his throat.

"Bloodmobile." Lips writhed in what might have been a sardonic smile. "Guess Welfare figured them poor hurt kids needed the blood more than *they* did."

"What do you mean?"

"Badges came, herded 'em all into trucks, bled 'em out."

"*Why?*"

"Maybe somebody ratted 'em off about you. Maybe Welfare figured it was time we sacrificed more for the good of the community." She shook her head. "Didn't have nothin' else *left* to give."

"Why didn't they take you?"

She touched her tattoo. "Hep. Injured kids don't need no tainted blood."

"Why—" He raised helpless hands. "Why didn't they *do* something? Why didn't they fight?"

"That's what they had you for, to do their fighting for 'em. Time came, they never raised a hand."

Black emptiness welled out through his pores to envelop him. *They relied on me, and I let them down again. . . .*

Then anger exploded from his core like a magnesium flare. *I didn't let them down! I was fighting for them, while they were submitting like so many sheep to the knife.*

"I couldn't protect you," he raged, spending his bitterness on the dead. ''Nobody could. Not when you wouldn't do anything for your own damn *selves.*''

He recalled, then, another thing *Guro* had told him: *Give a man a fish, you feed him one day only. Teach the man to fish, you feed him all his life.*

He had tried to give to the people, as he had been indoctrinated to throughout his life. What he had to give them had been spilled and wasted, spent on nothing—like the blood he let out of Zipperhead.

He looked at Cardboard Katie. She shrank from his expression. He nodded farewell. He had no more words inside.

Never again, he told himself. He turned his back on the sun, the dead, and heroic dreams, and walked on into the city's ruined heart.

I'd call this piece ''sociological SF,'' or ''political-science fiction;'' there's no techno-wow stuff in it, but it is still SF.

It's become a cliché that SF writers are not in the business of predicting the future. And I don't literally expect the future depicted here to come true. But given the current mood of bipartisan feelgood immigrant-bashing—what we used to call ''racism''—and calls for ''economic nationalism,'' we're headed toward it at warp speed, withal.

I study tae kwon do in the basement of the police station. My instructor is a homicide detective. Gives you an interesting slant on the arts.

One time more, the smiling face.

OOOOO

SHAPESHIFTER FINALS
a short story

Jeffrey A. Carver

The crowd roared as the first pair of wrestlers engaged in competition out on the center mat. "*Awwriiiiii-choooo-guyyyys!*" "*HUGGA-HUGGA-HUGGA-HUGGA!*" "*Wickety - (psicry!) - wickety - (psicry!) - wickety - (psicry!)*" Hog Donovan peeked over in the direction of the match, but tried not to get drawn into watching it. Neither of the contestants in the ninety-three-pound class was human, and better he should keep his mind on his own upcoming match.

"*Gaaiiee! Gaaiiee!*" "*Brackit-it-it-it-it-it-it-it-it!*" "*Wheeeooop-ooop-ooop!*" The assortment of cries from the stands was damned disconcerting, the crowd being over half extraterrestrials. It was the opening bout, finals round, in the 57,463rd Annual Games of the IntraGalactic Interworld Multicultural Amateur Wrestling League—and the first games ever to be hosted by Earth. Hog Donovan prayed that the human fans could drown out all the

ETs when he got to the mat himself. He was as nervous as a laboratory rat on speed, and he was going to need all the psychological boost he could get.

Hog paced the warmup area in his tights and warmup jacket, trying to still the butterflies in his stomach. It would be at least forty minutes yet before they called him to the mat, for the 138-pound finals. An eternity! Hog threw himself into his warmup exercises and tried to blank out everything else.

Bye-bye baby, baby bye-bye . . . The refrain of a popular song repeated mercilessly in his head, warring with the cheers of the crowd.

Hog grunted, working up a good sweat. Hog indeed! He was long and whiplike, and bore his nickname only because his old heavyweight friend, Hermie "Harmin' " Harmon, had dubbed him "Hog" in retribution for his jokes about Harmon's rhinolike neck. Those were the old days, but the name had stuck.

The crowd roared, and Hog was startled to realize that the first match was over—the victor a mercurial-skinned creature from Tau Ceti. The next weight class was up, and—hey!—this was the only other human finalist, a wiry little Brit named Johnnie Johnson, up against some sort of centipede from the Vega asteroids.

Hog ducked through to the sidelines to yell encouragement. "*Give 'im hell, Johnnie!*" he hollered as the Earthman trotted onto the mat. His voice was drowned out by a loud buzzing. Up in the stands, a large contingent of centipede fans were rubbing their upper limbs together, en masse, cheering on their fellow Vegan.

Hog suppressed a shudder as he watched Johnnie engage the centipede from a standing position. All those *legs*. And they were so . . . insectlike. And quick. With a chitter and a blur of speed, the centipede caught Johnnie's left ankle with several of its legs, and tripped him for a two-point takedown. The crowd buzzed in appreciation.

"*Get up! Keep moving!*" Hog yelled.

Tap tap. Hog started at the rap on the top of his head, and turned to see Coach Tagget urging him away from the sidelines. "But Coach—"

"Hog, go warm up. Don't fret over Johnnie, you're just scaring yourself." Tagget rapped him on the skull again. "Don't forget—"

"I know, I know, the brain is the most important muscle," Hog repeated by rote, as he turned back to the warmup area.

"*Think* about your match. *Think,*" Coach Tagget urged, as Hog resumed his stretches. After a moment, satisfied with Hog's progress, the coach left to go watch Johnnie himself.

Think, right. Think about the fact that he was about to wrestle an alien named Belduki-Elikitango-Hardart-Colloidisan, an Ektra shapechanger capable of assuming about a thousand different multiworld multicultural body configurations. He was thinking about it, all right. And he was having trouble keeping his knees from shaking.

Bye-bye baby, baby bye-bye . . .

He remembered how smug the Earth promoters had been when the IIMAWL rules committee had offered to make terran rules the norm for this tournament, in honor of the hosting world. Of course, none of the promoters had even *thought* about the fact that Earth's wrestlers would be competing against sentient bugs, snakes, gorillas . . . and shapeshifters . . . except that they'd finally decreed a return to the more modest, and protective, tights in place of skimpy singlets. In other respects, the referees' interpretation of Earth's rules had turned out to be a tad subjective, to say the least.

"*Johnnie—NO!*"

The single shout from the Brit's coach was drowned out by a rising buzz from the crowd. Hog jumped up, trying to see what was happening. The centipede buzz crescendoed. Hog ducked through an opening in the sidelines crowd to get a better view.

Uh-oh. Johnnie was in big trouble. The centipede had him halfway onto his back, with about six legs pushing his shoulders toward the mat. Hog knelt on the sidelines, twisting and arching sympathetically as Johnnie struggled against the inexorable leverage of all those limbs. Johnnie's coach, a wiry little man, was screaming, "*Scoot out! Scoot out!*" and making futile sweeping gestures with his arms.

Hog cupped his hands and screamed, "*PULL HIS ANTENNAS! PULL HIS ANTENNAS!*"

The match seemed to freeze abruptly, as the centipede cocked its head and glared across the mat at Hog with all four eyes. Its hairy antennas bristled. Hog gulped, regretting his impulsive yell. The thing looked as if it might just abandon the match and come on over and stomp him for his remark. It appeared to have completely forgotten its opponent.

Johnnie seized the opportunity. For an instant, it looked as though he might actually grab the thing's antennas—which would have been a definite foul—but instead, Johnnie managed to get an elbow inside the thing's legs and knock out several locked joints, loosening the centipede's grip. The crowd buzzed, and the centipede turned back to its opponent, but Johnnie was already wriggling quickly out of its arms.

"*That's it! That's it! That's it!*" screamed the coach, waving wildly.

Johnnie was frantically trying to complete his escape. He had one leg out now and was up on the other knee. The human crowd was screaming.

The centipede spasmed with rage and tackled Johnnie with a dozen legs. They fell together to the mat with a *whump,* knocking the breath out of Johnnie. Before Hog could even rise up on his toes to yell, Johnnie was on his back under the centipede, the ref was down on five elbows, peering to see if shoulder blades were touching the mat, and—*slap! tweeeeeeeet!*—just like that, Johnnie was pinned and the match was over.

The centipede humped its back and drew away from its human opponent, chittering triumphantly. Johnnie sat up, gasping. The centipede crowd went crazy rubbing their limbs.

Hog caught Coach Tagget's eye and turned away, sighing, to return to the warmup area. Johnnie had finished in second place. That meant the honor of Earth, wrestling-wise, rested on Hog. He swallowed, trying not to think about it. But how *could* he not think about it? He was the only human left in the finals. All eyes, and cameras, would be on him.

As he was stretching his hamstrings, Johnnie walked past, shaking his head. "Tough luck," Hog sympathized.

The Englishman paused, peering at him with dazed eyes. "Are you the bloke who got that thing as mad as a raving hornet?"

"I—well—" Hog spread his hands. "I was just cheering for you. You almost made it out, too. Sorry you didn't—"

"You know what those bastards *smell* like, when they're on top of you and they're mad?" Johnnie wheezed. "Cheeeeeeez-z-z," he whispered hoarsely. "That was what damn near killed me." Johnnie shook his head and wandered off toward the clutches of the TV interviewers. "It wasn't the bloody pin . . ."

Hog saw Johnnie's coach staring darkly in his direction. He went back to his warmups. Stretch left, stretch right, down, up . . .

"*Heyyaaah, earthman krrreeepy-krrreeepy—*"

Hog turned, wrinkling his nose at a sudden whiff of ammonia. The centipede was standing beside him, balanced on half of its legs, waving the claws on the rest of its legs in his direction. "Uh—?" Hog managed. "Can I, uh, help you?"

The centipede's antennas waved drunkenly. "*Hoho yassss,*" hissed the centipede. "*Krrreeepy-krreeepy earthman sso sssmart! Come sssee me lataaah.*" **Poot.** It made a loud spitting sound. "*Yahh-heyyy?*"

Hog backed up a step. "I don't know what you're talking about—"

The centipede chittered with laughter and sauntered away. "*Lataaaah, earthman . . .* "

Hog stared after it in disbelief. He jumped when he felt a hand on his shoulder. Then he heard the familiar sound of his coach tsk-tsking.

"Poor sportsmanship, Hog. That's all that is—poor sportsmanship. What do you expect from a centipede?" Tagget scowled at the Vegan, who was now parading in front of its fans, waving its arms in triumph. "Look, why don't you go on back to the locker room and clear your mind. I'll call you when it's time to come back out."

Hog nodded with relief. Yes. Back to the locker room. Forget centipedes. Have a swallow of honey for quick energy.

Bye-bye baby, baby bye-bye . . .

He trotted back to the locker room, shaking the tension out of his arms.

All things considered, it was actually pretty amazing that Earth had ever gotten nominated to host the IIMAWL tournament. After all, by A.D. 2008, the farthest any human had ever gotten from Earth was the Moon. But the interworld sporting federation liked to give a boost to a newly discovered worlds. And Earth was among the newest—not yet five years a part of the interworld community, since the Rigellians had landed and made first contact, and promptly proposed building factories here to employ the locals. In the eyes of the terran promoters, the tournament was not so much a sporting event per se as a promotion of tourism and general economic opportunity aimed at ETs who might want to spend money here. And in that respect, it was already successful, at least to the tune of a new sports complex for Cleveland and a good crowd of paying ET visitors.

The human wrestling world, on the other hand—the top wrestlers, the Olympic and AAU winners—had been pretty resistant to the idea, claiming that it was insane to pit oneself against aliens whose bodies were so different as to render competition meaningless. Mostly, the sportswriters echoed that position, denouncing the games as blatant sensationalism. Still, there were some good, if maybe not great, wrestlers who hadn't seen the obvious—and had wound up entering the competition that one wag, as *Time* was so fond of putting it, called the "crocodile free-for-alls."

That's the kind of wrestler Hog Donovan was: not great—but sharp, determined, and something of an iconoclast. He figured he only had a few good years of wrestling left in him, and he was determined to make the best of them. And the way to do that was to enter a competition so new, so outré, that the mainstream wrestling world hadn't caught onto it yet. And maybe, Hog figured, it would *become* recognized, and maybe it would even give *him* enough recognition so that once he'd hung up his tights and joined the working world, he wouldn't have to work on a Rigellian assembly line building Lotusflower roadsters.

Anyway, that was the reason he'd given his parents and his coach, though it was really only half the story. The other half was that he'd sacrificed and sweated blood at this sport for over seven years now, and by God, he wanted to be the best damned wrestler in the galaxy—okay, *one* of the best damned wrestlers in the galaxy—even if only for one brief, glorious moment.

To his own surprise, he'd done well, working his way through four preliminary rounds, and winning the semifinals just yesterday, narrowly besting a titanium-boned opponent with twice his strength and half his agility and intelligence. He was proud of that victory and the semiconductor medal it had assured him of, and the recognition it brought to his home planet.

But right now, he had to focus on just one thing—and that was how the hell to wrestle against an Ektra shapeshifter.

He paced in front of his locker and shook the tension out again. Peering around the corner of the lockers he saw one of the black-skinned African wrestlers warming up and he gave a collegial thumbs-up of encouragement before returning to his own spot. Wait a minute! he thought suddenly. There *aren't* any Africans in the finals.

He heard a loud *crack.* Uneasily, he peered around the corner again. The black-skinned being, which was *not* human, was separating its joints as if they were held together by rubber bands. It was pulling its right forearm out from its elbow, and dislocating its shoulder and stretching it way behind its neck. The creature grinned a gleaming grin, and Hog withdrew to his own corner, shivering. A *transformer,* he realized. Just like the toys that a kid could flex and twist until they'd changed from say, a spaceship to an atomic monster. What world was this creature from?

Don't think about it. Think about your opponent. How are you going to beat Belduki-Elikitango-Hardart-Colloidisan?

He'd only seen the shapeshifter once, briefly, in a preliminary round. "*Belduki's its name, and throttlin's its game,*" was how the *Plain Dealer* had put it, in pointed reference to its reputed predilection for near-strangulation of its opponents. That was obviously an exaggeration for effect; nevertheless, it unnerved Hog, who devoutly regarded wrestling as a gentleman's sport, safe and well regulated. He'd always scorned so called " " "professional wrestling" " " (he always mentally put several quotes around the phrase, to emphasize his disdain), in which contestants were slammed to the deck, or thrown against the ropes, or otherwise theatrically mistreated. Real wrestling wasn't like that; it was a sport of skill and conditioning and determination.

It'd come as a shock to learn that in the IIMAWL, there was not entirely the same sense of careful sportsmanship. Oh, sure, there were some protections: no contestants could emit chemicals toxic to the opponent, for instance. But with the contestants so morphically different from one another, monitoring safety was a lot harder than it was between human wrestlers. One contestant might turn blue with concentration, another with suffocation. Would a ref who heard that cracking sound of the transformer recognize it as the sound of breaking bones in a human? In the end, the IIMAWL claimed to be keeping the sport safe, but it was Hog's uneasy suspicion that they mostly threw up their hands, flippers, and toes, and said to hell with it, let's *try* to keep them from killing each other, but if a ref misreads a physiologic sign, what are we supposed to do?

Think about the Ektra, Hog thought, shooting a practice takedown in the empty space in front of his locker. *Think about the Ektra.*

The shapeshifter. Actually, he'd been more or less counting all along on Belduki-Elikitango-whatever being knocked out by Gazoom Gazoom the Indefatigable Baboon and returning champion, from Veni Five. After his own victory against Titanium Jimm, Hog had been carefully planning ways to defeat the baboon . . . ingenious ways, resourceful ways. And then the stupid baboon had gone and fallen right into the Ektra's four-armed can opener in the third period, and *boom*, right onto his back. *Slap! Tweet! (Psicry!)* The ref called the fall, and there went all of Hog's planning, out the window. And now *he* faced the shapeshifter.

Hog drew a deep breath and blew into his cupped hands. This was no good—hanging around the locker room, thinking about what could go wrong. He'd be better off out on the floor, soaking up the psychic energy of the meet. And where the hell was Coach Tagget, anyway?

Hog reached into his locker, took a long drag from his plastic honey bear, and slammed the locker shut. For just an instant, as his hand was about to close the combination padlock, he hesitated. What if he were knocked unconscious and they needed to get into his locker? Good God, man—stop it! He squeezed the lock shut with a decisive click.

As he strode up the echoing passageway to the gym, he heard shouts from the crowd and felt a surge of adrenaline. He broke into a trot, and darted past a couple of ETs who were half-blocking the end of the passageway, and jogged out toward the end of the arena.

The crowd erupted with a roar of approval. He smiled to himself, flushing with confidence, then peered over to see what they were actually cheering about.

Tweeeeeeeeet! Slap!

The 133-pound match had just ended with a pin. An alien that looked like a huge gerbil got up, shaking, from under one that looked like a leaf. The ref flagged the leaf as the winner.

And Hog was up next.

Bye-bye baby, baby . . .

Coach Tagget found him just in time to yell something incomprehensible in Hog's ear, shake his hand vigorously, and push him onto the mat with a whack on the rear. Hog shook off his irritation at the coach and stepped onto the mat with a glance at the ref.

A new referee had come out from the table, replacing the one who had just tweeted the last winner. This ref looked a little like a centaur with multijointed legs, and big paddle-shaped hands, great for slapping the mat. Good, Hog thought. The better to signal Hog Donovan winner by fall. None of this eking out a victory by points. Hog Donovan goes for the whole enchilada. Starting right now. This is for *Earth*, and this is for *Hog*. He swung his arms, huffing. Damn straight.

"You can do it, Justin! Tear his lungs out!" screamed a woman somewhere in the stands. Hog smiled a little. He couldn't pick her out of the crowd, but he knew his mother was waving her program wildly, endangering the eyesight of everyone within reach. His father was just as avid a fan, but he'd be too busy with the fastcam to spend much time yelling.

A blast of easy listening music filled the gymnasium from somewhere overhead—a sampler of Earth culture to entertain the ET crowd.

Hog's opponent streamed onto the mat from the opposite side, and gathered itself up into something resembling a whiplike tree. Its feet, if that was what they were, stretched out like roots, and Hog could have sworn that the roots were embedding themselves in the mat. What the hell kind of creature was this? Ektras didn't make up shapes; they always emulated real species that Ektras had known, somewhere in the galaxy. Hog puffed into his fist and looked at the ref, determined not to be distracted by unanswerable questions.

The announcer's voice boomed: "IN THE ONE-HUNDRED-THIRTY-EIGHT-POUND CLASS! FROM EARTH: HOG DONOVAN—HUMAN!" There was a murmur of approval, plus his mother's shrieks, but not exactly the thunderous roar Hog had imagined. He glanced up into the crowd, and saw a row of centipedes sitting on their legs. "AND FROM EKTRA FOUR: BELDUKI-ELIKITANGO-HARDART-COLLOIDISAN—EXTRA SHAPESHIFTER!" Hog held his breath, waiting for the cheers for his opponent. What he actually heard was more like a group indrawn breath of fear.

He noted that the Ektra had sprouted about a hundred suction cups on the ends of its tree branches. He was going to have a dickens of a time avoiding *those*. Hog danced in place, thinking hard—and coming up with very little, strategy-wise.

Fortunately, he was saved from despair by a voice that boomed out through the general noise: "HOGMAN, YOU PIN THIS WALKING JELL-O SALAD, AND DRINKS ARE ON ME FOR THE REST OF THE *YEAR*!" Hog grinned despite himself, and at that moment caught sight of Hermie "Harmin' " Harmon in the front row, shaking his hammy fists in the air. Harmin' now worked the graveyard shift at Lotusflower Assembly, hanging transaaactional warp modules under Rigellian interstellar roadsters. He hadn't wrestled in three years, and his physique now resembled that of a hippopotamus. Was that what was in store for Hog, after his wrestling career ended? Lotusflower Assembly, with the rest of the guys? Not if he could help it . . .

Hog frowned and stepped into a crouch, facing his opponent.

The shapeshifter waved its branches. The ref gestured with its paddles, and Hog reached out to grip the nearest branch in a handshake. The suction cups latched onto his hand, and let go with a *pop*. Hog shook off the stinging sensation. The ref leveled a paddle-shaped hand between the two contestants, then jerked it away with a *tweet!* on its whistle. The match was on.

Hog danced sideways, and forward and back, snatching in quick grabs at the shapeshifter's branches. He was just testing, seeing if he could get the thing off-balance. The Ektra waved its branches unconcernedly. Its feet remained planted. Hog circled, trying to make it lift its feet and follow. The Ektra didn't turn at all; it just waved different branches at him as he circled. Where the hell were its eyes, anyway—on the leaves? And what would constitute putting this thing on its back? he wondered.

"Cut 'im down, Hog!" he heard, in the dim distance of the sidelines. Harmin', cheering him on. His friend sounded as if he were miles away.

"You don't have all day, Donovan—go in after him!" he heard on the other side. Coach Tagget, offering helpful strategy.

Hog shrugged off a negligent grab by one of the branches, and, without thinking, launched his attack. He shot forward, low, grabbing for the base of the shapeshifter's trunk. It was a purely instinctive move—go for the single-leg takedown, whether the thing had legs or not. It worked better than he could have expected: the branches waved madly above him, and some of the suckers came down on his back. But he got a good penetration, and wrapped both arms around the Ektra's trunk. He got one knee up under him, and lifted, hard.

The Ektra didn't budge. It was holding itself down not so much by its roots as by a large sucker at the base of its trunk. Hog grunted, trying to break it free. As he strained, the Ektra's branches were clinging to his back, though fortunately the fabric of his tights top kept it from getting too secure a grip. Grunting harder, Hog dug his fingers under the edge of the tree's suction base. He heard his coach's distant voice: "—the *hell* are you doing?"

"Gaaaahhhh!" With a roar, Hog pulled up with his fingers. *Splook.* The Ektra came loose from the mat, and he had it in the air like a heavy Christmas tree. He staggered, turning with it, trying to tip it over. The tree was snatching at his back and his arms. Hog lost his balance and went over sideways, taking the tree with him.

Even as they fell, he could feel the thing changing shape. By the time they hit the mat, the Ektra was an extremely slippery snaky thing, sliding out of his hands. Hog tightened his grip, trying to keep it from getting away. But it was impossible; it had some sort of coating that made it slick as hell. He scrambled to follow it on the mat, desperately trying to hold on long enough to get the takedown points.

"Queeeeeee!" whistled the shapeshifter, and, with a convulsive jerk, slithered out of Hog's hands.

"No points!" brayed the ref, prancing alongside.

Hog glanced up in frustration. He was *sure* he'd earned the takedown points, even if he had to concede a one-point escape. Was this ref going to be an impossible-to-please type?

The glance was a mistake; it distracted him from his opponent. By the time he looked back, his opponent was gone.

Whufff!

His breath went out with a gasp, and he felt the snake's coils wrapping around him from behind. How could it have moved so fast? he thought uselessly, as he struggled to jam his elbows down into the coils to protect his ribs from the rapidly tightening pressure.

"Queee-ee-eeeee!" chortled the snake, in what sounded like a merry laugh. Prelude to strangulation? Hog wondered. The next coil whipped around his ankles, and he fell to the mat like 138 pounds of frozen meat.

"Two-point takedown!" whinnied the ref.

"Augggh!" Hog grunted, trying to keep from rolling onto his back. The snake was trying to get him to do just that, but it didn't have a firm enough hold on his legs, and he was able to scissor hard and gain some leverage, getting himself halfway up to his elbows and knees. "Hunhh! *Uunhh!*" He was struggling just to breathe. He could feel himself sliding a bit inside the slippery coils, despite the pressure. If only he could slide out . . .

In fact, he was moving a little, squirming in the coils. "*Unhhhh! Unhhh!*" He inhaled as hard as he could, held his breath a moment, then gasped it out and jammed his elbows hard against the coils. He pushed them down by about a foot.

The snake tightened like a vise around his hips. His progress stopped; the coils were smaller than his hip-bones. "Auuughhh!" Hog groaned, blinking at the sight of the ref leaning close, maybe to make sure he was still breathing. If he wasn't turning purple now, he never would be!

He heard a din and a stamping around him. The crowd was loving it—probably hoping he got squeezed to death.

Coach Tagget was yelling something, but he couldn't hear what it was. But another voice reached him through the cacophony: "HAWWWWG—SLAM 'IM TILL HE LETS GO!" he heard distantly.

Hermie. And good thinking. Hog huffed, raising himself on all fours, lifting the snake's weight. He suddenly went flat, hitting the mat as hard as he could, right on the snake's coils. He felt them loosen for an instant, and he squirmed frantically . . .

Tweeeeeet!

The snake gave a last squeeze, then relaxed its grip as the ref halted the action.

"Warning!" brayed the ref. "Slamming is forbidden! Warning number one against the human!" The ref waved his paddle-hands.

Hog gasped, trying to catch his breath. Warning or not, he had a fighting start now; they would resume the match from a one-up one-down position. As the coils unwound, he lumbered to his feet and walked in a brisk circle to shake off the effects. Then he knelt back down on his hands and knees.

"Shake it off—shake it off!" he heard his coach yell. "Now stay out of those coils!"

Hog glanced back to see if the Ektra would take another shape. But no—it could only change shape while the clock was running. That was a regulatory concession to the nonshifting wrestlers: the shapeshifters had the advantage of versatility of form, but they were momentarily vulnerable during the change, and for a few seconds following, while they "got into" their new forms.

"No delay!" called the ref. This time it was yelling at the shapeshifter. The Ektra seemed to be having trouble deciding how to situate itself on the top position over Hog: it had no hands or feet to place on or near him. "Rest your head on his back!" the ref instructed.

"Queeee?" protested the shapeshifter.

"On his back," repeated the ref. "No delay, please."

"Queeee," it answered.

Hog felt the snake's head touch the center of his back. He glanced over his shoulder and saw that the creature was arching over him from a base of coils on the mat, and was indeed touching him just on the center of the back. Good. He just had to move faster than the snake.

Tweet!

Hog launched himself up to a standing position, whirling away. He felt no resistance. "One-point escape!" called the ref. Hog spun around to face the snake.

"QUAAARRRRRRRR!" roared the creature that was facing him—no snake now, but an enormous, maned animal with a mouth full of large teeth. *(TERROR! TERROR! I'M BIGGER THAN YOU!)* Hog backed away, startled. He tripped on the heel of his sneaker and fell to his knees. "QUAAAAAAAAAA!" bellowed the Ektra, charging. *(BARE YOUR GNEEPHITZXX . . . !)* echoed its psicry.

For an instant, Hog was paralyzed with fear—like a man who'd stumbled in front of a rabid lion. *Do something,* he thought. *Get out of its way!* Then something in him snapped, and instead of using common sense and fleeing, he leaped straight at the charging beast with a bloodcurdling Tarzan yell. "AAAHH-AAAUUGGHHHH!" He was going to meet those teeth, and it would all be over before the ref could tweet his whistle, but he couldn't stop himself.

The Ektra lion halted in midcharge, bewildered by Hog's furious yell.

Hog slammed into it, grabbing it around the neck. The damn thing was all fur and air; it weighed the same as he did, but at three times his size. The Ektra went over like a bowling pin, perhaps too surprised to react.

BLAAATTTT!

Tweeeeet! "No points!"

Hog rolled away from the shapeshifter and leaped to his feet. "Whaaat?" he yelled. "I had him—"

"End of the first period!" called the ref, strutting away on its four centaur legs, ignoring Hog's protest. Hog sighed, wheezing for breath. Damn, this wasn't looking good. He had to do *something.*

"Ref, you blindfolded nag! If that wasn't a takedown, what was it?" came a scream from the sidelines. Hog kept his back to his coach as Tagget demonstrated proper Earth sportsmanship. Not that Hog didn't agree with him.

He turned and stared at the leonine alien, whose unreadable eyes were just shifting from Hog to the ref. *(I crush you.)* "Quaaaaaaa?" it asked the ref.

"Call the toss!" whinnied the centaur, holding an oversize poker chip in its paddle-hand. The chip was red on one side, blue on the other.

"Quaaaa," grumbled the Ektra.

The ref flipped the chip. It fluttered and landed red side up on the mat. "Up or down?" it asked, pointing to the Ektra, who had apparently called red.

"Quaaa," it said, with a shrug of its furry shoulders.

"Ektra up! Human down!" announced the ref, pointing to the center of the mat. Hog knelt and assumed the position.

"No teeth, shapechanger!" yelled Coach Tagget as the lion-thing positioned itself with two large paws on Hog's back and its mouth open, breathing hot, fetid air straight down on the back of Hog's neck. "No biting allowed!" shouted Tagget.

"QUAAAAAAARRRR!" answered the beast with a terrifying rumble. *(I SQUEEZE YOUR—!)*

"Get up and away from him!" Hog heard through the ringing in his ears.

The ref peered at the two, raising a flat hand. *Tweet!*

Hog scrambled, and felt the lion all over him. It felt heavy, and it was quick, and its breath made him reel. But it had to be tiring with all that movement, and maybe Hog could wear it out. He soon realized something, and the lion must have, too. Except for its teeth and claws, which it couldn't use, it had no good way to hold on to him other than hugging him in a smothering embrace and staying on top of him. If Hog could just shoot his legs out to the side and keep moving . . .

He felt the Ektra changing shape even as he did so. He made it partway out of the Ektra's embrace, then lurched to stand up. He turned, hopping back and away—and was nearly free when he felt a tentacle whip around his left ankle. He hopped harder, trying to jerk away, but the tentacle was faster. He managed to turn to face his opponent, and found the tentacle attached to something that looked as if it had crawled out of a very dark lagoon. God only knew what planet the original was from. It had a head like a moldy stump and two squidlike tentacles that sprouted from the head, and it was trying to snake its other tentacle around Hog's right leg. Hog hopped madly to evade it, and the lagoon creature responded by hoisting his left ankle to a ridiculous height, practically to his chin, with the first tentacle. Hog was hopping like a crazed ballet dancer, struggling not to lose his balance.

"Krrrreeee!" screeched the lagoon-thing.

"F-f-f- . . . says you!" gasped Hog. *No, don't talk to it!* he thought. *Save your strength, save your strength.* He jumped, trying to lever his weight downward to break free, but the tentacle's grip was tenacious.

"You can do it, Justin!" screamed his mother's voice, from somewhere.

"Get yourself out of there, dammit, Hog! How'd you get into that?" he heard, from another direction. He was completely disoriented with respect to the room; he could only focus on the mat, and this infernal creature.

He jumped higher. The tentacle went higher. He still didn't break free, and now his leg was up as far as it could possibly go, and his hamstrings were screaming.

"Krrrreeeee!" urged his opponent.

"Scree you!" Hog retorted angrily.

Tweeeeeeeeet! The ref strode forward, breaking the impasse. It turned to Hog and waved a paddle in his direction, while braying to the scoring table: "The use of abusive language is prohibited. One point penalty against the human!"

"*What?*" Hog gasped, limping away from the Ektra.

"Reference to the opponent's progenitors are strictly forbidden!" scolded the centaur with the whistle. "Assume the position."

"*Ref—you piece of Arcturan fungus!*" screamed a voice from the sidelines. "*You mold, you donkey! You wouldn't know a foul if it came up and plugged you—you—!*"

Hog ignored his coach's rantings and assumed the position.

The centaur was staring coldly in the direction of the sidelines, but it said nothing, until the shapeshifter had hunched behind Hog, its tentacles on his back. A little too *firmly* on his back, Hog realized. "Ref—wait a min—"

Tweet!

Hog was a moment slow in moving, and the shapeshifter had its tentacles around his waist by the time he was into his standup. He was on his feet, but he couldn't break free, and he began lunging one way and then another, trying to loosen the thing's grip. He dug his hands down under the tentacles to break their hold. Yes—he had them loose! "Aarrrrr!" He snarled, spinning and bracing his feet outward. If he could just arch, he could complete the escape. . . .

He staggered a little, as the Ektra pushed him backward off the mat.

Tweet! "No points!"

Hog cursed under his breath and returned to the center of the mat. This time he was ready.

Tweet!

He was up, turning, leaving the lagoon-creature on the mat . . . except for the tentacle that whipped out and caught his ankle and jerked his leg high in the air. "*GAAAHHHH!*" Hog roared, hopping . . . hopping . . . hopping . . .

Time seemed to slow and twiddle its thumbs as he danced, evading the second tentacle, while struggling in vain to escape from the first. He edged slowly toward the out-of-bounds, and the lagoon-creature slowly dragged him back.

Time took a coffee break. Time went out to an early lunch . . .

And Hog hopped . . . hopped . . . hopped . . .

Would the period never end? he thought desperately, throwing his weight up and down with fading strength. Would time never run out on this eternal second period?

BLAAATTTT! went the buzzer.

Tweeeeet! "No points!" called the ref.

Hog gasped, as the Ektra released his leg.

"Shake it off, Hog—shake it off!" "Go, Justin—!"

He gulped air as he staggered in a circuit around the mat, before going to assume the top position for the final period. "Whattza score?" he rasped to the ref.

"Three to one, Ektra," the ref informed him.

From somewhere overhead, the strains of country and western music filled the gymnasium.

* * *

For Earth, Hog thought dizzily, focusing on the form of the creature before him. Do it for Earth. Do it for wrestling. For wrestling. For the tricrystal medal. Just gotta do it, somehow. *You're on camera—the only human left.*

"FREE DRINKS, HAWWWG!" yelled Harmin'.

Tweet!

He hurled his weight into the lagoon-creature, hoping to topple it over. His only hope now was to turn it over for the fall. He felt its weight giving way . . . altering shape under him. What the hell was it going to be this time?

For an instant, he felt a disgusting slime under him, as the Ektra's form dissolved. Repulsed, he involuntarily loosened his hold a little, and as he did so, 138 pounds of Ektra bounced up into his chin. He almost lost his grip, but somehow recovered his balance and thrust himself against the Ektra with all the strength his legs had left.

Boing.

The Ektra bounced back against him.

Boing.

It bounced away from him, veering unexpectedly to his right, and doing a backflip out of his arms. He threw himself against it before it could get completely away, tackling it and carrying it out-of-bounds.

Tweeeet!

Panting, Hog took a good look at his opponent as it settled, more or less, into position in the center of the mat. It looked like a large coil spring inside a knotted sock, and it seemed unable to stop bouncing completely, even in the starting position. It bobbed and jittered at a sort of idle speed, reminding Hog of his Uncle Wainwright, who could never sit still, bouncing and gum-chewing his way through entire ball games—and who had often belittled Hog for choosing wrestling over basketball. Hog glared at the coil-springed Ektra, and imagined it shapechanging into his Uncle Wainwright.

With a silent snort, Hog settled behind the Ektra and placed his hands carefully on its trunk, prepared to tackle it as viciously as he could. The centaur-ref peered at him for a moment, seemingly unable to decide if his positioning was legal. Then it flipped its paddle-hand. *Tweet!*

Boing.

Hog lunged into the bouncing shapeshifter, and bounced with it, *boing, boing*, right off the mat. He got up glaring even harder. Time was running out, and it didn't do him any good just to hold the thing down, he needed to pin it. But how could he pin a coil spring? The one thing that encouraged him, as he watched it bounce back to the center of the mat, was that it was starting to look tired. Maybe all this springing was wearing it out.

At the whistle, Hog threw his weight into it again, and landed flat on his chin. For an infuriating, flustered moment, he thought he had lost the Ektra, and he scrambled to get up, looking around wildly. Then he realized that the Ektra was under him; it had splatted out into an enormous pancake with tiny, starfish legs around its outer edge. He pushed and hauled on it, but the thing was immovable.

"Turn it over! *Turn it over!*" yelled his coach, his mother, somebody.

He couldn't *possibly* turn it over—unless he got off it completely and tried to flip it like a throw rug. But that would be crazy . . . it was too heavy and too awkward.

"Warning—Ektra—stalling!" brayed the ref.

"*Hog—you're running out of time! DO SOMETHING!*" hollered Harmin', from somewhere very close to the edge of the mat.

With a snarl, Hog jumped off the pancake and yanked on the edge of the thing. It went "Querr*reee!*" and began contracting into a new shape. Good! Now he could go to work on it!

The change took place in a dizzying blur, and it was not just a physical blur. Hog felt a wave of confusion pass through his mind, and he blinked and found himself holding the hand of, and staring into the large brown eyes of, the most breathtakingly beautiful woman he had ever seen, or imagined. *(Come . . . come to me . . . now . . .)* whispered the psicry. She had long, golden brunette hair; and she was wearing a clinging silk wrap that did not altogether cover her breathtaking . . . her breathtaking . . .

. . . and she was breathing so hard, so *quiveringly* hard, and pulling him by the hand toward her with a smile that made his heart stop.

"Whoaaa—Hog! All riiiight! Go for it, man, go get it!"

The sound of Harmin's voice was strangely removed, as though Hog and his . . . opponent? . . . had been whisked into a private place for a special little tête-à-tête, with everyone else suddenly a very long way away, miles away, light-years away. *(Yes, yes . . . come get it . . . you will like it very much . . .)* And, for a fleeting instant, Hog thought that was fine, just fine, very fine indeed. For the glory of Earth fine. Oh yes.

And then maybe a whiff of oxygen reached his brain, or maybe a whiff of astringent alien breath, because the hypnotic spell slipped just a little, and his heart seemed to beat again, and with a start he realized that he was sinking to the mat, allowing himself to be drawn into the arms of this . . . about to pull this gorgeous creature on top of him, this . . .

"*Get that goddamn tramp off you, Justin!*" screamed someone, his mother.

. . . Ektra shapeshifter.

"Awwwww, jeeeez!" he panted, struggling to get his brain clear, and realizing he had about one second before he'd be flat on his back under this . . . sex-crazed . . .

The woman's weight was already shifting for the pin.

And his mind was still fogged . . . but not quite so fogged that he couldn't make one last, desperate, hopeless move.

He reached down and tickled her in the rib cage.

"*Breee-heee-heeeeeee!*" shrieked the shapeshifter, erupting into helpless laughter and losing its hold.

Hog scooted out from under it, but managed to keep his fingers in there tickling. He was gasping from the exertion, but his gasps were drowned out by screams of laughter. . . .

"Kreee-hee-hee-*(stop)*-hee-heee kreee*(stop)*-heee-hee-hee-*(please stop!)*-hee—"

Hog struggled to disregard the psicry pummeling his mind. He hugged and cradled this creature, far and away more gorgeous than any woman he had ever even fantasized about, cradled her in a fabulous embrace . . . tickling mercilessly.

"Kree-hee-hee-*(stop please stop!)*—"

"HOG, TEN SECONDS LEFT!!!"

The thing's laughter was contagious, and Hog fell on her, nearly laughing uncontrollably himself. And he pressed her back down to the mat, his left arm crooked in a careless reverse–half nelson, his right hand tickling just below those magnificent—

Whack! Tweeeeeeet! "Pin! The match goes to the human!" brayed the centaur-ref.

And he almost couldn't make himself stop tickling her now that he had her down, but the roar of the crowd was enough to make him look up in a daze, and the first thing he saw, past the four legs of the ref, was Harmin' Harmon jumping up and down like a dancing buffalo. His friend's voice was drowned out, but it hardly mattered. And the second thing Hog saw was the centaur bending down to look at him with apparent puzzlement in its eyes.

"Human, I am unsure how you did that," the ref said, waving its paddle-hands. "But congratulations. And if you don't get up off your opponent, it will be a shame that you will be required to forfeit the match . . ."

"Huh?" Hog released the Ektra with a start and sat back on his haunches, blinking in amazement at what he had done. He stood up shakily, and extended a hand to help his opponent up off the mat.

The Ektra-woman was pouting as it rose. But after a moment, its lips quivered and re-formed into a smile . . . and then into a beaming grin. *A grin?* Hog thought.

"Earth!" "Earth!" "Earth!" "Earth!" "Earth . . . !" A chant had started in the stands and was growing in intensity. They were banging their seats now. *"Number One!" "One!" "One . . . !"*

"WAY T' GO, HAWWWWWG!" bawled Harmin' Harmon, striding up and down the sidelines, fists in the air.

"Look at the camera, Justin—look at the camera!" His mother was practically on the mat, pointing up into the stands at his father and the fastcam.

Hog grinned weakly and looked back at the Ektra. It was still a dazzling creature, but her grin had continued to widen, bright teeth sparkling, until the grin seemed to take up most of her face. And then Hog realized dizzily that her face was slowly disappearing, leaving *only* the grin. And he stood, blinking, watching the grin fade last of all, until the Ektra was gone altogether. And Hog turned in bewilderment to the ref, who was looking toward the scoring table and didn't see any of it happen.

"Justin! Ask it to do that again! Your father missed it!"

Hog turned around, waving in confusion. "Say, uh—" he croaked to his absent opponent, "nice match!" And found himself thinking, Is it true? Is it really true? Did I win the tricrystal medal for Earth? *The only human in history to win a tricrystal?* And then the centaur-ref trotted back to him, and hoisted his hand in victory, and Hog forgot his doubts and waved triumphantly to the crowd. And when he turned, he saw a large, iridescent lizard rising up as if from the very substance of the mat and turning to shuffle away.

"Hey, Ektra!" he cried.

"Breee?" said the lizard, looking back. *(We like semiconductor medals better, anyway. (I lie!) (I lie!))* it whispered in a psicry.

Hog laughed happily and patted it on the back. "Great match, guy. Next time don't be so ticklish!"

"Breee," said the lizard. *(Done well. Next match I get the home crowd, okay?)*

"Okay. See you around." Hog trotted off the mat, waving again to the crowd, and fell into the congratulating arms of his mother and Harmin' Harmon. He hardly even heard their voices, or the voice of Coach Tagget. . . .

"Drinks on me, just like I said . . ."

"Where'd you learn to *do* that sort of a thing with a woman, Justin . . . ?"

"Donovan, just like I been tellin' you, the brain is the most important . . ."

But if he didn't hear what they said after that, he did hear the chants of *Earth! Earth!* and he could already feel the tricrystal medal glistening and breathing in his hand. And he heard a centipede voice hissing, "Kreeeepy kreeepy earthman—sssee you nexxxt yearrr on Meetsssnepp Fffive, hah-hahhh! Zerrrro grrravity unlimited, suckahhh . . . !" Only this time Hog just laughed out loud and didn't even bother to look as he headed for the cameras, as the Vegan's voice faded back into the waves of *HOG DONOVAN! HOG DONOVAN! TRICRYSTAL EARTH . . . !*

Bye-bye Lotusflower, Lotusflower bye-bye!

The act of writing this story brought back surprisingly powerful memories of my own wrestling days at Huron (Ohio) High School, more years ago now than I care to admit. Many elements of the story were lifted straight from my own experience. I don't think I'll say *which* elements; but one of my former teammates ought to recognize the hopping scene, since it happened to him.

This story was, in fact, something of a change of pace for me. I generally write novels not short stories—far future, cosmological, quasireligious hard science fiction about serious subjects. Artificial intelligence, first contact, transcendent encounters in space-time—that sort of thing. The last time I tried a purely humorous piece was in my prepublished days, and it was in place of a term paper in graduate school. The professor, perhaps not unreasonably, expected a more serious effort. The topic, as I recall, was something like: "Coastal Zone Management in a Marine Estuary System." A perfect subject for a humorous fairy tale, no? Well, it seemed so, at 1:00 A.M. the night before the paper was due. The professor's reaction was . . . quizzical. ("What the *hell is this,* Carver?")

That was in . . . let's see, 1974.

Nineteen years later, Roger Zelazny telephoned me one Sunday morning to invite me to contribute a wrestling story to this volume. (He recalled seeing a bio that mentioned my unsavory past as a wrestler.) In so doing, he accomplished three things. No, four:

1. He got me to write my first short story in almost ten years, and incidentally to try a humorous piece.

2. He got me to reflect back upon a sport that once commanded an astonishing amount of my energy and dedication, and in the process taught me a lot about life.
3. He left my wife starry-eyed with wonder: ("*Roger Zelazny*'s on the phone! He says he's sorry to interrupt your work time, but he has a question for you.")
4. He got me out of bed.

Thanks, Roger.

I wouldn't have gotten to see this story if it hadn't been for another story, by the same author. Glad we got to meet, Larry, albeit briefly.

ooooo

Heart of the Moment

Larry Segriff

I watched the four men spread out, surrounding her on the soft, white sand, and I wondered what she would do. She was pretty, with curly brown hair cropped close to her scalp and dark eyes that flashed as she watched her assailants. She was dressed in a white gi, tied with a black belt, and she held a katana in her hands. She spun slowly on the balls of her feet as her opponents scattered to the four corners.

I had a katana, too, but I didn't rush to her defense. I'd seen this scene too many times. I knew just how it would end.

Her opponents were clad in black leather, and all were armed. One held a six-foot staff, which he twirled casually in his hands. He was at the North. To the West, her opponent swung a pair of *nunchaku*, their evil whistling making them sound much more dangerous than they were. Next to him, across from the one with the staff, a man stood quietly, watching. He held a blade in his hands, much like hers, only straight and a little shorter. It was a ninja-to, the sword of Japan's feared night fighters. He looked as if he knew how to handle it, but I hadn't made up my mind about that yet.

The last opponent was the really interesting one. He held a pair of sickle-shaped objects called *kamas*. They were a dying art, difficult to master but deadly in the hands of an expert. I was very curious to see how good he was.

The man with the 'chucks moved first. It figured. There was something about that weapon. It seemed to call to the arrogant, cocky ones. On top of that, he waited until she was facing him before launching his attack.

He employed a classic technique, twirling the sticks in his left hand to distract her and then throwing a quick shot with his right-hand weapon. It didn't work. She timed it perfectly, leaning back out of range then cutting at his right wrist before he could draw it back. He grimaced and dropped that pair of 'chucks, and she slashed at his forehead before he could change his stance.

Total time: three-quarters of a second. Result: one dead opponent. Not bad.

She allowed the momentum of her strike to carry her forward into her fallen opponent's place, and then spun to face her remaining foes.

The man with the ninja-to went next, letting out a familiar, high-pitched scream and swinging hard at her head. Foolish. He was far enough away that she had time to get set for his blow. She caught it cleanly on her own blade, then flicked her wrists to throw his sword to the side and turned her parry into a cut at his head.

Time of that encounter: 1.2 seconds; total time since first move: 2.4 seconds.

She was good, but her two toughest opponents remained.

My own palms itched as I saw the staffer step forward.

He was using the six-foot staff—called a bo as opposed to the shorter, four-foot jo—and he kept it moving in a constant spin as he stepped forward. I wanted to call out to him, to warn him of his mistake. Better yet, I wanted to take his staff from him and show him how to wield it properly.

I did neither. Instead, I merely watched as he stepped in, tried to catch her blade in a traditional take, failed, and lost his head, all in nine-tenths of a second.

Three opponents down, in less than five seconds. I couldn't help wondering how well she would fare against somebody good.

The man with the kamas bowed slightly, came up on the balls of his feet, and then waited. I leaned forward, my curiosity increasing. Did he actually know what he was doing? Were we finally going to have a serious bout?

As it turned out, no.

She threw a cut at his head. He brought his right-hand kama up to parry, and swept his left-hand weapon out, searching for her wrist. The problem was, her cut had been a feint. There was no blade there for him to parry, and no wrist for him to slice. Instead, she picked up his attack and flicked it aside, and then treated him the same way she had her first victim: a quick shot at his leading wrist followed by a cut to his throat. He tried to bring his remaining kama over to parry, but she had all the leverage, and simply overpowered his defense.

Her katana ripped through his throat and that was it.

All told, just over seven seconds had elapsed from the beginning of the first attack until the last body hit the ground. Some people might have been impressed. I found it ludicrous.

I started clapping slowly.

Startled, she spun toward me, raising her blade.

"This is a closed practice," she said. She didn't lower her blade.

My katana was in my hands, too, but I kept it down.

She was too far away to pose a threat, and I didn't like to respond to empty posturing.

Instead, I shrugged. "Sorry. I normally have this room reserved at this time. When I found it occupied, I was curious."

At that, she lowered her blade. "Ah, then you must be Bob Sakai."

My eyebrows went up. "You've heard of me?"

She nodded. "Who hasn't? You're something of a legend at Chong's studio."

I waved that aside. "Studio," I snorted. "They used to be called dojos. Now, since Virtual Reality has taken over almost everything, they're studios. Like this one."

She heard the disparagement in my voice. "Don't you like VR?"

I shook my head. "It's not real. Don't get me wrong: I don't think you necessarily have to use real weapons or fight without padding, but I have found that pain can make a good incentive for making your parries effective. In here, there's nothing. It's all empty form. Face it, it's not hard to be a legend when motorized suits and specialized programming can do almost everything for you."

She nodded. "Ah, but that's why you're a legend. I've heard you don't use enhancements, and that you can still beat just about anything the computer throws at you."

I nodded. "I treat it as real. Besides, the computer's predictable. In battle, that'll get you killed."

"So why do you do it? Why VR, if you dislike it so much?"

I shrugged again. "It's better than nothing. I need a workout, so I come here, but I do it in an unenhanced suit, and out there, in the larger reality, I have a real blade in my hands. It's not ideal, but, since the advent of VR, it's the only game in town."

There didn't seem to be anything for her to say to that. At least, she didn't leap forward to proclaim that she, too, disdained the enhanced suits and the specialized subroutines. Instead, she gestured at her fallen foes and asked, "So, what did you think?"

I'd been dreading that question. At first, watching her fight, I'd been looking forward to taking her down a peg or two, but as we talked I found that desire fleeing. She didn't seem as full of herself as I'd expected, and so I didn't want to crush her. On the other hand, an honest question demanded an honest answer.

"It was interesting," I said. "You were using kendo moves, but this clearly isn't a kendo setting. It's rare anymore to see kendo used in anything resembling a practical environment. I've gotten used to it being a sport, a far cry from its roots as a serious, *martial* art. It's good to see someone else blending styles and training against other schools and other weapons."

She was frowning, though, and I could see my attempt at politics had been wasted. " 'Resembling a practical environment'?" she repeated. "I'm afraid I don't understand the qualification. I just took out four heavily armed and highly skilled warriors. I mean, granted, I'm not likely to run into these guys on the street, but, seriously, how could it be any more practical?"

I sighed, wishing I'd never gotten into this, and that I had simply waited for her to finish her practice.

"I'm not trying to be insulting," I began, but she held up a hand.

"No. It's not that. I really want to understand."

I nodded. "All right. To be blunt, your opponents weren't realistic. I don't mean just the fact that they were computer simulations—we've already talked about that and it can't be helped. No, what I'm referring to is how they acted. They all looked like bad actors in an old kung fu movie. Take the guy with the staff. He had all the moves down, but he didn't utilize his staff properly. Hell, it's six feet long. Your katana is only about forty inches. He had no business closing with you. He should have stayed back, using his reach, throwing quick little shots at your wrists and fingers. Same with the guy with the 'chucks. He had speed, and two weapons to your one, yet he walked right in and played to your strengths rather than his.''

I grimaced and shook my head. ''Look, what you were doing was no different than what most martial artists do. Watch a black belt in *tae kwon do* take on four brown belts and see how they act; watch an aikido instructor literally throw *himself* in a vain attempt to teach his students proper technique; watch any of them simulating a knife fighter in practice, and using clumsy overhand strikes and slow roundhouse swings, then contrast that with what real knife fighters do. It's not uncommon; it's just not real.''

I looked at her, trying to gauge whether or not I should say anything more. I'd given her an honest answer, but not a complete one. Looking at her face, frowning but not yet completely closed, I decided to continue.

''But that's not the biggest thing,'' I said. ''After all, to be honest, even with their limited tactics, each of your opponents posed a serious threat. For what it's worth, you did an excellent job against each of them. The problem is, that's not worth much. In a way, it really was just like watching any black belt in any discipline taking on multiple lesser opponents. Have you ever noticed how, for the most part, they all wait very politely, attacking the black belt in turn rather than together? Well, let me tell you, that's not how it works. Not in the real world.''

Her frown had deepened. ''I don't understand,'' she said. ''I mean, four people, all attacking at once—wouldn't they get in each other's way?''

I grinned. ''Want to try it?''

She looked startled, but only for a moment. Then she grinned back and nodded.

My own grin widened. ''Computer,'' I said, raising my

voice slightly. "Initiate Sequence SAKAI.TEAM-WORK.3 at my mark, using existing parameters."

The four fallen bodies vanished and four new warriors, identical in every way with the ones she had just vanquished, appeared in their place. They formed a small box, maybe fifteen feet across, with her at the center. For the moment, they were not moving.

I looked at her. "Ready?"

She assumed a guard stance facing the one with the staff, her blade held in a midline defensive position, and nodded.

"Mark," I said, then settled back to watch.

At my command, the four warriors shifted positions. Instead of attacking her individually, they moved together. The staffer and the guy with the 'chucks moved toward each other, and so did the other two. Now, instead of having one opponent at each corner, she had a pair of opponents bracketing her, the staffer/*nunchaku* team to her right, the swordsman/kama duo to her left.

Her instincts were good. She came about, presenting her blade directly between the two teams so that she could respond to whichever one attacked, but that was as far as she went.

The staffer moved first, raising his bo and taking a cautious step forward. Following his lead, the guy with the 'chucks started them spinning, and sent out a couple of very short feints towards her.

She responded in predictable fashion, starting to turn toward them. As soon as she did, the other team, now at her back, launched their attacks together.

It was actually pretty well choreographed. The swordsman stayed back, using his longer weapon to defend in case she turned on them, but she didn't. The first she knew of their moves was when the razor-sharp blade of one of the sickle-shaped kamas sliced across the back of her neck.

Total time: 1.8 seconds. Result: one dead warrior, no fallen opponents.

The computer-generated figures froze and she spun to face me.

"That's not fair!" she said. "Nobody could take on four guys like that."

I grinned. "Want to bet?"

Motioning for her to step aside, I took her place. "Computer, initiate Sequence SAKAI.TEAMWORK.3 at my mark, same parameters." I looked over at her as the computer reset the stage, "Or do you think it'll be too easy if I know their first move?"

She shook her head. "Even knowing it, I don't think anyone could stop it."

I only smiled, then let my humor fade as I slipped into readiness.

My mind quieted, all the turmoil caused by our conversation settling into stillness as I felt my way toward the calm, still center of the moment. I didn't like this setting; it was too artificial. I couldn't really imagine a situation where I would allow four armed opponents to surround me, but it was her scenario and I had to live with it. The sequence I'd summoned, Teamwork #3, simply told the computer how well the four should work together. The setting itself, the weapons they used, even their clothing, had all been selected by her.

I loosened my grip on my katana and raised it so the guard was level with my heart, blade pointing upward and slightly forward. My elbows were straight, and I, too, was facing the guy with the staff.

"Mark," I said, my voice soft and flat, and immediately went into motion.

My first step was toward the staffer, my blade coming up into a high-line attack, but as soon as my foot hit the sand I spun off toward the opponent on my left. He had the 'chucks, and he was the weakest link in the chain.

I had to angle slightly to my right to avoid any attack

from the swordsman on my left, but my first feint had pushed the staffer back a step and gave me room to maneuver. Directly in front of me, the guy with the 'chucks had already started moving to close ranks with the staffer. I cut him off and, staying out of reach of his shorter weapons, threw a feint at his wrist to get his hand moving and then cut at his head. I didn't really care if I hit him just yet; all I wanted was to get past him, so I could put all four of my opponents in front of me.

As it was, I got lucky and scored a shallow cut across his forehead. Not a killing blow, but the computer called it a valid hit and dropped him out.

"Lucky shot," she called.

I grinned at that. She was right, but the setup for the blow—and the fact that I hadn't been killed in the first moments of the fight—wasn't luck. Besides, this was her scenario. If it had been one of mine, he wouldn't have been taken out.

Once through their net, I continued on a couple of steps and then swung about to my left, trying to stay away from the staff. I needn't have been so cautious. They hadn't followed me closely. Instead, they closed up ranks, forming a triangle in front of me. The staffer had moved into the middle, and about half a step behind the other two, providing protection with his longer weapon. The guy with the kamas was on my right, and he was my next target.

The problem was, this time around he was using his weapons properly, keeping them moving so that I couldn't get an easy shot at his hands. If I was going to get him, it was going to have to be a compound move, something that forced him to commit to a defense and made him open up somewhere else. That meant I had to do something about that staff. Any kind of a long engagement with one opponent would get me killed by the others.

"Now what?" she called.

I didn't look at her. "Same as always," I replied. "Divide and conquer." Which was, in truth, the heart of my strategy. I had to take their numbers away, had to find ways to separate them long enough to take them out one at a time.

I knew I couldn't let them dictate anything. I had to carry the fight to them, and I had to do it on my terms.

I didn't hesitate. I shuffled left two steps, waving my blade slightly to simulate the beginnings of an attack. Again, I wasn't trying for anything overt; I just wanted the staffer to turn slightly to protect his swordsman. He did, and as soon as he started I was off, running full speed at an angle that would take me just outside the kamas' reach. The swordsman was too far away to do anything, and the staffer couldn't reach me without hitting the guy with the kamas.

I had my moment. There was just enough time for me to throw a feint, a parry, and then a real attack. If he parried my last move, I would have to disengage quickly or risk being picked off by the staff.

He didn't parry it. I threw a cut at his head, but pulled it up short and sent my blade in a sharp, fast circle. He had automatically brought one kama up to parry and sent the other out in a counterattack. I caught it just as my blade spun forward again, deflecting it off to the side and then cut along the inside line of his arm. His defensive kama was still over his head, and there was nothing between my sword's edge and his neck.

A moment later, I was past him and turning, ready to leap whichever way I needed to.

I didn't need to. His falling body was between me and my remaining opponents. They would have had to split up to attack me in that moment, and they chose not to do that.

Too bad. It would have made things much simpler.

They were learning, and quickly. I shuffled two quick steps to my left, toward the opposing swordsman, to see if I could put him between the staff and myself, but he didn't let me. He turned with me, but he also slid backward, staying within the protective circle of the staff.

All right. There was an answer for that, too. I took two more steps in the same direction, increasing my pace, and then doubled back. The staffer was racing forward, trying to keep me from cutting him off, and when he saw me change direction he swung his staff at me.

Perfect.

He chose a high-line shot, which made sense. He'd lifted his staff slightly while he ran, and he didn't have time to change position before swinging it. I parried it easily, and then reached up and grasped his staff with my left hand. I yanked on it, pulling him forward, and then ran along the outside of the staff, keeping a loose grip on it the whole time with my left hand.

Two quick steps and I cut at him. With the staff still at least partially under my control he didn't have a chance, and because his staff was still hovering between me and his partner, he didn't have any support.

Just that quickly, there was only one left.

We both came to a halt and saluted each other before assuming our on-guard stances once again.

"Computer, halt sequence."

I turned to her, my eyebrows raised.

She shrugged. "You've proven your point," she said. "It's one-on-one, now. Of course you'll beat him."

I nodded, and slowly lowered my blade. Sometimes, it took longer to come out of combat mode than it did to get into it.

"I'm curious, though, " she said. "I've seen a lot of styles, but I have to admit, I'm not familiar with what you were using. I recognized some kendo moves, and something that looked like kenjitsu, and pieces of other arts as well, but I can't put a name to the whole. Tell me, what art is it?"

I gave her a faint smile. "It's called 'Shurikendo,' the

Way of the Secret Sword. As you noticed, it takes pieces from all the arts, anything that's practical. I can use a katana, or a staff, or even a cavalry saber with a parrying dagger—in short, just about anything. It's more of a philosophy than a set of moves, and it's all based on what works."

She nodded at that. "And it does work, I have to admit. How many opponents can you face at one time, with a reasonable chance of success?"

I shrugged. "That depends a lot on what weapons they're using, how good they are with those weapons, and, most importantly, how well they work together."

We lapsed into silence, and I waited for her to ask the question I knew had to be on her mind. When she didn't, I grinned and said, "So, aren't you going to ask me to fence?"

She blinked. "What makes you think—"

My chuckle cut her off. "Come on," I said. "It's pretty obvious. You knew who I was; you were using the virtual room I always use, during the time I normally use it. Clearly, you were trying to meet me. Why else except to fence me?"

"Why else?" she said. "Why, to talk to you, of course. To hear about Shurikendo, and to see it. Besides," she added, "I've already fenced you."

That caught me off guard. "You have?" I thought about it, trying unsuccessfully to place her movements, her style. "Who are you? You're not Chong, are you?" That wasn't as silly as it sounded. I'd been to Chong's classes. I knew he was a little old man, but virtual appearances had little to do with physical reality.

She smiled and shook her head. "No, I'm not Chong. I'm not one of his students, either."

"Then—"

But I didn't get the chance to repeat my question. She lifted her blade and moved toward me. I smiled. This was what I'd been waiting for.

My smile didn't last long, however. When she got to within a couple of paces of me, everything changed. She didn't speak or make any gestures, but suddenly I was surrounded by opponents. I didn't have time to count, but there had to be at least a dozen, all of them exactly like her, and all of them just a step away.

She lifted her blade and flexed her fingers. Every one of her images did exactly the same thing.

I understood, then, what she was and what was happening. I also knew I was going to take her.

I never took my eyes off her, off the real her, the original her. I felt my mind go blank, and waited for the proper moment.

She took one more step and then picked her hands up and thrust her blade forward in the beginnings of a cut. I recognized the move. It was a classic kendo cut, very fast, but very linear, designed to go straight through my head. Normally, it would be easy to parry, but with a dozen or so other blades making the exact same cut at the exact same time, parrying was hopeless.

Instead, I merely waited.

The moment came when she committed to her attack, and that was the moment I'd been waiting for. I dropped into a low crouch, letting all the various blades pass harmlessly over my head, and then I thrust, straight for the heart of her primal image.

I suspected that if I could take her out, her reflections would also drop. I was betting that they had no independent life. After all, they had mirrored her moves exactly, and she had summoned them without a word or a gesture.

I was building an awful lot on two small observations, but I was fairly confident. Even so, I wasn't prepared for what happened.

My blade penetrated her chest and I saw bright red blood bloom on her jacket. She coughed, then, and more blood spilled from her mouth.

"What the hell?" I leaped forward to catch her as she collapsed.

The other images all vanished as soon as my sword entered her, but I barely registered that fact. I was only conscious of the woman in my arms.

"Hey," I said, "You can't die. You can't." And I believed that. She was the computer; she had to be. It was the only thing that made sense, even if I couldn't explain it. Besides, this was VR. Nothing in here was real. Especially death.

She looked at me, and I could tell from how fast she was fading that I was wrong.

"You said—"she started, but another coughing fit took her. "You said VR fencing was lessened because it wasn't real. I had to make it real, for me at least."

"Oh, God," I said as her meaning sank in. "I'm so sorry—"

She reached up and placed her hand on my lips. "Don't be. You were right. All those other times, none of it was real. But now, this time, it was. I lived, if only for a moment." She coughed again, a bright red stream, and then she was gone.

I looked up and saw that the virtual environment was unchanged. The network itself was still running. I looked down at the still form in my arms. I believed her when she said she'd made it real. So what was she? The heart of that network? Some fragmented portion of it that had developed a life of its own?

There were no answers to be found there upon the virtual sand, but I noticed my hand was trembling as I reached out and closed her eyes.

Did machines have souls?

"Computer," I said, "save all data from this session. Do not erase. Repeat, do not erase. Copy all data to my home terminal. Now, exit VR."

The world slowly dissolved, leaving me in a darkness

as limitless and profound as the questions that swirled within me.

Laying down my sword, I detached myself from the machine and went to see what answers I could find.

True story: we were putting on a demo at the University of Iowa. It was their ''Cultural Festival'' and there were a lot of groups putting on exhibitions. There were dancers; there were food vendors; there were various martial arts groups; and there was the University of Iowa Fencing Club.

Us.

Everything went along fine until a few of us pulled out shinais and started putting on a demo of our own blending of Eastern and Western styles and philosophy that we call Shurikendo—The Way of the Secret Sword. Then a guy came up and asked if he could join in. He was a black belt in kenjitsu, and he was very interested in some of our techniques.

Actually, I think he wanted to show us up.

Naturally, we let him in. We've tried on any number of occasions to cross-train with various other disciplines, including the Society for Creative Anachronisms.

This guy—his name was Jim—showed us a few moves and started telling us why what we were doing was wrong, and why our approach wouldn't work. After a few minutes of this I said, ''Let's fence.''

Well, obviously, if he had trounced me, I wouldn't be bringing this up now. The fact is, he was very good. His interior work was excellent, and I saw right away that if I let him have my blade, I was dead.

So I didn't. Put bluntly, I ran away. His whole style

was centered around closing with his opponent and using his superior blade work to score points. I didn't let him close. Instead, I stayed back, cutting at his hands and basically waiting for him to make a mistake.

We fenced for something like twenty minutes, and it would be a lie to say he didn't score any touches. He scored three.

That was not the birth of Shurikendo, but it was a big step forward toward the validation of it as an art. It is, pretty much, as I've described it in this story, but it's more than that, too.

And it's a lot of fun.

At this point, we have several standard fencers, a *tae kwon do* student, and a guy trained in kendo, all working with us. So far, we haven't found a style that's superior.

For the record, I still fence with the traditional Western weapons—I prefer the saber, I think—but my real love is Shurikendo. Any weapons. Any opponents. Any time.

A while back, Steve phoned to tell me that he'd run over on this story's length. I said, "That's okay. Is it by very much?" A silence followed. It was the same thing that had happened with Walter Jon Williams. We worked it in, too, and I'm very glad to have this tale right here.

ooooo

Sand Man

Steven Barnes

With thanks to Rex Kimball and Harley "Swift Deer" Reagan

1

The powder blue Impala chugged alarmingly, blowing steam and dust from the undercarriage. It pulled to one side of the rutted dirt road, sputtered, and died.

Brenda Jay Chase climbed out of the car into 102 degrees of New Mexican heat. The sweat on her forehead evaporated almost instantly. She was a slender woman of thirty-eight, nearly six feet tall, her aerobicized body sheathed in starched white denim. Even in the sweltering heat, her hair was impeccable.

Steam hissed from beneath the Chevy's hood. Brenda's sigh matched it.

From within the car came the pinging sounds of her twelve-year-old son's hand-held *Super Mario Brothers* video game. *Ping*. An anvil fell, and a tiny animated figure scooted to the side. *Ping, ping*. He had won it two weeks ago in a video tournament, playing an abominably violent, poorly programmed game called *Kung Fu Fighter III*.

Ugh.

She yanked up the hood, and stared at the engine. She didn't know much about cars. Computers, yes, but cars no. Still, she had no trouble interpreting the foaming green fluid sizzling from the radiator onto the parched earth below.

A tiny black lizard scooted toward the liquid, then flashed away into the shadow of a rock. Brenda thought it had the right idea. Just crawl off somewhere and sleep. She leaned her head into the coolness of the car. David was still immersed in what must have been his fiftieth game of the day. "I think we've got problems."

He didn't say anything, his fingers occupied with keys and tiny toggle switch.

"We might not make it home tonight."

That made him look up. A smile came perilously close to creasing his oval, walnut brown face. Another day in these hills, the last place where they had been a family together. The last place David and his father had . . .

He bent back to his game.

She *needed* to get back. There was a career, a life to resume. She had given David all the time she had, and he would just have to understand. Ten days roving around New Mexico and Arizona. It had been almost a year since Darryl . . .

Brenda bit her lip. There was a telephone back up the road, at a rickety little mom-and-pop eatery. They could drive that far. If she lost a day, just one more day, it wouldn't kill her.

She climbed back in. "Buckle up," she said unnecessarily. David was still immersed in the game. *Ping, ping*. Fastest fingers in the West.

"Tomorrow," the wizened little repairman said. "Get a new radiator sent over from Easton." Brenda thought he looked like a sun-dried hobbit.

"A whole new radiator?" Perhaps attracted by her frustration, David pocketed his game long enough to climb up on the bumper. The garage's shadowed interior was twenty degrees cooler than the furnace outside, which must have been 105 by now. An ancient fan ruffled miscellaneous bills and faded color catalogs, wagging back and forth mournfully.

The car elf raised his right eyebrow. "I could maybe patch it—but you already tried that, dincha?"

"Actually, I used some radiator stop-leak."

"Then drove through Arizona and New Mexico in July? Smart."

Brenda squashed a flare of anger. She *needed* this little gnome. Besides, he was right.

Outside the bay, a minibus emblazoned *University of California, Los Angeles* pulled up to the gas pumps. David wandered out. A thin, tallish, man with horn-rim glasses and pale peeling skin exited the van. He reminded her of a bifocaled stork.

"Tomorrow, then." Brenda kept one eye on her son. What was she worried about? That this stranger might grab David and haul him into the van, trundling him away to Never-Never Land? David was small but wiry, with sharp teeth, a green belt in Tae Kwon Do, and the energy of a wildcat. A load for any kidnapper.

"Tomorrow," the elf said. "Sadie's, right down the

road. Motel, restaurant. Right nice." He slammed her hood down. "Might give her a try. Price is right."

The microvan pulled away. David looked up at her challengingly. "So? Are we staying tonight?"

She ran her fingers through her hair. Her blood pressure felt dreadful, and she felt the beginning of a tension headache. But another voice inside her said: *This is the last summer vacation this twelve-year-old will ever have. The first one since I died. Next year, he'll be thirteen. A teenager. This is the very end of his childhood. There will never be a time like this again, for either of you. Be flexible for once, dammit.*

That was Darryl's voice. Darryl, gone only twelve months now. Despite the divorce, despite the ugliness of the last five years, still a void in her bed and her heart and her life. Still a wall between Brenda and her only child. Darryl, as usual, was right. She could almost smile. "Yes. We're spending the night. Why?"

He was flushed with excitement—even more hearteningly, he let her see it and share it. For the last year David had steadily become more withdrawn, relating more readily to video screens than human beings. He stopped shooting off the balsa wood and plastic Estes rockets he and Darryl had loved. Even the karate lessons withered to a ritualistic monthly embarrassment. "There's a dig of some kind going on right up in the hills. A mile, tops. Dr. Speakman said that they're letting tourists look around at the outside. Called it pre-atha . . . atha . . ." David shook his head. "Something or other. Can we go?"

NO.

She heard Darryl's voice so clearly in the back of her mind that she almost jumped. But David peered up at her, waiting for her to say no. His eyes blinking slowly between ears too large for his head.

"Let's see if there's a rental car. If there is, I guess we can stop in."

David whooped.

The ancient beet red rental VeeDub revived memories of Darryl's ancient bug. Of college beer runs and topologically improbable makeout sessions. Painful, and frustrating, and very very exciting. Much like Darryl himself.

It was still good masochistic fun to have her knees crunched up under the dashboard, and continuously worry about bruising her hip with the stick shift.

They rumbled down a rutted road, past a Nite-Spot motel that she marked as a possibility. Almost immediately she saw the UC minivan, parked among six or seven dusty hot cars in a rough turnout. A few people were scattered about. A couple of spindly-legged card tables stood beneath pale awnings. Behind them, red and grey rock spurs jutted titanically from the earth. Dr. Speakman, the tall man, carted a wooden box out of the minivan. Brenda's Beetle had barely stopped before David leapt out and ran over. Speakman raised one heavy eyebrow in greeting.

"Mrs. Chase?" Dr. Speakman held out a firm, dry hand. His pink hand was paled by dust, her umber skin darkened by the New Mexican sun. She liked his slightly exasperated expression. "Your son is quite the buff, isn't he?"

"I'm afraid so. This is the fourth site in ten days."

"You've been to the ones outside of Tucson?"

"Three days ago. Spent the last day or so just driving around in the hills. We were headed home, when . . . well, you probably heard the most of it."

The parking area was small and dusty. A tired-looking Indian woman sat behind a table, selling pieces of her heritage to bored tourists for exorbitant prices. A bad deal on both sides.

They followed a light trickle of tourists past a series

of ancient rusted campers. The path led though the base of a cliff, through a narrow pass lined with scrub brush, and into an open area guarded by another ancient brown woman at another dusty card table. The woman looked up at them with an automatic, tired greeting. Then she saw David, and the expression wavered. The smile was still in place, but something in the eyes had changed.

Her hands went to a turquoise necklace around her withered neck. "You take," she said, and offered it to him.

He ran his fingers over the individual stones. He looked up at Brenda cautiously. "Can I have it?"

"You have your allowance. Can you afford it?"

David dug small brown hands into his jeans pockets, and came up empty. He started to give the necklace back. She held her wrinkled palms up to him. "No, no," she said. "You take. You take."

A much younger man with the same general skin tones and Amerind facial features approached them, leading a small group of tourists. "Mom?" he said. The old woman spoke to him in a rapid-fire, staccato language, and he replied in the same. He smiled uneasily, and laid his hand on David's shoulder. "She says that you are in danger. She wants you to have it."

Brenda chuckled. "All part of the show, right? She gives one of these away every day?"

"Actually, no. I don't completely understand it. She's been a little funny ever since the UC people uncovered the old ruins."

"Old ruins?"

"They're not my people's," he said.

"Pre-Athabascan," Speakman said. "You have some legends that might fit, though, don't you, Julio?" The tall man had come quietly up behind them.

"Sure, Doc," Julio shaded his eyes and turned away a little, so that Brenda was no longer certain of his expression. "Why don't you take 'em on back?"

Julio sat down next to his mother, and watched stonily as Speakman put an arm around David and drew him down the narrow pass.

The cliff face was slashed with narrow ledges. Up above the first row were dozens of small cave mouths. Higher there was a second tier of ledges, and a single excavation hole.

"These don't look like cliff dwellings," David said.

"Good eye. There's no evidence that anyone ever lived here," Speakman said. "More like storage lockers. We've found pottery, and carvings. The nearest dwellings are almost a hundred miles away."

"Maybe it's a toxic waste dump," David said.

They approached a fenced-off area. Big yellow-and-black banners proclaimed **OFF LIMITS. ANTHROPOLOGICAL/ARCHAEOLOGICAL RESEARCH SITE.**

David peered around the banner. "So that's where you're working?"

"Yes. Up the cliff face. We're using rope ladders right now. See that hole at the top? Maybe it's a burial ground. But for just one person. Maybe a chief, or a respected shaman. Its old—*really* old. Hard to figure."

"Why?"

"Because we can't read any of the glyphs. This is one for the books." Speakman wiped his forehead with a long, sinewy arm. "There's no historical record, only some oblique references to a burial ground." He pulled a tarp away from a wooden table set in the shade. On it were displayed dozens of pottery shards and fragments. They were unusually bright shades of blue and yellow and a kind of glistening blood brown.

"Unusual," Speakman said, holding up a blue fragment the size of his thumb. "Really a unique polychromatic glaze. I think its Mimbrino."

"Mimbrino?" Brenda asked.

"They're extinct. They migrated around the southwest

in seminomadic bands, following game and available water. No one knows much about them. Here,'' he said, and handed the shard to David. ''It's your birthday, isn't it?''

''Uh . . . yeah.''

''No—'' Brenda said automatically. David's eyes pleaded with her. She clamped her mouth shut.

''Don't tell anybody.'' Speakman was delighted with his malfeasance. ''In a couple of days we expect to break through to the real site. We're going to see something people haven't seen for hundreds of years.'' He laughed. ''It will probably be open to the public next year. Come on back then.''

''We'll try,'' Brenda said.

David said nothing, staring at, and playing with, the brilliant blue shard of ancient pottery.

It was one o'clock in the morning in the Nite-Spot motel. The ancient air-conditioning hummed and clattered. David rolled out of bed and put the poor beast out of its misery. It was actually too *cold*—the thin walls and the desert night air simply didn't hold heat. He sat back on the edge of his narrow bed. In the other twin, Brenda snored steadily. David lay back onto his side, listening to the air-conditioning. Listening to the occasional roar of trucks hurtling along the two-lane highway just outside their room.

A sliver of moonlight shimmered on the bedside table. Its cool, bright finger touched the pottery shard, and the turquoise necklace next to it. The shard was so blue. So beautiful. It seemed to call to him. The necklace didn't shine half so much, almost as if the shard were draining its luster.

His heartbeat thundered. When it grew loud enough to deafen him he slipped on his pants, shoes, and a jersey.

David knew his mother's sleep patterns. Barring an earthquake, she wouldn't wake until seven, guaranteed.

He found the key and tucked it into his pants, and then slipped out of the door.

The room was quiet for a moment. Then Brenda whispered "David . . . ?" as if a feather of alarm were tickling the back of her neck. She climbed up near the edge of consciousness, but then fatigue pulled her back down into the pit.

"David . . . ?" Then her steady snoring resumed.

David waited for the headlights to pass, then scooted across the road, finding another shadow to conceal him. The full moon flamed silver.

No sound. He grinned. *Spiderman knew there was nothing to stop him from completing the mission* . . . He climbed across a crude, low gate, landing lightly on the far side. He froze. Somewhere in the distance, a coyote yipped over its kill.

The cliffs glared down on him, sheer and hostile. He wondered if they knew he was there. Wondered if, in some strange way, they were sensitive to his passage in the night. What would they think of him, sneaking in here after all the tourists and professors went away. Would they be honored? Insulted? He really didn't know, and wasn't certain that he wanted to find out.

He came to the yellow-and-black banners, and paused for an instant. He scanned in all directions. Nothing. No movement, only distant motor sounds. The nape of his neck tingled.

Super Mario watched for the appearance of the big toothy blobs, soon to bounce out of the shadows in search of power pills.

He waited, but nothing happened. He giggled. He hated his giggle, and was tired of waiting for his voice to change.

The moon above him was bright and half-full, pockmarked and stained yellow by dust suspended in the still desert air.

David continued. The path narrowed, then broadened again, and he was amid the new excavations. He searched the rock until he found a likely place for a handhold, and tested it. Weathered sandstone. He inspected several potential avenues, then decided.

It took a quarter of an hour to climb the first twenty feet. Twice, the sandstone crumbled, and he almost fell. By the time he reached the first ledge he quaked so badly he had to pause for five minutes, listening to the coyotes. He rolled flat on his stomach, and peered back down at the ground. This was getting too real. He pretended it was just another video game. *Lemmings,* maybe. *I made it to the second level. Where're my bonus points?*

A rope ladder made the second climb much easier. He guessed that the lower ladders had been locked away for security—and was mighty happy to use the rope now. A fall from this height would mean a broken arm, at the very least. No way to hide THAT from Mom.

He rolled over onto the second ledge, huffing but feeling that good wicked sense of clandestine accomplishment.

He fished in his right pocket and brought out a pocketknife rigged with a Flickit single-hand release. His left pocket yielded a Bic disposable flashlight. He flicked his Bic, and his blade, and growled impressively. *Ready for anything. What a stud.*

The entrance hole was only half his own height. *Must have been little people, used to stooping.*

The cave was higher on the inside, high enough for him to stand. He splashed the flashlight across the walls, noting the petroglyphs, excited. He'd never seen anything like this. There were symbols that looked like men, some abstract lightning bolts, maybe some bighorn sheep. A series of concentric circles. And then hovering in what might have been the sky was a cross between a jellyfish and an octopus. Nasty looking mother.

He heard his own giggle again, and still didn't like it

much. It sounded even worse here in the cave. Not even a laugh, really. More like a gasp.

In the very back he found an adobe wall, greyish in the Bic's flat, sharp light. Someone had been digging at it. What was it that Dr. Speakman said? A burial ground, or something . . . ?

The air was getting stale in here. He scratched at the wall with his knife, encouraged when the first mud scraps curled away. Holding the flat flashlight in his teeth, he scraped harder. He backed up a couple of steps, set himself, and kicked once, twice, three times hard.

It crumbled. Even though it was growing colder, he was sweating now. He shined his flashlight around in the crack.

It was black beyond the wall, but the Bic revealed a mound of earth, with a pot of some kind perched upon it.

Even in the flat light it glittered, shone, seemed almost to glow. More of the petroglyphs chipped around its circumference, similar to those on the wall.

He widened the crack until he could fit both arms in, and then pulled, tumbling out pieces of masonry. Keeping the little flashlight in his teeth, he crawled through the crack, and into the chamber beyond.

There was still no sound, and that was weird enough. The night was so still that it *hummed.* Maybe that *humm* was always there, but only when all of the background noise died away could you really hear it.

The *humm* grew louder, the closer he got to the urn, or vase, whatever the hell it was. Finally, it was almost deafening.

He touched the jar. There came sudden, complete silence.

For a while he crouched there, breathing the bad air, listening to his own heartbeat, fingertips barely brushing the smooth glaze of the clay pot. What was it? God . . . a burial pot from the extinct Mimbrinos? It could be worth twenty or thirty *thousand* dollars. David didn't consider himself a thief, but for that kind of money he was willing to change career tracks.

He rolled the pot onto its side. It weighed maybe ten pounds. He pulled it toward him, and tapped it. He held it up beside his ear. Nothing except a continuance of that vague, slow *humming* sound. The jar seemed COLD. . . .

An icicle slid into his heart.

David gasped, grabbed his chest, and the jar slipped from his hands. And shattered on the ground.

He sucked air, eyes watering, and for a moment the pain retreated.

What happened next was impossible. Red dots. Thousands of them. Some kind of glowing red bees—something, flooded from between the splintered fragments. David *shrieked* and backed away, hands in front of his face, palms out. It was too little, too late.

The cloud of red bees swarmed around him, biting, stinging . . .

He howled, and backed frantically toward the entrance. He managed to crawl out of the cave. The world consisted of nothing but pain and swollen sound. He made it to the cave's mouth. Blind, pain-maddened, David began his frantic descent. Blood-slicked hands slipped on the rungs, and he lost his grip. He slid, almost fell, managed to grip the rungs again, hung there for a minute, new agony in shoulders and wrists and elbows. The pain retreated again, and he made it halfway down before the pain slammed him again.

As he started to scream the red things flew into his mouth, down his throat, stinging and biting and tearing . . .

And up his nose, setting his brain on fire . . .

And feeding on his eyes . . .

He fell the last five feet, struck the ground, and staggered up. He ran, and crashed blindly into a wall. He slid to the dirt, fingers scrabbling at the rock.

Sobbing, he curled into a ball, and waited to die.

After an eternity, the buzzing stopped. The pain decreased, then vanished altogether. David opened his eyes, amazed to find that his lids still worked. He held his hands out in front of his eyes. In the starlight, they looked like engineers' gloves.

He groaned, a sound he hardly recognized as his own voice. He had to get to mommy. He had to get home. She would fix everything. She would make everything all better. . . .

He staggered toward the distant motel, arms outstretched, shuffling, burning up with pain.

But with every step, the pain diminished. With every footfall, the swelling decreased. Sensation returned to his limbs. By the time he sighted the motel, he felt almost normal. By the Nite-Stop's flickering neon Vacancy sign, he examined his hands. They bore no trace of what had happened.

He shivered, making the hardest decision of his twelve years.

Somehow, all of the swelling had vanished. There remained no evidence that the entire thing hadn't been the evilest dream of his life.

So. Choice One: he could tell his mother, and get the hell whaled out of him, and maybe get in trouble for breaking a priceless Native American artifact.

Choice Two: he could keep his mouth shut, and hope that whatever had happened to him would never happen again.

He stared at his hands. They still *looked* like the hands which had swung at the ends of his arms for the past twelve years. . . .

He unlocked the front door and slipped back into the room. He stood and listened carefully for the sound of her breathing. No snores, but definitely a deep, smooth drone.

David slipped off his shoes and pants, folded them and chucked them into the plastic laundry bag. Hopefully, she wouldn't notice the dust and stains. In the cheap flat motel mirror was the reflection of a normal twelve-year-old kid. A little scared, but otherwise a perfectly normal kid.

It was the last time that David ever saw him.

2

The woman in the white smock moved through the sterile white hallways of Westside Memorial Hospital with purpose and intention, that "unmuggable" quality which New Yorkers seem to possess from the cradle, and the rest of America learns only through hard, painful experience.

Her name was Annelle Trias. She was a muscular chunk of a brunette in her late twenties, with a Ph.D. in Developmental Psychology and a masters in Neuroanatomy. Her standard operational attitude was GO. At the moment, she was focused on one almost overwhelming problem.

Patient: David Chase
Age: 12
Height: 5'4"
Weight: 85 pounds

Painfully thin. His mother said that he had been losing weight, and sleep, for three months now. Pediatricians had been no help. There was nothing organically wrong with the boy, and nothing psychologically wrong . . .

Except for the nightmares. Ceaseless. Remorseless. Violent. Terrifying. And so he came here, to Westside's nationally recognized sleep lab, hoping for a miracle.

She charged through the last door, and into the children's rec room. It held a Ping-Pong table, a television set, one pinball and two video games, and a wide variety of toys, most chosen for their ability to give an observant therapist insights into a child's mind.

Trias had consulted with sixteen patients so far this year, and David was unique among them. He was the only African-American, he was the youngest, the smallest, and the frailest.

He stood before the room's most popular video game, intently manipulating Ninja Turtles as they clashed swords and nunchaku against the minions of an older, chunky blond kid. The blond kid's face was a mask of frustration. He bit his lip, slapped the side of the video game arrhythmically, and cursed under his breath.

The older boy stomped away. Brenda had been sitting against the wall, reading *Byte* magazine. She folded it carefully, and walked over to her son. "I'll try a game," she said brightly.

David ignored her, and shoved another quarter into the machine. *One Player or Two?* the screen asked. David chose *One*.

Brenda's smile flickered and died. She sat and opened her magazine again.

"David?" Trias said. He was lost in the game. "David?"

She waited until the animated sequence ended, then touched his shoulder. He faced her, and his eyes dropped.

He was even smaller than she remembered from the previous day's interview. He was one of those rare kids whose personalities are larger than their bodies. You remembered them as taller, stronger, more beautiful than they actually are.

In reality, David was quite a small child. And growing smaller by the week. In the eight weeks since his mother had first taken him to the doctor, he had lost twelve pounds. His facial bones were assuming a skull shape.

His eyes were fever bright. "We're ready for you, David."

He nodded. David absorbed in his computers, Brenda immersed in hers. The gap between them had once been bridged by a father, Darryl Chase. Divorced, then deceased. Trias could *feel* his absence.

Mrs. Chase looked up, stood, and smoothed her impeccably tailored business suit before crossing the room. She extended a warm, moist palm. "I'm grateful you could make time for us."

"Your therapist, Dr. Gage, is an old friend of mine. We were trench mates at Stanford. I respect his opinion."

David walked slightly behind them, saying nothing.

Brenda broke the silence. "Dr. Gage said you earned your degree when you were twenty-three. Wrote *Dreams* when you were twenty-four. Is that right?"

"It's amazing what obsession can accomplish. But then, you know that. How many female African-American vice presidents at DataComp?"

"You're looking at her."

Trias opened her office door for David, and noted how he walked. Stiffly, almost as if his body were animated from above. As if he was losing touch with it, and keeping it moving only by an effort of will. Odd.

She glided behind a mahogany desk. There was a large sign on the wall behind her desk, which read ***Am I dreaming NOW?***

"Please sit," Trias said cheerfully. "I want to check the statement we took yesterday, David. When did the nightmares start?"

"Three months ago." His voice was very quiet. She waited for him to continue. As with the previous interview, he just dropped his eyes to the floor, studying the rug pattern.

"We'd just gotten back from our vacation," Brenda prompted.

"Was it a good vacation?"

He nodded.

"Was it unusual in any way?"

He said nothing. Finally his mother spoke. "After Darryl . . . died, I don't think I handled things well. Things were coming apart at DataComp, and it needed my attention." Her hands were held tightly in her lap. "David needed it too. This was a chance for us to be together, in places where all three of us had been happy, once."

Dr. Trias nodded. "David. Tell me about the dreams."

He sank back into the chair.

"David?" Brenda whispered urgently.

He looked away from her. "They're always different," he mumbled. "The ones I can remember."

"Can you tell me the one that you can remember most clearly?"

"They're always different," he said. "And they're all the same."

"Tell me one that you remember." Brenda opened her mouth, but Trias raised a warning finger.

The office was silent for a long time. There was nothing but the whirring and churning of the air-conditioning. Then David began to speak.

"I'm kind of like a moth," he said. "I mean, I've got wings, and I fly around. Sometimes I'll pass something shiny and I can see myself, and I'll look like me. And sometimes I'll look down at myself, and I look like an insect, but it's OK, I like that too. And I'm flying through this garden. And I'm just looking at the flowers and things as I go through. And then I hit it."

"It?"

"Something sticky. I'm caught."

Suddenly, David wasn't talking about it anymore. He was *living* it. His body twitched. "I try to escape. I pull, and it hurts. It feels like I'm tearing my body apart trying to escape."

His shoulder rolled, and his left arm straightened, as if his fingers were stuck to his chair.

"Something's coming for me," he whispered. His body was almost vibrating, quivering, as if he were a bowstring drawn too tight, plucked by the hand of a clumsy musician. "It's coming . . ."

"Can you describe it?"

"Eight legs. Black, bulbous body. Oh, God . . ." His eyes snapped wide open, and rolled up. "The jaws, the *jaws!*" Then he screamed: "Mommy!"

Brenda started from her seat.

"Sit down!" Trias snapped. Then added: "Please." She smiled pleasantly, then turned back to David. "It's a spider?"

"Yes."

"Can you see that you're only watching the spider trying to kill the moth? That it's in your own garden?"

You could almost hear the gears grinding to a halt in his mind, stripping, trying to change direction. "Garden . . . ?" he asked finally.

"In your garden. Just a little spider. Can you see that? And that you could put your heel on it, crush it, if you wanted to?"

He gulped, and nodded, not totally believing, but trying to.

"All right, come on back to us," Trias said finally. "This is the dream which has haunted you?"

He stared at the ground. "Once I was a bird with a broken wing. A cat was getting closer. I was a minnow, and I was caught in a jellyfish of some kind. It really stung."

"When did you have *that* dream?" Dr. Trias asked.

"Two weeks ago."

"The pain seemed very real?"

He looked over at his mother, and then back at the doctor. "No," he said, and there was fierce intelligence in the young eyes. "You weren't listening to me. Nobody listens to me. I said that *it really stung.*"

Brenda swallowed hard. The boy stripped his shirt off.

His back was scored with five thin parallel lines. They looked as if someone had drawn a razor shallowly along his flesh, then rubbed alum into the wounds.

"How did that happen?" Trias asked.

"In the dream." He looked around the room, and then broke into tears. "I knew you wouldn't believe me. Nobody believes me." He bolted from the chair and out the door. Brenda started from her chair, and Trias shook her head. "One of the nurses will bring him back."

With one long fingernail, Brenda picked at the perfect cuticle on her left thumb. "What do you think?"

"Stigmata?" Trias smiled grimly. "There are documented cases of psychosomatically induced wounds. But that's still a long shot."

"What is it then?"

"This was your first trip together in three years?"

"Yes." She stared at the floor. "I had to try. After his father . . . my ex-husband passed away. And under such terrible circumstances." Her hands shook, and she blinked hard. She dug into her purse until she found a tissue, and wiped at her eyes.

"What circumstances were those?"

"Darryl had a heart condition. Quite serious. I begged him to slow down, but singing was his life."

"Singing?"

"Yes. He was a backup singer. Sessions. Did a lot of club work. It was exciting. He was always on the verge of 'Makin' it.' "

Brenda's smile was a sad, sweet one, regretful but not bitter. " 'We're makin' it now, Babe.' He used to get some little check, two or three thousand dollars. And say 'We're makin' it now, Babe.' "

"You were the primary breadwinner?"

"He made money, but it wasn't steady. One of us had to worry about the future. God knows Darryl wouldn't." She wiped at her eyes again. "He took an apartment after we divorced. A neighbor found him, dead." She was whispering now. "He was trying to reach the telephone. I think . . . I think that David believes that his father died because we weren't there to help."

"I see. You are very involved with your career, aren't you?"

"Are you implying that he's doing it for the attention?"

"It wouldn't be the first time."

"But he wakes up *screaming*."

"Something very easy to fake."

Brenda shook her head adamantly. "No. Ever since David was a baby, if he was having a nightmare, his breathing would change. He'd make a soft cooing sound before he'd start to cry. He'd be asleep when the change started. He does it now, before the nightmares. There's no way he could know he does that."

"He could tape himself . . ." Trias said thoughtfully.

She exploded. "Oh, come on, Doctor! What are you saying? I thought Westside *helped* people. Why the third degree? Isn't our money good enough for you?"

Trias smiled. "Yes. Quite good enough. In fact, I've already decided to take your case."

A blond male nurse appeared in the doorway, David in tow. His eyes were clear and bright, and he was laughing.

Brenda brightened instantly. "What? Have you two got a secret?"

"Larry's got *Sonic the Hedgehog,* Mom." For the first time he seemed truly alive.

"My kids love video games," the nurse said. "It's at home right now, but I can bring it tomorrow, and plug it in at the rec room."

"Solid," David said.

"Sit down, David," Trias said. He did. "How much do you know about our institute?"

"You do dream stuff."

"Very good. The process is called Lucid Dreaming.

Lucid dreaming is a state of dreaming where you *know* that you are dreaming, and can therefore control elements of the dream."

"I don't understand."

Trias frowned, and then brightened. "It's kind of like a video game. Most of the time, the machines just sit there, playing images by themselves, right?"

"Right . . ."

"But when you put in your money, and put your hands on the joystick, you start taking control of what happens. Would you like to learn how to do that?"

David nodded slowly and emphatically.

"Good. We're going to be using several techniques to teach you this. One of them is called Mnemonic Induction of Lucid Dreams. We'll call it MILD. It was developed by Dr. Stephen LaBerge at Stanford University. You are going to learn to ask yourself the question on the wall: ***'Am I Dreaming NOW?'*** a thousand times a day. You will learn to notice the difference between the dreaming state and the waking state. For instance: how do you know that you're awake right now?"

David looked a little uncertain. "That's a weird question. I'm sitting here."

"Yes, but a dream can feel just like reality. This could be a dream—and you and your mother would look just as real as reality. You would feel the chair, and see the desk."

David pinched himself. "Ouch," he grimaced. "See? I'm awake."

"Afraid not," Trias laughed. "If you pinch yourself in a dream, all that will happen is that you'll go *ouch.* It will probably feel like a pinch."

"So . . . ? How can I tell?"

Trias laughed and tossed him a paperback copy of *Dreams*. David snatched it out of the air.

"Nice catch. Now open it and read the top of any page."

David shrugged, and opened it at random. "—and the tendency for all mammals to dream an average of six to eight times a night implies that this is not a su . . . superfluous function—"

"That's enough. Now look at me. No, keep your thumb in the book. Keep your place."

David looked up. "What now?

"Now look back down at the page, and read those words to me again."

David stared at her as if she had lost her mind, but went ahead. "—and the tendency for all mammals to dream an average of six—"

"That's enough. Did you notice any difference?"

"No, of course not."

"That's right. And you won't. But if this had been a lucid dream you would have. If you were dreaming, and you read words on a page, and then looked away and back, the words would have changed."

David was fascinated. "Why is that?"

"Because in the waking state, your mind is constantly relating to the external environment, which is relatively unchanging. In a dream, the mind relates only to itself, constantly drawing new correlations, and creating new connections. So if you look away at anything, you trigger a new series of associations, and the dream page will shift to reflect it."

David's eyes lit up. "So I'd *know* I was in a dream. And then I could make myself wake up?"

"It's better than that, David. If you know you are dreaming, it is possible to take control of your dream. In a lucid dream, you can make literally anything happen, whenever you want it to happen. You could turn this desk into a pickle. You could fly—"

"Fly?"

"Yes—and the experience would seem absolutely real. In fact, flying is another test for dreaming. If you ever think that you are dreaming, and want to test it, jump up into the air. If you hover for even a second, it's a dream."

David was quiet, thoughtful. "You can teach this stuff?"

"I've taught *hundreds* of people," Trias said. "Although I admit that I've never taught anyone as young as you."

"And if I knew how to do this stuff, the next time a spider or something tried to get me—"

"You could turn it into a stone. Or you could be the gardener, and squash the spider. Or you could be a fly with super strength."

David was grinning now. "Wow! That would be great!"

Trias grew very serious. "But lucid dreams can be used for more than that, David. You can confront the monster, and find out what it wants. What it represents."

"I don't care about that," David protested. "I just want it to stop bothering me. Why in the world do I care what it *thinks*?"

"Well, like I said—the world of dreams is self-referential. In other words, it's created by your own thoughts and feelings. In other words, that monster is a part of you."

"Bullshit," David said, then covered his mouth sheepishly.

Brenda said "David . . ."

"Think about it. Sometimes you'll have a dream about a bully at school, or a teacher—only they don't look like a bully or a teacher in your dream. Now, you can turn that monster into a . . . oh, a snail in your dream, but you can't turn the teacher into a snail, now can you?"

"Well, no."

"So what you do in your dream won't help you very much in school, now, will it?"

"I guess not," he admitted.

"But if in your dream, you can turn the monster into

a friend, then you can see that that teacher is really an ally, trying to help you learn. And maybe that bully is just as scared as you are, and tries to hide that fear by making YOU afraid . . ."

"That really sucks."

"Yes, it does. But people are like that. You know they are."

"Yeah. I guess."

"So—do you want to play my game? It's more exciting than *Pac-Man.*"

"*Anything's* better than *Pac-Man.*" David thought for a while, and then nodded.

David was unaware of anything in his surroundings, not the lights flickering dimly overhead, or the leads attached to his limbs and head in the basement sleep lab. The cubicle was almost completely dark. It was two o'clock in the morning.

On the other side of the glass dividing wall, Nurse Larry slipped his glasses off and polished them on his shirt.

"How's our boy?" Trias asked, closing the outer door quietly behind her.

"Fine. Third REM cycle tonight, and he's fine."

In the past week, David had grasped the mechanics of lucid dream induction like a champion. Thousands of times a day, he asked himself if he was dreaming. He had gone through the sensory awareness drills, and visualization drills, applying himself like an athlete training for the Olympics. In that period, he hadn't experienced a single unmanageable nightmare.

Brenda had turned a cubicle down the hall into both office and bedroom. Fax and modem and cellular phone linked her to her office at DataComp. She not only hadn't missed a teleconference, her sleep hadn't been interrupted for three days.

"We're beginning a dream," Larry said.

"Is he stable?

Larry frowned. "We're getting a little rise in blood pressure," he said. "Heartbeat is accelerating. Skin temperature dropping."

He looked at the meters. "We're still safe—"

On the cot, David curled onto his side. His legs began to twitch.

"Unusual," Trias said. "Ordinarily, limbs are still during REM activity." This was true, an adaptation minimizing chances of attracting the odd nocturnal predator.

"Still, it isn't unique. Let's see what—" Larry leaned closer to the Sun work station running the encephalographic imaging program. The jagged white video line suddenly split into two different patterns, arcing and crackling across the display. "Damn," Larry said. "Never seen anything like this before."

"Shit," Trias said. "I like the old EGGs better. This new stuff is always malfunctioning—"

Suddenly David's eyes flew open. He stared, fingers crooked into claws, scratching at the sheets. He stared up at the ceiling. The veins in his forehead stood out until they looked like a road map.

"Jesus Christ." Trias rubbed her eyes. The fatigue, the stress. It seemed that there was some kind of *light* in the other room. Light that hadn't been there a moment ago. A halo or an aurora.

It was all too much. David's body arched under the stress until it seemed that every young muscle was stretched to its breaking point. He arched and then crashed down into the cot over and over again, eyes staring, crying *"Huuuhhh! Huuuhhh!"*

Trias frowned. "What the hell—"

The door behind them crashed open, and Brenda stormed in, nightgown trailing gauzily behind her. "What's wrong with him?"

"Nightmare."

"Well—wake him up!"

There was something wrong with the lighting, and the entire room began to *humm.*

Trias entered the sleeping chamber, and touched David's shoulder. His hand flew to her wrist, biting down upon it with a strength so ferocious that it barely seemed human.

His face, in that moment, wasn't the face of a twelve-year-old boy at all. It was the face of something far, far older, something looking out through David's face, pushing through that younger face, staring up at her, creating the bizarre illusion of two people living in a single body.

His nails were hurting her, cutting into her flesh. She jerked her arm away, his nails tearing furrows in her skin as she did.

Larry came to David's side. David's arm flew up and back, smashing into the nurse's face. His glasses whipped off, and flew across the room, smashing into the wall and cracking the plastic lenses.

For an instant, David sat up, staring, that terrible mewling sound straining between his lips. Then Brenda had her arms around him. He bit at her, scratched at her blindly. Then the terrible seizure seemed to pass and he collapsed, shuddering in her arms, a small dark terrified child, locked in the arms of his mother, a woman every bit as afraid.

"What did you see?" Dr. Trias asked.

"It was coming," David said. "It was coming to kill me, and there was nothing that I could do."

"What was it?"

"It was a tiger. I was a rabbit. I tried to turn it into something else."

"Did you do what I asked you to do?"

"I tried to run, but my foot was in a trap," he said, and the shuddering was more violent now.

Brenda touched the back of his hand. "Did you do what the doctor said?" she asked.

He stared at her. ''I tried to fight, and it didn't do any good,'' he said.

''David,'' Trias was growing exasperated now. ''Did you do what I've taught you to do?''

David stared at the floor, then snapped his head up. ''Did I ask what it wanted!? Did I ask what it wanted? Did I remember my lucid dream crap? That's what everybody wants to know, isn't it?''

He was so small, so fierce, like some tiny trapped forest creature, with only raw nerve standing between him and complete breakdown. He spit out the next words. ''Yes. I remembered. I woke up in the middle of the dream,'' he said.

''What was it like?''

''Everything was so bright, so vivid. Realer than real. And twisted in a funny kind of way. It was a forest—''

David woke up, looked down at himself, and saw that his black skin had been replaced by fine white fur. He was a rabbit, and felt a rabbit's fever-quick reflexes, and experienced a rabbit's extreme sensory capacity. A rabbit, in a forest of vines and ferns and moist green earth, crowned by trees reaching higher than the sky.

''I'm not a rabbit,'' he thought. ''I'm a human being . . .'' But there was something so placid about the experience that he was inclined to go along with it for the present moment. *Go along with it . . .*

And then he heard it. Something was coming up from behind him, along the jungle trail. *Flee.*

He hopped, and then ran, and . . .

With sudden, shocking finality a snare loop closed around his ankle. David pulled this way and that, struggling, and then at the last second calmed himself. This was a dream. This was *his* dream, and he could control it. The doctor said so.

It was hard to believe, but . . . he looked down at the

soil beneath his feet, and studied it, and noticed that the harder he looked at it the more it changed.

As he concentrated on his name . . . *Your name is David Chase. You live at 1356 Winona. Your name is David Chase*—very slowly, one tiny bit at a time, his body began to shift, began to reshape itself into a much more human form. Not so the creature that came through the leaves, directly toward him.

It was gigantic, as thick as a car, and with a wedge-shaped, mottled head. It seemed to grin at him. And it became a shape somewhat more like a human being. And the voice said: "So. Do you think that you know something now? Do you think that you mean anything to me? I will have you, little one. Through you I will enter into the world. I don't want you. I want what lies beyond you. In a week, the moon is full. Then, I come. Relax and live. Resist and die. Not tonight. No. Not tomorrow night. But we will grow close together, you and I. Very close. And then we will become one . . ."

It flowed closer and closer. The rabbit lashed out with a desperate paw, striking the thing's nose. It just laughed, and laughed—and then lunged down, and BIT—

The pain *burned* into him. Into his bones. Into his marrow. His scream drove him out of his own body, rising high above the forest, looking down as he watched the snake-thing eating him.

Eating him. Taking huge, bloody bites out of him, savaging him a mouthful at a time, and then—

Then he woke up.

There was silence in the office. Dr. Trias was the first to speak. "May I see those bruises, David?" she asked.

David raised his nightshirt, wincing.

There, in a half-circle that bisected his waist, was a ridge-row of red marks. His skin was badly bruised.

Brenda whispered, "What's happening, Doctor?"

"I'm not . . . really certain, Mrs. Chase."

"Isn't there anything you can do to stop him from dreaming?"

"The psychological consequences of dream deprivation can be severe. There are drugs which can inhibit REM activity, but I have never recommended them to my patients."

"Then I'll take him to someone who *will* prescribe them." Brenda's mouth was set in a tight, thin line. "I'd do anything to help David."

"Would you quit your job?" he asked quietly.

Brenda took on a very reasonable mother-to-child voice. "I'm on leave now, David. I'm with you."

"Just you and me and your fax," he said miserably.

"David, that's not fair."

"Nothing seemed to help," David whispered. "It was lucid, but I was just more helpless."

Trias closed her eyes. She needed to think.

"Before you do that," she said finally, "I would like to introduce you to a man named Tristan Worley."

3

Trias drove her silver Lexus north on the San Diego Freeway, through the Sepulveda Pass and the San Fernando Valley. The San Diego became the Golden State, and Trias took them east on something called the Antelope Valley Freeway, through communities called Canyon Country, and Lancaster, out into the high desert. She pulled off the freeway onto a street that had a number, not a name, and headed out into the scrub land.

"Tell me again about this 'Lightning Elk,' " Brenda said nervously. "Are you sure it's safe to leave David with him?"

"I met him at a dream conference in San Francisco. He has a masters in clinical psychology, and ran a youth center in Tehachapi before the state funds dried up. He spoke on Native American approaches to the dream world."

"What tribe is he?" David asked quietly. Those were his first words of the two-hour trip.

"He's a metis, or mixed blood, David. Irish, Cherokee, God knows what else. He's also what he calls a Twisted Hair, which means someone who blends different disciplines. In this case, traditional Native American teachings—what he calls the Sweet Medicine Sundance path, and martial arts."

"Martial arts. This Chulakua stuff?"

The road was bumpy and ill paved. The sun was high in the sky, and when Brenda touched the inside of the passenger window, it was unpleasantly hot. The air-conditioning in Trias's Lexus was blasting overtime.

"It comes from the Cherokee tradition, and was intended to teach their warriors to deal with fear."

"And you think it might help? Really?"

"I was impressed enough to ask him to the clinic two years ago. He's helped me out maybe six times. He's a little far-out on the Indian Juju, but he's great with kids. I mentioned your case. He was interested." She smiled confidently. "What have we got to lose?"

Shelves of blasted rock jutted out of the earth in seeming defiance of gravity. From two miles away, they stood in prehistoric relief, bisecting even more distant mountains. David pressed his face against the hot window glass, fogging it with his breath.

An old, blue forty-foot trailer was parked off the road near the rocks. Behind it loomed a geodesic dome perhaps twelve feet high, surrounded by a ring of white rocks. Between the trailer and the dome was some kind of flat tarp, anchored close to the ground.

Trias pulled them off the road and next to the trailer. As soon as the car stopped, David hopped out, stretching.

The trailer door opened, and an old man shuffled out.

"David," Trias said. "Meet Lightning Elk."

"You're the Karate instructor?" David asked quickly.

"Not Karate," the old man said. "Chulakua. Much older. Much deeper." He hefted a can of Jolt cola in his right hand, and grinned. "Anyone want a drink?"

Lightning Elk might have been a well-preserved seventy, or a wasted forty. It was difficult to tell. He chain-smoked black Djarums, and had consumed three Jolt colas in the two hours they had been at his home. His hair receded, and his hands bore terrible liver spots. The inside of the trailer was an incredible museum. There were crystal skulls, and eagle feathers in probably illegal array. There were bone pipes, kachina dolls, and paintings of distinguished-looking Indians gazing off toward far horizons.

David stared at them, especially at a photo of a pot with an unusual blue glaze. The design on it seemed to be some kind of octopoidal creature.

"I've seen something like this before," he said.

Elk was entirely casual. "Really? Where?"

"New Mexico. Look." David reached into his pocket, and pulled out the sliver of pottery. He handed it to Elk, who studied it, then held it sideways. "Can I keep this for a while?"

"Sure."

Another shelf stood on the far side of the room, this one crammed with martial arts trophies. David went straight to them. "Karate and Judo?" He examined a foot-high action bronze of two grappling athletes. The inscription read: "Grand Championship, Heavyweight. Salt Lake City Open Tournament, 1967."

Lightning Elk chuckled. Brenda watched as he shuffled over. He moved as if he had suffered terrible injury. Only his eyes were truly alive, but . . .

There was something in them that both frightened and comforted her. They were eyes that were gazing at life from a different perspective. A perspective closer to . . . some truth? Or just old and tired eyes?

"Not Judo," he said softly. "Ju Jitsu."

"What's the difference?"

"Karate is mostly striking. Judo is mostly grappling. Shorinji Ju Jitsu is the place where striking and grappling meet."

"Wow," David said. "Wow." He wandered around the trailer, touching this and that. Goggle-eyed, he circumnavigated the room. Lightning Elk chuckled.

"The name on the trophy says Tristan Worley," David said.

"That's my white name. Lightning Elk is my medicine name. It was given to me by Grandfather, and it has power." He shook his head. "White names have no power."

Trias rolled her eyes and chuckled.

The telephone rang. Elk didn't even glance at the answering machine as it took the call. This was the twelfth time in two hours that that had happened.

He stood very close to David, touched his face, his hair, seeming to drink him in in an almost-intimate manner. He walked around him, studied him, and then leaned close.

"Do you want to work with me, David?" he whispered. "It must be your decision."

"He needs someone—" Brenda began.

Lightning Elk looked at her sharply. "David," he whispered. "It must be your decision."

Slowly, David nodded.

"Come here, David," Trias said. She dug into her purse and extracted a package of Djarum cigarettes. David took them, and handed them to Lightning Elk.

The old man inclined his head gravely. "Ho," he said. "Well, now. We'll just have to see what we can do."

* * *

Brenda hugged David tightly, heart thundering in her chest. "I don't know what to do," she whispered. "I'm running out of answers."

She straightened, wiped her eyes, and looked squarely into Elk's face. "We're not rich people," she said. "But if you can help my boy, I'll pay you anything you want."

"This isn't about money," Elk said.

"I'll be back tomorrow night, David" she said. "I'll take you home, then, if you want."

He nodded silently, and watched as his mother and Dr. Trias climbed into the dusty silver Lexus. David held his rucksack in his left hand, looking out after them as they rolled away. Gently, Lightning Elk touched his shoulder.

"She wanted to go," David said somberly. "She couldn't wait to get away."

"It doesn't matter. This is not a thing for women," Elk said. "Come on. Let's go to the gym."

His flat, shuffling step was utterly unlike the athletic, springy stride of David's old Tae Kwon Do instructor. Just outside the heavy canvas of the geodesic dome was a huge tarp, held up by yard-long stakes. It was square, and fifty feet along each side.

"What is this?" David asked.

Lightning Elk peeled back a corner, exposing the largest sand painting David had ever seen.

It was a circle thirty feet in diameter. The colors were primarily browns and greens, with blocks of blue and red. Black lines of abstract birds, and a dozen dancing suns were positioned in a geometric design.

David stared at it.

"I've been making that ever since I bought this land, five years ago."

"But doesn't the wind . . . ?"

"Every day. And I fix it every day. I'll never be finished with it." He bent to a pot of colored sand, and extracted a handful of black. He poured a thin line down, touching up one of two humanoid stick figures. "See?

That was me, and my grandfather. He taught me many things.'' He pointed several feet left. There was another human form, this one blurred. ''Two weeks ago one of my students visited. I had him add himself to the painting. I fix him, but . . .'' He shrugged. ''He'll have to come back, and put himself back in. These are my memories. My life.''

''Why did you move here?'' David asked.

''There are places in the world that are special,'' Elk said simply. ''This one is special to me.''

Lightning Elk fished in his pocket for a set of keys, and slipped one into the chipped white door set into the dome.

David stepped across the threshold, into another world.

The dome was a little larger than it looked from the outside, and except for fifty square feet of mat in the middle of the floor, it was completely crammed with martial arts equipment, a weight machine, a climbing machine, and a stretch rack.

Elk took off his shirt to put on a black pajama-like gi top. But for a small, discreet potbelly, he was whipcord lean and powerful. His skin was wrinkled and loose, true, but the muscle beneath it moved as if he were some kind of an animal, and not a human being at all. He sat in an old black frame metal chair, and reached into a Styrofoam cooler. It was filled with water and red soft drink cans. He pulled out a can of Jolt cola and popped the tab.

''You studied Tae Kwon Do, David?''

The boy nodded.''

''Would you show me what you remember?''

The boy nodded, and faced off with one of the heavy bags, seven feet tall but only eighteen inches in diameter. A thick rubber ring was set at the five-foot level, as if someone had pushed the bag through an auto inner tube.

Eighty percent of David's weight was on his left foot, which was bent slightly to preserve balance. The right leg, in front, was also bent. The ball of his foot provided the balance point. David swung his shoulders, transferred weight from the rear to the front, and pivoted. That rear leg came up in a whistling arc, and smacked against the bag. It was beautifully done.

"Ho," Elk said. "Now—do the same thing, and get mad."

"Mad?"

"Angry. Think about someone hurting you. Or hurting your mother. Get mad."

David scrunched up his face, and faced off again, and yelled, and whacked the bag a little harder this time.

Elk shook his head. He took a sip of cola, set it down, and, with terrible effort, levered himself out of the chair.

"Not like that." Very casually, he slapped David's right cheek with his left hand. The sound echoed through the confined space like a rifle shot.

David's head whipped to the left, and his hands flew to his face. His eyes filled with tears, and they spilled, and began to run down his face.

Elk sneered. "What's wrong, sissy? Did that hurt mommy's little baby?" David stared at Elk as if he had gone insane. "Get out of my sight, you puling, sickening little porch monkey nigger bastar—"

David exploded. He was wild, he was uncoordinated, and he was also a whirlwind. For a single instant, all of his physical frailty was transformed into intention. His rear foot whipped off the floor and thudded into Elk, barely cushioned by a blocking arm. Elk scooped him off the ground and took him to the mat.

David landed hard enough to *whoof* the air out of his lungs, and send him into a blurred flurry of movement. Again and again Elk pinned him, and David just barely managed to wiggle away. He kicked out and almost caught Elk in the face with his heel. Elk rolled it, caught David again, and pulled him back just before he could escape the mat.

David was like a hot-eyed, desperate animal: denied escape, denied the resignation of certain capture. He gasped, his face reddened. Elk wrestled him onto his side. David hit him in the mouth with his elbow. Elk just barely rode it, then the boy eeled out of his grip, kicking and striking wildly, until exhaustion overwhelmed him. Then he was sobbing, all skill gone, and Elk had him down on the mat.

Somehow the grappling hold had become a hug. Elk held on to him tightly, and David screamed, and scratched and finally collapsed into a shuddering heap, tears streaming down his dark cheeks.

"Shhh, shhhh," Elk said. "It's been hard, hasn't it? There hasn't been anyone you could trust. No one."

David just trembled, like a little rabbit.

"Your father died. Your mother can't wait to get back to her job. And you make Trias doubt what she thinks she knows." David bit at him, and Elk twisted aside.

"I can help you, David. You're not crazy. I'll be here." David heaved against him, struggling to break free, and Elk just held more tightly, until finally, David quieted.

"I won't leave you," Elk said. "I swear I won't leave you, not until this is over, and you don't need me anymore."

David heaved again, but he wasn't trying very hard anymore, as if he had accepted the confinement.

"You won't leave?" David said.

"No. I won't."

"My father left."

"I know. It wasn't your fault."

"How can you help me? No one can help me."

"All human beings feel alone and afraid," Elk said. "These are merely the twin faces of Death. Chulakua teaches you to generate your emotions at will. To use them, and discover what each of them does to your mind, your body, your energy, your clarity. And as you become clear, we'll find out more about what is troubling you. It is my people's way."

David stared up at him. "You don't look so Indian to me."

"Been around white people too much," Elk said.

"Me, too," David said. And they stared at each other, and started to laugh, and laugh, and somewhere in the laughter David started crying again, only now he was clinging to Lightning Elk's chest. A small desperate child who, for the first time in months, was not alone.

Dinner was good, and hot. Fresh bread made in Lightning Elk's kitchen. A huge salad, and a kind of turkey chili. After a wedge of apple pie, David went through Elk's collection of videotapes, discovered a Sega Genesis video game and lured Elk into a match. They played until almost midnight, David driven by feverish energy. He beat Elk seven games out of ten, then sagged with fatigue.

Elk had been waiting for this. He walked David out to the dome and handed him his rucksack. "Find a place that feels right to you," he said.

"Out here?" David asked. "I'm sleeping out *here*?"

"Sure," Elk said.

David walked around in a circle, and then collapsed into a heap on the mat. Elk grinned, and helped him spread out his bag. "Do me a favor," Elk said. "Go and use the bathroom now. I don't want you to leave your sleeping bag again tonight."

David trudged off in the direction of the toilet, and while he was gone, Elk gathered several small leather pouches. When David returned, Elk sat him down.

He smiled again, but now the smile was stern. "You will not move from here tonight?" he asked.

David shook his head.

"Good."

Elk reached into his leather pouch, and produced a handful of white sand. He drew a circle around David's bag, and then a second circle outside that. A handful of red sand went between them.

He made several small sun shapes, and a rough bird shape, singing something unintelligible to himself. Then he took a feathered pipe, filled it, and lit it. He revolved it in his hand in an odd pattern, and spoke quietly, blowing smoke into each of the cardinal directions.

By the time that he was finished, David was asleep, curled up in the middle of the sand circles, snoring as the thin wisps of smoke wafted around him.

Elk watched him carefully, and then stepped out of the dome into the moonlight. He slipped the fragment of pottery from his pocket and examined it again, in the moonlight. "Mimbrino," he said thoughtfully. He looked up at the moon. "Six nights until the full moon." He lit a clove cigarette, dragged deeply, and exhaled. "What would you make of *this*, Grandfather?"

David was barefooted, dressed in grey sweats. They sat cross-legged in a cliff shadow in a dry riverbed. The cliffs towered above them. The sun was just now appearing above them, a piercing yellow eye into another, starker reality.

Elk had awakened him before first light. David, normally capable of sleeping until noon, found himself rested and . . . calm. The previous night had brought no dreams, nor the shadows of dreams. He felt healed. In Elk's battered old Chevy pickup, they drove out into the mountains to this river bed. Elk spread an ancient tatami straw mat out upon the sand, and set up three folding lawn chairs.

Lightning Elk sat in one of the folding chairs next to a duffel bag filled with martial arts weapons. David sat at his feet. Elk lit another in an apparently endless string of clove cigarettes. He hawked and spit into an empty Jolt can. "The trick is that it also works the other way. You can teach the body things that the mind can't understand. When you do that, you are taking charge of the whole body-mind connection. These are things that the old ones understood—things that we have lost as we became more 'sophisticated.' I'm not sure it was a good trade.

"Stand up," he commanded. "Rolls."

"Why rolling?" David asked. "What about punching and kicking?"

"All of that is well and good, but most fights end up on the ground. It is important that the Earth be your friend."

David stood, and Elk pointed to two folding chairs with a broomstick slung across the seats.

"Roll," Elk said. He punched a button on a ghetto blaster at his side. Rhythmic drum music and vocal chants boomed out of the chrome speakers.

David took two steps, dived over the broom handle and hit the mat rolling, and sprang to his feet.

He pivoted, and ran back the other direction, and dived, hitting the mat, rolling. Back and forth and back and forth he went, arcing over and over across the broom handle, turning the actions into a kind of grim dance. His little face was screwed up with tension, and he grunted with effort every time he hit the mat.

Finally he lay on his side on the mat, hair matted with sweat, panting. "Why . . . the music?" he asked.

"Because rhythm is coordination," Elk said. "It is also the doorway to the deep mind. You are tired now. Good. Stand."

David tottered to his feet. He was so tired and dizzy that he could barely stand.

Elk handed him a thirty-inch wooden dowel.

"What . . . what is this for?"

"You are going to learn about energy," he said. "Now. Relax." He approached a man-shaped dummy wired against the side of the truck. He regarded it for a few moment, and then exploded into action. So swiftly that the eye could hardly follow it, Elk performed a non-stop jazz drum solo on that dummy. The tip, the butt, the side of the dowel; his left hand, his elbow, knees, and head—all of them came into play in a pop-popping, thumping, jarring, teeth-rattling cacophony. In ten seconds, he must have hit it fifty or sixty times.

At the end of the performance, David's mouth was hanging open.

"Now watch, David." Elk wiped his forehead. "Every one of those strikes followed what we call an *angle of attack.*" He stroked at the one o'clock position. "That's a number one." He backhanded at the 10:00 position. "That's a number two." He curved the stick up at the 5:00. "That's a number three," and backhanded it at the 7:00. "That's a number four." And then he poked straight in in the center of the imaginary clockface. "And that's a number five. There are advantages to thinking like this." He swooped in along the 1:00 line again. "That's a number one," he said. He threw an overhand right at the bag, that followed the same approximate arc. "And that's a number one, too."

He backhanded with his left fist, once again following the same arc. "And that's a number one."

He stepped back, jumped into the air and spun. His left foot whipped up and around in a beautiful spinning crescent, hitting the bag in the exact same place, following the exact same arc. There was a hollow *p-Thoom!* that shook the truck.

"And *that* is a number one, as well. In other words, instead of worrying about what kind of kick or punch is coming at you, all you worry about is the *line of attack.* It simplifies your choices.

"There is another thing which works for us, boy." He picked up a staff, and whirled it like a willow wand. David was drop-jawed with astonishment. Elk whipped it up and around, smacking the dummy this way and that.

Then he threw the staff down and plucked up a blunt tomahawk.

And then a knife. And then a saber. And then double thirty-inch sticks. Short and long sticks. Two sabers. A stick no bigger than a roll of quarters.

And then his empty hands. And in all cases, the same basic patterns, the same blurring, eye-baffling speed, the same thunderous power boomed out of the dummy.

Elk stopped, panting now. He narrowed his eyes at David, who felt very, very cowed indeed.

"No matter what the weapon. No matter what the technique. There are only five different ways to hit. That means that you can use a knife, a tree branch, a rolled-up newspaper, your empty hands, or anything else, the same way. Do you know what else it means?"

David shook his head dumbly.

"It means that in the dream world, any tool that you find, you can use. Any combination of fang or claw you can find. Any kind of tool or natural weapon that is used against you, you can counter. This is not about the body. It is about the mind. It is the doorway to power. Can you see that?"

David nodded. "Sir?" he asked meekly.

"Yes?"

"That jump kick. You shouldn't really have been able to do that . . ."

Elk chuckled. "My body couldn't do it," he said frankly.

"Then how?"

"My body exists inside my mind," he said. "And my mind can do anything."

The sun was near the horizon. David worked in twenty-minute increments, resting, listening to Elk talk, listening to the steady beat of the music. He was so tired that he felt as if he were floating. Now he lay on his back, listening to the music, listening to the rhythm of Elk's voice.

"See it," Elk said. "Number one. See the line of fire." David visualized it, sharply, arcing toward him, as he had all day. Time wasn't . . . right, somehow, in this place. The mountains and the sun and the movement, and the slow, steady breathing through which Elk guided him all melded together to create a unity which seemed to peel away fatigue rather than add to it. "See it—" Elk said.

Then suddenly there was a flare. One line of light, or fire which was brighter than the others, and suddenly David was rolling out of the way, onto his stomach. Elk's staff rapped down right where his head had been.

David rolled up, panting. He had *seen* that light, a streak of phosphor, like a wooden match struck in the dark. *Seen* it. Hadn't he?

"I . . . heard you," he said.

Elk nodded his head. "I know."

David knelt there. The line of fire was still graven in his mind. Stark. Like a meteor fall.

"I . . . I feel a little nauseous," he said.

Elk began to fold the mat up. "It's time to stop for the day." David helped him carry it to the back of the old truck.

Just before he got in, David said: "I didn't really hear you."

"I know," Elk said, and started the truck.

Brenda's Impala pulled up in front of the trailer at about eleven that evening. Elk answered the front door wearing jogging sweats and a robe, his wrinkled belly protruding over the elastic band. Despite the belly, the muscles of chest and shoulders stood out in stringy definition.

She peered over his shoulder at her son. He was sitting in front of the television, cradling a video control in his hands. "Hi, David. Everything all right, darling?"

He barely glanced at her. ''Hi, Mom,'' he said, and continued blowing away animated terrorists on the TV screen.

Elk laughed silently and shook a clove cigarette out of his pack.

''How is he doing?''

Elk leaned back against the doorframe. ''I guess he's in pretty good shape. Coordination is good—he just beat me three games out of four at *Mercenary*. No problems there.''

''But . . . ?'' She heard the fear in her own voice, and hated it.

''Haven't you wondered,'' he said, ''why I took this case?''

''I thought that Trias was a friend.''

''Who thinks I'm a kook,'' he laughed.

''If it's a matter of money . . .'' She dug into her purse for her checkbook.

Elk laughed. ''No. I cancelled all of my other appointments. I was wondering if you had any idea why?''

She looked at this man's face, and then remembered the face of her son, an intense but innocent face, absorbed in his beloved games. Trying to remember the last time she saw that innocent child nearly broke her heart. ''No,'' she said in a small voice. ''I guess I don't have any idea at all.''

He laughed again. ''Not for you, or for the boy. More for myself, really.''

''What do you mean?''

''To Doctor Trias,'' he said, exhaling a long and pungent plume of smoke, ''the world of dreams is a phantasm. An engine chugging after the ignition has been turned off. And she deals with it in that sense. She is a good woman, but that is not my people's attitude.''

''What is?''

''The dream world, what my people call the Nagual, is as real as this one, which we call the Tonal. Perhaps realer. After all—in the Tonal, your mind can conceive of things that your body cannot actualize. A world, in other words, smaller than your mind. Do you know what my people say about this world?" He waved his hands out, pointing at the stars, the waxing moon, the dark titanic shape of the mountains.

"No, what?" She wasn't certain that she wanted to hear it.

"This is where our dreams overlap. Your dreams, and mine. What both you and I dream about in common, we can discuss. But if I tell you about my dream, and it doesn't match your reality, you call it illusion. Add a third person, and 'reality' is that which all three of us agree upon. The place where all three of our dreams overlap. Do you understand?"

"Consensus reality," she said.

"Ho. And we think that what a thousand or a million people agree upon is real, is realer than that which one person sees and feels. But is it?"

"I don't know," she said honestly.

"No," he said kindly. "You don't. Your son sees something in the dream. Every time he sees it, it is different, correct?"

"Yes . . ." Her brow furrowed. "Dr. Trias said that if you are in a dream, and you look at a page, and look away, and then look back, the writing will have changed. Because there is no external . . ."

"Referent. A nice, safe word. However, what she didn't say, and what you have to understand is that the page remains a page. The book remains a book. Do you grasp the significance?"

"I think so," she said. "The essence of the thing remains the same."

"Ho. What won't happen is that you hold a book, look away, and have it turn into a rose—unless in your mind, a book and a rose are somehow the same. Do you understand?"

"Like if . . . if both are a source of beauty?"

"Exactly. A book of poetry might turn into a rose. Now. Every night David dreams. Almost every night, he dreams of something coming to eat him. To kill him. The shape and form of the thing is the external factor. It will be influenced by images that he takes in during the day. He might see a dog or a cat. Hear someone say something about a lion. And so on."

"The external referent."

"Ho. But what doesn't change is the fear, the evil, the pain. The realism. And when he began to take control of the dream, the dream became more violent?"

"Why?"

"It is as if the dream was taking its time with him before. Lazily. Enjoying itself. Coming closer and closer. When he began to fight back, he took it by surprise, and it fought—showed him a lesson. Last night I protected him—"

"How?"

He smiled. "Sorry." He snubbed out his fifty-first cigarette of the day, and started on his fifty-second.

"What does all of this mean to you?"

"I live my dreams," he said. "This body is not my only body. This face is not my only face." He looked at her sideways, almost slyly, and then laughed at the expression of disbelief.

"Don't worry. I'm not crazy. I just talk that way."

"That's a relief."

"I listen to my dreams," he said. "And they tell me that your son is in trouble. Your son had a piece of pot from a people called the Mimbrino. He shouldn't have had it. Somehow, he has . . . caught a fear."

" 'Caught a fear'?"

"Something deep." In the darkness, his face illumined by the coal at the end of his cigarette, he seemed positively ancient. "In the old days, people talked about demons."

Brenda felt her face tighten.

"Oh, we don't talk about that anymore. I suppose that it's just a way of talking about those deep-seated, acute fear responses that Annelle Trias believes in. Things that warp the mind out of frame." His eyes were focused somewhere far away, and the words trailed off.

His face went through an eerie series of minichanges. Smiling and then frowning. Confidence, and then something that was very much like fear.

"Let's say that David is attacking himself. If you are starving, your body will eat its own muscle. David is starving. Emotionally. I know a little about you, and his father."

She turned away from him. For a few seconds she said nothing, and then: "It hadn't worked for a long time. We tried to hold it together for David's sake. It just wasn't working."

"David said that he can't remember ever seeing the two of you kiss, or hold hands, or make any display of affection. He feels like he was an accident that ruined both your lives."

"That's not fair."

"Nothing about this is fair."

"You started to say something else, Mr. Elk," she said quietly.

"Just Elk," he laughed, and exhaled a plume of smoke. "I started to say that if you weren't a businesswoman, hooked into the Tonal world, I would say that he was possessed."

She was very, very quiet. "Possessed?"

He laughed, and it was almost convincing. Almost.

"That would be crazy, of course. Who believes in demons, in this day and age?" Too casually, he asked: "By the way—where did David get that potsherd?"

She chuckled along with him, and found the sound remarkably unconvincing. "This summer we went to Arizona and New Mexico. We visited some old cliff dwellings."

He inhaled. "Just checking. That's what David said."

"If there were such things . . . such things as demons . . . visiting old cliff dwellings couldn't get you into trouble, could it?"

"If there were?"

"Just imagine with me."

"Well, then, I'd say no. Those old dwellings have been visited by too many people. Even if there had ever been some . . . *power* in them, it would have been dissipated."

Her next words were so soft that he could barely bear them. "What if it was a new one? Just opened?"

He flicked his cigarette out into the darkness. It spun, trailing sparks. "Where did you go?"

"About a hundred miles north of Phoenix. There was a new dig. A burial ground of some kind."

"Did he . . . touch anything? Any freshly uncovered objects?"

"What kind of object?"

"It might look like a pot," he said softly. "A sealed container of some kind."

"And what would be in it?"

"Broken, burned bones. Ashes. Not much." The desert was very quiet, save for a low wind whistling through the brush. "I'm going to tell you something. It is only a legend, of course. Grandfather said that the Mimbrinos were powerful wizards. That other tribes were afraid of them. They had stories about them. The Mimbrinos worked with spirits—demons, I guess. One of them was very close to the Western concept of the Sand Man—he who brings sleep, and dreams. If David came into contact with such a thing . . ." He exhaled powerfully. "It would kill him."

Brenda sank against the side of the trailer, little

strength left in her legs. "What could stop it?" she whispered.

"A warrior-shaman. One who can walk between worlds. Someone willing to die in order to kill. That's really the only secret there is, you know. Resist such a thing, and it will probably kill you—like resistance in an electrical line. There are stories of people literally burning up. Spontaneous combustion." He laughed again. "Just fairy tales."

"He's just a boy," she said. She looked back at David. He was sprawled in front of the television, now, asleep.

"And it's all just a fantasy anyway," Elk said.

"If . . . if there was something in him . . . why wouldn't it have taken him by now?"

"It might be on a lunar cycle," Elk said. "Its strength peaks when the moon is full. And every time it is, it takes more of him. Another week, perhaps," he said, watching the sky. "Five days."

"You told Trias that Chulakua was devised to help young warriors deal with fear," she said. "That's not exactly true, is it?"

He just smiled.

"If there *was* . . . something. Trying to get David. Can he learn to kick or punch a nightmare away . . . ?"

"It's the emotions that are important, not the moves. All of the kicking and punching, the throws and holds . . . ? All bullshit. Take any human being and place him in a focused, deinhibited state—insanity, angel dust, extreme threat to life or loved ones—and you will produce an animal response, an R-Brain response. He'd rip most black belts into pieces." He chuckled, and dropped his cigarette to the dirt at his side, then ground his heel into it.

"A good instructor will give you joy, and discovery. And then ecstasy, beyond fear or pain, or joy—pure sensation. Total deinhibition, flowing through a body strong enough and flexible enough and balanced enough to take that kind of emotional current without burning up. That is the true job of a real instructor—to prepare his students for death, and therefore, for life. Everything else is a shadow of the real purpose."

"Can you teach David that?"

"In five days? No. But I might be able to help him teach himself."

Brenda held David in her arms. He seemed small and cool—but at peace. More peaceful than she had seen him in months. Whatever was happening here, in this place, was good for her child.

"David?" she said softly. He stirred, and half opened his eyes. He pressed his cool mouth against her cheek.

"Mom," he said. And rested his cheek against her.

"David. Do you want to stay here?"

"Stay," he said. "Stay here. Feel . . . safe."

She nodded, and kissed his forehead, and walked back out to Elk. "I don't know what you're doing," she said. "But it seems to be healthy." She took his hand. "Help him. Please."

"I'm trying," Elk said. "I have to teach him enough physical technique so that the emotions can flow. I'm going to keep it simple. Rolling. The five angles of attack—"

She clutched his wrists. "I don't believe in demons," she said. "I *can't*. But I believe that *something* is hurting my boy. All I want to know. What I *have* to know is: Can you help him? If you can't, I'll take him somewhere else. Or I'll put him somewhere he can't hurt himself. I have to do something, and I'm at the end of my rope." Her voice was cold steel. *"Can you help him?"*

He met her eyes. They locked, and there was no more lying, no more circumlocution. "Yes," he said. "I can help him."

"*Will* you help him?"

"Yes," Elk said. "I will."

4

Yea, though I walk through the valley of the Shadow of Death—

From the tip of his toes to his kneecaps, David was covered with bruises. Bruises from hitting the heavy bag, bruises from blocking Lightning Elk's strikes with the rattan sticks.

His diaphragm was sore from the breathing exercises. Inhaling for three, holding for twelve, then striking on the exhale, exhaling forcefully. Or exhaling after that twelve count retention as Lightning Elk punched or kicked him in the solar plexus. The pain was extreme.

David dropped to his knees, sucking air. He looked out over the shelf of rock, down onto the desert below. They worked in shadow, rested and talked when the sun stole the shade. For the past four days he had eaten well, worked hard, and slept every night within the circle of sand drawn by Lightning Elk.

The entire world stretched out beneath them, the sky so blue and crisp and wide above them, expanding to an infinite horizon. He could feel the *pulse* of this place.

And his body and mind awakened to its rhythm. He dreamed of light lines crisscrossing in darkness. Lightning Elk drilled David's body and mind until those lines seemed almost to hover in the air around him. It was easy to imagine them, carving the air between the two of them. It was true—there was no human movement except along those lines, and he saw them more and more clearly with every passing hour.

In the city, it might have seemed absurd. But here, in this place—

It seemed perfectly natural.

''Last night,'' David said, ''I started to dream again. I couldn't help it.''

"How did it feel?"

"Like there was something behind a gate, and it was coming for me."

"Tell me about the gate."

"It's made out of sand. It circles me. Sandstone, maybe. But the wind is eating at it."

"What's inside the gate."

"Me, I think."

"And outside?"

"I don't know."

"Come on," Elk said. "It's time to work."

They climbed. Up through rock chimneys so narrow that David could barely squeeze through, and marveled at the fact that the old man could contort his body to pass. The bastard must have been made out of catgut. "I need . . . to rest," he gasped. He rolled over onto a rock shelf, and collapsed, panting. Elk zipped open his backpack and threw David a Jolt cola.

It was warm, and flat, and incredibly delicious.

He was tired, but sleeping in Elk's gym within a circle of sand was a strangely calming and energizing experience. And this place . . . in the distance, at night, there was the glow of a distant town. Aside from that, they were wonderfully alone in the desert.

"I used to go climbing with . . . my dad," David said.

Elk was braced in a rock fissure, feet against one side, back against the other, resting comfortably. "My grandfather did the same for me," Elk said. He popped open a Jolt can and sipped happily. "He taught me how to climb, and hunt. And he taught me about power spots and light lines."

"What?"

"You'll see." He waited for David to finish his can and then said: "Rested?" Affirmative. "Then let's go."

The last fifty yards were sheer. Elk attached a rope to David's waist, and shinnied up ahead of him, surefooted as a goat. Despite the absurdity of the emotion, David felt as completely secure as he ever had in his life.

They came out on a flat shelf of rock, separated from the main mountain by a deep defile. They were about three hundred feet above the floor of the desert. David had an odd feeling as he climbed up. He tingled. The air smelled—*electrified.*

Elk was grinning. "You feel it, don't you."

David nodded.

"There are places of power. Some of them are in the land. Some of them are in human beings: centers of balance, nerve centers . . . centers of energy. Throw a kick," he said.

David set himself, and threw a roundhouse kick into the air.

"Fine," Elk said. "Now, move around. Eyes closed. Find a place here that feels right to you."

David closed his eyes and walked carefully. He felt odd. He remembered watching a video about a man dowsing for water, holding a *Y*-shaped stick before him, and how the stick would begin to vibrate when he was near water. His body felt like that now. With his eyes closed, he ordinarily saw tiny specks of light floating in the darkness. Now, they were beginning to coalesce into lines. At this moment, the line was distinct. His breathing filled him with light, and the light flowed down to his feet and seemed to connect him to the earth, and balance was perfect. His arm shot up and he heard and felt **CRACK**! and his right foot flew out, seemingly of its own accord, and that light flowed from the ground and swirled around his hip and shot out **CRACK**! and he felt it connect. He opened his eyes.

His arm had blocked Elk's twenty-four-inch stick, and his foot had retaliated without conscious thought.

"Perfect," Elk said. "This is your spot."

* * *

They ate, and talked, and as the sun began to sink below the horizon, David felt his fatigue rising up in him in red waves. "I'm so sleepy," he said.

"You've fought for months, little one."

"Look!" David said, pointing at a red-black shape wheeling in the sky.

"A hawk," Lightning Elk said. "A red hawk. This is your place," he said. "And that is your name."

"Hawk?"

"Little Hawk. The spirits sent it to you," he said.

David smiled. "Little Hawk."

"You have fought alone, but I am with you. It is coming for you, Little Hawk. Soon."

"How soon?"

"Days now. I can help, but I can't fight it for you."

David's small, dark face turned up to him. "Why not?"

"This is your fight, Little Hawk. Every man has his own."

"I'm not a man," David said reasonably. "I'm just a kid."

"If you are a child, you are doomed. You must be a man."

"What's the difference?"

Elk sighed. He drew out his pipe, and packed it from a tiny leather bag. He drew on it. The smoke was sweet, and somehow dry. "A child thinks he will live forever. A man knows he is going to die."

"Why is that important?"

"Because if you cannot win against this thing, this creature which comes for you, you must be willing to die with it. To take it with you into the spirit world. Fear clouds the mind. To accept death is to accept clarity. And between warriors, the one who sees most clearly will win."

"Do I really have a chance against it?"

Elk nodded silently. He puffed the pipe, saluting to the

four directions, and then passed it to David. "Smoke. And say the words I have taught you."

David took the pipe gingerly. He turned toward the sun. "To the West. I ask my ancestors for physical strength." He inhaled sharply, trying not to get any of the smoke into his lungs, and exhaled to the west. He turned north. "To the North. I ask my ancestors for strength of mind." Again he puffed, and exhaled sharply. This time, a little of the smoke seeped into his lungs, and he coughed. "To the East. I ask my ancestors for strength of spirit." This time, a little more seeped into his lungs. He felt dizzy, and wanted to sit down. The setting sun, glaring at the corner of his right eye as he faced south, seemed to pulse. "To the South. I ask my ancestors for strength of emotion." He inhaled, and exhaled a long, sweet stream.

Elk spoke quietly. "And now to the Void."

David inhaled and held it for a beat, felt the world spinning around him, as if he were the hub of an immense and eternal wheel. He trickled the smoke out of his mouth, wondering why he didn't cough. He felt that he should, but he didn't. "To the Void," David said. "I ask my ancestors to take me, to change me as . . ."

"As they will," Elk said. "The Void is death. And life. Sexuality. And the core of your being."

David was glassy-eyed. He sagged down to the rock, and handed the pipe back to Elk. He didn't want to move. Or think. The world spun around him, the newborn stars transformed into streaks of fire.

Elk might have been reading his mind.

"The world was once a cocoon of light," he said. He set out several small clay sand pots, and began sprinkling grains around David, all the way around him in a circle. David's heart was thunder. The stars were lightning.

"All was light. Then Man thought his mind was God, and pulled back from the light, each man into his separate cocoon. Listen to your heart, live in your heart, and the separation vanishes. This is our secret, David. Your opponent is you. Follow your heart. Follow the lines of light, and you and your opponent become one. One body, one mind, one will. The one who most clearly sees the light controls both bodies. The earth is you. Find the spots in the earth where there is light, where there is power, and you are infinite, no longer separate from the source of creation."

David blinked. How long had Elk been talking? And there was music, although the old man hadn't brought his tape player with him. He swore that he heard music, although perhaps it was only his heartbeat. It was in rhythm with his heart. So strong now, so loud. It thundered through the entire universe. The world spun, the stars threads of light weaving themselves around him, joining with the painting that Elk created around him, surrounding him, here up on the rocks. David stared. There were men painted into the sand, and there were stars. There was earth, and sky. And there was light.

David's eyelids felt very heavy. He leaned over onto his side, and stared at Elk as Elk sat, smoking his pipe and chanting rhythmically.

Oh. That was the music. And yet . . . it seemed that there were many voices. Just as it seem that the stars had become threads of light. He wanted to drift away, and the feeling was one of separation, as if he were drifting up above the boy that was David, into the light. Surrounded by light.

He heard his own voice. Terribly small and vulnerable. "This thing in my dreams. It's real?"

"No, Little Hawk," Elk said. "It is not." He swept his hand out to the horizon, to the wakening stars and the setting sun and the desert and the purpling mountains. "And neither is any of this."

David was asleep, near sleep, at the far edge of sleep when Elk nudged him to wakefulness. "Stand," he said, and David stood. He rolled himself out of his sleeping bag, the breath constricted in his throat.

There was something . . . odd about Elk. He stood, naked to the waist in the starlight. The rock beneath David's bare feet seemed very cold. He wasn't completely awake yet. The dreams: dreams of light, dreams of threads of fire weaving the universe together . . . were still with him, overlapping into his waking world. He shook his head, trying to clear it. The stars resolved to points.

There was something in Elk's hand. A twenty-four-inch stick. Elk's face was expressionless.

The stick whistled at him, arcing in from the left. A number one line. It glowed, David barely got his hand up in time, and the stick smashed against his arm. He staggered back, mute with shock.

Elk's eyes glowed. The stick came at him again. David dodged to the side. It slid past his ear, missing him by a hair.

He wanted to run—there was nowhere to go. The entire shelf of rock was no more than fifty feet across. And Elk, his teacher, his safety in an insane world, had gone mad. David sobbed, diving, rolling—and then his foot tingled. It had touched a spot on the ground, and he felt it. He *felt* it, something that was light and hot, and strong. The stick flashed down—but the instant before it did he saw the line of light, and he moved before it manifested into a physical attack. He lost that precious footing. He scrambled and . . .

—and found another spot on the rock. He felt complete, alive, the stars spinning into lines of light again, the light connecting him with Elk and the spots on the ground that he could see now, shining like patches of wet grass in the moonlight.

The stick descended. David blocked. As it whacked against his arm he felt the connection and *kicked*, and his instep slammed into Elk's ribs. The old man huffed, and glared balefully at him, and a fist whipped out, taking David in the stomach.

All the air *whuffed* out of him. He staggered back, to the very edge of the rock shelf, balancing there, staring down at the desert floor wheeling beneath him. Elk's eyes were suddenly very very sharp and cold. "Come on, boy!" Elk's body eclipsed the moon, luminescently haloed, light streaks snaking in all directions as David fought for balance—

And he felt something touch him. Right between the eyes, just above the eyebrows. It was less a touch than a palpable sound, a *ping* like the snapping of a rubber band, and David was jerked back from the edge of the cliff, actually *propelled* away from it. He landed on his knees, staring up at Lightning Elk, who looked down at him, a being composed of light.

Then there was *only* light.

And then there was darkness.

David sat up, slamming from sleep to wakefulness in a fraction of a second. Elk sat ten feet away, still smoking his pipe. The sun was cresting the eastern mountains. The sand painting around him was complete, immense, twelve feet in diameter. There were no signs of footprints, no smears or smudges. He checked his right arm. It was badly bruised.

"This is a story." Elk gestured toward the painting.

David stared at him.

"It tells of a young warrior. One who accidentally became a doorway to a great and ancient evil." He set his pipe down, and lit another of his clove cigarettes.

"Did you sit there all night?"

"We are out of time, David," he said. "The moon is almost full." He drew deeply. "In two days your mother will come for you." He shrugged. "The rest is up to you."

David watched as Elk gathered his bundles and pots.

David stood in the middle of the circle. Elk said nothing to him. David looked down. There were spots of sand with a shiny look. Sort of like the rock in the previous night's dream. He stepped out, stepped directly onto the patches that *felt* right. Onto a hawk. Onto the sun. Onto the image of a boy.

None of the sand smeared.

Elk smiled. "Well done, Little Hawk."

David stood on an ice plain, the cracks projecting in all directions. The clouds overhead were things of frozen foam, casting cold shadows upon the frozen ground.

Something moved beneath the ice. Something huge and dark, something silhouetted against the ice like a gigantic bat wing. David stood there, his spear at the ready.

He had always been here, and as the shape came closer and closer, it covered the underside of the ice, until everything in the entire frozen world was this one shape, this one living darkness.

He turned his collar up around his neck. Something was trying to speak to him, something at the corner of his mind.

But he ignored it. He had to concentrate. There was so much fear here, and such importance. Was it the village at stake? He couldn't remember. It was vague. He had a strange and distant sense that he was young to be carrying so much responsibility on his shoulders, but carry it he did.

The shape loomed up, a whale. It had to be a whale. Enough food to last his family for a month. But there was something wrong. He thought that he was hunting it.

But . . . it was . . .

Hunting him?

Am

David watched by the hole as it swooped around under the water, reared back—

Am I

And headed up to the hole, and now David could see its teeth. They were too large, and something shot through David now, something more than adrenaline, more than mortal fear.

Am I dreaming

And the face of the whale wasn't a whale's face at all. It was more like something octopoid. Some mollusk form, and as he watched it shifted. Now wolf. Now tiger. Now mantis. He knew this thing, *knew* it, and it thrust up through the ice, shattering it in slow-motion, and David knew that he had made a horrible mistake, knew that he was not the hunter at all. He had never been.

Am I dreaming NOW?

As if an electric cable had been rammed up his spine, David jolted to wakefulness within his dream. And in the moment that he knew it, he also knew that he was well and truly screwed.

The whale was coming down at him, looming with unimaginable speed and force and—

*It's **my** dream!*

The harpoon. He took a step to his left, set it into the ice and pole vaulted, just the way he'd seen on television a hundred times. He sprang out of the way of the thing, and whirled to see it leaping across the floes, crashing through sky and ice with every jump.

He fought to control the images. This was his dream, he could make anything anything he wanted, right? So why was this image, this thing in his own mind, fighting back, almost as if . . .

Almost as if it wasn't his dream. As if it was a shared dream. Both of them were dreaming. Both of—

His focus was off, way off. The thing was almost on him. Then he remembered again, realizing that it was coming at him from the left, arcing down . . .

A number one stroke. Huge, powerful, unstoppable.

But still just a number one stroke.

He saw the flare of light, the arc of the movement, and knew exactly where it would land. Even as he thought, the harpoon sucked ice from beneath his feet, became an angled wall in the shape of one of Elk's blocks. The creature smashed into it at an angle so that it glanced away, glanced off and thundered into the ice, and it flopped and twisted and looked at him and snarled—

So. You have learned Chulakua. The old man is a charlatan, trying to teach what he has never experienced. The woman Trias is a child, finger painting with the blood of gods. I will deal with both. Next time. Soon I take you, and through you, your mother—

The thing's mind opened, and suddenly David *saw*, and it was like dropping into a sea of raw, flaming sewage, evil and need and hunger ancient as the stars, and vaster still.

He *screamed—*

And sat up in his sleeping bag, in the gym, in the circle of white sand. He sobbed, hiccoughed, and vomited all over his bag. When his eyes focused, he saw that Elk was seated there, watching him. "It—it almost, almost got me."

"Did you fight back?"

"I tried. I tried."

"What happened?"

"I stopped it once. First I remembered that it was a dream, and I started changing things."

"Wasn't that better?"

"Yes . . ."

"And when you fought back, you actually turned it away . . . ?"

"Yes," he said. Elk tossed him a cloth, and David swabbed at his mouth. "But only because he didn't expect it. It's as if there is something actually alive in there, and it knows all about Chulakua. And it was waiting."

"Tell me the truth now, David. Tell me everything."

Haltingly and in a very small voice, he told Elk about the night in New Mexico, stealing out of the room, the climb, and the entrance into the cave.

"Mimbrino," Elk said soberly. "You came into contact with something which has entered your dream."

"It's not my dream!" he screamed. "It's *his* dream. He said . . ."

"What did he say?"

David could barely speak.

"David? What did he say?"

David told him everything, even the most terrible things, and by the end of it, was sobbing incoherently.

"David," Elk said slowly, "I was wrong. I thought this was a demon. I think that it is a man, an evil man. I think that his tribe killed him while he was asleep, and in the dream world. Do you understand? He is dead, asleep, dreaming that he is still alive."

Elk lit a cigarette. His hand was shaking.

"Elk?" David asked. "Is what he said true? You've never dealt with a demon?"

Elk's expression was dark. "It's the truth, Little Hawk. Grandfather trained me. I've prepared all my life for something like this." He exhaled a long stream of smoke. "Maybe in my heart I thought that the world had moved on. That such things didn't happen. The Great Spirit has a sense of humor. Maybe you're just here to show me how wrong I was. You're being punished for my sins."

Back in the mountains, a coyote howled. David wiped his hand across his forehead. It was clammy with a thick, foul perspiration. "Do I have any chance at *all?*" His voice cracked on the last word.

Elk stared off into the sky, eyes fixed, body very still except for the arm that took the cigarette to his mouth again and again. Finally, with a very measured voice, he spoke.

"Life must have been sweet for this Mimbrino. He has clung to it for a very long time. He may have lost . . .

perspective. He may be afraid to release life. If he fears, that will be your moment."

David wiped his face. "The moment to do what?"

"Awaken him. Fully. Remember: he is dead, asleep, dreaming that he is alive. Give him fear, and make him look at himself. He must know that he is dead. And return to the spirit world."

Trias stood with Brenda in the yard between the trailer and the gym. For twenty minutes Elk moved around the yard with the boy, holding a cushioned pad while David kicked and punched against it, face screwed in desperate concentration. Trias's expression grew more and more perturbed.

When the display was over, Brenda applauded politely. Trias cocked her head in puzzlement.

"David," she said, "would you come here, please?"

David walked unsteadily to her, and stood passively. Trias took his arm and studied it. "These bruises," she said. "When did this happen?"

She didn't wait for an answer. She examined his leg. From climbing, from striking the pads, from grappling and striking, David was a mass of bruises and contusions.

Trias's lips were a thin line. "Elk . . . I don't understand. What have you done to this child?"

"Taught him," he said bluntly.

Brenda drew David to her, looked carefully at the bruising. It was swollen, and tender. David yanked away when she tried to inspect it. "You did this?" she asked.

Elk nodded.

"How *could* you?" The pain, and betrayal and fear loaded into those three words was crippling.

"I don't understand," Trias said. "I assumed you were helping him to deal with his dreams, and teaching him some martial arts skills."

"That's what I've been doing."

"You never bruised any of my other patients. If you had, I assure you I would not have brought David."

"It was never necessary before," he said simply.

The fury in her voice was barely controlled. "Mr. Worley," she said, "what I see comes very close to child abuse. If you don't explain yourself more clearly, I'm going to insist that David return with us."

David froze. "Mom!" he screamed. "You've *got* to leave me with Elk. He's coming back. He's coming through me."

"What is?"

"Mimbrino," he said. "The dream demon. The Sand Man."

"Worley," Trias said bitterly, "I can't believe this. You were supposed to help him deal with his fears, not terrify him even more."

David clung to his mother. She seemed undecided, confused. "Mom," he said frantically, "it doesn't want to kill me. It wants to come through me. It wants you—"

"*What?*"

The words tumbled out in a rush. "It said that it wants to come into the world through me. It wants to have sex with you, through me, and to bring back its tribe—"

Trias was utterly speechless. Brenda snatched David's arm, pulled him next to her, and turned a withering blast of rage onto Elk. "What kind of *filth* have you been telling David?"

"My God," Trias stammered. "Just what the hell has been going *on* out here? This child is bruised, and hallucinating, and fantasizing about relations with his mother?"

Elk looked at both of them, in silence.

"Mom, Elk didn't tell me that—the Mimbrino did. In my dream."

"This is *over*," Brenda said.

Trias's face was a mask of fury. "I'm taking this child back to the hospital for examination. I now understand how you lost your funding. I'm shocked, disappointed, and ashamed of myself for suggesting you, Elk. If this child has been harmed . . . well, he's already been harmed, hasn't he? I have nothing more to say to you."

David struggled and bellowed as his mother hauled him back to the car. He glanced back at Lightning Elk, and squealed: "No!"

Elk stood very quietly, watching. David tore free from his mother's arms and ran to his teacher, and hugged him tightly.

Brenda and Trias were momentarily frozen. Elk returned the hug for ten seconds, and then carefully peeled David away, and held him at arm's length.

"Good bye, Little Hawk," Elk said.

David stared at him, something like resignation clouding his eyes, until at last he lowered them to the ground. "It's going to get me, isn't it?"

Elk shook his head.

"No," he said, raising David's chin until their eyes met. "No. It's not." Then he gently handed David back to his mother.

Elk watched them drive away. He lit a Djarum and sat on the porch of his trailer, staring out at the desert.

When he was finished with the first cigarette, he lit a second one. Then he spoke quietly. "I've done what I could, Grandfather."

The lie was there in the words. There was nothing that he could do to hide it. "She's his mother. She has the right to take him home."

She gave him birth. ***You*** *gave him his medicine name.*

He sighed. Whether you lived in the Tonal or the Nagual, sometimes there were no easy choices at all.

5

It was 2:48 in the morning.

"Mother," David said. His voice grew softer even as she listened, "Don't let me go to sleep. Please." He was back in the cubicle at Westside Memorial, wired to the machines, protected only by sheets and blankets. There were no circles of sand on the floor. Small things, perhaps—but without them, he felt full-blown panic.

"David," Trias said wearily. "We've gone as far with this as we can. You have to sleep. Your mother has to sleep."

He ignored Trias, and grabbed his mother's arm. "Elk swore he wouldn't leave me. He *swore*."

"It wasn't up to him, David," Brenda said. "We made a bad choice. We shouldn't have taken you there."

"He'll get me."

"You're safe from Elk now—"

"The Mimbrino! The Mimbrino will get me—"

Trias looked at Brenda with despair. "I'm sorry."

"David," Brenda said. She was so tired she could hardly keep her eyes open. "You'll get through all of this. And you'll get back to your life. Remember the way life used to be before all of this? Rock climbing, and Nintendo, and Screaming Yellow Zonkers? Remember?"

His small white teeth were set firmly in the meat of his underlip.

"It can be all of that again."

"When he comes, Mom," he said, flatly. "You can't help me. Neither of you can. I'm going to remember everything that Elk taught me."

"Please, David." She felt contempt for the derision in her own voice. "If this doesn't work, we're going to have to take you somewhere. To a hospital. Somewhere they can watch you all the time."

"Then you could get back to your job, right?"

"That's not fair, David."

"But it's true, isn't it? The only reason you're here is because . . ." His lids were so, so heavy. Too heavy. God, so heavy. Closing now.

"Because you need me," she said.

"I always needed you . . ."

And then his small hand had lost its grip on her, and David fell away and away and away, into sleep.

A man-shaped shadow moved through the bushes planted alongside Westside Memorial's north wall. It melted into the bushes a moment before a roving guard rounded the corner on his hourly patrol.

The guard was overweight and underpaid, an ex-cop named Cash. Cash was thinking about a bustling strip joint he had attended the previous evening. There, he had watched a blond with a round face and tight little titties bump and hump as Linda Ronstadt asked the musical question "When Will I Be Loved?"

Cash had had too many beers. In direct consequence thereof, he stood and yelled: "How 'bout right *now*, bitch?" fumbling for his fly to the general hilarity of the customers and the irritation of the club's three jumbo bouncers. As Linda wailed in the background, they had him by the armpits and Cash was on his butt on the sidewalk.

People just didn't understand.

He was about to fantasize about the dancer's berry-sized nipples for the hundredth time, when something caught his eye. Paper. Green paper. A *ten-dollar bill*, lying in a slash of light shining from a second floor window.

God *Damn*. He bent to pick it up, and never even felt the wiry arm slither around his neck.

Lightning Elk carefully lowered Cash to the ground. With that nerve strangle, the fat man would be unconscious for about three minutes, and would wake up intact save for the mother of all headaches. He might not even realize what had happened.

Elk slipped Cash's key ring off the guard's web belt, and slid over to a side door, testing keys until he found one that fit. He opened it a crack, stuck a branch in to keep the lock from springing shut, and reattached the keys to Cash's belt.

As an afterthought, he picked up the ten-dollar bill, and slipped it back in his pocket. Strange. He had intended to let the man have it, but after looking at him, he just couldn't do it. Maybe it was judgmental, but for some reason the guy just looked like an asshole.

David flew.

Not as a bird flies, or as a balloon flies, but in the manner that a small dreaming boy flies; with motions vaguely reminiscent of running, with arms and legs flailing at the clouds. His dreaming eyes were wide with wonder.

Los Angeles was far beneath him. He could see his old neighborhood. There was the schoolyard where he had played since he was six, when his father stopped . . .

Father . . . ?

He flew down and down, through the houses, then touched ground without remembering the last few feet of flight.

The puzzlement fading after a moment or two. Someone sat on the front porch of his old house, a tall, thin, dark man he recognized. He began to run, yelling "Father—"

"We're in REM sleep," Trias said. The line bleeped across the video screen. Her small blue eyes were chips of ice.

"Do you think he's all right?" Brenda asked.

Trias rubbed her eyes and leaned back into her chair. "There's no evidence of abuse, if that's what you mean. Maybe we overreacted. But *something* just told me to get David the hell out of there. It was a judgment call."

Brenda brushed David's forehead with her fingertips. "I just want my boy back."

"Look," Trias said. "He's smiling."

"Daddy?" David said.

His father sat dressed in jeans and a *Natalie Cole Live!* T-shirt, epoxying a tail fin onto a red-and-white plastic model rocket. David recognized it—it was called an Egg-Lofter. He remembered constructing one with his father, remembered twisting in the solid fuel engine, and twisting the two little wires down at the bottom. Then he and his dad went down to the schoolyard and shot that puppy off. At ignition, it accelerated too quickly for the eyes to follow, carrying its precious cargo into the sky. At zenith it *popped*, and a red-and-white parachute flared open. David and his dad watched it float safely to the ground. He felt his father's heavy arm across his shoulder, and knew that everything was well.

"It's been a while, David," his father said. And smiled. It seemed to David that his father's teeth were whiter and larger than he remembered them.

Am

"I thought that maybe we'd go out and fire a couple. What do you say?"

"I'd love it," David said, and felt as if he must be dreaming.

Am I

And the moment he thought it, he must have blinked, or fallen asleep and Dad must have bundled him off in the Impala. They were in the desert now. The mountains wavered in the heat, and the salt flats were hard and crisp beneath his feet. The Chevy looked bright, as bright as his father's teeth. And eyes.

They set up the Egg-Lofter. Dad took one of the igniters, and pushed it into the bottom of the motor tube, bent the wires back, and fastened the igniter clips.

"It's been a long time, eh, Tiger?" Dad said. "How long has it been since Mom took you out and fired a few with you?"

David smiled uncomfortably. "Well, she doesn't." He carefully thrust igniters into another motor.

"She's pretty busy isn't she, David?" Dad's teeth were huge, his smile so large that it looked like the smile on that guy the Joker, the one that Batman was almost always fighting, the one who had fallen in the vat of chemicals, and came out as a pasty-faced leering caricature of a human being. The one who looked like a clown, but the only jokes that he told or thought or laughed at were jokes about death and mutilation.

It was *that* face he saw, for just a moment.

"She's always too busy, isn't she, Davie-boy?" his father said, and reached out a hand for him. The arm was long and muscular, exactly like the brown arm David remembered, backed by the burning black eyes in his father's brown face. And all by itself, the rocket leapt off of the scaffold and into the sky, trailing smoke, and—

Am I dreaming—

Dad took him by the neck. They peered up into the sky together. The clouds burst into flame as the Egg-Lofter exploded. Chicken feathers and chunks of burnt fowl and live flaming birds fell screaming from the air. His father's face was very close to him now.

"You are powerful, David. *We* are powerful. We don't need your mother anymore. She never loved me, anyway—you know that. That means she can't love the male part of *you*. You and I don't need anything but each other. We don't need that old fool Elk, *that's* for sure. There isn't any need to fight—"

The teeth were so large, and so white and so near—

Am I dreaming Now?

* * *

"His skin temperature is 98.4," Trias said. There was just a hint of nervousness in her voice. "His blood pressure has risen slightly. His heartbeat has accelerated." She sipped at her coffee. "I would say that he's just entered a nightmare."

Dad's hand had grown into something very like a claw. It bit deeply into his shoulder. David spun, freeing his collar from the grip, tearing and spinning loose just as the head came down. The head was a human head on the body of a spider, grinning and leering and chomping, teeth clicking shut just an inch from David's throat.

"You're not my father," David yelled.

"But I *am*," it whispered sweetly. "I am what your father is *now*. You can join him." The thing made another absurdly delicate step forward, and David suddenly remembered that this was *his* dream—

A tomahawk appeared in his hand.

He swung it at a black, jointed leg. Green glop spilled out of the wound. The creature plunged down onto one knee. David raised the tomahawk and struck again and the thing howled—

"Curious," Trias said. "We've got a spike here."

Brenda came close, looked over Trias's shoulder at the video encephalograph. "What does that mean?"

"Not certain. He is undergoing an emotional stress of some kind. . . ."

"Are you certain that that isn't the machine?" she asked. "It seems to be humming a little more than usual."

Trias looked at her in surprise, as if she had just noticed that. "That's not the machine," she said uncertainly. "That's *David.*"

The spider disappeared. David stood in a hall which receded as far as his eye could see. Candles flickered in ornate holders on the walls, and the walls were covered with precious paintings. Complex piping tones echoed down at the far end.

The music soured as he approached a heavy wooden door. Light gushed from beneath it in waves of smoke. He pushed it open, and entered a maze of computers and drives, printers and monitors, and at the center, surrounded by a massive keyboard, labored Brenda. Her face was suffused with a kind of ecstatic intensity. He had seen it far too often. As her fingers stroked the keys, the piping flowed out, each note rising in the air like a crystal bubble. She worked the keyboard like a master pianist. The closer he came, the more intensely she bore down, stroking, and pounding. Sheets of paper flew out of the printers.

"Mom?" he said. "Mom?"

She worked on.

"Mom? I'm scared. I don't know what's going on here."

He came closer. There was something wrong with her face, that beautiful dark face that he knew so well.

"Mom?"

She whipped her head up. She had no eyes, only empty pits within which flashed a cathode display, an endless blankness with numbers and letters flashing across over and over, on and on, and as he watched, she smiled to him sweetly, and said:

"I have to work, David. It's for both of us. I need it for both of us."

"We have enough money," his lips fumbled over the words. "From Dad's insurance. You said so. I don't need money. I need *you*."

She smiled, as if there were so much more to life than his poor little brain could conceive of.

"David, there's work. And when the work is done, there will be time for us."

"There's never time. Dad had to *die* for you to make time, and then it took you a *year*—"

"Now go out and play—"

David turned, and almost died. He teetered on the raised and fractured brink of a volcanic pit. Far beneath him, hazed by heat, a river of lava crackled and boiled. *Things* moved in it.

"**Mommy**—"

She was gone. The computers, the printers, the entire room itself was gone. Flame lashed up around him. "**Mommieee!**" He screamed, nothing alive in him now except fear. "I needed you dammit, and you needed your work more than you loved me *or* Dad. I hate you. I *hate* you. You left me here and I wish you were *dead!*"

Brenda stumbled back, and one small hand went to her chest. She sucked air through her pursed, pinked lips, and shook her head.

Trias watched her carefully. "Mrs. Chase?" she asked. "Are you all right?"

Brenda stared, momentarily sightless, and shook her head an emphatic *no*.

The flesh around David's chest wrinkled, and something climbed out. It looked like a warped and twisted human infant, crimsoned by placental tissue. It grinned up at him, its head webbed with red threads, blood glistening on its white, white teeth, and dripping from the corners of its wide, white eyes.

"David," it said. "I'm here."

It crawled the rest of the way out of him, and fell heavily to the ground, heaving. With every breath it became just a little larger. It balanced on stumpy, wobbly stumpy, legs, growing still. It was a five-year-old David, naked save for the slick of gore. Then it was a twelve-year-old David, his twin except for a tighter, fuller sheath of muscle and outsize genitalia. Then it was him as a teenager, animalistically muscled and fully aroused. And then—

His father.

"David," the glistening father-thing craned its head. "You have cried for me, and I came. I have been within you the whole time."

Lava splashed sparks against the peak. Shrieks of the damned wafted from below, loud at first, then more distant.

"Father?"

"Your mother can't protect you," the thing said. "She doesn't really want to. Don't be afraid of me."

David was numb, and silent.

"I am you. I am what you want. What you feel inside is the child being devoured by the man. Your mother will try to keep you a child. Her dyke shrink will try to keep you a child. Lightning Elk *knows* he can't stop me. All his life he has played in the shadows of reality. I am the sun. Bow before me, David. Bow, and I will give you what you want."

"What is that?" David asked.

"Power," it said.

The room lights flickered. Trias stood over Brenda, a Dixie cup filled with water in her hand. She straightened and looked back over at the couch, the flickering lights alternately shading and exposing the suddenly deep lines in his face.

"Shit," she said quietly. Twin brain scan lines wavered on the monitor. One was a jarring forest of angry spikes. The other was David's normal boyish arcs.

Brenda felt as if someone had hit her in the center of the chest with a sledgehammer made of raw rage and grief. She felt as if she were imploding.

She barely noticed the alarms ringing in the halls outside. Running feet slapped the tile. Men were yelling.

Trias murmured, almost babbled, as if there were no

one in the room with her. "If the leads had slipped, I would think he was suffering an epileptic seizure. Or that there was damage to the corpus callosum, and the halves of his brain were no longer communicating with each other. Or . . ."

Trias's voice was a squeak. Her eyes were wide and fixed on David's body. The groaning, churning vibration had increased. "There is something going on . . . that I hadn't anticipated."

The monitor screen burst, sparks and shards of steel and glass fountaining into, and through, the ceiling.

Through the pain in her chest, Brenda managed to gasp: "Wake him up! Wake him up, damn you!"

One halting step at a time, Trias stumbled toward David.

"What do you want?" David stammered.

"What do *you* want?" his father asked in return. "Do you want things to go back to the way they were? Your mother has no time for you. It is time to be a man. To be a human being is one thing. To be a man is another."

"What are you talking about?"

"Men and women are not human beings," his father said, and licked its lips with a red, slimy tongue. "To be a man is to crush, to destroy, to raze. In balance with the woman-force, it makes a human being. Either by itself is partial. Your mother seeks more of the male. Obsessed with the male. *That* is why she divorced your father. That is why he died alone. There is no room for a man in her life. Any man. Not even you."

It stretched out a bloody hand to him. "Take it," Father said. "I could have chosen a thousand others. I chose *you*. Within you lies the seed of a great warrior. I will make you a man. A *real* man, unlike the milkwater whining things that think they are men because penises dangle between their scrawny thighs. I will show you the truth!"

And it dug its fingers into its own chest, and pulled it

open, exposing the beating heart. And that heart was alive with light.

Trias had opened the door to the sleep chamber, and was almost to her patient when the impossible happened. From within his chest appeared a shaft of silver flame. It danced at first, then gushed forth in an unending flow.

It slammed her back against the wall, and she crumpled. She managed to say: "I—" and then the words froze, her mind froze, and in that instant Annelle Trias, Ph.D. in Developmental Psychology and masters in Neuroanatomy, author of two best-selling books on lucid dreaming, went quietly insane.

Still clutching her chest, Brenda fought her way to her feet, screaming silently into the light.

And out of that light flowed . . .

David, and his father.

David rose up, piercing his own shadow. He looked down at the husk of his body, and felt a great calm. The figure beside him, one arm around his shoulder, was magnificent. He saw how the black woman quaked, and the white one crawled against the wall like a crab, babbling. The black one was . . . *mother.* Yes, he remembered now. Mother. For the first time, her air of superiority was completely gone. Completely. She stretched out her arm to him, beseechingly.

"She wants to hold you, David. She wants to stop you."

David looked up at his father, all-wise and

Am

knowing, and felt his heart surging with

I Dreaming

love like he had never known

Now?

The thing with its arm around his shoulder was dead,

long dead, the remnants of flesh twisted about its chipped and blackened bones like blood-slimed beef jerky.

Brenda teetering on the edge of insanity, her entire world turned inside out and upside down. The unconscious David had opened up like a melon, spewing . . . David. A waking David and a *thing*, a rotted, maggoty abomination. For a moment her boy was transfixed. Then he fought back, lashed out with one small foot. It stuck to the thing's cavernous belly. He kicked with the other foot. It stuck as well. Screaming, David punched it, and then again, and then he struck it with his head, and it laughed.

A chaos boiled in the hall. Someone screamed, and a man's voice said: "Hold it, you son of a bitch—"

There was a gunshot.

Brenda turned in time to see a body fly past the open door to the hall, smashing into the wall hard enough to dent plaster.

And Elk was there. His shoulder bled, and blood streaked the side of his face. His eyes burned. A guard tackled him from behind and Elk shrugged him off, somehow got the man's arm in a twisting grip. Bone splintered.

"Little Hawk!" Elk commanded. "*Fight him!*"

Two more guards tackled the old man. He got one off, and the other hit him in the head with a flashlight. Elk's head snapped sideways, but his elbow connected hard enough to shatter teeth. The guard went down, still holding on—

Then the guards looked into the sleep room.

And they saw.

And froze.

Elk lurched to his feet. "Fight!" he thundered. "Find your power spots. Find the lines of light!"

David's scream was the howl of a dying hurricane. "I can't!"

Elk staggered forward, dug a shaking hand into the leather pouch at his waist.

''Hold him, David. For your mother.'' He pulled out a handful of sand.

Trias stared at him, fist stuck against her mouth, wordless and wide-eyed. Her lips moved without making words.

Elk drew a line of sand completely around David's cot. He sat heavily on the floor, drew his pipe from his knapsack, lighting it with shaking hands. He calmed as it came to life.

The thing on the bed howled, turned, grabbed David's face—and crawled into his mouth, distending his head horribly, forcing his lips impossibly wide. Brenda heard the bones creak, saw David's mad eyes staring into the ceiling, saw its head and shoulders disappear, watched David's throat swell as it passed, and at last saw the thing's blood-smeared skeletal feet disappear between David's crimsoned lips. The waking David disappeared back into the sleeping David's chest.

David vibrated on the bed, his body distending as if being struck stupendous blows from within. His screaming seemed to be coming from farther and farther away.

Elk blew smoke to the four directions, and then to the sky.

The scream boiled back up at them, but now it was a demon's scream. It grew louder, and louder, and peaked, and David's entire body spasmed, throwing him into the air.

Then he crashed back down, and was still.

Nothing. Then . . .

The floor began to shake, the red-and-black tiles cracking, separating as they watched, as if some terrible pressure were pushing from beneath.

Brenda took a step forward, and Elk grabbed her arm. ''Stop.''

''What's happening?'' She looked shell-shocked.

"It's just beginning," Elk said.

"Didn't you kill the thing? The demon?" The glass window in the door shattered, and the plaster split along the wall in a ragged vertical seam.

"Only David can do that," Elk said. "All I could do was confine him to David's body. David's dream."

"What?"

"Think, woman! The Mimbrino was coming into our world. Through David. There's no one alive who knows how to deal with something like that. There hasn't been anyone for five hundred years who knows about these things. Really *knows.* David is the only one on an equal footing with it."

Two of the guards had made it to their feet. They stared at the boy, and at the petrified Trias, at the buckling floor, unable to move or think. The alarm bells shrieked. They ran.

"This is David's fight," Elk said. "It's always been."

"What can I do?" Brenda asked, desperately.

"Let your boy be a man," he said. "That's all that there is."

"That is my mother! Those are my friends!"

David roared it, snatched his hand from the grip of the cold dead thing that walked in the form of his father.

It recoiled and hissed at him.

I gave you a chance, boy, because I saw something in you that I could have used. Now, I'll rip it from your body!

David watched the Mimbrino melt, turn into a wave of energy that peaked and crested like a tsunami and rolled in to cover him

A bungee line of light snatched David out of the way, to a spot that glistened as if wet—but felt dry.

Some little thing in the back of his mind said: *He's lying! He didn't destroy you before because . . .*

He's too weak. All the strength he has, he takes from you, and the more you fight him, the more he'll get!

Ants. Ants everywhere and they bit like fire. David concentrated, and the heavens burst with water, carrying them away. . . .

And in the water they flowed into a thousand thousand piranha, biting, tearing, and David grew a shell and watched their teeth breaking against his shell—

And they shook, vibrating like a million operatic sopranos, and he felt his shell vibrating and cracking, cracking, and he split into a thousand smaller Davids, each one whole, and scurried away as the sound turned into a synthesizer gushing out a techno-pop, cut and scratch rap version of the Death March.

David deliberately soured his notes, and the synthesizer cracked and shattered. Suddenly he was sound ripples vibrating in a water funnel swirling around and around and around and sucking him down into hell—

Brenda turned to look at Trias. The doctor had vanished. Brenda whipped her head back toward the door and saw the doctor in the hallway, tearing a fire ax from the wall. When Trias turned back, her lip was bitten through, her eyes wide and crazed and fixed on David.

Those mad eyes flickered from David to Brenda. "It's the only way," she said, very, very reasonably. "He'll destroy us all!"

Brenda screamed and threw herself between Trias and her intended victim. She grabbed the ax handle as Trias stepped, as the weapon came up, and held on for life and love.

Then Elk was there, striding through the crazy-quilt sliding world of Westside Memorial's sleep lab like an avenging angel. Elk grabbed the ax just beneath the head, and spit out his words. "You ignorant, cowardly, self-righteous bitch! We're supposed to *help* him!"

Elk twisted, and Trias's ax was in his hand. Brenda

flew one way, Trias the other. The doctor slammed into the wall, and slid down, gibbering. Elk strode up to her, the shifting whirling colors painting his face into a death mask. He raised the ax and slammed it down—

Next to Trias's head. Trias soiled herself, and fainted.

Elk turned just in time to see Brenda heave herself up, and crawl the last foot to the edge of the sand circle before he reached her. "No! Don't break it!"

Brenda lost control, words tumbling out in an avalanche of grief. "I'm sorry. I'm sorry. David, please. Come back to us. God in heaven, I'm so sorry—"

David, halfway down the funnel now, stretched out his hand to her, reaching nothing, finding nothing, but hearing her words and finding in them, as he swirled toward an eternity of blood and madness, a line of light—

A widening pool of light.

An image. A memory.

He and his mother, on the road together. Laughing.

He and his mother, sharing barbecue at a roadside restaurant. And there was the whisper of a sadness in her eyes. It was—

He and his mother and his . . .

And his . . .

Father. Road trip. New Mexico. Camping. By the river. Just a moment, one moment. He was five years old, and asleep. He yawned awake, and crawled out of the tent. Mommy and Daddy were—

There, in the moonlight. Holding each other. On a blanket spread out in the moonlight. Naked. Sweat-slicked. Kissing, groaning into each other's mouths, oblivious to the rest of the world. And in their eyes, unmistakably—

Love. So deep and complete and scathing that it burned into his soul. A fire bright and hot enough to consume its own substance in years instead of decades.

David crawled back into the tent, eyes wide and wondering.

One moment. One memory. One and only one. Whatever had happened later, love had lived between Brenda and Darryl. Between his mother and father.

Love.

A bridge of light. A bridge upon which he could make a stand.

Deep within David, something bared its teeth.

Now.

If he tried to shift again, the Mimbrino would have him. Every time he shifted, it shifted. Every time he won, it just upped the ante, changed to a new . . .

Level?

Like in a video game . . . ?

Can I do that?

Why not? It's MY goddamn dream . . .

The roaring stopped. Brenda, sobbing, reached out and touched David's limp arm. It *hurt* her. She snatched her hand back.

"He's burning up," she whispered.

Elk grabbed Trias and pulled her to her feet, shaking her to wakefulness. "Have you got ice?"

"Ice?" she mumbled.

"Yes, dammit, ice! Frozen fucking water."

Her eyes wouldn't focus. She spoke as if explaining something to a child. "No. Why would we have ice here?"

"David's found a way to fight back," Elk said. "The Mimbrino is using everything against him. His resistance will create heat—David could literally burn up. We have to cool him off, and give him a chance to fight."

"No ice, no ice," Trias babbled.

Brenda shook her head, fighting to clear her mind. She looked up, and then at Elk. "Give me your cigarette lighter."

"What?'

"GIVE IT TO ME!"

He fumbled it out. Brenda pulled a chair to the middle of the room, stood on it, lit the cigarette lighter—

And held it to the fire sprinkler sensor overhead.

It *popped,* and the room was filled with rain. Steam rose from David's body.

Brenda laughed hysterically.

David dropped a mental quarter into the mental slot, and instantly found himself at the controls of a tiny blue fighter jet. Enemy planes were everywhere, zipping in from all quadrants. It should have been frightening, but he felt oddly at peace. He knew this. He *knew* this world, the world of *Super Mario Brothers*, and *Sonic the Hedgehog,* and *Lemmings*, and *Commando Task Force.* He knew this world, and the Mimbrino wouldn't.

Still, his enemy was adapting fast. It sent ships at him, probing his defenses. . . .

But as if David had gained some kind of bonus powers, the ships glowed before they fired, were connected by lines of light to his own weapons. He literally couldn't miss.

David blasted wave after wave of enemy fighters out of the sky. Death rained on the flat, two-dimensional landscape beneath.

He fired and fired and fired, and was strafed in return. He could actually feel the light building inside him.

This was his kind of war. It was death, and destruction of a different kind. It was fighting that he understood, because he had always used it. Passive/dynamic resistance, an emotional weapon against his mother.

A weapon.

A *weapon.*

"Look," Elk said quietly. "The water is washing away the sand."

The rumbling had died. The floor, the walls were crooked, as if struck by an 8.7 tremor. The air was muggy, clouded with steam. David lay quiet, struggling to breathe.

Brenda stared. "What's happening?"

"He's leaving his body."

David took another long, slow breath—and stopped.

Without a word, Brenda shoved Elk out of the way, and stepped across the scattered grains. She arched David's head back, opened his mouth and cleared his air passages—

"Hurry!" Elk screamed. "He's in the other world now. His mind, his spirit are locked with the Mimbrino. His body is forgetting how to breathe!"

She lowered her mouth onto David's, and blew.

The world was a world of fire. The spaceships had mutated into a jungle of mercenaries. David fought them, leaping from rock to moss to patch of grass through a video jungle, each footprint glowing in advance, shining in its turn.

Power spots.

The jungle mutated into a world of tangled pipes and wires from which cascaded electric, razor-fanged furballs. David felt the lines of light connect him to their vulnerable underbellies, and spilled their computer-animated intestines. The Mimbrino changed the game to a racing track. David was chased by demons riding piggyback on motorcycles, howling, hurling Molotov cocktails at him—

David jumped to a power spot. And when he was there, the light lines appeared like crazy quilt rainbows. He blew enemy motorcycles into junk until the spot began to fade, then moved to the next one, and devastated the demons until *that* spot faded, then he moved to the next one. This one was so powerful, so filled with magical essence that David felt himself swell, and he *willed* the next change—

Silence.

David stood in the middle of a tiled floor. All around the edges, receding into the darkness, a crowd of leather-jacketed bikers and their tattooed Mommas cheered him on. He looked down at his arms. They were massive with cartoon muscle.

On the other side of the floor, another ponderously thewed cartoon figure manifested.

The Mimbrino.

And for the first time, his enemy's expression was . . . confused.

David grinned. He was right, just exactly where he wanted to be.

"Hey, Mimbrino," he yelled. "Welcome to *Kung Fu Fighter III,* you stupid *fuck.*"

Brenda held her son, crying and remembering everything she could about the proper resuscitation rhythm.

Elk worked David's chest while she breathed for him. There was no movement. There was no response.

David hurt. He was tired. But he had been hurt and tired before. He didn't care. Elk had shown him what that space was, the space on the far side of fatigue, and pain, and fear.

It was simply death.

David, 450 pounds of cartoon muscle, stood in the center of the ring, trading thunderous blows with the behemoth Mimbrino. He saw the light flashes before the blows landed, and felt the laser bungee sensation that snapped his own limbs onto target.

The Mimbrino's first manifestation growled and raged, but finally crashed to the earth, defeated. And another appeared. Tougher. Stronger. A humanoid rhinoceros.

The lines of light guided David directly onto the weak point—the Rhinoman's horn. He glided across the floor, finding one power spot after another, punching and kicking, slamming and jamming, hopping and bopping into flying, tumbling, jumping, paroxysms of ecstatic motion.

And then another opponent. And then another. The Mimbrino tried to change the dream, tried to shift the game, but David held on for dear life. When the edges started to shift, started to peel away into nothingness, he concentrated, and held the Kung Fu biker bar scenario in place.

Punch. Kick. Jump. Over and over. He knew this world. He was the *best* at this game, and the best part about it was that, after ten bruising rounds had been played—

Letters, blessed letters flashing red and black in the air between them said:

Game Over

Over and over again.

Game Over.

The Mimbrino, in the form of some gigantic shark thing in blue tights, looked up at the display. And blinked.

"Game Over, man!" David yelled. "We're going down together. You can't have my mother. You can't have my friends. You can't take over the world. You're just *dead.* We're both *dead.*"

The Mimbrino stared at him as the darkness swarmed in to take them both. It looked down at itself, at its hands, and saw its bones through its skin. Its eyes literally went as wide as saucers. It groaned.

With his last strength, David spun light out of the specks in the air, spun them into mirrors. Mirrors that surrounded the Mimbrino. It turned this way, and that, and wherever it looked, it saw its own death. Its own putrescence. Its own burnt limbs. For the first time not a thing of awesome power, not the lord of nightmare, but a man, a man afraid of dying.

The Mimbrino shrieked. Light flashed from those mirrors, flame hundreds of years old, and this time the Mimbrino's mind received the full horror of its own death, could not escape into dream. Its mouth stretched wide, and it said: "But you're just a *boy*—"

Then its flesh peeled away, its bones exploding into charred powder. It whirled, collapsed, became a smoking heap.

David crawled to it, pushed the ashes together into a pile, and spun a cocoon of light around them. The cocoon took the shape of a pot, of a spirit bowl, its circumference etched with pectroglyphs.

The urn dwindled to nothing, and was gone.

David rolled onto his back. The darkness was almost total now. The cartoons were gone. He was himself again, on an evaporating video stage. He felt so very, very tired.

He turned onto his side and felt his eyelids force themselves closed. "I was always a man," he murmured.

"I just needed my mommy and daddy. That's all."

His eyes closed. He was no longer a warrior, a streetfighter, a scourge of evil. He was just an exhausted twelve-year-old boy, dying alone in the land of dreams.

GAME OVER

DEPOSIT ANOTHER QUARTER

YOU HAVE TEN SECONDS. NINE. EIGHT—

"David!" Brenda puffed into his mouth, waited, puffed, waited, puffed. Her mind, that focused business thing that she was so proud of, was completely gone. She was nothing but a mother now, as desperate as any woman who has ever watched her child slip away into darkness.

"David!" She screamed—
Into his open mouth—
Shivering his teeth and jawbone—
Vibrating his skull, and making that three and a half pounds of jelly called the human brain quiver in its casing—

David . . . ! reverberated that infinite video stage, just as the last dot of light winked out.

Blackness. Then . . .

GAME RESUMED. ONE OR TWO PLAYERS?

The still, dark child in Brenda's arms turned his head and coughed, gagged, and coughed again. His hands flailed, then found his mother's arms and relaxed. He said two words, then folded against her chest, smiling. She held him tightly, tears streaking her face.

"Too damned close." Elk exhaled harshly. He dug into a pocket, and pulled out a clove cigarette with trembling fingers. He flicked his cigarette lighter twice before he realized that the overhead sprinklers were still going. "Shit," he said, and tossed the sopping butt to the floor. "Oh, well . . . what did David say just then, anyway?"

"Two," Brenda sobbed, holding her living child. "He said 'two players.' "

6

The powder blue Impala pulled off the dirt road, squealing to a stop in front of the old man's battered trailer. The sun was low in the sky, brushing the mountains. Lightning Elk sat in a folding lawn chair, watching it set, seemingly oblivious to the fact that the car had arrived. The passenger door swung open, and Elk managed to get to his feet a half second before David reached him. The boy leapt up, grabbed him around the neck, and hung on for dear life.

Brenda stood an arm's distance away, holding a shopping bag in her arms.

Elk set David down and smoothed his hair. He glanced questioningly at her. "What do you have there?"

"I did some research," she said. "We wanted to bring you medicine gifts." She pulled a yellow Pendleton blanket from the bag, and handed it to David. David gravely gave it to Elk, who inclined his head in thanks.

"Ho. You make my heart happy, Little Hawk," he said.

Brenda fished deeper into the bag, extracting a carton of Djarum cigarettes. Elk grinned. "Great. Almost out," he said. "Stores out here don't stock 'em for shit."

"Got the new *Jurassic Park* game, David," he said, almost nonchalantly.

David shrugged. He wandered over to the great tarp, and lifted a corner. The gigantic sand painting stretched before him, still larger than the trailer itself, still unfinished. But there was a new figure drawn into it, the figure of a boy looking up into the sky.

"What's he looking at?" David asked.

"I thought maybe you could tell me."

David grinned. "Can I?"

"The pots are over against the gym," Elk said.

David unlidded a pot, and drew out a handful of red sand. Very very carefully, he began to sprinkle it in a bird shape. Within moments, he was completely absorbed.

Elk sank into his lawn chair and lit up a cigarette. He motioned Brenda toward a chair leaning against the trailer. "Pull up a seat."

They sat there for a time, and then Brenda scratched a line in the dirt with her toe. "You saved his life," she said. He nodded, still gazing at the sunset.

"And more than that, didn't you?"

Elk said nothing.

"Trias is still on leave. They say she'll be back to work in a week or so."

He nodded. "She's basically a good woman. But I think she was searching for something she didn't really want to find."

The silence between them stretched as the sun sank closer to the mountains. Finally, she couldn't stand it any longer. "The . . . Mimbrino. He's dead, isn't he?"

Elk inhaled deeply, and let the smoke trickle sweetly out of his nose. "Always was. Just didn't know it."

"Now he does?"

"Now he does." He reached into the battered Styrofoam cooler at his feet, and removed a can of Jolt cola. He shook the ice water off, and offered it to Brenda.

"Are there more of them?"

He peered down. "At least four."

"That's not what I meant."

"Don't ask so many questions," he said, not unpleasantly. "Get on with your life, Brenda. Love that boy of yours. He'll forget most of what happened, unless you keep reminding him."

"Is that a good idea?"

Elk smiled. "You don't want to live in my world," he said.

"Do you?"

He took another sip. "It's my world. You have yours. David will make his own."

"What if he wants to come back to you. Sometimes. Just for a visit?"

"Door's open," he said.

Brenda looked back between the trailer and the ribbed dome of the gym, where her son sprinkled a handful of sand onto Elk's vast canvas. Twenty feet across, with hundreds of symbols and images, the panorama of a lifetime. It would never be finished. Every day, it had to be redone. Each animal, each tree, each mountain renewed. And now her son was a part of that tapestry. Just above the spot where her son worked, loomed a shape. It might have been a cloud, or a jellyfish, or an octopus. Whatever it was, it made her chest feel cold.

"Yes," she said quietly. "The doors *are* open, aren't they?"

Elk gestured again with the soft drink can, and this time she took it. She sipped. It was good. And just as good to watch the last sliver of sun disappear, and the western mountains begin to phosphoresce as night fell softly across the desert.

People don't practice the martial arts for the same reasons they take up table tennis. In the majority of cases, there are fear and power issues to be dealt with, often strong enough to be emotionally crippling if unprocessed. The question remains: once these basic issues are resolved, why continue the practice? The answer: sometimes for fun, sometimes for fitness, sometimes to teach others.

Then there are those who continue because the martial arts, like Yoga, offer a bridge between Mind and Body unlike that commonly found in Western sports. Additionally, some believe that Eastern movement arts offer a "Threefold Path," linking Body, Mind, and that mysterious quality known as Spirit.

Is there a reality beyond the phenomenological universe? I don't know. I *do* know that walking the Threefold Path is one up of the most satisfying things in my life, a wonderful way to busy up my days. And that, for now, is quite enough for me.

Everyone else in this book has written an afterpiece to his or her contribution. None here, though, as I asked calligraphy sensei *Kazuaki Tanahashi to write something to serve as the afterpiece to the entire book.*

OOOOO

A Small Circle

Kazuaki Tanahashi

What if a super warrior had a clumsy student? After all it was a time when everyone was confused, humiliated and poor. Japan had just surrendered and been occupied by the Allied Forces. All the martial arts had been prohibited. This old man was growing rice and yams in a country village and was teaching his underground class in a small dojo surrounded by young pine trees. He had about five kids at the nightly training. That was the time when I studied with Morihei Uyeshiba, the founder of Aikido.

A thirteen-year-old boy who loved the dense smell of Western philosophy, I was not at all physical; every movement I made was destined to be chaotic. While my fellow students were beautifully thrown down by the master, I would cling to his arm so he had to shake me off. After one of us rolled on the wooden floor, Morihei would kneel and keep him down with a little finger making no effort whatsoever. I had no idea how this short man with a white beard could do such a miraculous thing, and there was no clue for me to get the secret of the art.

Several years later martial arts became legalized as Japan regained independence. My fellow students started teaching the art in schools and community centers, and eventually all over the world. The number of practitioners increased to thousands, millions. Meanwhile I became a painter, after studying with the master for one year. I was a complete dropout from the warrior's path. I moved to the United States in 1977.

The scale of my brush has increased over the last thirty years. Its shaft was as thick as a finger, then a thumb, an arm, and finally a human body. The movement of the brush became ever more sparse and decisive, to the point where I would create a large painting with a single stroke. Decades after the death of the master, often without my knowledge, I was still in the process of learning from him. Through art, I gradually experienced what he was demonstrating in his subtle movement—intensity, effortlessness, and the spirit of accepting all the energy coming against him and turning it in a positive direction.

In the early 1990s I was mainly using black paint on white canvas. But when asked to participate in an exhibition at the Zen Hospice, a residential program in San Francisco for patients with AIDS, I thought a black-and-white painting would not be appropriate, as it might not be pleasing or healing for the residents. So I decided to use color. A multicolor Zen circle on a canvas scroll was the idea I settled on.

In June 1993, I stretched a canvas, about five and half feet wide and seven feet tall, over a wooden panel which was set up on the floor of my basement studio in Berkeley. After priming the canvas with gesso, I put together strips of felt with raffia straws, enough to draw a line over one foot wide, and bundled them up around a wooden shaft. I poured generous amounts of acrylic paint here and there on the canvas. Overlapping spots of paint altogether formed a circle, which touched the sides of the canvas. The top of the circle was red, yellow and golden, and the bottom had darker colors.

I wet the "brush" with light parchment–colored paint, stood on the canvas, and traced over the circle with the brush almost in one breath. The paints washed together, forming a complex mixture of all colors, yet retaining an uninterrupted flow of the brush movement. I thought it was a magnificent representation of a world with joy and hope.

While I cleaned up and went away for a cup of tea, the paint on the canvas was still moving slowly, creating marblelike patterns. The very dark blue puddle in the bottom found a path into the center of the circle and started running toward the upper right. I could have stopped the traveling of paint by vacuuming or blotting it, but I just watched it. It seemed that the circle was sending a message. After several hours, the circle stopped changing, having become a sort of *Q* shape. The painting was no longer pleasing or healing, but disturbing and alarming.

I thought of giving the painting a dark and ominous name. But finally, I decided to name it "A Small Circle" in honor of the very tiny class my master taught in the village. It also meant that I was hoping to create a larger circle.